T0378922

This special signed edition is limited to 750 numbered copies.
This is copy 668

Howard Waldrop

George R.R. Martin

Bradley Denton

WALDROP · H'ARD STARTS

HOWARD WALDROP

H'ARD STARTS

The Early Waldrop

EDITED BY GEORGE R. R. MARTIN
AND BRADLEY DENTON

H'ard Starts: The Early Waldrop
Copyright © 2023 by Howard Waldrop.
All rights reserved.

Dust jacket illustration & end-paper illustrations
Copyright © 2023 by D. C. Potter III.
All rights reserved.

Jacket and interior design by John D. Berry.
Typefaces used:
TT Marxiana (text and headings)
Eames Century Modern (display type on dust jacket)

First edition.

See page 359 for individual story copyrights.

ISBN (print): 978-1-64524-116-4
ISBN (ebook): 978-1-64524-117-1

Subterranean Press
PO Box 190106
Burton, MI 48519

subterraneanpress.com

Manufactured in the United States of America

For Ms. Ellen B. Brody of Chestnut Hill, MA,
who must have been about seven years old
when the first of these pieces appeared.

CONTENTS

PREFACE

Whatever the eventual title of this book is, the subtitle should be *What I Wrote Before I Could Write.*

I was amazed by a lot of the stuff Jeremy Brett and his colleagues at the Texas A&M Special Collections Library found amongst my papers.

I had absolutely forgotten that I had used certain people, places, ideas, and situations in various published and unpublished works that I also used in later published pieces.

But as Fantasy, Inc. v. Fogerty proved, no matter who holds the copyright, you can't plagiarize yourself.

I had vowed from the beginning to never write the same story twice, and so far I never have.

This book couldn't exist without the efforts of lots of people, chief among them George R.R. Martin and Brad Denton.

George has been my friend since I sold him Brave and the Bold #28, which contained the first appearance of the Justice League ("vs. Starro the Conqueror"), in 1962 for twenty-five cents. (It's worth approximately $12,000.00 now.) We've been pen pals and friends since then, sometimes exchanging letters so long and heavy it took four cents to mail them. George always thought there were masterpieces buried in a trunk of my papers somewhere. I hope working on this project has finally disabused him of that notion.

Brad recorded the conversations we had about what I remembered of stuff I had written fifty and sixty years ago. I've known Brad since the early '80s when he and his wife Barb lived in Baldwin City, Kansas, before they moved to Austin so Barb could finish her library degree. I showed them where to not live in the Austin of the time, which had maybe 250,000 people.

The best way I can sum up this book:

I walked into a party at the 1981 Denver World Science Fiction Convention wearing a T-shirt with silk-screened arms clawing up from the beltline.

Someone asked me, "What's that down your pants, Howard?"

Without missing a beat, the late Terry Carr, over in the corner, said —

"It's a good writer, trying to get out."

I laughed so hard I fell down on the floor and couldn't get up for a couple of minutes.

That's what you see in this mélange of early stuff.

A good writer, trying to get out.

your old pal
Howard
November 22, 2021

WALDROP · H'ARD STARTS

1. The Four-Color Fanboy

HOWARD'S FANZINE STORIES

INTERVIEW, PART ONE

1. "A Lovely Witch" and
2. "Well of Chaos"

BRAD: We'll begin with two of your early fanzine stories, the Wanderer tales "A Lovely Witch" and "Well of Chaos." I'll also want to ask you a little about your Wanderer collaboration with Paul Moslander (writing as Victor Baron), "Sound the Hell-Horn."

You were seventeen when "A Lovely Witch," featuring your character the Wanderer, was published in *Cortana* #1. You told me the other day that you were the Art Editor for that fanzine, right?

HOWARD: Right, Art Director. I did the cover of my own character, you know. And I did most of the interior art. Occasionally, Bigglestone would pick up some odd illustrations from other people. But I illustrated most of the stories, except for the people who illustrated their own. Because there were lots of artist/writers at the time.

BRAD: You were still in high school, right? Did you know Clint Bigglestone (editor of *Cortana*) from school, or did you know him through fandom?

HOWARD: He lived in San Francisco, and I lived in Arlington, Texas. It was all in correspondence. I corresponded with George (George R.R. Martin) from 1962, and I corresponded with Bigglestone and (Paul) Moslander from 1963 and '64. And Bigglestone and I had a common interest in Conan and Robert E. Howard.

BRAD: Was the fanzine his idea, or did you come up with it together?

HOWARD: He was part of a bunch of people including Moslander and a guy named Steven Perrin. And Johnny Chambers, who later did the "Little Green Dinosaur" cartoons for underground comics. They had a semi-loose publishing collective type of thing. Moslander published a fanzine called *Jeddak*, which is from *A Princess of Mars*, of course. And then Bigglestone had the idea of publishing a sword-and-sorcery fanzine. That was *Cortana*, named for Ogier the Dane's sword, I believe. In whatchacallit, the Charlemagne crap, right?

BRAD: So he came up with the idea to do this fanzine, and he invited you to participate as Art Director?

HOWARD: Right, we had been corresponding about *Amra*, a fanzine that was dedicated to Robert E. Howard and the Hyborian Legion.

BRAD: Was Clint Bigglestone also in his teens?

HOWARD: I believe he was maybe twenty, tops. But he was almost the same age as me. Oh, and his girlfriend was the first female mail carrier in San Francisco since the war. Later, when I went out there and met them, she was still workin' the job.

BRAD: As for the story itself, and the other Wanderer stories — I have a memory that you once told me you decided to start writing fiction after reading a terrible sword-and-sorcery book by Lin Carter, and telling yourself that you could do better. Is that right?

HOWARD: Yes, exactly!

BRAD: Did you read his book and then immediately sit down to write a better story?

HOWARD: Pretty much. I think that was a little bit later. I had already started writing some stuff, but once I read Lin Carter's *The Wizard of Lemuria,* I knew I could write better than that. That was when I started going from being an artist to being a writer. It took about five years before I completely left one for the other.

BRAD: It seems as if that's one of the two ways people start writing. People start writing either because they admire somebody and want to be like them, or because they think, "I can do better than this shmuck."

HOWARD: Exactly! Lin Carter was a great nonfiction writer. He did all these Lovecraft essays and stuff. He was a good scholar and nonfiction writer, and he was a good editor. But when it came to fiction, he couldn't write for beans, you know?

BRAD: So he was like a fan himself, except that he managed to get his stuff published at a professional level.

HOWARD: Right. And they started a series of "Forgotten Fantasies" at Ballantine because of him. He's responsible for a lot of great things in the field ... but his writing isn't one of 'em.

BRAD: What do you remember about collaborating with Paul Moslander on "Sound the Hell-Horn?" That was going to be a serial, right?

HOWARD: It was gonna be a serial novel. God knows how we would have done it. But we thought we could, right?

BRAD: So you kind of jumped in without a plan, like young writers do.

HOWARD: Exactly. The thing was, I wanted to collaborate with him because he was the best writer around at the time. He could write better than either me or George, at the time. This would have been around 1965 and 1966.

BRAD: Way back.

HOWARD: Way back! See, I went out to visit all of them in 1966. I took a bus trip to San Francisco, stayed at Moslander's house for a week, and met everybody in sf fandom, pretty much, in San Francisco at the time. I met Johnny Chambers, who drew the Little Green Dinosaur. And I met Clint Bigglestone, of course, who was the editor of *Cortana*. I met everybody who was in comics and sword & sorcery fandom, all at once, in that one week. It was the year *before* the Summer of Love, of course. But I still saw plenty of people like I'd never seen before, because the early hippie movement was starting there.

BRAD: You were twenty years old, or about to turn twenty. So you just went out there on the bus to meet all these guys?

HOWARD: Well, I had broken up with a girlfriend, and I was pissed off and depressed and stuff. And I decided I needed a trip to San Francisco to meet everybody I'd been corresponding with for years. So I took a forty-four-hour bus ride. And I sat in the exact same spot on the bus back to Texas as I'd sat in on the bus going up to San Francisco. It was right over the back wheels of the bus, too. So I was really tired of that view by the time it was over. Eighty-eight hours of it, right?

And I got to San Francisco with a dollar and twenty-eight cents in my pocket because the Greyhound people had told me the wrong fare. So when I got on the bus, I only had like twelve dollars for the entire trip. And of course I had to buy food two or three times on the way. So I got to San Francisco with a dollar twenty-eight. Buddy (Saunders) had taken me to the Greyhound station, and I told him to send money to Paul's address for me. So he did. He sent fifteen or twenty bucks, I think. But this was 1966 *real* money.

BRAD: Yeah, in 1966, you could live for a week on twenty bucks.

HOWARD: Pre-Vietnam money! Real American dollars. Anyway, he sent the money — and it came on, like, Thursday, before I got on the bus and went back home on Saturday. So I didn't get to enjoy it. But I had a round-trip bus ticket, of course, which was a good thing.

Anyway, Moslander and I talked about collaborating on a serial. And we decided it would have to be set post-apocalypse. One of his characters was a Nazi who turned into a werewolf.

(Laughter.)

But it was deeper than it sounds, knowhaddamean?

BRAD: Hey, I'm not gonna knock it. When I was in college I wrote a story in which the Lone Ranger was a werewolf hunter. Because of the silver bullets.

HOWARD: Sweet! Anyway, that was one of his characters. And his medieval character, Drom Halliburt, was an actual medieval person, right? And I said it would have to be post-apocalypse, because the Wanderer was post-apocalypse, of course. So there would be all these prophecies, and these characters would wind up having to team up. But only the first chapter was published.

BRAD: Had you written more than the first chapter?

HOWARD: No. We wrote the first chapter for what would be the last issue of *Cortana.*

BRAD: So you discussed this collaboration while you were in San Francisco?

HOWARD: A little bit. And then the rest was in correspondence. We were corresponding all the time, like I was corresponding with George all the time.

BRAD: So I take it that if *Cortana* had continued, you might have gone ahead and finished the serial, or at least written another installment or two.

HOWARD: Yes, we would have. But everybody just essentially went different ways and did different things all of a sudden.

I met Bigglestone again, right before he died, at BayCon in nineteen ninety-whatever. That was the first time I'd seen him in almost thirty-five years, right? And he was the same guy.

3. "The Soul-Catcher"

BRAD: You self-published your story "The Soul-Catcher." That was in March 1966, right?

HOWARD: Right.

BRAD: You were just nineteen. So if you don't remember all of the details, it's understandable.

HOWARD: Well, see, the used bookstore in Arlington on Main Street — the guy who ran it was real nice. In a forlorn hope, he opened a used bookstore in downtown Arlington, Texas, in 1965.

And it was going okay. And he had a mimeograph at the store. Occasionally I would go in and help him with stuff, move boxes and things like that, so we got pretty friendly. He was running off something on the mimeograph at some point, and he said, "Why don't you do something, and I'll run it off for you." And I said, "Sure!"

So I wrote "Soul-Catcher," and I used orange construction paper for the cover, back and front. Then I ran it off on the mimeograph. And I believe I did an illustration on the front cover, or maybe it was the title page. Because I was still trying to be an artist at the time. Anyway, I did that on a mimeograph stencil, too. It was the first time I had ever worked with mimeograph stencils, as opposed to spirit duplicator masters.

BRAD: The "young folks today" — we were talking about this earlier — tell 'em what you had to go through to run off copies of something back in 1966, and it's like you're from a different planet. Because now there are xerox machines, and there's publishing online . . .

HOWARD: See, with a spirit duplicator, what you do is, you type up on a master that makes a reverse, a negative, of what you type. And then you put the ink and stuff in, and it prints off directly onto the paper. Whereas with mimeograph stencils, you cut a hole in the stencil itself with the typewriter, and the ink comes through from the *other* side. They were opposite processes of each other.

BRAD: So with a mimeograph machine, you're literally typing letters that are holes in a piece of paper.

HOWARD: Yes, exactly. But with a spirit duplicator, you're just typing, and picking up ink on the back of the master where each of the keys hits. And that's where the ink comes off and prints on the blank paper. But essentially, yes, you poke a hole in the master for a mimeograph stencil. And "corflu," correction fluid, you put over it and type the letter again if you type the wrong letter. So then you put the right hole in the stencil.

But yeah, you tell people nowadays that you didn't just throw something in the xerox machine ... See, if anyone had xerox machines at the time, they were expensive. It cost a quarter a page or something. And that was in 1966 money.

BRAD: That'd almost be like spending $2.50 now.

HOWARD: Right. So everybody ran stuff off on either a spirit duplicator or a mimeograph.

BRAD: And "The Soul-Catcher" ... Let's see, this says you did twenty-five copies.

HOWARD: Right, twenty-five copies, and I mailed them off to different fanzine editors and people I was tryin' to impress. And (decades later) somebody got hold of one, and Lawrence (Person) ended up with it at a fanzine auction at some convention. [*BD Note: It's thanks to writer/collector Lawrence Person that we have "The Soul-Catcher" for this collection.*]

BRAD: Yeah, that's incredible — because I'm guessing you didn't have any copies at that point.

HOWARD: I think I maybe had *one*, and of course the construction paper cover ate itself eventually, as construction paper does.

But that's the way fandom was at the time. On my San Francisco trip (to visit Paul Moslander and other fanzine luminaries), I walked into a house I'd never been in before, and on the wall in the living room was a piece of art I had done for some other fanzine editor like six months before. They traded art and stuff (along with trading fanzines back and forth). Now, with the internet, people aren't surprised by stuff like that.

Back then, like I said, there were twenty-five copies of something, and the fact that one or two of them are still around is incredible to me.

BRAD: That's what amazed me — that Lawrence was actually able to lay hands on a physical copy of this when you had only made twenty-five, and it was so long ago.

HOWARD: Obviously somebody had hung onto it for some reason, right?

I believe there was a little introduction to "Soul-Catcher" on the inside front cover that said there were twenty-five copies, and when it was done, and all this stuff. And I said something like it was the third Harry Smith story. The first two were not fantasies at all. The first two were political thriller type stories.

BRAD: Yeah, your little intro gives the titles of the first two. One was called "Sawtooth by Starlight," and the other one was called "Moonlight on Claw Lake." These stories had gone out to be published in other fanzines, right?

HOWARD: As far as I know, they had. But whoever had them never published them. They went out of business, or gafiated, or whatever. That's the chance you took back in 1966.

BRAD: Right, because ... Just because someone is publishing a fanzine this month, that doesn't mean there will be another one, ever.

HOWARD: Or even like *Crawdaddy. Crawdaddy* went out of business like right after I sold to them.

BRAD: So I'm guessing if you sent the first two Harry Smith stories to Paul Moslander or whomever — if they didn't get published, they're just gone now.

HOWARD: I'm *sure* they're gone now. And I can't imagine subjecting anyone to them now anyway. Because that's me at like nineteen, right?

BRAD: Yeah, but they'd still be interesting. I thought this one, "The Soul-Catcher," was an interesting story. It's not a *great* story. As you say, it's a nineteen-year-old's story. But it's a story by a nineteen-year-old who obviously knows something about what a story is, you know?

HOWARD: (Laughs.) Right, right, exactly. But like I said, that doesn't make it *good*, right?

BRAD: No, it doesn't make it super good, but it at least makes it worth somebody's time to read it. And I think I told you before when we talked about it, one thing that did strike me about the story was the setting. In fact, you say in your introduction, "The setting of this story is the same as the first two stories, a place called Haram's Corners, Texas, a Central Texas town, population 2667."

That was one thing in reading the story that kind of struck me. The small-town Texas setting reminded me of years later when you created the small-town Texas setting of "Night of the Cooters."

HOWARD: Right, it was sort of Pachuco City in miniature. I had forgotten I had set it in that small a town. It was so long ago.

Of course, Arlington, Texas was a small Texas town back then too, right? I remember the day they got their fifty-thousandth person in town, which they knew because of hooking up their utilities and stuff. They got free stuff for the rest of their damn life!

BRAD: I was gonna make a joke about how they threw that person a parade — but it sounds like they kind of did.

HOWARD: They really did! The whole town turned out, you know? I was at a track meet, and I heard over the public address system that the merchants had given them free diaper service for ten years or whatever, and they were getting all this stuff from the grocery stores and the banks, and all that kind of stuff. It was a big-cheese deal, because when I moved there, the town had seven thousand people. And then by 1965 it had fifty thousand. I'm sure it probably has half a million now, in the area.

When I was in the Army, there was the mayor of my hometown on national TV, because the Washington Senators had just become the Texas Rangers.

Anyway, like I said, I had forgotten I had set the story in that small a town.

BRAD: One last thing I'll mention about "The Soul-Catcher." You probably don't remember this, either. As we've said, you wrote and published the story, and sent it out, when you were nineteen. But in, like, the second paragraph of the story, Harry is talking to his friend, the deputy sheriff. And Bill the deputy sheriff says:

"'You know, Harry, you're a lucky kid, having a wife who can cook like that, mighty lucky.'

'Bill was only twenty-three, but to him I was still a kid, since I was a year younger.'"

What struck me was that you were writing the story at nineteen, and you're writing about the grown-up adults who are doing grown-up adult things, and they're twenty-two and twenty-three.

HOWARD: (Laughs.) Exactly, exactly! Beats me, like I said.

BRAD: Well, everything is relative, isn't it? From our current perspective, twenty-two and twenty-three might as well be twelve, you know?

HOWARD: All of that is so long ago, right?

BRAD: And given that it was so long ago, I'm just amazed that we've got the story now. That's pretty cool.

HOWARD: I know. It's unbelievable that one of 'em survived.

4. "Vale Proditor!"
5. "The Adventure of the Countess's Jewels"

BRAD: You were still a teenager, barely, when "Vale Proditor!" came out in *Star Studded Comics* #9. You were nineteen. Had you joined the Army by then?

HOWARD: No, I wasn't drafted until 1970. This was after the lottery. What General Hershey (L.B. Hershey, director of Selective Service from 1941 to 1970) did, because he couldn't meet the quotas, is he said, "Anybody who hasn't finished four years of college within four years of the date they entered college ... is eligible for the draft." They later proved it was illegal. But that's the way they got me, and that's the way they got George, too. But George did his alternative service as a VISTA volunteer. And like I said, they later proved it was illegal, but whatcha gonna do? Sue them after the fact? Lyndon Johnson tried to get me twice, and then Nixon tried to get me twice — before he *got* me. The good thing was that because I was drafted in '70, I got out six months early in '72 because *everybody* did. Nixon was trying to convince everybody after My Lai that he was ending the Vietnam War, so he gave everybody a discharge six months early.

[*BD Note: Howard's date of discharge from the U.S. Army was May 1, 1972.*]

BRAD: So you were in a total of eighteen months, then?

HOWARD: Eighteen months and one day! They did that on purpose so you couldn't get an Army Commendation Medal for your service. Because you had to have eighteen months and *three* days for an Army commendation. That's how petty they were.

BRAD: Oh, Jesus. Okay, back to the story —

You told me that the editors of *Star Studded Comics* were Buddy Saunders, Howard Keltner, and Larry Herndon.

HOWARD: That's right. The "Texas Trio."

BRAD: The Texas Trio. And they were all local in the Dallas-Fort Worth area, is that right?

HOWARD: Except Keltner lived in Gainesville, which is about seventy-five miles north. Right on the Texas-Oklahoma border.

BRAD: Right. Now, these guys you did know personally, I assume.

HOWARD: Oh, yeah. I had known Buddy since seventh grade. And we were both at the same high school the first year. But then they split the high school into two, and all the people on the east side of town went to the new high school. We had moved three times while I was in junior high, once in each junior high district. By the time I got to high school, they split that in two. So I knew everybody in both high schools.

BRAD: So you were kind of in on the ground floor of Texas fandom at that time. You knew everybody.

HOWARD: Comics fandom, right.

BRAD: You mentioned the other day that "Vale Proditor!" was based on an illustration by somebody else. How'd that come about?

HOWARD: Landon Chesney sent in a full-color illustration. They were gonna put it on the back cover, but they needed a story to go with it — because *Star Studded Comics* was all comics, all strip stuff, you know? And we thought that to have a comics fanzine, you had to have all comics stuff ... except for one "text" story, as we used to call them at the time. See, the reason they had to have a text story in every comic book was because that's how they got their Second Class mailing permit. You had to have at least two pages not devoted to comic strips.

BRAD: More petty government rules!

HOWARD: Exactly. To get a Second Class mailing permit, which all the comics publishers had, every comic book had to have one two-page text story in each issue. That's how Mickey Spillane started. He wrote Human Torch text stories in *Marvel Mystery Comics* in the 1940s.

BRAD: Wow, I did not know that.

HOWARD: His first published works were two-page text stories about the Human Torch in 1942.

BRAD: You and Mickey Spillane, man.

HOWARD: If you read the Wanderer story, it's post-apocalyptic, of course. And you remember, he learned to read from Mickey Spillane novels? Because anywhere you went in the world, there would be old trashed-out paperback copies of Mickey Spillane lying around. I figured that was the most prevalent reading matter that would still be around after the apocalypse. Like Stephen King now, or J.K. Rowling.

BRAD: Now, I'm assuming you weren't paid, at least not in dollars and cents, for any of these.

HOWARD: No, we weren't paid. What we usually got was a quarter-page free ad in the "Comics Wanted" section of most fanzines.

As a sidebar: We tried to pull a hoax. We tried to make up a comic book company of the '40s that nobody had ever heard of. So we all started putting ads beside the real ones for comics we wanted ... You know, "Wanted, *Brave & Bold* #14" and stuff. We put in "Wanted, *Cosh Comics* #3 and #5." We'd make up these titles and we'd put 'em in all our "Comics Wanted" free ads.

BRAD: Just to mess with people.

HOWARD: Just to mess with people! And they finally published the "Cosh Comics Story." One of the fanzines put out a special edition devoted to Cosh Comics. And I did some of the illustrations for that, too.

That's just one of the things you did if you had a fanzine collective.

BRAD: This is foreshadowing for the "M.M. Moamrath" stuff later.

HOWARD: Oh, yeah, sure, right! But this was like 1966, just as the collective was breaking up. See, a lot of 'em, Moslander and other people, got into Diplomacy fandom.

BRAD: Diplomacy fandom?

HOWARD: See, back then, Diplomacy fandom was carried on through the mail. What you would do is release press releases about what your armies were gonna do and this kind of stuff. And you'd send 'em to each other and play the game through the mail like that, you know?

BRAD: So, military strategy games —

HOWARD: Sort of, yeah.

BRAD: Only diplomacy.

HOWARD: Right. They got off into that, and most of 'em quit publishing fanzines.

Then other fanzines came along to fill up the gap. And I did stuff all over the place for everybody for a while, you know? And there are a couple of my covers that are actually *good*, believe it or not. I've still got a couple of those, and they're still good!

BRAD: I also wanted to ask you about the other non-Wanderer fanzine story that we have for the book, "The Adventure of the Countess's Jewels." It's a Three Musketeers pastiche, right? What year would that have been?

HOWARD: That would be sometime between '64 and '67.

BRAD: I'm sure we have the date. But when I first saw that we had this story, and that it was a Three Musketeers pastiche, my initial thought was, "Oh, you were inspired by the Richard Lester movie." But you weren't, because that movie came out in 1973, and your story was several years earlier. Had you read *The Three Musketeers*?

HOWARD: No, I was inspired by all the earlier movies. And I just made it up, you know? Like Monty Python did with *Ripping Yarns.*

(Laughter.)

BRAD: Anything with swashbuckling and swords!

HOWARD: Right, exactly. Like I said, I was under the sway of the Hyborian Legion at the time, which George Scithers ran. He ran *Amra* for years, before he became the editor of *Asimov's.* Somewhere in the stuff I gave Texas A&M, I have my Hyborian Legion certificate. You sent in like ten bucks, and took a Hyborian Legion name, and they printed it on a diploma-looking piece of paper. It was really neat.

And there's another story that was in a Larry Herndon fanzine. It was set in ancient Britain. It was about a bunch of Celts and stuff. And I can't think of the name of it.

BRAD: I guess we don't have that one.

HOWARD: No, you don't. But there was stuff everywhere, right? I had art everywhere and stories everywhere. Just to anybody who would take 'em. Anybody who asked, in other words.

BRAD: Back in the teenage years, it was "whoever would take it, whenever they'd take it."

HOWARD: Right! Like I tell people now who try to get my stuff for free: "You gotta stand in *line* to get my stuff free, man!"

(Laughter.)

But back then, you did it because somebody asked. "Could you do a story for us for the next issue?"

BRAD: And of course, you were flattered that they asked.

HOWARD: Of course. "All the glory you can eat!" as Steve Utley used to say.

But yeah, "The Adventure of the Countess's Jewels" just came from watching old Musketeers movies and stuff like that. And back then, when George read my stories, he'd say, "Cardinal Richelieu? What superpowers did *he* have?" Because he was writing essentially prose versions of comic strips, and I was writing, you know, *stories*, right?

6. "Apprenticeship"

BRAD: The next thing I want to ask you about — and this is another one we talked about before, when I wasn't recording — I want to ask you, real briefly, about "Apprenticeship." Your different-incarnations-of-Jesus story.

HOWARD: Right. It was written sometime in the way-early '70s, I'm sure. And I probably sent it to one of those David Gerrold anthologies, where it was rejected. It was finally printed about 1980 in Lew Shiner's *Modern Stories*, a one-shot fanzine he did.

BRAD: Do you remember how it came about that you dug it out and gave it to him for that?

HOWARD: He asked for it. He had seen it, I think, at a very early Turkey City. [*BD Note: "Turkey City" was, and is, an infamous Texas sf/fantasy writing workshop.*] He had seen it or heard about it, and he called me on the phone — he was just across town — and asked me if I still had a copy of it, because he wanted to look at it. So I sent it to him, and he published it.

BRAD: You know, most of your stories are not super long stories. You have written some longer things, like *A Dozen Tough Jobs.* But most of your stories are between 5,000 and 15,000 words. Your basic "story-length" story. But this one is one of the few things I've seen from you that could qualify as what they now call "flash fiction." It's like, one page. One page, and you're out.

HOWARD: Well, I had also written a Feghoot. [*BD Note: A "Feghoot" is a short-short sf/f story that generally ends in a pun.*] And the punchline is a play on Tom Reamy's name — like a lot of Feghoots end, with a science-fiction person's name. Anyway, I had written a couple of things like that and sent them off, and nobody bought 'em. So I think "Apprenticeship" was during that period of time, when I was trying to write shorter and shorter things to see if I could do it. Because a lot of magazines were picking up stuff like that.

I think I told you about the night Steve Utley and other people and I wrote all these things together. *Mirabile dictu*, as I called it. The night our wives were at a baby shower, and we were all over at Buddy Saunders' part of the duplex while the wives were over at my and my wife's part of the duplex, right? It was me, Utley, Buddy, and George Proctor. And there was a tornado warning at the time, so we were all waiting for the house to get blown away at any second, right? We sat down and started playing with Buddy's new IBM Selectric II typewriter, and we started writing stories together. We wrote two two-way collaborations and two three-way collaborations, all in one night. And we sold *all* of them, every time, first time out. I think my take for the night was one hundred and twenty-five dollars total, you know?

Everyone else made the same amount of money. There were four pieces of fiction, and we wrote 'em all in a couple of hours.

BRAD: That's amazing. Do you remember which stories those were?

HOWARD: I'll look it up in my story logs. We sold one of 'em to *Vertex*, which was edited by Don Pfeil. They paid more than other people did at the time. I think he paid us a hundred bucks a piece for stuff that was *short*, right?

[*BD Note: Howard checked his story logs, and found that the two two-way collaborations from that night were his and Steven Utley's stories "Rex and Regina" (which was published as "Crab" in the semi-pro magazine* SF Eternity*) and "Willow Beeman" (which was published as "Sic Transit" in the Ballantine Books anthology* Stellar 2, *edited by Judy-Lynn Del Rey). One of the three-way collaborations was a Waldrop, Utley, and Saunders story called "Time and Variance" (which appeared in* Vertex*), and the other was a Waldrop, Utley, and Proctor story called "Up Uranus" (published in* Adam, Vol. 19 No. 1, *under the pseudonym "Franklin Dale Wyatt" — the three authors' middle names).*]

BRAD: So all of these stories you wrote in that one night were short-short things.

HOWARD: Right. I think one of the longest ones was the one Utley and I wrote together, and that was probably like five pages total. But the rest of the stuff was two and three pages. And like I said, it all sold first time out. Because people needed short stuff to fill out the pages in their magazines.

BRAD: I'll bet you wished you could have repeated that experience a few times.

HOWARD: Of course! But you tell the young kids now about something like that, and they don't believe you.

A LOVELY WITCH: A WANDERER STORY

> "In other places I have told of Wanderer's adventures, and of how he overcame great odds as suited his somewhat mercenary outlook on life, and of how the Pharaoh was angered with him. Once though, that benign old despot my master found need of the swordsman, which behooved and vexed his spirit greatly for having need of one so lowly; but nevertheless Wanderer was called forth and sent into the burning, barren land where once the metal towers of unknown purpose raised their gleaming silver sides to the night sky..."
>
> Chapter II: *The Canticles of Chimwazle*

Wanderer's eyes peered out from a face stained brown by wood oils, beneath hair made black by dyes. The wind whipped sand and stinging grit into his eyes; his lips were covered with dirt and grime, and the robes he wore could have stood stiffly up by themselves if he had set them down. On his head, he wore a headband of one of the short, swarthy desert tribesmen. His clothing was yards of robes and cloaks, which rubbed his back raw, and which stunk terribly after four days of travel across the glittering sand and scrub thorns. Under the cloak he wore his own short sword Boarkiller, but strapped at his side was a curved, golden scimitar which swung and banged against his thigh as he rocked back and forth on the back of the camel, which beast was making about half-a-mile an hour across the sands. The wind rose in a gust, which burned Wanderer's face, and lifted the headcloth over and up across his head. In trying to grab it, which he finally did just before it flew out of reach, Wanderer almost fell off the camel's back face first.

Damn the Pharaoh! Here Wanderer was, trudging across the sands on some idiot mission, sent by an old rascal who hated him, wearing hot, sticky clothes, and a bulky, curved sword which was good for nothing except trimming cactus. Wanderer could feel his brains cooking under the hot desert sun, which shimmered the purple horizon and made it seem to flow and move. Sweat ran down his face, forming huge drops, mixed with wood stain that made his tanned face the color of dark varnish.

Wanderer wanted to go off somewhere and giggle, preferably a place with gallons of water, beautiful girls, and tons of food with barrels of wine. The heat made him giddy and he caught himself swaying. Knowing he couldn't let his mind wander, he bent all his thoughts to ways to make the Pharaoh suffer when, and if, he made it back. The more he thought, the madder he got.

He swopped the camel with the camel stick in his right hand. It began to move a little faster, settling into a jog-trot. Wanderer was ready to accept it, then he thought once again about the Pharaoh. The old boy had been nice about it, after a dozen or so Civic Policemen had grabbed Wanderer in a tavern and drug him to the presence of His Most Elevated Tyrant. He had given Wanderer the choice of going on the mission, returning safely, and collecting a huge reward, or of refusing to go and being beheaded on the spot. Wanderer, of course, had decided that he would love a trip into the desert for a change of scenery and climate, and had accepted the Pharaoh's agreement.

As soon as his escort had turned back, near the Sini border, Wanderer had thought that a trip to one of the seacoast strongholds would be nice, or perhaps a trip even to the war-gutted Forbidden Lands across the Middle Sea. Something told him, though, that the wily old ruler would have spies somewhere along the way, and surely as soon as he was seen on the seacoast, he could begin looking for a small army to come after him. Now, grumbling about his stupidity, he was slowly realizing what an idiot he had been for going through with his end of the bargain.

Just for spite, he swatted the camel twice across the neck as hard as he could. Off it went, looking like some gigantic spider clam — racing up and down the small dunes, and Wanderer hung on for dear life.

Inside the walls of Fata el Ercha, the people moved about quickly, shouting to each other as in a holiday spirit. All houses were lit, even the most humble. Of course, the sons of Ishmael did not drink, being faithful to the Prophet, but none checked the fruit juices to be sure that some had not fermented, and therefore the proceedings were doubly spirited.

A fat merchant swaying down the street mumbling to himself was bumped into by two spike-helmeted soldiers, who then sat down and laughed until they cried at the plight of the merchant, who was vainly trying to find his legs so that he could get up. The porcine one finally lay face down and cried into the dirt, shaking all over and calling on Allah to give him back his legs.

Elsewhere were a few more somber people, especially near the center of the town, more especially in the outer works of the palace of the local sheik who called Fata el Ercha his domain. Guards paced back and forth on the wall of the palace as well as a double guard on the grounds. The soldiers wore light mail shirts and cloaks, and seemed extremely nervous, always lingering their scimitar hilts or holding halberds at the ready. The night carried tension.

Just as the moon rose, a lone figure riding a camel was spotted by the guards on the city walls. The figure rode up to the wall, then seemed impatient when the camel halted before the closed gates.

"Since when are the gates of the town closed to the sons of the desert? Or are you afraid that the faithless Egyptians will swoop down upon your city!" shouted the figure. Wanderer knew good and well that they were afraid of just that. But telling an Arab that he was afraid of an Egyptian was inviting a chest full of quarrels. Since the Great Fire Wars, when the first Pharaoh had come and established his own religion, and the sons of the Nile had renounced the religion of Mohammed, the Arabs were sworn enemies of the Egyptians. Hence Wanderer's desert costume, and the challenge he threw in the faces of the guards.

One of two things would happen. He would hear crossbows twang and then he wouldn't hear much else, if they thought he wasn't an Arab. Or the gates would open to let him in. He knew that most Arabs could bluff themselves out of anything, and he was trying his best to look, think, and even smell, which he did, like an Arab.

The gates opened. Cold sweat broke out on Wanderer's brow, He swatted the camel, and it walked through the gates. One of the guards came lightly tripping down the steps from the wall.

"State your business. The city is full of too many desert jackals who come to watch the Egyptian girl be executed to suit either I or the sheik. Come, come, if you haven't a reason, I'll turn you back into the desert," he said, trying to put on an official air.

Wanderer leaned down. He glared at the guard, trying not to laugh. "Have you looked at my trappings? Or cared to look at my sword?"

The guard looked at each. Then his eyes widened. His mouth fell open. His official air floated away.

"Ahab Alrashim! But we thought you dead in the holy war against the Egyptians almost two years gone. I cannot ..."

"Silence, imbecile! I have enemies everywhere. I have been in Egypt these two years, and am on my way to Mecca to the Caliph. I have stopped to rest. Not one word that I am here, or I shall seek you out and let you taste my sword edge!" said Wanderer, glaring.

The guard turned green. He stepped back and let Wanderer pass by, making all sorts of bowing signs.

Wanderer let the camel trot down the street. He was pleased with himself that the ruse had worked. True, the trappings of the camel and the scimitar were those of Ahab Alrashim ... sword and trappings taken by Wanderer as victory spoils after he had killed Ahab in a sword fight when the Arabs had tried to take Khufu two years past. Wanderer had gone into that battle, not out of patriotism for Egypt, or love for the Pharaoh, but because his sister had lived in Khufu then and he hadn't wanted to see her under Arab rule, or worse. The Arab Legions had seen Wanderer and Ahab skipping across the dunes, then the Egyptians had routed, and the only talk heard on the long trip back was speculation on who killed whom. Some diehard Arabs still swore that somewhere out near Khufu, Ahab and the accursed Egyptian were still at it.

Wanderer knew that the guard would keep his mouth shut. Ahab had been hated by as many as idolized him, and it was known that his vow was as good as written scripture in the Koran. If possible, Wanderer would have to swing this deal so that the guard would still be on duty when he got ready to make his getaway.

It was good that everyone knew of Ahab's sword and the trappings of his camel rig. They were better than a pennon or a band or trumpeters when Ahab Alrashim had gone into a battle or had settled a blood feud. In fact, he was known more widely by them than he was recognized as a person. A good thing, too, for Wanderer might have been unlucky enough to have picked a guard who knew Alrashim.

Wanderer turned the camel down a narrow side street. First, he had to get to a livery and find a couple of horses ...

A soldier walked along, his light mail shirt making faint tinkling noises. He was in a particularly bad mood. The captain had called out all guards who had been off duty more than five hours, because the desert men had become so spirited that they wanted to lynch the captured Egyptian girl before dawn. He shifted his pike to his left hand in order to navigate a sharp turn in the narrow street. He saw a movement from the corner of his eye before someone brought the hilt of a scimitar against his ear ...

A few minutes later it was Wanderer who walked down the street near the palace — with slight tinkling noises. The pike felt very uncomfortable in his hand; the thing would be of no use in fighting because of its heaviness. It didn't matter, he didn't feel that he would take on too many pikemen anyway. Oh, Hell, why had he taken the Pharoah up on this deal! He knew finding the girl would be easy enough; getting her out would be impossible and there was no chance at all of him getting her back to Egypt. The Pharaoh wanted her for some special reason; something that he had left to Wanderer's imagination.

A horn blared out, piercing Wanderer's ears. Behind him, he heard the stomp of running feet. He wheeled around. He knew the guard couldn't have gotten out of the ropes so soon. Instead, he saw guards, dressed like himself, running at him, but instead of laying on, they swept past him, running towards the sound of the horn. Wanderer stood a moment.

"Whatsa matter with you," came a deep voice, "didn't you hear the horn?"

Wanderer turned. By his insignia, the man facing him was the captain of the guards. He was a big man, wearing a breast-plate and chain mail, and carrying a huge scimitar in his left hand. He had a broad face, covered partly by a huge beard and mustache.

"Come on, boy. Those hopped-up desert scum are trying to get at the girl. We got to take her to the palace, so they can execute her officially. Orders are orders! Let's go!" he yelled, tugging at Wanderer's arm, nearly pulling it off.

Wanderer, even as he ran, was grinning all over. He murmured a sort of thankfulness to any Egyptian god in general who happened to be listening in.

The mob gathered near the gate was giving the palace guards a hard time trying to get inside and to one of the corner turrets which served, Wanderer guessed, as the prison tower. Lots better than a dungeon; somebody might tunnel out of a dungeon, but not the upper part of a tower. After that, Wanderer didn't have time to think. He and the big captain began applying the pike butts to some heads. Other guards were running to join them, both from the palace grounds and the other parts of the city. In a few seconds the crowd had drawn back, most of them rubbing aching heads or holding battered arms. Wanderer stood with the captain, facing the crowd.

"Why don't you go back into the desert! It'd do us all good. At least, you can pretend you're civilized, and wait until the Egyptian girl is tried and then you can see an execution. The Sheik has promised good entertainment!" roared the big, burly captain.

"We want the girl!" came a shout from the crowd. Others took it up.

"She's a witch! Sorceress! Egyptian scum! Kill her!"

The crowd pressed forward again. Pikes bristled from the line of guards. Big heavy nightsticks leaped from their thongs. In a few seconds, there was a melee of screams, curses, and dull thuds in front of the gate.

"You!" screamed the big captain, as he kicked the legs from under a short man trying to get by him, at some of the guards. "Get to the barracks, call out the charioteers, and come break this up. You three" he hollered at Wanderer and two others "come with me. We'll get the girl out!"

They sped off across the palace grounds towards the turret. Two guards stood in front of the door. The captain opened the door, began running up the steps. Wanderer clambered up after him, after dropping his pike outside. Around and around they went, up the spiral steps. The captain opened a door, and jumped in, Wanderer behind him. A fat, half-naked guard leaped to his feet, then settled back as he saw the captain.

"What's up?" he wheezed.

"Give me the keys. Some of the people got their fingers on some juice and are trying to get to the girl. Stay here and make sure no one gets up here," the captain said, running to the other door with the jangling keys in his hand. Wanderer went after him. The door swung open.

A girl jumped up. Wanderer didn't have time to look at her. A job was a job. He had a glimpse of a tattered dress and darkish hair. Then the captain's big body blocked his vision.

"C'mon girl. You're going to the palace with us." The captain grabbed her roughly and pulled her around. Then there was a noise like a rotten egg cracking, and the big captain doubled up like all the air had been let out of him. He fell limply to the floor, and his helmet, dented above the temple, rolled across the room.

Wanderer threw what was left of the stool in the corner. He grabbed the girl. "Play along with everything I do," he said, pulling her to the door.

He pushed her out before him, making it look good. "Get down the stairs, scum! You're putting us to a lot of trouble." He grabbed her arm and pulled her towards the door that led to the stairs.

"Wait!" grumbled the huge guard. "Where's the captain?" He stepped closer to them, then looked into the other room, saw a pair of feet sticking out. "What's going on here?" He unsheathed a huge sword. "You're not leaving here." He stepped forward, and stood near the stair door.

There was a flash of silver and a meaty *chunk!* filled the air. The guard writhed once, then dropped the sword with a clatter. He didn't fall, though. He was pinned to the wall by a dagger through the neck.

"What — what are you doing this for? Do you want to torture me yourself?" asked the girl, shivering.

"Our old friend the Pharaoh wants to see you bad enough so that I've got to do a lot of dirty work. Now, just be quiet and go along with me."

The girl's eyes widened at the mention of the Pharaoh.

They clambered down the steps and out the door. The guards waited for them. Wanderer began yelling as soon as he got out.

"The captain said to help those at the gates till the chariots get there. I'll take the girl to the palace." Oh, damn, he thought, don't let them wonder why the captain's not here. It was settled a few seconds later when a noise from the gate brought their heads around. A few of the drunks had broken through and were pointing at them. Off went the guards with brandished night sticks, and in a few seconds there was a flurry of arms, legs, and headcloths. Wanderer pushed the girl towards the edge of the wall. They ran off through the low inner walls and lost themselves in the palace gardens ...

The guards on the city wall were leaning on their halberds and watching the proceedings with unfeigned interest. What went on inside the palace grounds was none of their business unless the Sheik himself called on them. Besides, the royal guards never got any exercise. It would do them good. While the guards and many of the townspeople watched the scrap, one other saw two figures disappear into the gardens. He happened to be standing on one of the verandas of the palace, which was quite all right, since he owned it. Growling, he went off down the steps.

Minutes later, Wanderer and the girl sat panting under a tangle of growth where they had stopped to catch their breath. Near them, set in the wall, was one of those ornamental windows, flower-shaped, which decorated the open gaps between the flowers. Wanderer had planned to use it as a means of escape once he caught his breath. The chariots had rumbled off a few seconds earlier, and screams floated back, telling them that the palace guards were getting the drunks in shape. Wanderer knew the girl would be discovered as gone soon. Questions would be asked. Then Wanderer would probably fight the last fight of his life.

She leaned on him, breathing hard, her lips parted so that she could get air. Her hair, he noticed, was lighter in color than most Egyptian girls', and was cut short. Her nose was a little larger than it should have been, but it took nothing away from her beauty. Her shoulders, and other parts of her body, were heaving as she breathed. She would be a good catch for any man. Wanderer had to put her aside from his mind; there wouldn't or would be other times to think about it, depending on what happened next. Right now ...

Brush crackled. Wanderer leaped up; the girl muffled a scream. He tore the scimitar from its sheath; he had no time to grab for Boarkiller strapped out of sight at his side. A figure loomed up, dressed in mail from head to foot, wearing the head-cloth of a sheik.

"Abu Hrasham!" choked the girl.

Wanderer knew then who he faced. He crouched low, unused to the weight and heft of the scimitar in his hand.

"So, the Pharaoh was bold enough to send someone for the girl anyway. I think he'll get both of you back. But without your heads."

He leaped, swinging his sword. Wanderer parried, then spun and sent his blade licking out in a flash of silver. The sheik replied smoothly, brought his blade over Wanderer's guard. Wanderer stumbled and somehow got his blade up in time to save his shoulder. He was fighting blindly now. He caught himself backing, tried to correct it. Each time he tried to circle, Abu deftly stemmed his advance. Wanderer knew he would be backed into the shrubbery, where the sheik could carve him to pieces while he tried to get room to swing. If he could only get Boarkiller — no time for anything but back and back and try to keep that silver death from touching him.

Both problems were solved at once. For an instant, Wanderer forgot the weapon he used. A slight opening came while the sheik tried to chop downward. Forgetting that his point was almost useless, old fighting sense made Wanderer lunge. The sheik, unused to the attack, parried wildly. He got better than he hoped for. His own point caught the hilt of Wanderer's sword, and it went sailing over and over into the bushes. But the sheik was still backpedaling.

Wanderer ripped Boarkiller out. It seemed to snicker evilly as it came out of the sheath. It was not the desperate Wanderer who had but a moment before been fighting a futile battle. It was a cool, level-headed swordsman with the one weapon that he could use as if it were part of his body. He had found the sheik's weak spot, and he made use of it.

Wanderer came in, swinging Boarkiller in and out, around and up and down the blade with which the sheik could barely use to parry. He bored in, teeth clenched, stance light and high on the toes, at his ease now.

It was over in a split second. The mail was made to withstand an edge, not a point. The sheik had swung high. Boarkiller changed course twice, then disappeared into the sheik's side before he could parry either feint. The scimitar jumped from nerveless fingers, and the sheik Abu Hrasham gurgled and went down, clutching his side.

Without a second look, Wanderer caught the girl's arm gently and pushed her to the window.

They made it to the horses, hidden behind a row of shabby houses near the gates. Wanderer got into the garb of Ahab Alrashim once again, except the camel trappings, which he stuffed into the horse's saddle bags. So far, so good. He put a riding cloak on the girl. His biggest task lay ahead of him. He rode beside her slowly until they came within sight of the gate. He leaned over and squeezed her hand.

"You are the sister of Ahab Alrashim. You live near the Nefud Desert, and you were here visiting relatives incognito for fear that someone would swipe you to get revenge on Ahab, since he was supposed to be dead. Your name is Talwa," he said.

He saw that his "friend" at the gate was still on duty. Then he spurred his horse, came charging out of the darkness leading the girl's horse. Halberds came up and crossbows levelled at them.

"What's the meaning of this! Oh ... it's you," said the guard; then he lowered his voice. "Does the desert call?"

"Mine enemies have found me. My sister and I must leave. If any come looking, you have never seen me. Understand? Hurry!"

said Wanderer, taking on the gruff tones he had used before.

The guard signaled to open the gates. They began swinging open, showing the desert under the cold stars. Nothing ever looked better to Wanderer.

A horn blew. The guards stiffened. Clanks of mail and spears and the sounds of running men filled the air. "No one leaves the city. The girl has been stolen!" yelled a guard rounding a corner at the head of a dozen others.

The guard looked into Wanderer's eyes. "I'm sorry. You'll have to stay! We ..." He never finished. Wanderer shoved with his foot, and the guard went tumbling onto his back.

The gates were beginning to close. Wanderer spurred, and his horse leaped through the narrowing aperture. His arm was almost jerked off as the reins of the girl's horse became tight. She leaned low and kicked. The horse flew through an instant before the gates clanged shut. Off they went into the darkness of the desert, quarrels and spears showering around them. Something hot and wet trickled down Wanderer's left arm. He looked and was surprised to see a quarrel buried in the muscle. No time to worry about that ...

Five days later, Wanderer lay in the shade of a date palm, surrounded by grass. They had stopped after a day-and-a-half of riding and had gone into a fitful sleep. Both were rested as were the horses. There only remained the short trip to Alexandria. Wanderer's arm was still sore, but was healing. Somewhere, they had shaken the hordes that had poured from Fata el Ercha after then. Now, he sat in the shade, with the water trickling from the spring in the middle of the oasis. The girl was sitting beside him. He put his arm around her almost before she knew it.

"You know, girl, that I don't even know your name. Here we've been together for the better part of a week! And I've been too busy to really notice you, something I shall never forgive myself for." Then: "It seems strange that a girl like you should want to live with some old fool, even if he does run the greatest nation in the world. Why ... "

The girl giggled; something she hadn't done before.

He went on. He knew she wouldn't be able to resist his next line. "Why not stay with me a while? I could offer you the desert stars, the burning sands, wine, ale, anything your heart desires and I can steal. You won't get that when you're locked up in a stuffy castle with rats and worms and cold stone, and an old man for a consort."

Then he kissed her. Almost. She pulled away at the last instant. "I wish you wouldn't," she said quietly.

"Why, am I that bad?" he asked, moving closer again.

"No, but General Nayak and fifty of his men are watching you," she said matter-of-factly.

Wanderer looked up. Somehow, the Pharaoh's brother and his men had come within fifty feet of them and were looking on with quiet amusement.

"Ha! I see he brought you back, Tula. We didn't think he'd make it. No one did," said the general, grinning from ear to ear.

Tula ran up to the general, put her arms around him. "It was the most wonderful thing anyone has ever done, Uncle."

Wanderer was confused. Tula? He'd heard the name many times. Who was named — Uncle Nayak!! But Nayak was the ...

"Don't worry, Wanderer. Daddy's said lots worse things about you that I shouldn't have heard," she said, mounting her horse.

All the way to Alexandria, during the triumphal procession, and the banquet in his honor, Wanderer was in sort of a pinkish haze.

He smiled when he should, had good manners, spoke when he must, but he didn't remember any of it afterward.

When he finally went to sleep that night, he dreamed of a girl with brown eyes and hair cut short, even though the girl resting on his arm had green eyes and blond hair that hung down past her shoulders...

THE WELL OF CHAOS: A WANDERER STORY

> "In this time of turmoil, though it be two centuries since the fear and superstition following the Great Fire Wars broke out, demon cults have sprung up, devoted to dark gods and hideous rites involving human sacrifice and mass orgies. The Pharaoh has tried to detain them, his Civic Police have taken thousands prisoner, but to no avail. Where a cult is destroyed, another springs up, sometimes worse than the first. The cults draw their following by way of fear rather than through devotion. This is prompted by certain disappearances among the unfaithful. These cults practice taking chosen ones to be given to the gods in the rites on the dark of the moon.
>
> "To one of these worships came that sand-footed rogue The Wanderer, to do dating aces while attempting rescue ..."
>
> Chapter II, *The Canticles of Chimwazle*

Down, down into the mouth of the pitch black well wound the grim procession, their chanting tunes carrying the feeling of impending evil. Smoking torches gave only enough light to dispel the Stygian darkness a foot or two before them. Their steps echoed on the slime-covered stairs where rats and lizards grudgingly scurried away into the fungus-crusted rocks. Darkness here was never broken save at noonday, then only the top of the hundred-foot mouth of the well was lighted to any degree. It was as if night took refuge here during the daylight hours and flowed out over half the earth at night. The circular stairway wound ever downward for nearly two hundred feet to stop at the edge of a platform fifty feet wide.

It was towards this platform that the procession moved, the priests sweating under their cowls in the thick black robes they wore. Masked priests followed, stripped to the waist, and carrying in their hands the ceremonial axes of the cult. The golden blades gleamed evilly when struck by torchlight. Following these wound the sacred dancers, musicians, lesser priests, and finally the faithful, their voices lifted in chanting.

Down they came, perhaps two or three hundred in all. The priests stepped onto the platform, causing eerie echoes to reverberate evilly across the slimy, stagnant pool of water which took up the other half of the well. The priests continued onto the altar, which strangely faced the well instead of the congregation. The faithful formed a rough line behind the altar and stood. It was then that one other person was roughly pulled to the raised dais. The sacrifice.

She was a girl of nineteen or so, pretty in her way. Her eyes red from crying, she did not struggle, but went with a sullen defiance to the platform beneath the altar. Her hands were tied with leather bands and she had found long ago this night that struggle was useless. The girl trembled as the ceremony began, knowing that she was the 'chosen one' tonight and destined to meet the dark god Gresh in his lair of slime and muck.

The priests began chanting a strange, birdlike cry, punctuated by the musicians' eerie tunes and wild drum beats. Faster, faster went the music, louder and louder became the chant. The congregation took it up and echoed the priests.

Then it stopped. The entire gathering stood frozen in the nerve-shattering silence. The high priest mounted the altar and looked out over the slimy, dark water. His face was wrinkled with age and his eyes showed malevolent reflections from the twin torches which lit the altar. A horned skull cap of the high priest of Gresh adorned his head. He raised his withered arms to the sky, facing the altar and peering into the water.

"Oh mighty Gresh, lurker of the Deep Well, we bring you this night a Chosen One, so that you may appease your hunger and need not come from your lair. Take her and show us your mercy, Oh Mighty One. Hail, Gresh the Destroyer."

The girl was pulled to the altar by two brawny masked priests, who then dragged her to the edge of the platform. As she looked down into the water and remembered all the tales of her childhood, she wept and fell limp.

"Gresh, whose wrath be vented hopefully upon this chosen one, take thee this offering we give. Long live Mighty Gresh."

Upon these words, the two masked priests bent slightly, then rocketed up, flinging the girl outward and upwards over the slimy, stagnant pond which Gresh made his home and waited for offerings.

Her limp body reached the apex of its flight and started to arc downwards. Then ... it stopped with a jerk in midair, swung left to right dizzily, and began a slow, deliberate movement towards the starlit sky above the well mouth.

Cursing himself, Wanderer heaved for all he was worth on the rope at the end of which the girl dangled perilously, several feet above the water. Sweat broke out on his body under the light purple tunic he wore and his hands were being chafed to ribbons by the rope he tugged on.

Three days ago he had come into this country from Alexandria, and had been ill-received by the people. Then, one night at the tavern, he had been sought out by an old man named Galt, who offered him all his worldly belongings if only he could save his daughter. It seemed that Nila, that was her name, was to be the sacrifice to the pool-god Gresh. The old man told him that long ago, Gresh had been born in the pool at the bottom of the well, in the dark days following the Great Wars and the Silent Death. In the years following he had ravaged the lands, seeking blood to satisfy his devilish thirsts. Upon finding its lair in the huge well, men had kept it fed with animals. Of this had come the cult, which fed it each day but had begun to use rites once a month at which humans were thrown to the thing called Gresh. The cult had drained the lands of cattle and people had begun to live in fear of each other, lest the priests choose them for the dark god's hunger. Such it was when Wanderer had come to this cursed place.

He had known he was a fool to get involved in devil worships, but had believed the old man's tale, strange as it was. The old man had said there was growing unrest, but that all were too afraid of Gresh's wrath to openly defy the cult.

So this night, with hundreds of feet of rope on his shoulder, he had made his way to the Well of Gresh with the foolhardy idea of rescuing Nila from the clutches of the demon-worshippers. He had, while the elaborate ceremony began, come halfway down the spiral steps in darkness, perhaps fifty feet above the heads of the celebrants. There he had attached his rope contrivance to one side of the well. He then crossed to the other side, perhaps thirty feet higher up the spiral stops, and had attached the other end of the rope. Dangling from the middle was another length of rope, which he had pulled in and looped. As soon as the girl left the arms of the priests, a snakelike noose had flown silently downward from his hands, neatly catching her across the middle. A dangerous chance, but it had worked. Now, he panted as he drew her up by means of a third rope attached to the noose. Wanderer had made it look dramatic. It did.

The priests stood, paralyzed, peering into the darkness above, and seeing nothing. Gasps came from the faithful. Axe-wielders began swarming up the stairs. Someone had the sense to light an oil-soaked arrow and fire it upwards into the gloom. Its dim light showed Wanderer straining at the rope. Cries went up.

"Blasphemers! Kill him!" rose from the priests. "Death to the unfaithful! Sacrilege!"

Wanderer pulled the girl's limp body to the steps beside him. She began to move, awakening. He cut her bonds with his throwing knife, shaking her to movement. She looked at him dazedly, then shook her head to clear it.

"Come, Nila!"

The axemen had already come one flight below them. Arrows

whizzed up, knocking loose chunks of bricking. He tugged at her, pushed her in front of him.

"Make it to the rope, two flights up!" he yelled at her. "Then they can't possibly get you! Run!"

The girl ran. Around the spiral they went. Halfway. One flight. The girl was nearly two flights up when she dropped to the fungus-crusted steps, panting.

"I — I — ca — can't make — "

Wanderer didn't let her finish. He bent, snatched her up from the steps and ran. His tired muscles bulged and his arms hurt from that eighty-foot pull. He lifted her and ran for the rope which leapt up to the top of the well. It would save them three flights of steps — if they could make it. Already the axemen were across the well from them and gaining in their fanatical haste.

Wanderer stumbled to the rope, set the girl down, then lifted her once again.

"Climb, Nila. At least make it to the second stairway. Then run as far as you can. They won't get by me. Pull the rope up behind you; don't let them get to it or they'll catch you. Climb!"

He shoved her upward. She caught at the rope, began to inch her way up towards the next flight of steps. He helped as much as he was able, pushing her until he could reach no higher.

Then Wanderer turned and drew his short, thick sword Boarkiller. His eyes began to gleam. Wanderer in the midst of a fight was a fury, a human machine of destruction. He crouched low, waiting for the first axeman to reach him.

The high priest had wasted no time on the chances that the axemen would overtake the fleeing pair. He turned, and paused statuelike, his arms upraised in a sign of invocation. His cracked lips gleamed evilly in the light of newly lit torches.

"Oh Great and Mighty Gresh. See you these blasphemers, and know them for what they are. Come forth, Gresh! Destroy them. Kill! Kill! Arise, Gresh!" he cried hysterically.

For a few seconds the faithful awaited, eagerness in their eyes.

Gresh had never been seen since the cult had arisen. Never had he been called forth before.

The stagnant water, evil, stinking, was placid. Scum and algae floated on top, undisturbed. Slimy fungus grew at the water's edge, over onto the platform. Then, slowly, the water near one edge began to swirl, as if a school of fish had been startled. Scum floated to one side. Bubbles began to rise. The water seemed to turn darker, danker at the spot.

Gresh appeared.

A great yard-wide head came up, crusted with slime and algae, dripping slaver and black rot out from the long, daggerlike teeth in its open mouth. One claw lifted out of the water. Handlike, it had webs between the fingers, and six-inch claws for nails. It swam forward ponderously, a bulky, loathsome thing unused to travel. Gresh came to the edge of the pool. It clawed the wall of the well, began to inch its way up. Its hind legs appeared, manlike but deformed; too short for its twelve-foot body. The feet, too, were webbed. It had a short, stocky tail. Leeches and suckers clung to its body, where there was no fungus. Its body, greenish in the dim light, was huge — too fat and bulky. It stank. Gresh looked above, saw Wanderer, and began to climb its way up the well's wall.

Wanderer played havoc with the sacred guards. The first's axe had looped over his head, ready to send a blow that would split Wanderer from head to navel. Boarkiller went between his ribs and through his spine before the swing half formed. The second parried Wanderer's sword, swung a blow that brought blood from the swordsman's arm. He got a blade in the throat for his trouble. The stairs were too narrow for more than one at a time.

The axemen had no room to swing, while Wanderer thrusted and parried with ease.

One axeman abandoned his axe for a sword. It snaked in for Wanderer's ribs, caught on Boarkiller's hilt. Wanderer's sword flashed too quickly to follow. Back and forth they danced, in and out went the swords in playful death-games. Then, Boarkiller's point appeared on the other side of the axeman's head and the fight was over.

Wanderer waited. But the others had run, screaming, away from him, throwing away their weapons in panic.

Wanderer looked down, and saw Death groping upwards.

He went up the rope with a bound, climbing in a haste he didn't know he had. Up, up to get away from that loathsome thing that followed him. For one of the first times in his life, Wanderer was afraid.

Nila had reached the second flight. She pulled herself over onto the steps as Wanderer came up, panting from his climb. She tried to stand and nearly fell. Wanderer groped his way over to the edge.

Just as he reached her, she half-stood and looked down. At the sight of Gresh she screamed, her eyes rolled in fear and exhaustion, and she slid over the edge.

Somehow, through a haze, Wanderer grabbed her wrist with his left hand. They hung there, supported only by the strength in Wanderer's right arm, dangling while the dripping horror climbed ever towards them. Tiredly, Wanderer got his legs on the rope. Tiredly, he inched his way up to the edge of the steps. Dazedly, he pulled Nila up onto the stairway and pulled her onto the slimy steps, away from the edge.

This is the way all heroes die, thought Wanderer, as he pulled his throwing knife from its sheath. He thought of the camels he had stolen, the money he had squandered away, the girls he had rescued, the swordsmen he had conquered. His mind went to his days as a cut-purse, his first getting his sword Boarkiller from the wizard. Through a daze, he finally saw the monster's gleaming toad-like face below him. Its mouth opened, and a stench of death rose into Wanderer's face.

"This is the way heroes die," he thought again. He kicked himself away from the wall, flew out towards the evil, slimy thing below him. Its mouth gaped in anticipation. Wanderer's knife arced down. The blade buried itself in the thing's eye to the hilt.

It clawed — the knife flashed again — slime flew — the claws again — falling ... falling — the knife again — spattering blood ... falling ... falling ...

Wanderer jerked up in bed and gasped for breath. The thing, where was it? Then he saw Nila and Galt who had started when he had come up.

"Oh, swordsman, the fever broke. You will live." Wanderer hoped so.

"How did I get here?" asked Wanderer, feeling his bruised, clawed, and cut body.

"'Twas most heroic, Wanderer," said Galt, "to see you launch yourself upon the god Gresh, and slay him as you fell. Never had I or anyone else seen such bravery. And it broke the fear over us. As one, we rose up against the demon-cult.

"The monster was not dead yet. Its death throes were terrible to see. Some of us fished you out, while the others fed the priests to the leeches. I myself had the pleasure of tossing the high priest in on his ear. The once-god Gresh, in its madness, bit him into separate parts before it died. The whole place stank for days afterwards. You ... "

"For days?"

"Yes," affirmed Nila, "you've lain here for over a week in a fever. You were quite mangled by Gresh. It's a wonder you weren't killed by the thing." Her eyes showed wonderment in their green depths.

"It's going to be a nice long stay here," thought Wanderer as he looked at Nila. "A nice stay, indeed."

THE SOUL-CATCHER

Notes on this Publication:

This is the third Harry Smith story, chronologically, and the first in order of appearance, which might present a problem to anyone who has not heard of the character before.

The first story, "Sawtooth by Starlight" is a short fantasy, and is presently in the capable hands of Paul Moslander, and was at first to appear in *Jeddak* #VIII. The plans were changed and it was to be my second story in *Magnum* #1.

The second story in the series, "Moonlight on Claw Lake" could only be called adventure fiction or possibly an espionage tale, although the spy element is kept to a minimum. It is a very long novelette (for a fanzine) and will appear in a later *Batwing*, and is the hands of Larry Herndon.

Like the other two Harry Smith stories, this one is being written in the heat of inspiration. (The first took me somewhere around 45 minutes, and the novelette was written in one day straight last summer while I was suffering from an abscessed tooth.)

The setting of this story is the same, Haram's Corners, Texas, a central Texas town, pop. 2667. Harry Smith, after unsuccessful tries at being a private eye (his life-long ambition was to set up an office in Houston), returned to Haram's Corners after his father, mother, and brother were killed in a car wreck. He now works for the D.A. as a legman. But to tell any more would be spoiling the other two stories.

Let Harry tell you about it.

Howard Waldrop
Limited edition 25 copies
The VORPAL Press March 1966

Everybody's still talking about the night the green star fell. Ann and I had been married for two weeks, and we had just got back from our honeymoon in Dallas. Don't ever go to Dallas for a honeymoon; it's too noisy and everybody wants a tip. We were all sitting on the front porch — all of us being Bill Soames, Ann and me. We had invited Bill — he's the deputy sheriff — over for supper that night. I wanted to show off Ann's cooking, but she outdid herself that night. They nearly had to carry me out to the front porch, I was so full of chicken and mashed potatoes and peas and salad.

"You know, Harry, you're a lucky kid, having a wife that can cook like that, mighty lucky." Bill was only twenty-three, but to him I was still a kid, since I was a year younger.

"Ummhum," I mumbled. I was too full even to talk. Ann and me were sitting in the porch swing, she had her head on my shoulder and was tickling my nose with some honeysuckle she had pulled off the porch. I sneezed, clawed for her hand, then gave up while she tickled my nose some more. Bill was leaned back against the columns on the porch, with a content smile on his face.

Funny thing about sitting on the front porch on a hot summer night. It's one of those things everybody in town does, but you don't mind doing it, too. I mean, you hate to have to go shopping every week, mainly because everybody else does the same thing. But sitting on the front porch after supper is different. You get away from the heat inside the house, and the wind outside blows cool across your head, and you can hear everybody else along the street sitting on their front porch, talking and cooling off. Away off somewhere a dog barked; the moon had come up an hour ago but wasn't giving off much light. Bill jerked up.

"Say, you know the carnival is coming to town day after tomorrow? I almost forgot to tell you. They were tacking up posters all afternoon up and down the street. Why don't I get Jeannie, and us four go together Friday night, huh?" He almost yelled.

"Oh, Harry, tell him we'll go," Ann squealed. "We can ride all the rides, and I can wear my new dress you bought me last week and I can go find a pair of shoes to match it and we can — "

"Okay, Bill, we'll go with ya'll. If — "

Ann grabbed me and kissed me. "You big hunk of man, you!" she whispered, and started biting my ear. That's when the porch swing tipped over and both of us fell out — kerplunk thud! — onto the porch. I lay there laughing at Ann while we tried to untangle, and then started up. The swing swung back in and cracked me across the head. I just lay there laughing like an idiot because I was too big to cry. Bill and Ann were laughing, and when I got up Bill slapped his knees and doubled over. His chair went over and he fell off the porch backwards and out into the flower bed. I had the last laugh on Bill. When we all calmed down, Bill stood up and thanked us for the dinner, and apologized for leavin' so early.

"I've got to drop by Jeannie's a while before I turn in," he said.

"You know what I think," I said. "I think you ought to marry that gal. Why, just look what Ann's done for me in the last two weeks. I've never felt better before in my life. You wouldn't think by looking at her — "

That's when her fist got me right in the eye. "Shush up, Harry. Oh hey, don't you dare — hee hee, quit tickling me, you big ox — " she giggled, while I paid her back.

"I can see ya'll aren't listening, so I'll just mosey along," Bill started. He had taken about two steps when the sky turned green.

At first everything went green, then faded, and it was deathly quiet, and the only sound was the intake of breath along porches up and down the street and all over town. It was "Ooooo" like a tonguetied kid saying "lady sheep." Ann and I jumped off the porch beside Bill and looked up at the sky.

The stars were there, and what part of the moon there was,

but something else was there, too. I could feel it run up and down the hair on my neck and arms. The feeling told me that something was coming. It came. It appeared suddenly, a long green streak down the sky, at the tip end a whistling, cracking ball of green flames, splitting open the sky, making it bright as daylight; only a weird, terrible, green daylight. The fireball at the end crackled like a high tension wire as it screamed by overhead, and there was a shower of sparks cascading down for miles around, burning themselves out before they hit, like snow melting before it hits unfrozen ground.

The green star seemed to hang in the sky for eternity, when it was only a couple of seconds. Then it disappeared over the mountains, way off over Sawtooth Ridge, out past Claw Lake, and further. For a few seconds there was complete silence, then from far off came a tremor, like when a jet leaves a sonic boom, only this was deeper, way down in the ground, like Texas was trying to expel the intruder which had burrowed itself in its skin in some not too far away place.

It was a few seconds before things began to move again. The green glow faded from the sky. Slowly, up and down the street, people were closing their mouths which had hung slack open for the last minute — you could hear them click.

"Gaw-aw-aw-lly!" said Bill Soames, looking up at the sky. "I ain't never seen a shooting star like that one. Man, 'at was bright as day. Wonder how far away it hit?"

Ann was hanging on for dear life. I put my arm around her and she was shivering. I think maybe I was a little, too. You don't see a sight like that, then walk off and forget it. Not for long old time.

Later that night, when Ann and I had crawled in bed, with all the windows open to get some cool air in, she ran her finger down my cheek and whispered:

"Harry, have — have you ever stopped to think about things like that green star? Makes you sort of feel puny, doesn't it? I mean, like you didn't amount to anything, anyway." I said, "Don't let it bother you, you good-looking hunk of woman." I ran my fingers down her ribs. She reached over and pulled a bunch of hair off my chest.

What with one thing and another, I had almost forgotten about the green star that night.

"See The Green Star" was the big sign over the entrance to the carnival that Friday night. Bill and me and Jeannie and Ann were suckers like everybody else, and we paid a dollar each and stood in line an hour and a half to see it.

The carnival had had luck on its side the night the green star fell. They were in Quincy, thirty miles south that night, and the meteor had fallen in the north part of the land they had rented outside town for the carnival. Shook things up, and nearly closed the place down because of the shock wave. Quincy had been without power, because the meteor had taken most of the town's lines down just before it hit. It was a miracle the thing hadn't landed smack dab in the middle of the thing — it was right at the busiest time, and everybody in town was at the carnival.

Then some enterprising soul had gone down into the small crater and had found the chunk of rock we finally got to look at — to me it looked like any other rock, with veins of greenish-gray substance all through it. We heard all about the story from the barber who finally got around to showing us the rock — the green star. He also told us that scientists from U.T., Rice and the New York Museum had got there the next day to test anything buried in the crater, just as the carnival was leaving for Haram's Corners.

When we came outside the packed tent, Bill said, "Boy, that sure was big let-down. To think that that teeny-little old boulder made all that noise and light the other night."

Ann shrugged. "I feel the same way, too. I just couldn't imagine anything so terrible caused by such a little thing."

"There's probably a lot more of it down inside that crater he told us about," Jeannie said. "Most meteors bury themselves deep or explode on contact, provided they don't burn up first in the atmosphere." Jeannie was a brain anyway; she pushed her glasses up on her nose and smiled at Bill.

"Say," I said, "I've got a friend I'd like you to meet." I pulled on Ann's arm, made sure Bill and Jeannie were following, and walked as best as I could to Nicky Castava's Portrait Corner.

I had gone to school with Nicky until the time he ran away with a carnival when he was sixteen. He had been a camera nut then, and now he was the photographer who did portraits. Nicky used to stop and see me every time the carnival came through; I was surprised when he hadn't shown up that afternoon. Nicky used one of those old-fashioned cameras, even to the flash powder, plates and long black accordion lens which he would toy with endlessly. He had grown a handlebar mustache and wore spats, and old suits with a gold watch chain across the vest. He had done fairly well for himself; even though you had to wait a couple of hours, you got your money's worth. Nicky was a craftsman, no doubt about it.

When we came to the Portrait Corner, the place was full. I had wanted a portrait of Ann done pretty badly, so I told them to wait. I went in, mumbling some sort of excuses, getting dirty looks from guys twice my size, till I came into the makeshift studio inside the old-timey circus wagon proclaiming *Likenesses Twice as Natural as Life* on the side.

Old Mrs. Fringle was sitting for a portrait then. She was a neighbor who made sure she knew exactly what Ann and I were doing every minute. I sort of smiled at her, and stood against the wall. I was expecting to see Nicky, rotund as ever, taking pains with her, getting her in the pose that would show her best features. He'd had to have done some mighty good posing. Instead, I saw him rush the last subject off with only a terse "pitcher'll be ready in a few hours." That wasn't like Nicky. He started giving

Mrs. Fringle the rush treatment, then he stopped, shrugged a little, and began posing her. Still, it wasn't the same old Nicky.

As soon as he was through, he seated the next subject, poured flash powder in the trowel, held it aloft, and pulled the cord. I walked over to him while everyone in the line outside was still blinking.

"Hey, Nick, long time no see," I said.

He looked at me for a few minutes, almost casually. Then his eyes focused, and he dragged a palm across his head. "Harry — Smith. Haven't seen you in a long time — got to excuse me a little bit — I've got a headache that won't quit. Big rush tonight. You'll excuse me, huh?" he said, licking his mustache.

"Oh, yeah, sure," I said. "How soon do you think you could get a shot of my wife?" I expected him to descend on me like the Furies when I said that. If they had taken a poll in high school of who would most likely to be married, I wouldn't even have been last. They would have left me off entirely.

"Oh, maybe an hour or two. Pretty busy!" he called back over his shoulder while he filled the trowel with powder again. I left him and went back out into the lights and madness that made up a carnival. The Tilt-a-Whirl was running full speed, screams were pouring out of it like water in a rapids. Ann was waiting there for me, so I decided to ride the thing once. I shouldn't have, not after three hot dogs and four cotton candies. I wasn't feeling too well by the time the ride stopped. All three of them thought I was pretty funny, all white and green in the face, they said.

We were getting off when the panic started. Someone had run screaming onto the midway, drowning out the cries of the barkers. It was a girl; she was half-hysterical with fright. Bill got there first. The girl could only point between the booths and jabber "woman, woman, woman." Bill and I went around the corners quick as we could. When I came up, I wished I hadn't.

It was a woman, as it had a woman's body. It was more like a demon, a terribly stricken soul, something like, but more frightening, than a chicken with its head cut off. Because this woman was intact. It was her actions ...

There were floppings, and tearings at the grass, snarly, ragged breathing, gnashing of teeth, the limbs sprawled awry, doing impossible contortions.

"Epileptic!" Bill hollered, dragging off his belt. Suddenly the body went still. "May be choking," he hollered as he jumped down beside the body. I grabbed the limp figure and turned it over so that Bill could get at the tongue if he had to. Those eyes — it didn't take a doctor to tell me she was dead — Mrs. Fringle's eyes — stared up in cold death at me.

"Go call Sheriff Johnston, Ann," I said, without looking up. "Tell him to get the coroner and an ambulance out here. Tell him to bring our stuff with him."

I heard her footsteps fade away. Bill looked up at me. "What do you make of it, Harry?"

I pointed down to the tiny hole the size of an icepick just between her eyes. There was no blood, only a tiny round black hole. "I don't know," I said. "I just don't know."

Bill stood up, looked at the crowd that had gathered around. He turned to one of the barkers. "Where's the manager of this outfit?" he asked. The man pointed, and Bill left. I took off my coat and covered Mrs. Fringle's face with it. In a few seconds, the loudspeaker system squawked to life.

"Ladies and gentlemen ... " it began. It was drowned out by another scream from somewhere on the midway. I got over there as fast as I could go. And in the middle of the sawdust lane, a white-haired old man, surrounded by an ever-widening circle of people, began the same dance of doom as Mrs. Fringle had. My eyes went to the faces of the people backing away — no, no murderer there, only shock and fear and horror.

Someone shouted, "Oh, it — it doesn't have a soul. Its soul's been taken, it's a mad thing ... " and ended in a scream of shock.

Sheriff Johnston came from somewhere, he may have had the

siren on; I was too shaken to have heard. He, too, stopped at the circle of people, stopped and watched the body finally relax in death.

"Nobody leaves!" he bellowed. Bill and the manager were coming out of the announcer's booth. Ann came from somewhere, threw her arms around me, and cried. I tried to comfort her. All she could keep saying was that it was the Green Star's fault, that we all were crazy, crazy, crazy. I hauled off and slapped her a good one, and she broke down crying. Jeannie came up, and I handed her over to her.

The crowd was on the verge of hysteria. Any minute they would panic and trample each other to death in an attempt to get away from the murderer who struck openly in the carnival.

Don't ask me why I did. I walked over to Sheriff Johnston, he nodded and handed me my .44 Magnum and the holster for it. I checked to make sure it was loaded. Then I grabbed the manager by the arm.

"Who went and got that Green Star?" I screamed.

"Who — man, you're crazy, there's people dyin' — "

My eyes must have shown him that I would have wrung his neck if he didn't humor me. He gulped down air. "Why, two of the tent boys got the big chunk of it. Somebody else got the one we show ... "

"Big chunk? What big chunk? Where!" I was stark raving mad, and I knew it. But I couldn't listen to Ann screaming.

"Well, we had a bigger chunk. Not as pretty as the little one though. They took it over to Nicky's. He wanted to take some pictures of it ... "

I was walking towards the wagon advertising *Likeness Twice as Natural as Life* on the outside before he finished. Two steps, four steps, each one getting me closer to the wagon. The wagon where Mrs. Fringle had her picture taken. Where the old man who died was standing in line when I left. Nicky hadn't been himself lately. Hah.

Ten steps, fifteen. Nicky's got a headache. Nicky's got more than a headache. Nicky rushed people into poses, only took his time with the old ones like Mrs. Fringle. Nicky took pictures. Nicky posed the people. Nicky used charge after charge of powder in the trowel of the camera. Nicky took dozens and dozens of pictures. *Nicky never once changed plates.*

I stopped outside the deserted wagon and drew the .44 Magnum. When will man ever learn? When will he learn that there are some things that shouldn't be played with? When would he learn his lesson? Always too late.

From inside I could hear voices. Nicky's voice, and something — else. "Now — they'll get us — you couldn't wait. Had to have food *now*. You — could have — waited," said Nicky's voice. Something else answered, something I could feel in my brain.

"Foodoldonesweaker — thantheyoungoneschildrenfightbacktoo-mucholdonesgoodfoodweamindedtogrowstrongermustgrowquickpick-meupanruntheycan'tcatchyounowwhileI'mstillweakmustgetawayto — eatagaintakebrainsoutofthemthroughboxsomeonesoutside!"

The last thought filled me with cold dread and fear. The hackles on my neck rose up stiff, adrenaline pounded into my bloodstream, and with a scream I smashed the door down with my foot. Flying shards caught Nicky Castava as he was pouring powder onto the flash trowel, spinning him around clutching at his eyes and down to the floor. The powder went into the air in a ghostly film that began settling even as it rose.

The Indians and African natives were on the right track. A camera was a place to catch an enemy's soul, imprison it, tear up the image and destroy the person. A trap of dreams and reality in one. White man's magic. What happens to the white man, though, when something comes along that treats him as if he were a savage, something that can really capture his soul and destroy it utterly? All this went through my head in a split instant. Then came the groaning, twitching command deep in my soul, that rose from my toes up through my head until I felt like exploding into a million fragments:

Look at the Lens, Harry Smith.

No, no, no, I screamed inside.

Look at the Lens.

No, no, I screamed inside.

No, I screamed inside

Look

"Damn you to Hell, Soul-Catcher!" I screamed, and pulled the trigger of the .44 Magnum. I remember seeing the lens flying to a million pieces and the back of the case bulge and explode and a slick black wet spatter all over the back of the wagon. Just before I fell, I saw for an instant a death-writhing wet black tentacle grip and ungrip the tripod of the camera while stickiness ran down in greasy plops to the floor ...

A few weeks later, Bill and Jeannie were sitting on our front porch with us after a supper both the girls had cooked.

I put my arm on Ann's shoulder. "You know what I think," I said. "I think you ought to marry that girl, Bill."

"Don't let him fool you," Ann said to Jeannie. "Look what being married has done to me. Made me a nervous wreck, gave me emotional scars, and we've got a $700 doctor bill. Let me tell you, it's not worth it."

"Sure, it's not," said Bill, winking at Ann.

With the tip of her toe, Jeannie kicked him and his chair out into the yard.

APPRENTICESHIP

The Entity first came to earth in 356 B.C. Then, he was named Alexander.

He went out and conquered the world with the sword. He cut the Gordian Knot, went to the edge of the world and wept. He started home and died, aged thirty-three years.

The second time, they sent the Entity back as Jesus. He bided his time, as per instructions. When he was thirty, he began to conquer the world anew, this time with wisdom and compassion rather than the sword, spear, and hoplites. They nailed him to a tree, and he wept that time, too. Aged thirty-three.

The third time the Entity came back as a baby in 1855. He grew up and was a famous lamplighter in London. Those were times when everything was bad. He became a notorious murderer of prostitutes and other broken persons. They called him Jack and Leather Apron and hunted him while he lit their lamps in Whitechapel. They never caught him because he developed consumption and died, weeping and coughing, aged thirty-three years.

The Entity was awakened again in 5127 A.D. This time, the Entity Master told him, he'd be born a three-eyed mutant. But he'd have a wonder mind and would lead the remnants of near-men out of bestiality, would set them back on the path of civilization and the way to the stars.

"There's only one thing," said the Entity Master.

"What is it?" asked the Entity, tiredly.

"They'll stone you to death when you're thirty-three. After you give them civilization and all. Mutants will be very out that year."

The Entity shrugged his shoulders.

"Well, that's not so bad." He smiled. "At least I'm learning a trade."

THE ADVENTURE OF THE COUNTESS'S JEWELS

My companion, Jean Anton du Provence, and myself were making our way through the darkened streets towards the villa of the Countess Ronceveaux, who was giving a ball to celebrate the victory of her husband, at the front line of the army during their recent triumphs, when he suddenly stopped me with a tug at my sleeve. Fearing trouble, I brought my hand to my rapier hilt, but Jean Anton only laughed.

"No, my friend Charles, there is no danger!" he said, twirling his mustache with his right hand. Jean Anton had always reminded me of a panther, or some other fearsome beast. He was always ill at ease when in confined spaces, and preferred country villas to the crowded, narrow streets of Paris. Even dressed as he was tonight in a broad-brimmed plumed hat, knee-length coat, and high, roll-topped boots, he moved with the ease of some animal. Shorter than average, he looked formidable in the moonlight, with a silver buckled sword belt over his right shoulder and rapier hilt protruding from the silver sheath at his left hip. Jean Anton was, in fact, a tremendous swordsman, and wore the weapon as other men wore clothes. He lodged at the barracks of the Brotherhood-of-Arms, for both he and I wore the scarlet plume of the Brothers.

Jean was a particular favorite of the nobility; he was one of those rare people who put all near him at ease. His sense of humor and personal charm well suited him to the life of a Brother-at-Arms.

"Forgive my nervousness, Jean," I said. "Perhaps too many things press upon my mind. You meant to say?"

"I merely was going to ask your opinion of the recent thefts of various valuables from the homes of nobles. Does it not strike you as strange that each time, the deed was not discovered until well into the next morning?" asked Jean, his teeth shining between his tiny beard and mustache.

In truth, this was one of the things that was preying heavily upon my mind. As one of his Majesty's personal emissaries, I had carried messages from the King to various nobles in recent days concerning these affairs. It seemed that after certain social occasions, gems and jewels had disappeared from the houses of the hosts. But guards were posted at all doors on those occasions, and none were trying to enter. It had therefore become a mystery of highest importance, and a matter of great dissension among the nobility. Contingents of the King's picked guards were dispatched to an affair only the last night. No suspicious person had been seen, nothing had disrupted the affairs, but nevertheless, the next morning gems and a large sum of money had been found missing.

I had just started to voice my opinion, when a scream rent the air, coming from a narrow cross street to our left. Without an instant's hesitation, both Jean and I hurled ourselves towards the sound. The scream had come from a woman, possibly a young girl, and where either was involved, neither Jean nor I were ones to stand idly around when they screamed for assistance.

We turned the corner, and stepped into a trap.

Instead of a young girl, we found a young woman standing in the doorway, smiling devilishly at us. But we were too busy, after a glimpse of her, to worry about young ladies.

There were perhaps eight, maybe ten of them. I had not so much a glimpse of men, but only a flash of forms coming at me from doorways. These were street rabble, in tattered clothing. A glint of steel showed me that they were armed with daggers; others had clubs. I drew my rapier while leaping back to gain a small amount of time. A form came in low, trying to get inside my guard. Balancing on one foot, I readied a stop-thrust that pierced the head of the first attacker.

From the corner of my eye, I had a glimpse of Jean Anton in action. Always the practical man, Jean had not drawn sword but had instead reached for his pistol. There was a muffled roar, a blinding flash, and one of the nearest attackers pitched forward limply. With one hand Jean reached his dagger and parried a slash at his throat. He reached his sword just as another attacker came at me.

There was no time to think, only a time for instant action. I was forming a thrust when I was hit on the shoulder by a thrown club. I felt my rapier start to slip from my fingers, and quickly I changed hands.

A voice roared in the background: "Take the tall one alive!"

I had never fenced much with my left hand, but I thought perhaps Jean and I together could hold them back until a chance to summon aid or to flee presented itself. With rapier in my left, I stepped into those attacking me, and swung a furious, whistling blow which caused them to step back. The sword felt clumsy in the wrong hand; I could not maneuver it deftly.

Jean Anton was attempting to withdraw his rapier from the chest of a writhing man, while trying to keep two attackers at bay with his dagger. One, armed with a long dirk, went down screaming, his arm cut bone-deep near the elbow. Jean brought his arm up to fend off a club swing, but the man in which Jean's sword was lodged toppled and pulled him off balance. There was a dull thud and Jean went down.

"Jean!" I shouted, and began hacking my way towards him. My attack was more bravado than skillful swordsmanship, but it made the three facing me draw back.

"Get him, you fools!" ordered a voice from the shadows. Then a figure stepped into the moonlight, drawing sword. This was no street rabble, but a person dressed in the rich garments of a noble, and the sword which came out in his hand was highly decorated. He came at me soundlessly, and I found myself facing a tremendous swordsman.

He feinted, and I formed the parry, but quicker than I could follow, his blade appeared before me, and he was lunging in a blow that would enter my shoulder. Left-handed, unaccustomed as I was to it, a parry was impossible. My only chance I took instantly, that being to throw myself to the right and bring my blade up in hopes that it would possibly hold him in check. In doing so, I landed at the feet of the rabble, and my last vision was of a club, swinging downwards towards my unprotected head.

I woke up to face — myself!

I was sitting in a chair, my hands and feet bound. Around me were various of the type of rabble and cutthroats that infest Paris. Between them I could see that I was in one of those dank, underground taverns at which types such as these were always to be found. But the figure before me was a mirror-image of myself!

Long face ending in a double beard, gray eyes, hair growing to his shoulders, he was wearing the same costume which I had on, except that the sword, I noticed, was the same as that of the swordsman who had so skillfully backed me into a headache. The effect was terrible on me; he was a perfect duplicate of me! Why, not even Jean Anton would have been able to tell us apart!

As soon as he saw the startled expression on my features, he turned to the men standing or leaning near the tables.

"Good, my friends!" he laughed, a twinkle in his eyes. "Tonight we trim the King's beard! I must away to the Countess Ronceveaux's house, there to be entertained most heartily!"

The cutthroats laughed gruffly and waved goodbyes to him. At the top of the stairs, he turned and called to a huge fellow lounging at a table. "My friend," he called, "please see that our 'guest' is well taken care of!"

The rabble laughed again and raised farewell toasts to my mirror-image, who was turning to go out the door. "One more night's work and we will all be rich!" one of the rabble yelled, from the back of the tavern.

In a few moments, a smallish, ragged cutthroat wearing an eye patch came in the door. He came jouncing down the stairs lightly and announced: "The master would like some of you to go up and stand watch. Someone may have trailed us here, or found the other cavalier's body!"

These words unhinged me, I could not believe it. My friend, Jean Anton, dead! It was impossible! I jerked at my bonds which held my hands, almost causing the chair to overturn.

The two who had grudgingly gotten up to stand watch stopped on mid-stair and looked at the big fellow,

"You'd better do something with him!" one said, jerking a thumb at me. Then they went out the door.

The big fellow clambered to his feet. He was huge, with big rolling muscles under hairy forearms. His nose, as evidenced by its crooked slant, had been broken several times, and his ear was adorned with a huge ring made of gold. He crossed the floor towards me, flexing his huge hands, and a grin beginning to spread across his ugly face.

Just then, the small, one-eyed one came up to me.

"Ha!" he laughed contemptuously. "So this is the brave Charles? A fine cavalier, scourge of all who oppose justice. My, my, aren't you ready to carve a few of us up in defense of justice?" He scowled, then spat, narrowly missing me.

The four or five rabble left in the place laughed heartily. Even the big fellow roared with mirth; his laughter shook the building. Once more he came at me.

The small one-eyed man turned and walked away, passing the giant. "Get him for me, big one!" he said, patting the giant on the side as he passed. The big fellow stopped, then stiffened visibly. Slowly he looked down at his side, seemingly amazed at the dagger hilt protruding from his flesh. He grunted once, like a bull, then fell like so much dead weight. Chairs and tables splintered beneath his bulk.

But the small fellow hadn't stopped to watch this as all the others had. While they stood frozen, watching the giant fall, he reached inside his ragged vest and brought out two huge flintlock pistols. He fired once and the face of one of the cutthroats nearest him disappeared in a welter of blood. The other pistol barked, and another crumpled, choking, over a table.

The noise brought the other two rabble to frenzied action. But before the first could get to his sword, one of the huge pistols caught him on the jaw. With a groan, he tumbled backwards.

The other drew sword, but finding himself all alone, decided better of it. He was on the third step when the one-eyed madman plunged his rapier into his back. He writhed for a few seconds, then stopped and slid backwards down the steps. Withdrawing his sword, the one-eyed fellow came towards the chair to which I was tied.

He stopped before me and sheathed his sword. Then he took off the eye patch and his nose. Before me stood the figure of Jean Anton. Grinning, he cut my bonds and helped me restore the circulation to my arms and legs, all the time keeping a wary eye on the door and a hand on the pistol tucked into his sword-belt. As soon as he was sure that I could navigate, he took me to the top of the stairs, and drawing the pistol, he opened the door. The two guards were gone; they must have thought better of staying to try to stop us.

Jean motioned my queries to silence. "Now we must save the most valuable jewels in France," he said, leading me to horses down the street.

We mounted and rode like the wind from the tavern, heading for Countess Ronceveaux's villa. In a matter of minutes we were dismounting in front of the entrance.

Two of the King's picked men were on guard. "Halt, les amis!" one called out. He eyed Jean's ragged clothing and my crumpled costume. Then he squinted at me. His eyes went wide with amazement.

"My good Charles!" he stammered "But a few moments ago

you entered! How can — " His eyes goggled wider as he recognized for the first time who Jean Anton was. "But you, Charles, said Jean had been struck ill when you came in before! And you were accompanying Mademoiselle De Maret this night!"

"Stay on guard!" snapped Jean. "Let no one leave until I say so!" He and I flung ourselves in the entrance.

"My sword will not be of much help, Jean," I said as we ran. "My arm is still injured from ... "

"Stay near the door, Charles, and let none leave," he called, as he went into the milling throng in the ballroom. At the sight of what appeared to be a peasant entering, the musicians stopped their playing. A gasp went up from the crowd, and couples stopped dancing. Jean peered around the room, while several of the gentry made their way towards him. They were outraged that a peasant should interrupt their party.

Before they reached him, however, Jean's eyes picked out their quarry. "My good Charles!" he called to my impostor-twin, who, upon seeing him, had tried to reach the stairs to the second floor unnoticed. "One moment, my friend," Jean said. "I would like to know why this night I am sick, as you have been telling everyone. I would also like to ask your reason for trying to dispose of myself and your twin, who stands in the doorway." Jean pointed at me.

Heads turned towards me; gasps went up from the hundreds of assembled guests. Eyes went back and forth in disbelief at what they saw. Some of the Brothers-at-Arms were exasperated; evidently the impostor's disguise had been near-perfect, even to their keen eyes.

The crowd was frozen. Jean stepped towards the stairs and the impostor went into action. He turned quickly and ran headlong up the stairs. There was a large window at one end of the open corridor along which the stairs connected. The impostor, gaining the corridor, headed towards this escape route. It was then that several of the Brotherhood stormed up the second set of stairs at the other end of the open, railed corridor. The impostor, seeing his escape cut off, turned back.

Jean Anton stood, hand on his rapier hilt, at the head of the stairs.

Too late to shout warning, I saw my twin reach into his coat and come forth with a pistol. His fingers closed on the trigger, there was a roar, and smoke and fire belched forth. Jean crumpled to the floor.

I started forward. A movement from the corner of my eye attracted me, and I stopped short. A young woman, veiled, was hurrying towards the door. I stepped to her side, rested my arm upon her elbow. She gasped.

"Would the Mademoiselle desire company for the evening?" I asked. She struggled for a moment, then resigned herself with a sigh. Still holding her, I turned once more to the scene above.

The impostor had run towards Jean Anton's body, evidently to get past him to one of the second floor rooms, and escape through the windows. There was no hope of the Brothers-at-Arms getting to him before he could reach and lock the door. He stepped across the body of Jean.

Jean came to life in a blaze of action. His foot swung up, catching my twin in the stomach. The impostor doubled over and fell. Jean came to his feet just as the impostor rose and drew sword. He stepped back, drew his rapier with a smooth motion and parried the impostor's thrust. It was impossible, but somehow the shot fired by my twin had missed Jean. He had only pretended death to catch the impostor off guard!

All eyes were on the combatants; never had I seen such swordplay! The impostor skipped back. Jean feinted, then bored in with motions too swift to follow. The impostor lunged, and Jean barely saved his face with a parry from the basket-hilt of his rapier. The high whine of steel on steel filled the ballroom as the two players of the deadly game moved and danced. Then the impostor thrust, and Jean's sword flew in under his guard. The bloody point of Jean's rapier came to sight between the impostor's shoulder blades. His arms went limp, and Jean stepped back, empty handed. His sword, like an arrow, was thrust through his foe's body.

For an instant, my mirror-twin clung to the rail. Then he fell back, his feet came off the floor, and he fell twenty feet to the ballroom floor, landing with a dull thud. Jean's rapier snapped under the impact.

Later, as Jean and I made our way back to the barracks, he explained to me how he had found me in the tavern.

"When I was hit on the head," Jean explained, "I went very limp. My friend, I consider myself a brave man, but I have never thought it becoming to me to be dead. I have always thought that I could do more for people alive, so I lay very still until all of our attackers had left, thinking me dead. Then, following you to the tavern, I ... eh ... acquisitioned some garments from one of the lower class there. Obtaining some putty and the eye patch, I modeled my face after that of a delightful little rogue I once dueled. Quite simple, really," Jean said, twirling his mustache.

"But how did you discover the identity of the impostors?" I asked.

"You remember that each time jewelry was stolen," Jean started, "it was after an affair of state or a ball that it was found to be missing? That, and the fact that no one of low character was seen at these affairs led me to believe that some noble or military person had perpetrated the robbery. The more I thought on it, the clearer it became that it was the work of a master impersonator. Then I remembered something that had slipped my mind for days. Unfortunately, I thought of it at a most inopportune time: during the attack in the alley. Do you remember that frightful affair we attended last week? The one thrown by that Duchess visiting her summer villa?" he questioned, a twinkle in his eye.

"Ah, yes!" I answered. "But it wasn't so frightful, as I recall. There was a young la... yes, I remember it. Why?"

"Do you remember the Duchess telling us how wonderful it was to see you and me, Anjou, and the other members of the Brotherhood?"

"I vaguely remember," I said, still failing to see the point.

" ... and how nice it was to see Pierre and the young lady with him?"

I clapped my hands to my head. "Pierre! Pierre? But he had hurried off late that afternoon, telling us that he had received word that his mother was ill! Pierre was nowhere near Paris! Why, that was the impostor! But why should they pick me? Why didn't they detain me by some other means?"

"For one thing," Jean said, "this was to be their last theft. They needed someone who could be trusted by all. Not even the Count would object to your being upstairs, for as everyone knows, your honor is spotless. For another thing, he had to study your face carefully. We owe the solving of the thefts to your impossible face!" Jean laughed. He dodged, and my fist just missed him

"But come, Charles," he said, unconcerned, "we must go by the weaponer's. I fear I have broken my best rapier. And," he said, scratching his sides, "I want a bath and to get out of these dreadful clothes!"

VALE PRODITOR!

Prologue

Geldric came frothing like a mad dog into the kitchen of the great hall, cursing and raging in his anger, and behind him the noise of pursuit closed like the sound of doom, each scream or shout or sound of blows making him wince and throb that much more.

The kitchen maid dropped the knife she had been using to peel potatoes and screamed at the sight of the wizardling in such a rage. She put her hands to her face as a shield and tried to think what she could have done to deserve the beating she was expecting, such as the ones Geldric sometimes handed out to those too slow for his liking.

Instead she saw the haunted, wild look in his eyes and heard the mumbling from behind his bearded chin as he stepped past her and went to the larder where he flung open the cabinet doors. Then dimly to the girl's ears came the skirl of steel on steel, screams of agony, shouts of joy, and the padding of running feet. The maid then dimly realized the cause of the uproar — Lord Bruce had returned to claim his own.

Three years before, she remembered, the Duke of Westsan had gone away to the Holy Wars with Richard Coeur de Lion and the other lords and nobles of England and Eire, leaving his younger brother, Geldric the Scholar, with the duties of the kingdom. Geldric at first had given nominal power to the old retainer lords who owned manors on Lord Bruce's estate, and to the Duchess, so that he could have more time for his studies, and ever and anon would messengers come from the great monasteries and centers of learning, bringing with them books and documents which Geldric read ravenously. At times between the messengers, he would pace the halls of the castle and watch the horizon for sign of riders. Then slowly a change had come on Geldric. A new light came into his eyes. The messengers who brought the books were no longer from the monasteries, but from places not named, and when asked they would say, "I come from my master in the East, far beyond the Holy Lands." Geldric then had taken more and more of the tasks of the dukedom on himself, until his power equaled that of the Duchess.

The maid remembered the day that Geldric received the messenger dressed all in mail and still wearing the accoutrements of the Crusader. After the conference, Geldric called together all the people of the dukedom, and from the high seat of the great hall he told them that their lord Bruce lay dead in the Holy Land. As was his right, he took then the title Duke of Westsan and began his reign. In a few weeks, he had hired mercenaries from Gascon, had forced the people into submission, and had taken the Duchess as his wife, forcing the abbot from a nearby poor monastery to perform the wedding.

Then had come the reign of fear and darkness in the land, and the old retainers were pushed off their holdings and the Gascons in Geldric's favor were appointed to them. Geldric was seen less and less, keeping to himself and his books. The Duchess was virtually imprisoned. No more were there feasts in the great hall, nor were the people happy under the mismanagement of the foreigners who lorded over them.

The maid's reverie ended as a shout from outside startled her. The din and clash of chaos drew nearer beyond the kitchen door in the great hall. She was sure she heard the shout of even the oldest of the retainer-knights as they fought alongside their lord come back. She watched, stunned, as Geldric withdrew two white objects from the pantry. Cursing towards the din outside, he went through the side door of the kitchen and out into the courtyard, his mouth a-writhe and his eyes wild like those of a wolf at bay.

The maid turned and watched through the doorway as he half-ran down the path that led to the smith's shop,

A scrape and crash behind her made her shriek. She backed against the wall and watched the coming of death. A man was standing in the doorway, his back to her, seemingly staring out into the great hall. By his armor and surcoat, he was one of Geldric's mercenaries. In his right hand was gripped a sword.

Fascinated, she watched the Gascon's left hand grip and ungrip the stones of the doorway facing, turning pale and then back to red as the grip relaxed. The right hand slowly unflexed and lost the grip on the sword hilt, and it slid to the floor with a dull clink and rattle. She saw that, just in front of one of his feet, a small red puddle was spattering and growing. The man slowly turned towards her, his left hand dropping from the doorway. As he turned, he began sinking to the floor ...

The maid screamed and screamed again. The body had turned and the hands had gone up to a gash where a face had once been, where now there was only a staring eye and the corner of the mouth with protruding teeth remaining to show human semblance. The corpse sank to the floor and a pool of blood seeped out onto the stones.

Stepping across the body came Lord Bruce, his sword a-drip, covered from head to toe in blood-spattered mail, with the crest of the Duke of Westsan showing through. Lord Bruce towered over the girl like a giant, his eyes showing blue as steel through his mail cap, above the tangle of his red beard. There was only the battle-lust at the depths of his eyes to show he wasn't the same gentle lord he was when he left — battle-lust and vengeance and animal rage now tinged those eyes.

The girl sank to the floor, weeping, relief flooding over her for the three years of suffering as she realized that her master, her true master, had come back. Geldric was no longer a threatening tyrant; aye, no longer a threat to Westsan or the Duchess or the people. Soon, Geldric would be a threat to none. She pointed down the path to the smithy, and as Lord Bruce followed her pointing finger, she slumped to the floor.

Lord Bruce, like the juggernaut of doom, turned and walked out the door and down the path.

Geldric had just finished placing the two objects he had taken from the pantry behind a barrel, and was wiping out three concentric chalk circles as Lord Bruce came through the doorway.

Geldric drew his own sword and pulled a shield from a pile of repaired weapons stacked in one corner of the smith's shop, then looked up at his brother with his wild, mad eyes, and laughed. The laughter echoed like mirth from the halls of hell through the room. Then he came across the smithy floor, shield up, sword to the side and level.

"So, my brother comes back to see my end? Surely, surely, you wouldn't kill your only brother?" Again Geldric laughed, and the bark of the demon hound was in his voice.

"I kill my only brother as he would try to kill me, except that I am man enough to do it myself. I send no hireling to stab you in the back with a poisoned dagger and leave you sick for a year and too weak to come back and claim your own, do I, brother?" Bruce gritted out between clenched teeth, the anger and impotent fury of a year of sickness and grim vengeance coming to the surface. Then he charged, his two-handed broadsword swinging up and back.

Geldric was small and tight muscled, and quick as a fox in his movements. He brought the shield up and skipped to the side, and Bruce went off balance as his sword ricocheted off the shield's rim. Geldric swung his own sword at his brother's exposed side, but futilely, as his armor gave him full protection from the sword's edge, and Geldric grunted as his sword stopped dead. Lord Bruce slowed his swing, reversed his blade, and brought an underhanded sweeping cut up under Geldric's shield. Blood spattered on the ceiling as Geldric's left arm went limp, and the shield fell away from fingers grown numb where tendons were severed.

The younger brother backed off, babbling. His eyes went from demonic pinpoints to wide-eyed desperation. He jumped to the top of a bench above Lord Bruce and screamed.

"Yes, yes, you'll kill me, brother, I already know. But I have something far better than death planned for you, Bruce — grief! And you won't get to see it. No!" Then his words fell away to the demonic laughter once again.

Geldric jumped from the bench to the pile of unlit coals heaped in the forge.

"Not your sons, Bruce, but your sons' sons will pay for this. In fifty years Westsan will be as dead as Troy or Carthage, only it will never be rebuilt! They'll say, 'Geldric did this, and Bruce couldn't stop him!' Remember, Bruce my brother, it'll be your name that will kill Westsan! Ha!"

Lord Bruce went into a red blind rage. He swung his broadsword two-handed at Geldric's feet. The younger brother's parry came too late. Bruce felt his blade bite through cloth and skin and bone, and Geldric screamed and somersaulted onto his back in the dust of the smith's shop, blood covering him from knee to foot.

"Your sons' sons, Bruce! Remember ... !"

The taunt ended as Lord Bruce leaned both hands on the pommel of his broadsword and pushed the blade through his brother's neck. He turned and walked out into the fresh morning air, where his victorious followers and the freed Duchess waited for him.

Lord Bruce never told what happened in the smithy. Over the years the smith shop was abandoned because Geldric had died there, but part of the walls stood, and the roof was left, and it became choked and grown over with weeds.

The Tale of Dermott

Lord Dermott looked down from the small hill above the keep of Westsan and watched as the funeral procession wound to the churchyard within the outer walls of the castle. Smoke was still drifting up from here and there about the castle, and the walls around the windows were blackened and sooty. A few carrion crows were picking over what the fire had not taken. The morning mists hid the village at the foot of the hills, but the smell of cinders and ash was heavy in that direction. The people of the castle and the town were at the funeral, most of them with their few belongings tied to their backs. Dermott watched the procession. As the bodies of Duke Robert and Duchess Eleandor came below him, he turned away to look at the unicorn which stood cropping grass beside him.

He patted the animal's sides and neck, rubbed its flowing mane. He was still a little awed each time he saw the spiral ivory horn projecting outwards two feet from the unicorn's forehead. Dermott knew, though, that he should hate this animal more than anything in this world.

Somehow, still, respect for the beast overcame the resentment he felt. Now that Helen was gone, it was the only thing of value he had left to him. Dermott's world was turned against him because he was different from the rest of humanity.

His mind went back to those days a half year ago when he and his brother Robert had been the two greatest knights of their time, fighting with the best of all the lands.

Then one morning before all and sundry of the nobles and ladies were to set out on a stag hunt, a peasant had come screaming at the top of his lungs that he had seen the Lady of the Unicorn on a hill above one of the huts that morning. As one, all the nobles and knights had set out in search of the Lady. The Lady of the Unicorn was a shadowed being, for each time she had been seen there followed the next day a calamity of catastrophic proportions. The Lady had first been seen one morning three years before, the day before the battle of the Five Kingdoms in which Dermott's father, the old Duke of Westsan, the son of the first Duke Lord Bruce, had been killed; and Dermott and Robert had to fight like fallen angels to retain some semblance of a barony underfoot. And the Lady of the Unicorn had been seen near the keeps of each of the barons who had died in that battle. So the legend had started.

Nor had she been seen again until that morning three years later when the peasant had shouted the news. Some of the knights, the most gusty of the fellows, wanted to capture the Lady and find what made her appear as she did. Others were for setting traps and capturing the unicorn. It was agreed by all that chase should be given, so the whole mounted party had made a path straightway to the wooded hill where she had been seen.

They searched futilely all that day and half the night, Duke Robert and Dermott riding side by side during the hunt, with neither they nor anyone else catching so much as a glimpse of the Lady. That night they camped in a clearing, and slept with the chill till the dawn.

Well did Dermott remember the next morning and the pain that came with it, for it still ached in his head. He had awakened early, as if by some noise, to see on the hill above them the Lady astride her magnificent animal. No one else was astir in the camp. Dermott sprang on his unsaddled mount and spurred it up the hill. He was dressed only in his tunic and pants with his sword at his side. The Lady of the Unicorn wheeled her mount around and it took off as if shot from a catapult.

For the first time Dermott actually saw the beautiful rider and her magnificent animal. He dug his heels into the horse's flanks. The Lady's hair danced in the wind like a pennon as she tore down the other side of the hill. The beast's hooves pounded across the draw below, its two-foot horn gleaming in the early sunlight like a lance tip.

As Dermott reached the summit of the hill and thundered down, there arose shouts and the whinny of horses below in the camp. Dermott took this to be the noise of others waking to see him go after the Lady and the attendant fuss and bother of the others, mounting and following his lead. He heard his name once or twice, but gave no thought to it as he bent over his horse, intent only on the chase ahead. He grinned at the thought of the two prizes, the Lady and the unicorn, and wondered at the enigma of what the Lady was and why she lived such a phantom life.

The Lady looked back, and an expression of intent crossed her face, her lips set tight. Dermott had never seen a girl as beautiful even with such an expression. The unicorn was no farther than three lengths ahead of him. Then the Lady kicked her mount and as if by magic the distance began to grow with each of the unicorn's strides.

Dermott saw his dream evaporating with distance. Desperately, he spurred his mount to even greater speed. Its hooves resounded like hailstones on the grass. Inch by inch he overtook the phantom. They flashed over a small rise and down a draw. Soon they were galloping parallel to the bank of a small stream which ran twelve feet below the trail in its bed. Suddenly the Lady turned the unicorn sharply and set off across a field. Desperately, Dermott tried to do the same.

For an instant he hung suspended in the air as the horse's hooves scrambled futilely in the gravel at the bank's edge. The mount and its rider cartwheeled off the high bank, the horse neighing in terror, dropping towards the shallow, rocky streambed. There was no time to get out of the saddle or kick away; the world turned twice, and Dermott hit as the horse came down on top of him. The breath flew out of him and he blacked out ...

Dermott awoke unfeeling. Then pain washed through him from his leg and chest. He slowly dragged himself from under the horse, whose back took a right angle where it had broken.

The mount had hit partly on hard rock while Dermott had landed partly in the water with mud and silt under him. He was still pulling himself together when the shadows of men fell on the ground beside him.

Dermott remembered that moment. His brother Robert and all the knights of Westsan stood looking at him. Most of them were cut and bleeding and bruised. Others were missing. Two of them carried his armor.

Dermott remembered the sham trial that was held then. On the spot he heard accusations against him. One of the party had heard something, awakened to find an arrow buried in the ground beside his hand. He sprang up to see himself and his comrades being attacked by robber-barons and men of the forests, and a glimpse of Dermott going out of sight over the top of the hill. The man had shouted and awakened the others, but Dermott had not come back despite their cries. A hard-pitched battle had followed, it being about equal, since the knights were neither mounted nor armored at the time. There had been much loss on both sides, but the brigands had been defeated.

Then Duke Robert and his followers had followed Dermott's trail, still fresh, and found him.

"But I was after the Lady of the Unicorn! She was on the hill; I gave chase in hope of catching her!" Dermott pleaded.

"Why did you not awaken us?" asked one of the men.

For this Dermott had no answer. He had not thought of it in his haste. Then he spoke:

"If you say you followed my tracks, then you were sure to have seen the tracks of the unicorn."

The knights and nobles looked at him. "We followed only the tracks of a man driven by fear and cowardice," one said.

"If you found no tracks it is because the unicorn is an otherworld beast. Surely you expect it not to leave a path," Dermott said. "We were looking for this being and its rider. You must give me the benefit of the doubt ... "

"Tell that to my son who lies full of quarrels in the glade," spoke up an old retainer. "He lies there because you did not wake him."

"I had no idea of what transpired, I didn't know that any robbing bands were about in these woods, I only wanted to catch ... "

"You ran, Dermott."

Dermott reached for his sword, which had been taken from him when he was found. "I'll prove my truth in combat against any one of you."

"When you ran, Dermott, you lost all your rights. And could it be that though you would face anyone here armored, that you were afraid of the robbers unarmored?"

"You ingrates!" Dermott's temper sprang up at last. "Have I run before, when my brother and I had to fight to keep what was our own? I helped save half your homes. But you forget, don't you? I did not run from battle. I can say no more, except that I am innocent."

Knight and noble and baron all looked at Duke Robert. Tears were in his eyes as he spoke. "Dermott, you rode on when we called for you to turn back, before you were out of earshot. That in itself is enough to justify what we do now." He paused and swallowed. "Vale, proditor."

At that, a knight stepped forward with Dermott's spurs in his hands and broke off the spikes. Two of the lesser lords began beating his breastplate with axes and stripping the crest off his shield. One took his sword and smashed the flat against a rock until it broke a third down the blade. Dermott's clothes were stripped off him, and he was given his surcoat turned inside out.

"Walk only in streambeds and in the middle of the roads. Only there are you safe from attack. Stray from the road's center and you are prey for any man. Take the shortest path out of the Five Kingdoms and never turn this way again. Many died today because of your dishonor," said Duke Robert.

Dermott sank to his knees on the riverbed and wept. But no

one spoke to him. They watched as he got to his feet and limped down beside the stream and walked away.

The shout came from behind him as one voice: "Vale, proditor!"

News spread rapidly in the kingdom. When at last he waded to a bridge over the road, it and the road were lined with people. They cursed him as he walked eastward down the center of the road. The knights trotted on their horses behind him. The peasants began to throw refuse at him. They taunted him, insulted him, waiting for him to leave the center of the road.

Three youths pelted him with rocks. One hit him in the face, and Dermott saw a blind red rage and grabbed the nearest youth and strangled him to the ground. Then the peasants came upon him with clubs, while the knights rode around him and the thrashing of arms and legs and shouts from the peasants.

Screaming in rage, Dermott fought his way to his feet. He smashed a face with his fist, then kicked another down, taking the man's club away. First left then right he swung the cudgel till the attackers drew back in a circle, afraid. Then a lance butt smashed Dermott to his knees, the club dropping in the dirt. There was a flurry of horses' legs closing in on his vision as the knights, at last able to avenge the death of their comrades, rode him down. A lance point came towards his chest. Dermott watched, fascinated, as it came nearer and nearer ...

Suddenly it was gone, the knight dropping it as he spilled off his horse beside the girl whose mount had bored his horse in the lungs with a bloody twist of its polished horn. The Lady of the Unicorn spurred her mount and it stepped forward to stand like a watchful demon over Dermott's slumped figure.

Her hands reached down to him. "Lord Dermott, get up. Take my hand, quickly!" she said, and her voice was like the wind through the pine trees. "Quickly!"

Dermott saw groggily that the knights were still, in a circle around him, dumbfounded with their mouths agape at the awesome beast and at the beauty of the rider. Dermott leaned up and over the unicorn's back. He swung his legs over, not caring or feeling what he did anymore. He put his arms around the Lady's waist and the unicorn gave a loud, unearthly neigh, as if a thousand horses voiced one cry.

The horses of the knights bolted then, bucking and cavorting off the road into a ditch, across the meadows, tumbling over the knights and stampeding through the peasants. Curses rent the air as the Lady of the Unicorn, dressed all in black velvet habit, spurred her white beast. It dashed away like the wind, leaving no hoofprints in the dirt of the road.

A dismounted knight stood in the way, drawing his sword. Dermott watched as the unicorn went over him like water through a sand dike, and the man's blood ran like oil through his armor where the hooves battered it flat from front to back. Dermott and the Lady bent low as the unicorn sailed over a tree trunk and went for the low hills across the fields.

Arrows and quarrels flew like birds from behind, spurting up grasses and weeds or quivering in saplings. In a few seconds they would be out of range. Suddenly, a quarrel arced over Dermott and sank into the Lady's shoulder. She slumped down, blood staining the velvet a slick red. She would have fallen had not Dermott grabbed her with one hand and the reins with the other. The unicorn was heading somewhere; Dermott let it have its head.

Dermott vaguely remembered a flight like the wind as he tried to steady the Lady with one hand, hold the reins with the other, and keep mounted at the same time. The beast's breath came in ragged sobs as it went through field and up hill, over stream and valley and through thicket, until it came to a dead stop on a hillside. Only then did it slow to a walk, but still continued uphill until it came to the entrance of a cavern set deep beneath the tall pines. There the unicorn stopped. Dermott dismounted and took the Lady, still unconscious, to the ground. Set in the cave entrance was a strong door, and when Dermott opened this, he found it led into a room, furnished for a lady, with bed and stools, and kitchen and fireplace. Dermott placed the Lady on the bed. With the coming of the night, he lit a candle and shut the door at the cavern entrance after seeing to the unicorn outside. The creature's pale purple eyes looked at him inquisitively, then went back to cropping grass.

By candlelight Dermott took the quarrel from the Lady's back, hardly noticing her dark-skinned beauty for his tiredness and concern. He found a larder and ate bread and cheese, then sat on a stool near the bed. Dermott waited and listened the whole night through. It was early the next morning when the Lady first stirred, then opened her eyes. When she saw Dermott she began crying like a child.

"Oh-ooo, Lord Dermott, I-I didn't mean to have you hurt this way. Ohh ..." she moaned, and the wet tears rolled down her face.

"Lady, Lady, cry not else you'll open your wound again." Dermott came to her side and held her hand. "What I have done, I have brought on myself."

"No, my lord, no. I was a fool to think that I could change The Way Things Be. If I had not come to the hilltop yesterday morning, none of this would have befallen you. If ..."

"If you had not come? Do you not divine events and come to forewarn of them? Why do you foretell disasters?" Dermott asked, but the Lady had lapsed into unconsciousness again.

Gradually, Dermott remembered, he had gotten the story from her that afternoon. She had awakened and then told him:

"You can see that I am not of the same people as you. My mother was born on an island to the west. It was the island Bladud and his followers settled centuries before. My mother was involved in a scandal brewed up by jealous rivals and was exiled to this barbarian island with her pet and a few belongings to live as best she could. At first, she appealed to the people here for help, but her differences" (here she had closed her purple eyes) "were feared, and she was cast out as a witch. It is true that she had the Powers, as do most of the people of the West, but she was not evil.

"That was twenty years ago. She wandered about with her mount half starved, until she was found by Sir Percival de Naon, the outcast highwayman, who was so overcome with her that he took her off to get married. Here," she indicated the room-cavern they were in, "he built her a home, and continued his highwaying, as everyone knows. I was their only child.

"Four years ago, you remember he was killed. Soon after that, my mother died of grief. I was left alone, except for the Beast out there. My mother did have a hand mirror, a magic mirror that can see events that will come to pass. I was left to a life of thieving by night and staying close to the deep woods during the day. One night I was looking into the mirror when it filmed, and then I saw all the armies of the Five Kingdoms in a battle. I knew some disaster would come to pass, so I rode to each of the Five Kingdoms to warn the people. But each time I got near one of the keeps, the peasants ran away from the Beast. They say a great battle took place the next day.

"I hardly used the mirror again until three days ago. I ... I first saw you, Lord Dermott; and I knew that something would happen to you. So in an attempt to warn you I came near your keep, but again the yeomen fled. And I watched you while you hunted for me. Yesterday, I knew that I had to get back to you and get you away from the danger. What a fool I was! Instead, I caused you to be shamed and degraded ... Oh-h ..." and she began crying again.

Dermott soothed and comforted her, and after a bit she fell asleep. For the next week Dermott cared for her, cooking their meals and mostly burning them. He slept only fitfully. His wounds were healed, but Helen's, as her name was, had not healed. She was fevered and chilled. and only partially awake at best.

The unicorn stood watch outside, its purple eyes always watching, and sniffing the air. One day it came inside, barely getting through the door. It stood beside her bed, and she patted its scruffy mane and head while Dermott watched. He marveled at the animal's magnificence; its heavily muscled body and head, and the ivory horn like a lance from its forehead. The animal turned its eyes on Dermott; for an instant they seemed to look on him as an equal. Then the look had gone.

Dermott fell in love with Helen, and she knew it though she was only half conscious. One afternoon Dermott came in to find her sitting up, her eyes as bright as a squirrel's. He sat on the bedside and held her hand.

"How do you feel, my Helen? You seem better this day."

"No, Dermott, only more free, or something. I do not know how I feel." She lowered her eyes. "My lord Dermott ... will you stay with me for a while after I get well? I mean ... if you would like to ..."

"I'll do better than that. I'll hunt up some priest if you want to be legal. Of course, it'll have to be one who hasn't heard of my actions ..."

"Oh, Dermott!" She threw her arms about his neck and kissed him soundly again and again. "Quickly, go to the cabinet there and get my father's old armor. It should fit you. Hurry."

Dermott did as he was told. He found blue-polished armor and mail, with a crested helmet, and a long light sword, a breastplate and spurs. He put them on. They were a little loose, but at least they were not too small. Dermott looked once more like the man he had once been.

"You look handsome, my lord," Helen laughed. "I must sleep now, but I'll get well soon for you." She kissed him, turned over and closed her eyes.

She died in less than an hour.

Dermott buried her in a grave under the pines that he dug with the sword. He cut a cross from wood and placed it on the rocks covering her grave, and wept. Then he mounted the unicorn, which gave no protest. They walked away with their heads hung low, and with many a look back.

Dermott came out of his reveries, and his eyes were wet with tears with the thoughts of Helen. He mounted the unicorn and patted its neck. He watched as the body of his brother and sister-in-law and all the others were placed in a mass grave. The people gathered their belongings and began to walk westward.

Dermott rode down to the people. Some of them ran from him, thinking him back to exact vengeance. Others thought the same but did not run; they turned their vacant eyes to him as if to say, "go ahead and try to hurt us more."

He came upon one of the brothers of the monastery hurrying along.

"Ho, father!" The priest looked up, turned ashen. He crossed himself. "Dermott, the outlaw! But this is no time for holding a man's past deeds against him. Come, we must hurry away from this accursed place, lest they come and tear out our very souls."

"I've been six months in hiding, father; six desolate months in the hills. And now I return to desolation. Only two days ago I heard that calamity had come on Westsan. I have come back to attend to what is mine."

"Stay here and attend to what is yours and you'll be a dead king over a dead land," the priest said, then turned to walk away. Dermott drew his sword, touched the blade to the priest's neck. "One more step, father, and you are the dead man."

"You — you would not kill a holy man. Surely ..."

"What matters it to me who I kill now?" Dermott's eyes went away for a moment, then came back. "Tell me what happened to the people of Westsan!"

The priest looked eastward and licked his lips. "Three days ago a kitchen girl from the castle went looking for guinea eggs in the old smithy where old Sir Bruce killed his wizardling-brother Geldric fifty years ago. We know of this because she lived until the second day of terror. She told us that it was dusk, and in the dim light she saw two huge eggs in the corner. She muttered something like, 'I must show these to Duke Robert,' and then the evil came on the land."

He crossed himself again.

"The two huge eggs cracked, and then disgorged their nauseous spawn, the spawn of hell. They spread their wings over the smith shop and the girl fled, screaming. She ran to the castle with the things behind her. On their batwings they flew throughout the castle and rent flesh and bone from noble, peasant, knight, and lady alike. Duke Robert gathered men on the drawbridge as one of the things flew out of the castle with the body of Lady Eleandor in its claws. The men loosed their spears while we watched from the shelter of the monastery, which we managed to seal off. Others fled across the fields. The castle caught fire from the inside and the first of the things we had seen was joined by its mate on the drawbridge. They tore the knights apart, then took Duke Robert and quartered him while he was yet alive. Then they flew to the peasants' huts. Where doors were barred, they flew down the chimneys, through fire and all. We blocked the monastery chimney with tables and the inside doors. When they found they could not reach us, they flew off to the ruins of the old castle of Westsan on high Camrain Hill. We watched them sitting there in the early dawn.

"For two days we watched them. In the daylight, they sit like lizards soaking up the sun. Then at nightfall, they climb to the sky and circle in the moonlight, killing all living things; cattle, birds, dogs. Westsan is becoming a dead land, Dermott. This morning, when we were sure that they did not fly at day, we came out and buried the dead. We are trying to get away from them before sundown. They seem to know the boundaries of Westsan and fly only over it; or so some peasants from Oread's holdings said that the things turn back on each flight at the borders. It's as if they are trying to clear Westsan of all living things. We will go to Oread's keep, and hope they will not follow. Come, Dermott!"

Dermott looked far, far eastward to Camrain Hill, and the hulk of old ruins at the top.

"Go, father," Dermott said, and turned the unicorn towards the hill.

The priest shuddered. "You're not going ... surely not, Dermott ... You can get away with the rest of us ... " He gave up and hurried after the others who had slowed as they saw Dermott go towards Camrain Hill.

Dermott turned.

"Tell them I've come back to claim my own."

Tears came down his cheeks as he turned towards the old hill and castle; tears for himself, for his homeland, tears for people who had once been his friends, tears for Duke Robert and his wife Eleandor who had once been happy together, but most of all tears for Helen and her loss, which had hurt him more than anything in the whole world, the whole cruel world into which he had been born and lived in and turned on by. He rode towards the hill and castle; the unicorn with great magnificent strides taking him closer and closer to the curse put on the land before he had been born.

He was last seen before he went over a hummock, the sunlight gleaming on the armor of the father of a girl who had been killed because she had loved him. Then he was gone.

When the morning sun shone down on Camrain Hill the next day, it fell on four dead, blood-spattered bodies; one in mail, one horned and hoofed, and two others.

Westsan became a dead land.

2. The Filthy Pro

EARLY PROFESSIONAL SALES

“Lunchbox”
“Onions, Charles Ives, and the Rock Novel”
“Love Comes for the YB-49”
“Mono No Aware”
“Billy Big-Eyes”
“Unsleeping Beauty and the Beast”
“My Sweet Lady Jo”

INTERVIEW, PART TWO

1. "Lunchbox"

BRAD: Now we come to your earliest professional sales, in the early 1970s. This is when your name started appearing alongside names like Isaac Asimov and Anne McCaffrey. We're talking about "Lunchbox" in the May 1972 *Analog.*

"Lunchbox" was your first professional sale, right?

HOWARD: Right. It was written in '68, and I sent it to Ed Ferman (at that time the editor and publisher of *The Magazine of Fantasy and Science Fiction*), like I always did. I sent everything to him first, and I *knew* he would buy it, right? And I would always count the days. I'd wait ninety days, and I'd get a letter back saying, "No." I did that for three or four years.

So after Ferman rejected "Lunchbox" — I could go get my logbook and tell you who I sent it to next. See, it was written in '68, and I marketed it all through '68 and '69. And then I sent it to *Analog,* like, two weeks before I was drafted. I went in for the draft on October 27, 1970. And I was in my fourth day of basic training when I got a letter from my wife with a xerox of the check stub in it, you know?

BRAD: Wow!

HOWARD: We were standing in formation and had mail call, and I got that. I got to enjoy it for like thirty seconds, and then I had to do a hundred push-ups or whatever we were doing at the time.

BRAD: (Laughing.) I shouldn't laugh, because that's awful. But in retrospect — In the movie of your life, this would be a big scene, you know? Your first sale, and you immediately have to "Drop and give me a hundred!"

HOWARD: "One, Drill Sergeant! Two, Drill Sergeant! Three, Drill Sergeant!" But that's what I had to do, right?

BRAD: And you just covered the next two or three questions I had. But it leads me into the next thing I was going to say: I think "Lunchbox" is a swell science fiction story, but it doesn't yet display the voice and the sensibility that your readers would later come to call "Waldroppian."

HOWARD: Right. See, the thing was, I sold it to Campbell (John W. Campbell, then the longtime editor of *Astounding/Analog*) in October of 1970. And then Campbell dropped dead in May of 1971. In the interregnum, Ben Bova was appointed editor of *Analog*, and he wrote me a letter that was forwarded to me by my wife — by then I was at Fort Bragg, probably — and he said that the nomenclature of the actual mission to Mars (the situation and setting for "Lunchbox") had changed in the meantime. Originally it was the Voyager mission, and they changed it to the Viking mission. So he wrote me a letter saying, "Can I change the nomenclature in the story to match what NASA's plans are?"

I started to write back a snotty letter saying, "No, Ben, just publish it like it originally was so I'll look like a *dork* when it comes out!" But I didn't do that. I said, "Of course, Mr. Bova, sir!"

"Lunchbox" went into the Army with me — like I said, I got the acceptance letter four days after I went in — and it was published the month I got *out* of the Army because Nixon had given us that six-months-early out, right? So it came out in May of 1972 along with *me*.

BRAD: That's a pretty typical publishing lag, even now. About eighteen months.

HOWARD: But of course that one was complicated by the fact that Bova wasn't the editor when I sent it in.

BRAD: So it might not have been the very last story that Campbell bought, but it was certainly *one* of the last stories he bought.

HOWARD: Right. But I always took credit for killing John Campbell, just like I later took credit for killing magazines when they bought stories from me ... and then died.

2. "Onions, Charles Ives, and the Rock Novel"

BRAD: Let's talk about your essay "Onions, Charles Ives, and the Rock Novel" — which was in *Crawdaddy*, right?

HOWARD: Right. It should have appeared in the original *Crawdaddy.*

BRAD: Because you actually sold it to them before they switched?

HOWARD: I sold it to the actual *Crawdaddy* when Chester Anderson — who wrote *The Butterfly Kid* and all that stuff, a trilogy with him, Paul Williams, and T.A. Waters as protagonists of three different books. Anyway, *The Butterfly Kid* was the one that got the most press and stuff. He was the editor of *Crawdaddy* at the time. His acceptance letter said, "When I saw the Grand Prairie, Texas postmark, I thought my past was coming to get me." Because he lived in Grand Prairie at one time.

BRAD: The address on the manuscript that we have says Arlington.

HOWARD: But I think I mailed it from Grand Prairie. Anyway, Chester Anderson thought it was some of his past coming back to haunt him. He had accepted it, and then the issue of *Crawdaddy* that was on the stands was Number 33, I think. My piece was supposed to be in Issue 34 or 35, but then Number 33 stayed on the stands for three or four months. And I said, "Uh-oh," right? That's always a sign that the distributor hasn't gotten a notice from the publisher to put the next issue out. Then it finally disappeared, and a year later when I was in the Army — ready for this? — I got a Third-Class envelope. I opened it up, and it was copies of the first two new *Crawdaddy*s. And there was a sixty-dollar check in between the two issues.

Me and my wife were on our way to a friend's house in Newport News, Virginia from Fort Gordon, Georgia. We were going to visit them because they had moved from Arlington, Texas to Newport News. He was restoring an organ in his house, a big pipe organ he'd gotten from a church. Anyway, I got the *Crawdaddy* issues from the mailbox as we were on our way to Newport News, Virginia — and there's a photograph of me holding them up with a check, right? Because as far as I knew, *Crawdaddy* had died with my article.

The article itself came out of a PBS performance by an orchestra performing Charles Ives' previously unperformed Fourth Symphony. His Third Symphony was what won him the Pulitzer Prize in 1947. Then he wrote the next one in '48. [*BD Note: Howard's article says that Ives' Pulitzer was awarded in 1947, but that his Third Symphony was actually written in 1911 ... with the Fourth probably having been written between 1911 and 1914.*] But it had never been performed in his lifetime. So they got an orchestra together (in 1969) and performed it. And while I was listening to it, the idea for the article came to me.

The article was about the "rock novel," as they called it. And Chester Anderson's letter to me said, "I think the Who have a 'rock novel' out called *Tommy*."

BRAD: That is exactly what I was going to ask you about.

HOWARD: Right. I wrote the article before *Tommy* came out. Anyway, what I called a "rock novel" is what everybody calls a "rock opera" now, of course. But at the time, everybody was talking about the possibilities for "comic book novels," "graphic novels," and "rock novels." That was the terminolgy people were using at the time.

BRAD: And that's what you talk about in the essay. I thought it was very prescient — but only a few months prescient, you know? Because I think you must have written this essay in early '69, and *Tommy* came out later that same year.

HOWARD: Right, like in May or June.

BRAD: And yeah, what you describe in the essay is what Pete Townshend was trying to do in *Tommy*. Whether you feel he was successful or not is another thing, but that's clearly what he was shooting for.

HOWARD: Exactly. And that's what I was thinking about when I heard the Ives piece performed.

Ives was big on counterpoint and cacophony, you know? Counterpoint, to the point of cacophony. His thing was, like, he had a thing in there where two marching bands are coming towards each other. And the tunes they're playing, for a while, syncopate up with each other, then become cacophonous as they get closer together.

Anyway, like I said, just listening to that made me think about the "rock novel." And I didn't know about *Tommy* yet, since it hadn't been released.

The essay is pretty self-explanatory, if I remember correctly.

BRAD: It is. And as I say, you were a few months prescient, because what you describe is pretty much what the Who attempted to do.

And then of course other people tried to do it as well, with varying degrees of success. I remember, maybe just a year or two after *Tommy*, Jethro Tull did one called *Thick as a Brick*. And then even a few years later than that, do you remember — oh, I forget the guy's name. His first name was Jeff ... I'll look it up. But he did *War of the Worlds*.

HOWARD: Yes, he did! What's his name ... I'll think of it in a minute.

[*BD Note: Neither Howard nor I remembered the name during our conversation, but the musician in question was Jeff Wayne, and his musical version of* War of the Worlds *was released in 1976.*]

BRAD: But yeah, he did a whole concept album that was basically musical-novelizing, or opera-izing, *War of the Worlds*.

HOWARD: And of course Andrew Lloyd Webber did *Jesus Christ, Superstar* and *Joseph and the Amazing Technicolor Dreamcoat*.

BRAD: So it all morphed into Broadway, and double albums, and all kinds of stuff.

HOWARD: You know, it (*Jesus Christ, Superstar*) was originally conceived of as just an album. And then it became a play, you know? If I remember correctly. We all thought Andrew Lloyd Webber would be something besides an institution, when he started out. You know, everything he did in *Jesus Christ, Superstar*, he and the other guy had done in *Joseph and the Amazing Technicolor Dreamcoat* beforehand.

Anyway, like I said, my thinking about it (the "rock novel") was all from the PBS film of the orchestra doing Ives' Fourth Symphony, which was broadcast either late in '68 or early in '69, if I'm not mistaken. At least on *our* PBS station.

BRAD: So that's "Onions, Charles Ives, and the Rock Novel." You were clearly on to something. But it sounds like by the time it finally came out in *Crawdaddy*, the other things (like *Tommy*) had already started happening.

HOWARD: Oh, yeah, it didn't come out in *Crawdaddy* until '71. Because it was delayed across that year and a half.

3. "Love Comes for the YB-49"

BRAD: Now we're going to talk about "Love Comes for the YB-49." I mentioned to you the other day that I love this essay, because even though I'm twelve years younger than you, I was obsessed with the same things — just different models of the same things. As a ten-year-old, you were fascinated with the early X planes, but by the time I was that age, I was obsessed with the X-15.

HOWARD: Right! You remember Jules Bergman, who was the science editor for ABC News, wrote a book on the X-15.

BRAD: I may have actually seen that book when I was a kid. But what I remember for sure is that two of the magazines my parents got at the house were *Popular Science* and *Popular Mechanics*. They were essentially the same magazine with different titles. But that's where I remember reading about the X-15, and how I became obsessed with it.

So I wanted to ask you: In the essay, you mention that the Flying Wing was featured in some of the movies you loved when you were that age, and I'm wondering if the first time you became aware of the Flying Wing was from those movies.

HOWARD: No, I knew about the Flying Wing before that. As I say in the essay, we lived in Arlington, Texas, which was near Carswell Air Force Base in Fort Worth. It was a Strategic Air Command base. So what I saw flying over me were B-36s. If the world had been different, it wouldn't have been B-36s, but YB-49s.

Out in California, Edwards Air Force Base is named for a guy who was flying a Flying Wing. The plane had some, whatcha-callit, "drag problems." Because it didn't have tail surfaces and stuff, it crashed. And they named the Air Force base after him.

But I was aware of everything, like the X planes, and Chuck Yeager, and the YB-49, and everything. And I knew they had flown the scale models of the YB-49, which were exactly the same plane, but scaled down for just a single pilot. They had flown that in the '40s, you know. Then they adapted that design to the Flying Wing, which was supposed to have a crew of thirteen, six of whom could sleep at a time. So it could stay in the air for something like eighteen hours.

I was fascinated by it. First because of the fact that it didn't look like any other plane that had ever been built. And you know, when they finally built the Stealth fighter and the B-2 bomber, they were essentially updated versions of the Flying Wing. Because Northrup had the right idea: The more surfaces you can get rid of, the less it shows up on radar.

I believe they showed it to Northrup when he was in his nineties, right before he died. They took him to Lockheed and showed him the Stealth fighter, even though they weren't supposed to. But they had adopted all his ideas — thirty, forty years later. So he was vindicated, you know?

But I knew about all that stuff. X planes, rocket planes, stuff like that ... just fascinated me when I was a kid.

BRAD: What was your medium for finding out about all this? Was it comic books, or magazines, or — ?

HOWARD: Well, in America in the '50s, you got everything from TV, or the radio, or you saw *LIFE* magazine. It came to the house every week, and there were pictures of the YB-49 there all the time. And if Stuart Symington (first Secretary of the Air Force, from 1947 to 1950) hadn't been such a dipshit, we would've had YB-49s flying out of Carswell rather than B-36s.

What he tried to do, was he tried to get the Air Force to adopt the B-49, but only if Convair would get the contract for the engines. My theory is he had some fingers in some Convair pies. Convair is what became General Dynamics eventually, by the way. So we wound up adopting the B-36.

If you see the movie *Strategic Air Command* with Jimmy Stewart and Harry Morgan, they take a tour of the B-36. Stewart plays a baseball player who's called back up to service and becomes a Strategic Air Command pilot just as they're about to adopt the B-47 medium bomber, you know? But they fly to the North Pole and back a few times early in the movie, and you get a lesson on what the B-36 was like.

But like I said, I'd rather have had them flying the YB-49.

BRAD: I'm struck again by the parallels and differences between you and me, being a dozen years apart in age. I grew up near Wichita, Kansas, which was the home of McConnell Air Force Base.

HOWARD: Another SAC base!

BRAD: Another SAC base, that's right. And what *I* saw flying over all the time were B-52s.

HOWARD: Right. They were just gettin' ready to adopt the B-52 when the B-36s were phased out. I even remember the B-58, which had a brief, about a one-year, operational life. That was the delta-wing bomber that had different pods you could stick on the bottom of it. One was an anti-radar pod, another one had a thermonuclear bomb in the pod, and another one had other stuff. One of 'em was a pod full of chaff to screw up the radar everywhere instead of just jamming it.

They only flew those for about a year and a half. But the B-52 was the workhorse once it was adopted, because they were still flying those even in Desert Storm, you know?

BRAD: Yeah, those things were probably held together with duct tape at that point. But they still flew. They'd probably still be flying now if not for the B-2.

HOWARD: There were guys in the Air Force who flew nothing but B-52s their entire career. They'd come in, they'd get into a B-52, they'd fly it for thirty years, and then they'd leave the Air Force. And that B-52 would still be going with different crews.

But like I said, that could have been the YB-49, if things had been different.

When *Crawdaddy* was revived, I sent 'em the YB-49 article, and that was the only one of mine they managed to publish before they went out of business again.

BRAD: That was the next thing I was gonna ask you about. This essay was published in *Crawdaddy* in 1971. Had you sold it before you even made your first professional fiction sale?

HOWARD: Lemme see ... Yeah, I believe I had sold the YB-49 article before I sold "Lunchbox" to *Analog*. I had sold Paul Williams two articles. The other one was "Onions, Charles Ives, and the Rock Novel." Neither appeared in the original *Crawdaddy*, which was printed on slick paper. Then the new *Crawdaddy* was printed on newsprint.

BRAD: So you just sent these in as cold submissions, right?

HOWARD: Oh yeah, sure.

BRAD: That's kind of wild, because I don't think there are any journalistic magazines at all now that would take a cold submission.

HOWARD: Well, even then, *Crawdaddy* was different from any other magazine around it.

But a lot of 'em did take cold submissions back then. It was a different world, right? The world I grew up in, and the world we live in now.

BRAD: My last real question about "Love Comes for the YB-49" is this: You finally have a Flying Wing model! (An AMT/Ertl 1/72 scale model, re-released 1995.) How did you finally get your Flying Wing model, and do you think you'll put it together?

HOWARD: If my eyes hold up, I will. The Revell kit from the '50s was reissued in the '90s. They were on a kick of doing that, because people would be saying, 'Why don't you do a reissue of the Sabrejet model' or whatever, you know?

Anyway, Ed Bryant sent it to me as soon as it was reissued.

BRAD: He just bought one and mailed it to you?

HOWARD: Yes, exactly. Because he had read the YB-49 article when it came out in *Crawdaddy*, more than twenty years before. And he knew how fascinated I was with it. And this was the first version since the 1950s that they put out as a model kit.

BRAD: That was a really cool thing for Ed to do for you.

HOWARD: It really was, and I was sorry I never put it together while he was still alive, so I could send him a picture of it. You can put it together so that it's flying, or so that the landing gear are down and it's on the ground. I was gonna do it as an on-the-ground model and take pictures of that.

But at the time, I didn't have a place big enough to set it on once I'd put it together, knowhaddamean? It's a big-ass model.

BRAD: You know, if you want it put together, and you don't trust your eyes to do it, you could probably get one of your friends who still does models to do it for you.

HOWARD: Of course, then I'd have to ship it both ways, and count on it not being fucked up by the new Postmaster General, you know? Who they still have to get rid of, and soon.

You might put that in the interview too, right?

BRAD: (Laughs.) I'd be happy to.

4. "Mono No Aware"

HOWARD: Like I said, "Lunchbox" went into the Army with me, and then came out with me. But I had also written all these stories while I was in the Army and of course none of them sold — and then the last month I was in the Army, I sold my second story. That was to, I think, a David Gerrold anthology which it later didn't appear in.

BRAD: Really? Which story was that?

[*BD Note: Howard didn't recall the answer to that question during this interview, but did in a later one. His second sale was "All About Strange Monsters of the Recent Past." That story's rights reverted when the anthology wasn't published, and it eventually appeared in* Shayol. *It was reprinted in Howard's collection* All About Strange Monsters of the Recent Past.]

HOWARD: There were also two "lost stories" while I was in the Army. I sent one to Damon Knight, and I sent one to Samuel R. Delany, and I never heard back. I wrote to 'em about the first one, and they said, "We don't know. We'll look around the place for it." The other was a story I sent to Chip Delany, who was editing *Quark* at the time. It was a paperback-original anthology series. I wrote him, and he says, "I'm taking off for Italy — " or maybe it was Greece, or wherever " — tomorrow, but as soon as I get back, I'll look around and see if I can find it." And eight months later or so, I got the story back. He had found it in the crap in his house after being away for six or eight months or whatever.

I thought they were good stories, but they've never been published anywhere. Because I didn't think they were such good stories that they should be in one of my collections or anything. One was called "The Great American Dreamers," I think. It was a, whatchacallit, a "corpsesicle story" as Fred Pohl later called them. You know, a cryogenic preservation story. And the other one was based on the Fisher King. That was never published, either. So I had copies of both of those stories, but I still considered them "lost" because the original submissions had literally been lost in those two cases.

BRAD: Was "Mono No Aware" one of the stories you wrote in the Army, or was that just after you got out of the Army?

HOWARD: That must have been just after I got out — because I got out in May of '72, and I got the acceptance in June of '72 by Special Delivery letter.

They had announced the magazine (*Haunt of Horror*), but I don't think they had announced the editor yet when I sent in the story. Look in the May '72 issues of Marvel comics, and you'll see the ads for the premiere of the magazine. So I had written the story fast enough to make it into the first issue.

BRAD: Yeah, the first issue was out in '73.

HOWARD: Witchcraft and sorcery was what the magazine turned into. It was taken over by somebody besides Marvel, and that's the direction it went then.

BRAD: Your story, "Mono No Aware," does *not* fall into that category. In fact, it's kind of an unusual story to be in a magazine called *Haunt of Horror.*

HOWARD: Right! But I sent it to 'em, and they bought it. I thought it was a good story at the time ... but when it came time to collect the stories in *Howard Who?*, I didn't think it was good enough to be in there.

BRAD: Well, that was your call. I think it's a pretty good story. I had not seen it before we started putting *this* book together, but I liked it quite a bit. As I said earlier, "Lunchbox," while it's a good science fiction story, isn't really what people would now call "Waldroppian." But in "Mono No Aware," it seems to me that you were starting to make some moves towards a more "Waldroppian" kind of story, because you would later write a lot of what could be called "alternate history." And although "Mono No Aware" isn't really an alternate history story, it's about a guy who's trying to *create* alternate history.

HOWARD: Exactly! Anyway, I thought it was a good story, and I'm sure I sent it to Ed Ferman first. And for some reason he rejected it in time for me to submit it to *Haunt of Horror.* Usually, he took ninety days to say "No," but this time he only took a week or two. Because I know I wrote it *after* I got out of the Army, and it was bought in, like, June of '72, which was just the next month.

BRAD: I remember you telling me a long time ago that you used to send Ed Ferman all your best stuff, but he never bought any of it.

HOWARD: That's right! For twenty years. Even after *Omni* started buying my stories, I'd send some stuff to Ed Ferman first, just with the idea that I was gonna *make* him buy something from me, you know? But then I asked myself, "Why am I waiting ninety days to hear him say 'No' when I can send it to Ellen Datlow and hear 'No' in a week?" I mean, if that's what was going to happen.

BRAD: I understand it, though, because there are editors that you *want* to sell a story to, regardless of whether you're gonna get a penny a word. My first sale *was* to Ed Ferman, and he would continue to buy my stories ... but at the time, who I wanted to sell to was Gardner Dozois, and Gardner turned down everything.

HOWARD: Of course! The one you can't have is the one you want. Datlow was paying five times the money that Ed Ferman was, but I was just gonna write stories good enough that he *couldn't* not take 'em, you know? And it never worked.

BRAD: But you know, I can see why you would have sent "Mono No Aware" to Ed Ferman first, because I could easily have seen that story in *F&SF*. That was the kind of story I read *F&SF* for. It wasn't a story I would have looked for in *Haunt of Horror* — and yet, there it was.

You did eventually sell to *F&SF*, but it was after Gordon Van Gelder became editor.

HOWARD: Right. Ed Ferman was still writing the checks in the early days (after Gordon became editor), before Gordon bought the place. And the first time he wrote me a check, Ed said, "Glad to see you in the magazine!" And I started to write back to say, "No thanks to YOU!"

(Laughter.)

Of course I didn't. But you know, it was thirty years from the time of my first sale to the time Gordon finally bought something of mine for *F&SF.*

5. "Billy Big-Eyes"

BRAD: Now we come to "Billy Big-Eyes" from *Berkley Showcase #1.* You and I talked about this story the other day, and I told you that I thought Cordwainer Smith was a heavy influence on it. And you said, "Well, of course!"

HOWARD: Of course! Like I said, it was originally written because ... See, after Roger Elwood, all these publishers who had never published science-fiction anthologies before ... well, got ideas for science-fiction anthologies. There was a mostly scholarly, Christian-type publisher called Unity Press that contracted with George Zebrowski for a book called *Biogenesis*, about possible future biological mutations of human beings. So I came up with Billy Big-Eyes, who could see the music of the spheres, as we say.

BRAD: Who could basically see every wavelength *except* the wavelengths visible to human eyesight.

HOWARD: Right. Then I came up with a story for that, which was based on "The Party at Jack's" by Thomas Wolfe, from *The Web and the Rock.* That's the one where they were having a party for rich people in a high-rise penthouse, and while the party's going on, the building catches on fire. It was an analogy to that. I was thinking about a big party in the future, where there are mutants running around. So Billy Big-Eyes fits right in.

BRAD: When I first mentioned to you that George wanted to include "Billy Big-Eyes" in this book, you said something to the effect that you weren't sorry you wrote it, but it wasn't a story you'd write now.

HOWARD: Right. I don't think it works. My problem with it is that after all the crap I went through with it for three years, it didn't work like I wanted it to.

BRAD: It didn't match the "Platonic ideal" that you had in your head of the story.

HOWARD: Yes, exactly.

BRAD: Because when we start to write a story or a book, we all have this vision of what we know it's gonna be, of what it *should* be. And we measure our success by "How close did we come to it?"

HOWARD: Right. And I don't think, even after all the drafts I did — two hundred thousand words of drafts, believe it or not.

BRAD: And what did the story come out being? Twenty, twenty-five thousand words?

HOWARD: Eighteen or twenty, I think. Something like that.

Tom Reamy looked at it, because neither Zebrowski nor I could figure out exactly what was wrong with it. And Tom said, "The stuff on page 8 belongs on page 32." And he was right. Some piece of information, some info dump, was in the wrong place, and screwed the whole story up, see? So I put it where it belonged, and then it worked *better*.

BRAD: Well, I like the story. I understand why you're maybe still not happy with it after all these years, because it's still not quite the direction that your voice was going to take. Certainly, deep-space science fiction wasn't going to be your milieu, really.

HOWARD: (Laughs.) *Métier*, as we say.

BRAD: On the other hand, I think there *were* some "Waldroppian" touches anyway. The way the characters talk to and relate to each other, and the basic weirdness of the "Big Eyes" clan themselves. There was clearly a bit of a Cordwainer Smith influence, but —

HOWARD: — because there are five families that control all the "big eyes," you know. They were all named for people I knew at the time.

BRAD: That, I believe.

HOWARD: Except for "Big-Eyes," of course.

But just like in Cordwainer Smith, I figured there would be a division of labor between the clans, you know? Some would have control over some things, and some would have control over others.

BRAD: Almost like far-future guilds. Only clans.

HOWARD: Exactly.

Anyway, I don't think it worked like I wanted it to work. Which is my disappointment with it, after all that work.

BRAD: After the George Zebrowski anthology fell through, did you send it to Victoria Schochet cold? How did it wind up at *Berkley Showcase*?

HOWARD: I think I did send it to her cold. I think Tom had sold something to 'em, and he had mentioned 'em. So I said, "Oh, okay, I'll try to send it to them, then." Because the Unity Press thing had just fallen through. They had decided to end their line of science-fiction anthologies. I don't think we had ever been paid. I think we had signed a contract, but hadn't been paid yet. So when they went out of the science fiction business, I had a story that didn't have a home. And I had done so much damn work on it that I sent it out immediately when Tom told me about the market.

BRAD: Victoria Schochet isn't a name that I know outside of *Berkley Showcase.* Was she a Berkley book editor who just did this series for the house?

HOWARD: Yes, she and John Silbersack were editors at Berkley before the Berkley/Ace/Doubleday acquisition happened. And they had been acquiring work for Berkley, and decided to do *Berkley Showcase* as, well, a showcase for the work they would be publishing in the next few years. That was the idea behind it. But I sold to them anyway, even though I didn't have a book coming from Berkley.

BRAD: They probably didn't have enough stories from writers whose books they were publishing to fill out the anthology every time.

HOWARD: Exactly right. I think there was one more issue, a second *Berkley Showcase.*

BRAD: I looked online, and it seems like there might have been three or four before they stopped.

HOWARD: But I was only in the first one. So after that, I stopped looking.

I think Tom must have told me about it just before he died, because the book came out three years after he was gone.

BRAD: *Berkley Showcase #1* came out in 1980, and that was just about the time your writing career started to change. Because "The Ugly Chickens" came right after that, and things went in a different direction for you.

HOWARD: Right, I consider "Billy Big-Eyes" to be my last ... my last not really . . .

BRAD: Your last "apprentice" story, maybe?

HOWARD: Right, exactly. There had been others, too, that I didn't put into *Howard Who?*. It took until 1986 for *Howard Who?* to come out, even though my career was fifteen, sixteen years old at the time. I had my second novel before I had a short-story collection, you know?

BRAD: Well, even taking that long, it was still kind of a triumph. Because not many people, even then, were getting short-story collections published. Certainly not by major publishers.

HOWARD: Like I've said before — At the time, Pat LoBrutto, at Doubleday, could buy any book he wanted for two thousand dollars. If he went above two thousand dollars, he had to go to the editorial board. He was a good, good editor, you know?

6. "Unsleeping Beauty and the Beast"

HOWARD: Say, did you want to talk about "Unsleeping Beauty and the Beast," too?

BRAD: That's the one in *Lone Star Universe,* right? I know George wants to include that. But I don't have it yet, and I've never read it.

HOWARD: You'll be disappointed, I'm sure.

BRAD: (Laughs.) What year was *Lone Star Universe* published?

HOWARD: 1976. That was a watershed year, too, right?

BRAD: Oh, it was the same year as MidAmeriCon in Kansas City.

HOWARD: And also of "Custer's Last Jump" (written with Steven Utley).

BRAD: So yeah, '74 through '76 were kind of big for you.

HOWARD: Yes, they were. Anyway, "Unsleeping Beauty and the Beast" was a cryogenic story. The unsleeping beauty is in a state of suspended animation. And the thing was, I was interested in a woman, and she was an expert on fairy tales and stuff. We were at an Aggiecon, and I called her at 9:00 in the morning — and it was too early, because she was still knocked out from the night before. But I wanted to go down to breakfast and talk with her about the story, you know?

So I did all this research for it. And let me see, if I'm not mistaken, it was supposed to appear somewhere else before the idea of *Lone Star Universe* came along. Something happened, so it wound up being an orphan, and I wound up giving it to Utley and Proctor for *Lone Star Universe.* So many of my stories have appeared somewhere they weren't supposed to, right?

[*Howard checks his old story logs.*]

All right, "Unsleeping Beauty and the Beast" went to several places. Then it was under consideration at *Galaxy* for about five months. And then Baen (James Baen, then editor of *Galaxy*) wrote me a letter saying he was gonna publish it. Then two years went by, and he never published it, so I withdrew it. He hadn't sent me a contract or paid me any money in two years.

I had forgotten completely about the *Galaxy* thing. But now I remember, I was pissed off because he kept it over four months before he told me anything, and then it was in inventory for two years.

So it was written sometime in '73 or so. I got it back in early '75, then sent it a couple of places, including Damon Knight at *Orbit* and Don Pfeil at *Vertex.* But they turned it down. And then Utley and Proctor told me about *Lone Star Universe,* and I handed it to 'em.

It had already been sold, essentially, for two years without any money or a contract. It's the usual Howard Waldrop story, right?

But anyway, like I said ... when you see "Unsleeping Beauty and the Beast," you'll admire it, but you won't like it, knowhad-damean?

BRAD: Tell me a little bit more about *Lone Star Universe*, which was an anthology devoted to stories by Texas science-fiction writers, and edited by Steven Utley and George Proctor. I knew Steve in later years, of course, and knew his writing. But I never met Proctor, and I don't know anything about him.

HOWARD: Proctor lived in Arlington, and he wrote novels under pseudonyms for many years, but he put his own name on several fairly good ones. He was a friend and protégé of Andrew Offutt.

BRAD: Oh, another guy who wrote a lot of books under different names.

HOWARD: Right. And Proctor was also a reporter for the *Dallas Morning News*. That was his day job.

He was a good guy. He died in a scuba-diving accident something like fifteen years ago in the Caribbean.

BRAD: That might explain why I never met him.

HOWARD: Yeah, he died before Utley did. He was one of the original members of the Turkey City group, and he came to nearly every Turkey City workshop for the first five or six years. He was a good friend to everybody, and he and Utley were fairly tight. They put together *Lone Star Universe*, and it ended up at Heidelberg Press, which of course ended up in receivership from Lamar Savings and Loan.

So for years, people would write to Lamar Savings and Loan trying to get copies of *Lone Star Universe.* Sometimes they'd fill the order, and send the books and a bill. And sometimes they'd say, "This is a savings and loan operation! We're not a bookseller!" They ended up selling it to some small-time distributor in Tennessee somewhere. So copies of *Lone Star Universe* started showing up in used bookstores all over the South for several years. And that was about the only way you could find 'em.

BRAD: Looking at the Table of Contents, it had just about everyone who was in Texas at that time. You, and Neal (Neal Barrett, Jr.), and Lisa Tuttle . . .

HOWARD: *Everybody*'s in there. It's a good book.

Although "Unsleeping Beauty and the Beast" is one of *my* lesser stories. But I liked it at the time, you know?

7. "My Sweet Lady Jo"

BRAD: That brings us to "My Sweet Lady Jo" in Terry Carr's *Universe 4.* You and I were talking the other day about how

Cordwainer Smith touched on the same theme in one of his stories.

HOWARD: "The Lady Who Sailed the Soul." I thought that story was essentially going to turn into "My Sweet Lady Jo," and you would realize it was his mother. But then it wasn't, and I said, "Well, I'm gonna finish the job that Cordwainer Smith wasn't man enough to do!"

(Laughter.)

BRAD: And what I said was that, at the time Smith was writing it, it probably occurred to him — and he probably realized that if he had done that, he couldn't get it published.

HOWARD: Right, it was in the late 1950s, in the later part of his career. He was writing all these *great* stories, you know?

BRAD: So you were writing "My Sweet Lady Jo" almost twenty years later. And in 1974, you could get away with things you couldn't in 1958.

HOWARD: Well, and because it was Terry Carr. The main reason I wanted to be in Terry Carr's anthologies ... Remember, *Universe* started off as a paperback series, right before Carr left Ace. The first two were paperbacks. And they were illustrated by Alicia Austin, who did these great frontispiece illustrations for each story. And the reason I wanted "My Sweet Lady Jo" to be in *Universe* was so I could have an Alicia Austin frontispiece. But in the meantime, Carr's *Universe* switched to being a hardcover from Doubleday. So they had quit using the Alicia Austin illustrations by the time I sold to him, see. So I was disappointed in that fashion.

BRAD: It seems that with a lot of your stories, we can talk about how you were disappointed by the publisher in some fashion or other.

HOWARD: Right, exactly! Anyway, once I sent the story to Terry, he said, "I think there's something wrong with the time-dilation line." So he and I sat down and worked out the time-dilation line so that it came out right.

BRAD: That's interesting, because my next question here on my piece of paper is, "Had you talked with Terry Carr about the story and its theme ahead of time, or was it a cold submission?"

HOWARD: It was a cold submission, but once he bought the story, he knew there was something wrong with the timeline. I forget what it was. It was something about ... You know, she had gone out once, and come back. And then there was the story. And there was something about the way I had set it up so that the timeline didn't work out quite right. But Terry helped me work that out. It was a cold submission otherwise.

BRAD: It's cool that he saw what the story was supposed to be, and wanted to make sure that you got it right so the science nerds wouldn't jump on it.

HOWARD: Right! Anyway, like I said: I was able to finish the job that Cordwainer Smith wasn't man enough to do.

Of course, I was very pleased when Terry bought it. Did I tell you, Terry sent me my first royalty check ever? I had gotten paid for stories, but Terry sent me the first royalty check.

BRAD: That's very cool.

HOWARD: Three dollars and seventeen cents! And I kept that check up on my wall for two weeks until I needed it.

BRAD: So that would have been in 1975 or so. And in 1975, three dollars and seventeen cents — that was some money.

HOWARD: Like they said in the Laurel & Hardy documentary, "There wasn't a man alive who could live to what that could buy!"

LUNCHBOX

It came down on a flame towards the gray and red landscape, hissing through the thin air, lower and lower as the dim sun rose up the edge of the planet. The ground below was turning from shadow to sunlight, and the metal eye of the craft reflected the eye and heart of the sun.

It dropped more slowly still, and the pillar under it changed from bright orange to nothingness and shimmer as the propellants burned away and the nitrogen pressure tanks were emptied in the last twenty feet of the drop. It settled with a small thump, and the legs made the machine plumb level inside their hydraulic casings.

The planet was quiet and still.

The sun beaded the horizon in the deathstill frosty calm of dawn.

Man's first claim to daybreak on Mars.

The noise rose from stillness to roar to pandemonium inside the Mission Control Room. Cigars were passed around, papers were thrown into the air, the unloosed tension went from desk to desk. Checklists fell like snow in the cyclone of the room.

Then the men resettled at their consoles, ready for the Big Broadcast of 1977. Above them, television commentators were telling the public that what they had just seen was a celebration by the men at the consoles because the first of the Viking series had landed on the red planet, Mars.

Krvl, resting in their den, heard the scream of a ruined xr. Parts of Krvl roused, other parts remained dormant, others were reproducing in a random manner, ready for the formation of a motherbud later in the day.

Krvl shifted himself sluggishly, aware that something was amiss. Xrs roamed at night, and by the slight pulsing in its head, Krvl knew it was dawnlight — when xrs should be dying. They did not scream when they died. And what but an xr went about at night?

And what, except the Kind, destroyed xrs?

Krvl paused/moved to the chute-tube of the den. It availed themself of an xr pouch and slid out, leaving its reproducing self behind.

Outside, it was a wonderfully murky morning.

The first photographs from Mars showed a hummocked landscape of powdered sand and clay/grit sized particles. The scanning lens mounted atop the module showed the hummocks. The close-up lens in the bottom of the Viking showed the clay sized particles.

The scanning camera on top turned completely every two minutes. It recorded a scene each twenty degrees of arc and sent them back after two minutes of rumination within the devices that made up the innards of the Viking.

The pictures were marvelously sharp and clear, and showed a rolled landscape of dunes. Readings gave back a temperature of –27°F but the temperature was slowly rising in the fairly bright morning sunlight.

Krvl seeped across warm dunes. He would have to hurry to gather xrs before they died completely in the hot burning sunlight that would come in an hour. Krvl liked to hunt in the morning better than the evening, though chances of getting a near-live xr were much less. This morning, Krvl also wanted to find the thing that had made the xr scream. He had heard a small sound like it often when he retrieved a half-live xr for his meal from the ice vein that ran through his den. But never from above, in the open, at night, that loud.

He struggled down a dune. Already it was warmer. In thirty minutes the heat would become unbearable. He would have to hurry. Krvl liked the summer least of all the times.

He came into view of the xr crawl.

The close-up lens of the Viking began to turn slowly, photographing then relaying pictures back to Earth. First was a photograph showing the third leg of the Viking which showed a discoloration, a darker smudge protruding from beneath the landing leg. When the photograph was relayed a matter of minutes later, the interpreters became tense for the first time. They immediately sent signals to the machine to take a much closer series of pictures of the third leg of the craft.

The scanning camera, meanwhile, showed a patch of darker smudges in a dip between two dunes.

Excitement ran high. The bottom of the Viking opened and a long sticky string uncurled on the ground. The interpreting people got down to work.

They tried to get the long string as near as possible to the third leg of the craft. They tried, but got no closer than four inches.

The string withdrew up into the craft like a long tongue.

The xrs had shifted a lot during the night. Krvl came over the dunes and saw the thick webbing of them strewn over miles and miles of desert.

He opened his pouch and began gathering them up, putting them inside with the small ends up. He would look back every so often, and those that had not moved their large ends up, he took out and dropped back to the desert. The sun was very very warm now.

He would have to hurry, or they would lose the rebirth fluid into the air through evaporation.

The instruments in the craft showed a temperature at minus eleven degrees Fahrenheit as the first of the sample gatherers was fired towards the darker smudge between the two dunes. The small rocket was propelled by liquid nitrogen pressure, and as it left, the nitrogen compressor, powered by the same nuclear generator which ran everything on the craft, sucked in more air from outside, to compress and liquefy.

The small rocket arced out, between the dunes, and landed amidst the darker tones of the camera lens. It sat a few moments, the last of the nitrogen bubbling off, and then a small grapple and net affair slid out, scooped, opened and closed. An activator signaled for the craft to start the winch that would draw the collector back.

Krvl straightened at the sound. A high thin pop, and then a thud quite near. He looked in the direction of the sound.

There was a slight hiss. He saw deepfrost form around a depression in the midst of the xr crawl. As he watched, xrs began crawling towards the depression, first a few, then more and more, then a virtual riot of them. And with the sun blazing.

All thoughts of xr gathering were forgotten. This was a new and strange thing. As mysterious as the xr scream early this day.

He/she/it walked towards the moving xrs. Krvl scanned the horizon for other signs of strangeness. Out a ways, between the nearest dunes, he saw a much larger depression, and a solitary, curiously flattened xr. More newness.

He stopped. A group of xrs was being gathered, folded, compacted, crushed into a tight mass before him. The folding stopped. Then the mass moved, without walking, towards the edge of the xr crawl.

Krvl looked and watched and followed, but could not decide what or how this thing happened.

An invisibility. He reasoned.

Krvl pulled out his twelfth and thirteenth Haze eyes.

He stopped at what he saw. His Haze eyes were good only when the air cleared and the Hazelight came down. Using them now, though, he could barely make out the countryside, but was taken aback at the other thing he saw.

A creature sat far off between the two dunes. With one of its feet it was standing atop the crushed xr, and had extended a claw from itself into the xr patch, where the claw had scooped up some of the things and was pulling them back towards itself.

Carefully, Krvl followed the claw as it was pulled back into the Haze creature. It had no business bothering his crawl.

The scanning camera showed the collection rocket being pulled back into the Viking. Then the series of landscapes as the camera rotated. Then the rocket, winched closer, and behind it the drag path where the grapple had slid through the sand.

Then more landscape. Then the rocket, still closer. One of the interpreters asked that the camera be frozen on the winching process next time around; he thought he had seen some interesting phenomena. The camera came around. The rocket was close, closer. There were marks behind the dragging grapple which did not seem to be made by its passage. Then the rocket was pulled within the innards of the craft. Then there were more markings on the ground,

The interpreter leaped up.

Some of the monitors showed activity within the spacecraft.

The last picture was sideways.

All was black.

Krvl had followed the claw until the creature pulled it inside itself. Then he looked at the Haze creature, sitting very high on its four appendages. It looked at him through its single eye.

Krvl gave it a universal greeting, while he assumed a warning stance. It did not move.

Krvl touched it. Nothing happened. Perhaps it was dormant while digesting its food.

Krvl pulled at its leg, lifting it from the ground.

Immediately the creature hissed, and sent its leg forward to the sand. A shower of dust flew up, and the creature rocked and settled on its legs again in the same relative position.

Krvl was very wary now. He asked it why it had entered his domain without respect. It did not answer. He pulled at its leg again. This time it moved violently, rocked towards him and back, sending up a great geyser of sand.

It would not do, Krvl decided, to have a mindless creature threaten one's food supply.

Krvl took action. The eye was always a good place to start.

On earth, consternation.

That afternoon, a Kind called Mrgk stood respectfully at the edge of Krvl's crawlpatch and asked to come visit.

Krvl was happy to see them again. Mrgk came in and smelled the xr smell, cold and delicate, on his sensors.

"To devour the xr," said Mrgk.

"To devour the xr," answered Krvl. "I have a new thing to show."

"What is it?" asked Mrgk.

"You will have to use your Haze eyes," said Krvl.

They went into the den, to the back, near Krvl's xr bin.

"Here," said Krvl.

It lay on its back, legs up.

"This is most strange," Mrgk said. "What can it be?"

"I think it some sort of creature of the Haze," answered Krvl. "I found it raiding my crawl this morninghunt."

As they watched, the creature let out a hissing scream. Its legs thrashed in and out, moving up and down, trying to find footing in the air. Just as suddenly, it quit.

"Can it hurt us?" asked Mrgk.

"I think not," said Krvl. "I blinded it before I brought it back to my humble denning. Or I thought I did. It struggled fiercely much as you just saw, on the way back. I later found a smaller eye on its nether side, which I also removed."

"It has no other appendages?" asked Mrgk. "Four seem such a small number."

"It had," answered Krvl. "Six more clawlike devices, tightly wound inside. I discarded those also, fearing they could be harmful." He indicated a tangled pile of loops and grapples. "I believe it to be fully incapacitated now, though seemingly able to live somewhat, like the xr. It moves from time to time."

"This is a most wondrous creature. We shall have to tell the other Kind."

"I will take it to the next Meet," said Krvl.

"Very strange indeed."

"I have not yet shown the best part," said Krvl modestly. "After rendering it helpless, I cracked its shell. Inside I found a wonderful newness. Note its stomach is very cold?"

Mrgk bent close, saw the deepfrost forming on its insides.

Krvl dropped a stiff xr into the body. In a few seconds, it swelled, grew, moved, began running about, trying to climb out the slick sides.

"Simply marvelous," said Mrgk.

"I think this Haze creature was able to make its stomach very cold, so that it could ingest fully live xrs. Imagine," said Krvl.

"But will it not lose this ability?" asked Mrgk.

"I think not. It remains the same as this morninghunt. It has lost none of its coldness," answered Krvl.

"Then it is a wondrous find. Wondrous. We shall be able to place xrs in it and then ingest them fully live ourselves. Oh, I can imagine the taste already!"

Mrgk paused. "Do you realize every Kind will try to find one of these Haze creatures, so they will be able to rejuvenate their xrs? You'll start a craze, Krvl, a positive craze."

Krvl was pleased. Buds formed quickly on his back.

In front of them, between the four legs, the nuclear generator hummed and the compressor pockpocked, making more liquid nitrogen. The legs suddenly hissed and moved, searching back and forth for footing in the air of the den.

ONIONS, CHARLES IVES, AND THE ROCK NOVEL

My wife is in the garden planting onions now, and I'm out there with her, preparing for the Great Pratie Famine later this year, but my mind's not on the leeks. It's back last night on Charles Ives, his music, and what he's done, and on the threatening possibilities his Fourth Symphony opens up for Rock.

The work was broadcast last night (7:00 CDT) over the NET outlet from Dallas, Channel 13. I expected music, good music, when I tuned in. A friend (who works for the S part of NASA) has a demo record he went wild over and set me down one rainy night two months ago to hear it. I had no choice but to listen (the friend outweighs me some 100 lbs) to the record. The Ives work there was *Putnam's Camp*, part of the longer work *Three Places in New England*, and I was immediately taken by the sound montage and the use of the sleep effect in the music. *Putnam's Camp* concerns a twelve-year-old boy who falls asleep by the river one Fourth of July listening to the concerts and marches from the park. In the dreams and partial awakenings, he "hears" American history, the Civil War, the Revolution.

I was impressed, needless to say, and looked forward to the symphony when it was announced in the TV guide. I didn't quite know what to expect; if I had, I might have run away.

When Linda came home from supporting us at Sears, my eyes were hanging out and noises were still running around inside my head. I went missionary, didn't give her a chance to catch her breath; I ran around waving my hands, pointing to invisible instruments, making noises and being generally incoherent and unintelligible. When I finally slowed myself down, she was looking at me and tapping her foot. I started all over again, slowly.

I told her that I'd just seen and heard one of the best pieces of music in the world. Three conductors for an orchestra and chorus. Half the violins sawing away, the others barely moving. Different times; three or four melodies at once; sound like the bridges in "A Day in the Life," eight or nine of them. I told her about a soft waltz melody line being played, then there's twelve bars of anarchy over it in the brass, and the screaming stops and the waltz melody is still going quiet as ever. I told her of the stretches with sounds like silence with "Yankee Doodle" playing over it and spaces with Sousa over an earthquake of percussion.

It was beautiful; it was the strangest and one of the best pieces of music I've heard anywhere, anytime.

I told her all this, and I don't know what all else, everything that came into my head, I suppose. I talked about it until I went to sleep.

It is today, though, not last night, and I've been thinking. Which is a disease common to too many people. Reflection sobers, and sober reflection sobers absolutely. And frightens, if you're in the music business.

This morning I'm glad I'm not in the biz. The possibilities opened by Ives' Fourth Symphony are too big, too deep, too intense and soul-searching to ignore. If you're a musician, listening to the Fourth Symphony is akin to reading Agee's *Let Us Now Praise Famous Men* for the first time if you're a writer. You're humbled. You marvel at both the feeling and the technique. Your own stuff begins to look kiddygarden. A little humility is good. Agee, by the humanity and goodness of his work, and its brilliance, humbles most other writers, even reporters, who are notoriously unaware of genius when they see it. Ives' music scares. It frightens the Bejeezus out of most people.

It should. There's no telling when it was written. Ives died in '54. The Fourth Symphony was discovered in his papers; it was wrangled over and discussed for ten years, first performed in '64. Most guesses place the writing between 1911-1914. (Ives' Third Symphony, which won the Pulitzer in '47, was written in 1911.) These were the last of Ives' most productive years. This smacks of genius in my book, but I'm no judge of anything that nebulous. The Fourth Symphony disturbs me. It should scare hell out of Rockheads; it was written so long ago, and Rock has produced nothing near to it in the five years since its virgin performance.

The purpose, the major intention of all these words is not about Ives but about Rock, about music itself. There is talk in "comic book" circles of the graphic story novel; a long, long work of major importance told in panels; the major arguments being whether or not it should have words, or to what extent words should augment the panels. Talk of this in a form so inimical to length in the first place; the comic strip's strength lies in its ability to tell a story quickly and simply in a small number of pages, and to give a punch to the reader at the end. If it so chooses. The graphic story novel would not choose to do so, instead would make up in length and depth what it passes over when it sacrifices its brevity and gosh-wow. The idea was put forth collectively by Bill Spicer and Richard Kyle of *Graphic Story Magazine*; work has been started on several graphic story novels, mostly by young Westcoast writer-artists like Jim Gardner or George Metzger and others.

The graphic story novel is on the way: It's time for the Rock-Novel.

A work of music, a rock symphony, if you will. A work with or without words. (The words of "In-A-Gadda-Da-Vida," for example, are only an envelope for the music; whether or not it would be complete without them is open for debate.) A work composed of songs, of music of all types, of all times. Counterpoint "Battle Hymn of the Republic" with "Sad-Eyed Lady of the Lowlands," "Adeste Fideles" with "Get a Job." Not those songs, but those modes of music. The classical, the religious, the simple ballad with the most inane 4/4 lyric; the ridiculous with the sublime, all together with original compositions for orchestra.

For Orchestra. Therein lies the rub. The Rock-Novel could only be performed, in my mind, by a full orchestra, plus guitars, maybe harmonica, amplified or not. Even with this, though, I think the first Rock-Novel will be written not by a classical composer but rather by some Head tunesmith, or an aggregate of them, or by several Rock bands working together to give Music a newer form.

There are very few geniuses running loose; even fewer are at work in the field of music. Lord knows where the talent to write a Rock-Novel can be found. But I know it's there somewhere. The Rock-Novel is a personal vision of mine — it sprang forth full grown out of my head this morning after thinking on the Ives concert last night.

Not enough is known about music to do it, maybe. (But the Fourth Symphony stifles that, I guess.) We haven't found out all about music yet. Not in all the thousands of years we've been upright, not in all the years since someone beat on a log and liked the sound. We've been trying. People talented that way have been at it for centuries.

"What would happen if I made this sound" (twang) "at the same time I made this sound" (twung).

So they go (twang twung) and made a chord. Maybe it was a bad one, but at least he wouldn't do it again, consciously.

(I digress. I am too close to my subject, I realize. Digression is good for the soul; it clears the mind like ice water on the bare spine.)

The Rock-Novel as Theme and Form

With all the mishmash of sound in the Fourth Symphony, Ives manages not to lose sight of the music or his aims in all the acoustics. The moods change brilliantly; one form merges into another, or one form stops and another begins. The bombardment is total; no one will go to sleep on Ives (as they can for short stretches on Wagner or Richard Strauss). The mind keeps alert.

As one of the musicians said in interview before the symphony, that through all the gaiety of Ives' works, under the "Yankee Doodle" and the Sousa, you can hear a sadness ... He was right; there is a bittersweetness under the music, though it be fierce, unsubtle, or hammering — a remembrance and grievance for things past is the best way I can describe it and its mood — not mournful, not sentimental; though parts of the music approach it, there is another melody going reminiscent of rag or chaos under the sentimental line.

The Rock-Novel can have theme and form rather than being a collage of sound, song, and noise.

I envision the Rock-Novel as long as the longest symphonies, probably longer, with no break. You've got to have grit if you want to hear music, real music, all the way through. Something like the Rock-Novel should be for everybody, anytime, for as long as they want to listen; it should have a unity that carries through like a symphony.

The themes can be as varied or more so than any symphony — alienation, good times, melancholy, space and the Universe, love; whatever the composer or composers think is important enough to devote his energies and the energies of an orchestra, choristers, and other musicians to; to make a statement or leave a feeling on.

It's all there, it *will* all be there, in the Rock-Novel. I'm sorry all I can do is envisage the Rock-Novel, that I can't do any more than write about it. Were to God I were a musical genius. Ives has pointed the way, has put it all down on paper; people have played it. It's up to somebody with the grit and talent to take it from Ives' Fourth Symphony to the first Rock-Novel. It's coming, and soon, soon.

LOVE COMES FOR THE YB-49

It was 1954 and we were all a little in love with science and the Flying Wing.

I was. All my friends were, and even though we lived near Carswell AFB and could see B-36s fly over at any hour of the day, we figured you could stick all the B-36s in the world in your eye without making a dent. The Flying Wing was and would always remain our plane.

I think every kid in the world loved it. The people in Hollywood knew it, too. When they saw what Northrop Aviation had done, they put the big airfoil in movies time and again. We saw it in the opening of *Captive Women Invasion* and *USA* and George Pal was no fool because he had it drop the H-Bomb on the Martians in *War of the Worlds*, and wow, if we wanted anything to stop the Martians we wanted the YB-49 to do it. Not just any old bomber. *Our* bomber.

You remember the Flying Wing. There were two of them. One was the YB-35. It had four engines driving eight propellers, and carried thirteen men and could go 10,000 miles without flinching. It came out in 1946.

The other was the YB-49. It had eight Allison jet engines, and it really did look like a bat out of hell and it carried nine men and was the most awe-inspiring sight in the galaxy. They were both nothing more than gigantic wings and we loved them like nothing else. Both were tried by the Air Force and Navy and were found wanting.

But in 1954, before we knew about things like performance and fuel consumption, before we even knew what kept a plane up, you could have said to us, but it doesn't do quiet right, and has trouble climbing, and sometimes there's trouble handling it, and we'd have looked at you like you had just pushed out our pet goldfish.

Anyone who said something like that was guilty of the rape of our dreams. We *wanted* to be able to grow up alongside the Flying Wing. It had been born the same year that we had. It meant science fiction and space travel, and something new and different. It was our symbol of the future and they took it away from us.

There were other planes, too. We loved the X-series of aircraft, the rockets and jets: the X-1, the X-2, the X-3, the Douglas Skyrocket. They were also symbols of what we needed to grow up with and dream about. They were all shiny and white and there was nothing we wanted to fly more, expect maybe the YB-49.

But I think the Flying Wing was a symbol, a goal in itself. It didn't *have* to do anything. The X planes did. They were powerful things, dropped out of the bellies of B-29s, rising up and roaring off on a quiet thin pencil of flame into the dark upper sky. We read about them in the papers, first 60,000 then 80,000 then 110,000 feet up they went, at 1000 then 1800 and finally 2000 miles an hour. And we were there, in the closed canopies with Yeager and Kinchloe and Goodlin.

We wanted to grow up and fly one of the rocket planes. Or maybe go up in one of the StratoLab or ManHigh or Farside project stratosphere balloons, way up in the middle of the air in a plastic bag full of gas, inside a gondola the size of a beach ball. Heroically, teeth gritted, taking readings in the thin air, wiping frost off our googles, breathing through oxygen masks. Looking down and seeing the shrouded landscape, looking out and seeing the curve of the horizon, looking up and seeing the black black sky with the stars shining in the middle of the day.

And we watched our V-2s and Viking missiles rise up from White Sands Proving Grounds and fall back to explode and burn like hell, and pretty soon the whole thing was looked on by most of the people at worst as a waste of money and at best as the finest joke to come down the pike in a long time.

And the movies we let ourselves see. If it had planes or rockets or spaceships or flying saucers or submarines in it, we were there. Staring, wide-eyed, mouths open, hands on invisible rudder controls and trim tabs, ready to reach for ray guns, as we sat in the middle of the darkened theater, watching meteors that glowed and sparkled in a space with no air resistance to make them burn, spaceships that shot sparks and smoke out the back end, wobbled on wires and roared like freight trains in the vacuum, traveling mattes that moved when they shouldn't have. Enlarged pictures of horned toads and grasshoppers the size of barns superimposed and supposed to be scary.

And the comic books we read in the days between one Saturday and the next to keep us going. Comic books about airplanes, and spaceships and Mars, especially Mars.

In 1956 when I was ten, there was a favorable opposition of Mars on September 8th. My mother and father were bringing my sister and me home from summer vacation that night. I stayed awake all through that autumn night, listening to the car radio because the news broadcasts kept mentioning astronomers and Mars. I suppose I was expecting them to see people through the telescopes opening the locks on the canals or something.

And the airplane models we put together. Any jet, any German plane from WWII. Japanese planes, B-36s and B-29s. The model rockets, the Nikes, The Loons. The space stations, the Vanguard satellites, the moon ships, the space taxis, even models of the moon itself.

And of all the models we had, nobody had a Flying Wing. I don't think one was made. The plane we worshipped was never put into the $^1/_{72}$ reality of clear and colored plastic, never made solid; always to remain a phantom on celluloid and cold gray newsprint.

The science we loved carried over into our reading, and we

began to read science fiction, and take off on a new thing, and it all tied together and made sense: the airplanes, the balloons, the films, the models, the comic books, all of it. It was a shapeless unbundled mass called childhood. It was good because all the things gave us something to work for, it was bad because we did not understand the society that could produce comic books at one end and the H-bomb at the other.

Someday I'll go back there. It will be a cool gray day, I think. A West Coast fog will be rolling in and the fence around the place will be wet. (I do not think I could stand a sunshiny day.)

I will be there, wherever the last Flying Wing is sitting forever, if there is one left anywhere. There has to be. It will be standing on the concrete on its high undercarriage, a beached monster of a plane, with its glassy cockpits covered with latex, as if it had shut its eyes against the dampness. The morning will be quiet.

Somehow I'll get to go inside. I'll look out through the wing turrets, stand in the tail cone, and finally sit in the cockpit and put my hands on the wheels and throttles. I will sit for hours, remembering.

Then you will be able to hear a shout of joy at the edge of the Universe.

MONO NO AWARE

There are shadows in Hiroshima.

The city was levelled and rebuilt after the war. All traces of that hot morning in 1945 are gone but the Atomic Dome, the Peace Park and the shadows.

They lie there, along the bridges which span the Ohta River. Shadows of railings burnt into the bridge road itself, indelible. Scorched there in the light of a thousand suns.

And on the steps of the Sumitomo bank. One of the nameless 70,000 statistics huddled there against the bomb burst which turned the city white with heat. His shadow is there, now part of the stone.

The city has been remade. All that remains of that day are the Peace Park, shadows and bridges and buildings. And the memories.

Inoshiro Nowarra rubbed his eyes. Lack of sleep left them gritty and burning. Still he worked, tightening the cockpit latch which had hung. The most minor thing now, he thought, the most minor thing might hold me back. It cannot be. Not after this work. Not now.

With a snap, the cockpit canopy slid closed. Nowarra squeezed graphite into the slide. He opened and closed the canopy three times. It worked smoothly, with barely a click.

He jumped off the wing, stepped to the hangar doors. He slid them back, revealing sky and stars. The August night was warm.

He jumped into the tow tractor, cranked and put it into gear. Looking back over his shoulder, he pulled the A6M Zero from its metal house.

It was in the morning, and his father was going to work. As his father came out of the house, they heard an approaching plane though there was no air raid siren. He ran to his father.

His father held him while the airplane flew over. It was a Zero, flashing yellow and red in the morning sunlight. It circled and wagged its wings. They waved.

It flew away.

"There are not many planes left, are there, Father?" he asked.

"No," said the father. "Soon there will be none. Stay near the house today, Inoshiro."

"All right, Father."

His father patted him on the shoulder and left.

He turned to go in when he saw a caterpillar on the lawn. He stooped to watch it.

He studied the caterpillar while it crawled over four or five feet of the lawn.

He looked up at the street. A man was looking at him. The man wore aviator's garb. Being six years old, Inoshiro did not know which held the greater mystery, the aviator or the caterpillar.

He finally looked back down to the caterpillar.

Then the sky turned red and the house fell down.

"Mother, Mother!" he screamed, but there was no answer.

"Mother!" he screamed again.

There were more explosions as buildings burned and died.

"Inoshiro, is that you?" asked a voice in the darkness.

"Here! Here!" he cried, though he was pinned and did not know where he was.

"Keep talking, Inoshiro," said the voice. "I will find you."

"Who is it? Who is there?" he asked.

"It is Mrs. Namura," said the voice. "I will find you."

"Where is my mother?"

"I do not see her," said the voice. "Keep talking, Inoshiro, I will find you."

The ground rumbled again. A scream came from somewhere nearby.

Inoshiro began to cry as the shock wore off. It was pitch black. He was twisted, pinned in the debris of the house. He could not breathe in the darkness.

"Mother, Mother!" he cried.

He heard hands scrabbling above him and saw lightness near his arm. He tried to move but couldn't.

"Mrs. Namura!" he yelled, struggling. "Here, here!"

The hands were near. They caught him, fumbled, pulled him. Then they pulled him again and he came loose. He cried; it was almost as dark outside as under the debris. The air was full of moving, blinding dust.

"Mrs. Namura," he said, "Mrs. Namura," and hugged her and looked up at her.

She had no eyes.

He pulled the Zero onto the grass landing strip. The stars shone bright and light wind blew. He stopped, disconnected the tractor. The Zero hulked in the starlight, roundels barely visible on its wings.

Its clean lines were broken where blast ports of two Mauser Mk 21 30mm cannon protruded, and where a supercharger thrust from the engine cowling. Two more cannon bulged in the wing roots. The canopy was shortened aft of the pilot, with just room for the oxygen bottles and regulator behind.

The plane was pale yellow, the engine cowling and roundels red. It stood high on its landing gear, nose pointed towards the ocean and Shikoku.

The Inland Sea was still.

He had grown, like thousands of others, in the shadow of the bomb. He saw the old ones die from the slow ravages of the atom, and heard of the stillborn. He watched his playmates wither away. He grew up while the children folded the paper cranes, while the city was rebuilt by the Allies, the Children's Monument erected and the country reshaped.

Mrs. Namura died two days after the blast. His mother and sister were found weeks later when the block was cleared by the crippled and dying. His father disappeared at the hypothetical point above which the bomb burst.

Inoshiro was shunted from hospital to orphanage to school. He was one of the *hibakusha* but he did not know it; the effects of the blast did not manifest themselves until he was sixteen. Then, it was not as leukemia or bone cancer or baldness. It happened one night as he lay sleeping in the school dorm.

The sleeping forms around him melted, wavered, changed. He found himself among the old, the dying, the dead. A doctor moved from bed to bed, unable to do anything but kill pains while bodies died. He saw the hospital as he remembered it, two days after the blast.

He screamed and wakened.

A week later, it happened again.

Three nights later, a third time.

Then one afternoon, in class. The walls faded away; he saw the countryside as it had been before the school was built.

He began to read everything he could find on the Bomb, Hiroshima, World War II, atomic fission and the air war.

He walked through the streets of the city as though he had never seen them. He visited the shadows on the bridges, the Peace Park, the museum, the airfields, the airports, the barracks.

He became a civilian employee of the Japanese Self-Defense Force. He watched the peace riots of the late Fifties and early Sixties, and still he read.

The phrase he most often found while reading of Hiroshima was *mono no aware*. The words meant the traditional acceptance of all bad things in the past as inevitabilities, but with sadness tempered by distance in time. In use with the Bomb it had a special meaning: It is sad this terrible thing happened, but then, it was sad the whole war happened. Let us accept it, and see what the future will bring.

No, thought Inoshiro. *Mono no aware is wrong, accepting what happens as what happens. There must be a better way than to be six years old and have the sky explode and kill your family.*

That night, he walked the rubble of Hiroshima. From a hill in the nearby country, he watched it burn. He cried for his lost mother and sister and father, and the eyes of Mrs. Namura.

The trouble had been that there were too few planes and not enough fuel. And those with fuel had not been able to reach the altitude at which the B-29s operated.

The Japanese Army dug in for invasion in those last days, an invasion which never came. Secretly, just after a rainstorm one day in mythical New Mexico, the sun touched the ground, fused sand, shook storefronts in Reno, Nevada.

Instead of an invasion, two bombs would come calling for the Allies.

Nowarra had been a frightened six-year-old then. He was a man, now.

Buying the plane had taken his time and most of his money. The hardest items to obtain were the cannon parts. While he learned to fly, he also learned more about his atom-bomb affliction. On his first visits, he spoke to no one, carried no equipment. Then he began taking small things back to the flaming inferno which raged for the first few days after the bomb was dropped.

Months passed before he could carry something as small as a lunch pail. Then a shovel, then larger things. He awoke after each trip, haggard, unable to go back for days, sometimes weeks at a time. Then for longer stays. He roamed the days between the bombing and the Occupation, always careful to avoid the flames of the city.

He tried for a long time to go back past the bombing.

Inoshiro succeeded in November of 1965.

He convinced himself of something else that month. There was a building he passed each day, one of the shadow-places. He knew each mark, each scratch. That night, he took a small square of paper back to the morning of August 6, 1945. He taped the square of paper to the wall. He woke next morning feeling worse than he ever had before. He dressed hurriedly, walked to the building. On the wall was a new white square, with two little tabs where the tape had held it in place.

Inoshiro stared at the building a long time. The past, evidently, could be changed in a small way.

The calendar in the hangar read August 6, 1973. Dawn greyed the east over the Inland Sea. The stars paled until only Venus was left. Inoshiro slipped into his flight jacket, sword at hip, headband across his hair. On the headband was the insignia of the Rising Sun. Over this, he pulled his aviator's cap and goggles. He wore no parachute.

The time was 6:45. Inoshiro climbed into the Zero, tested his oxygen regulator a last time, turned it off. He cranked the Zero, sat within the cockpit while the engine warmed. The Zero taxied to the end of the runway and lifted into the sun.

His plane appeared on the radar of the nearest airbase. A check on local airports revealed no flight clearance. Call went out for the aircraft to identify itself. The plane continued without answer on a southerly course towards Kyushu.

At 0702, the radar ran around the trace without a return.

The weather plane sent to check the target city would be over Hiroshima now. He did not want the weather plane to report hostile aircraft. As soon as the B-29 turned out to sea far ahead, Nowarra pulled into a spiral and levelled out at 5000 feet. An hour out in the Pacific, between his Zero and Tinian, a flight of three B-29s came towards him.

The first was named *No. 91.* Like the others, its rudder was painted with the circle and arrow of the 509th Composite Group. Behind flew the *Great Artiste* and the *Enola Gay.*

All, Nowarra knew, had been stripped for the mission, with only tail guns functioning. The planes contained instruments, not weapons. The *No. 91* held cameras, the *Great Artiste* telemetering devices to test blast effects. The *Enola Gay* carried the "Little Boy" deep within its bowels.

The official mission reports read: No flak, no fighters. They were not expecting interception. Few Japanese planes could perform at 31,000 feet; flak could not reach that high.

Nowarra banked the A6M for a last look at the city. Hiroshima lay below him like an outspread fan, the River Ohta branching to the sea. Just short of the main river bridge would be the hypocenter of the blast.

Inoshiro's head swam; he fought to hold himself still in time. He had to concentrate to keep himself back this long before the blast. *I have made it back with my plane,* he thought. *I have come this far. Do not let me fail now.*

The time was 7:43. It would take nine minutes to rise to the altitude of the bombers. The sun stood east. The B-29s would come at him out of the sun.

Inoshiro continued his look at last things. He looped the Zero over the city. He turned towards his home. Down there, near the third and fourth branch of the Ohta, was his house and that of the eyeless Mrs. Namura.

He remembered that morning. The Zero swept low over the rooftops. There — his street, his home, a child playing in the yard. Inside, his mother and sister. His father had not left for work yet. He would be eating the last of his breakfast as would so many fathers on that day. The wives would be scooping coals into corners of cooking pots. These pots would be responsible for much of the devastation beyond the blast area. When the shock wave came, they would fly with the other debris, setting fire to paper, wood, clothing.

Inoshiro circled. He saw the child run to his father. He banked, came back, wagged wings and began his long climb up the air.

The sky was three-tenths cloud. He rose, the engine straining. He pulled away from the city and cleared his cannon.

Doom Doom Doom Doom the four 30mm cannon said to the bright morning.

Can there be no change to what has happened, only regret? wondered Inoshiro. *Perhaps not this time, not this day.* He turned towards the Inland Sea.

7:59. The three silver bombers would be in their run over Shikoku. In seven minutes, they would pass over a convoy in Fukuyama Bay.

Nowarra put his mask on at 14,000 feet. Tension made his shoulders hunch, his head began to hurt. For an instant, vision wavered. *No!* he told himself. *I have been here this long. I cannot falter now.*

Still he nosed the A6M up the eastern sky, towards the sun. He reached 23,000 feet and settled into a shallower climb angle. Hiroshima lay behind like a dream; a few minutes ahead were the B-29s.

His head hurt more. The sky shimmered.

The landscape altered slightly. The altimeter showed 28,000 feet. 8:09. The bombers should be only three or four minutes away, only a few thousand feet above his altitude.

The sky was darker blue. He cut the supercharger in. The plane lurched ahead. *Where are they?*

A reflection of sunlight ahead. Two of them. The *Enola Gay* followed by the *Great Artiste. No. 91* had turned aside to film the drop twelve miles away.

Nowarra leveled the Zero for his run.

Time shimmered.

They were gone! His watch said 8:13. Two minutes. *There they were, past him.* He had moved ahead in time.

The Zero came around at full speed. The *Enola Gay* and the *Great Artiste* were on their final runs. He edged the Zero's nose over to gain speed.

The wings screamed in thin air. The supercharger whined like a bee in a tin hive.

8:14. Near Hiroshima now. 31,000 feet. Seconds left, only seconds. Already the arming tone of the bomb was being heard in *No. 91*, far away. The tone would stop as the bomb left *Enola Gay*.

Close, but not close enough to fire. *They have not seen me. They worry about the bomb. Too late. Too late.*

8:15. Hiroshima lay below, a real city in a real time.

Nowarra began to fire while too far away from the *Enola Gay*. Already the men inside would have their goggles on.

The Zero closed, still firing.

Tracers crawled up towards the bombers.

8:15:17. The *Enola Gay* lifts, breaks for the right. The *Great Artiste* banks left. Three parachutes blossom on the air.

A cheer runs through an anti-aircraft battery on the ground. One of the two planes veering away must be in trouble; the crew must be bailing out.

The three parachutes carry telemeters to send blast data back to the *Great Artiste*.

The sky ahead was empty, a silver bomber to left and right. Inoshiro's tracers laced between. His finger left the button. He turned away from the doomed city.

Inoshiro looked up at the street. A man stood in aviator's gear. He was watching Inoshiro.

Inoshiro looked down at the caterpillar crawling across the yard.

The man in the street watched the two planes turn away high overhead. The parachutes began to blossom.

He counted to forty-three.

Purple instant of death.
Mono no aware.

BILLY BIG-EYES

"To hear the sun —
What a thing to believe.
But it's all around
If we could but perceive.
To know ultraviolet,
Infrared, X rays,
Beauty to find
In so many ways."

"Om"
Mike Pinder
The Moody Blues

The technician turned away from the plotboard.

"Very good," said the man down in the middle of the room. "Now could you please light it in something I can see? Ultraviolet, infrared?"

The plot analyst looked sheepish. He switched his console to a higher mode. "Sorry, sir."

"Forget it," said Maxwell Big-Eyes from the floor. He put one arm under the other elbow. With the fingers of the supported arm he tapped his teeth, studying the board.

Maxwell Big-Eyes was Chief of Scouts Emeritus. He had given thirty years of active duty to the Service and had distinguished himself.

He was retired and kept in consultant capacity, called only to handle special problems. His other duties were largely ceremonial in nature.

Beneath the well-known masked face was still the mind of

a Scout, the same which had charted unnumbered sectors, led rescue missions, advised and questioned the leadership of the Systems for three decades.

All the bureaucracy, speeches, ceremonies and dinners in the worlds had not dimmed his enthusiasm for the jobs at hand. His first was to make the Systems of worlds a safer and better place in which to live. The second, and most important to him, was the welfare of each and every Scout in the Service.

Maxwell Big-Eyes was stocky of build. He was dressed in red tight trousers, a vest of purplish satin, a russet cape. A leather and plastic mask covered his face from nose to forehead, leaving mouth and hairline exposed. The straps of the maskpiece extended over the back of his head. Where the eyes on his face should be were two opaque lenses the size of grapefruit.

"This was the last position?" he asked.

"Positive," said the plotter.

Maxwell turned to the man in the white smock behind him. "Snorkel, I'd like you to get my niece Dierdre up here, and readings on the conditions of the missions of the other Scouts. But ..." — he put up his hand — "I'd like to talk to Billy myself."

"You think it wise to let him know? His mission is on critical status right now."

The two men were of the same age though Doctor Snorkel was much taller, had a mustache, carried himself more erectly and was not Sighted. His hair was solid iron-gray; that of the shorter man was peppered.

Maxwell turned to the plotboard which to the two others in the room was dark.

"We'll wait and see what he finds before we contact him, then."

Snorkel put his hand on Maxwell's shoulder. "Max," said the scientist, "mightn't it be better if we didn't let him know?"

The old Scout turned to face his friend. There was no expression on the blank, large-orbed mask, but the mouth below was a tight line. The tight line opened and closed.

"I know why you're saying that, Otto, so I'll let it pass." Then the short old man sighed. His mouth grinned, relaxed. "I'll do it when the time comes. He's my great-nephew. If anybody has to be upset, let it be me."

From his ship *The Argus*, Billy Big-Eyes had been watching the suspicious plasma cloud for some hours.

To normal human eyes the night around him would have been black, broken by points of stars, a smudge of dust cloud, perhaps the solitary dot of a comet rounding a sun nearby.

Billy was not watching with normal human eyes, and he was not looking at darkness. He scanned the cloud in several spectra, ultraviolet, infrared, long radio, X ray, those further above and below.

The night in infrared was a dull glow like heated metal, pulsing in the light of interstellar hydrogen. There were tight points, like holes punched in paper, where certain stars gave off no IR radiation. There were others with streamers and long flares like painted brushstrokes. The whole of space was covered with the light as if a colored scene from one of Dante's hells.

In the ultraviolet, the stars and space became draped velvet curtains and the light itself was frozen and black. Stars were dull balls of fur, gas clouds became scrim curtains behind which the suns beat coldly. With a few seconds' concentration, Billy could see through all the other gases around him.

The plasma cloud ahead was different, though; still opaque.

X ray held the strangest view of all; sleeting points of light flew in every direction, away, towards, tangent to him. Some appeared just before his eyes and receded forward, cosmic rays which had passed through the ship and his head. The space around him roared in that spectrum. The sleet moved like an aurora, a shimmering wave through which at first he could see only a few kilometers.

The stars slowly took form through these garbage hazes. In the X ray they were hollow, like glass ornaments or fishbowls, and they spun slowly as he neared them. Then they hove to on the sides and receded as if they were crystals pulled on wires away from him. Gas clouds were in view only a few seconds before he looked through them to others beyond.

And so on, up and down the spectra, each view having its own problems and wonders and needs.

There was one range in which Billy could not see.

Visible light.

To normal humans, Billy Big-Eyes was blind as a bat.

Using the Scout Relay, the people in Control sent out the last known position of the *Nightwatch*, its probable course, the possible dangers in the sector it had been assigned.

The Scout Relay was a remnant of the old Snapshot system. It had once been used to connect widely separated points by means of Kerr black holes. Scanners from orbiting relays sliced across the Planck lengths of these rotating black bodies every 10^{-33} seconds, finding the minute wormholes which opened and closed in those frequencies. Messages sent into these vortices came out somewhere else; that somewhere was inside a Scout ship.

The Snapshot system had been built by the first of the great old solid state intelligences, when man had lived on Earth. It had worked then, and continued to work. Communication across light-years was instantaneous and unerring. It was like talking to someone in the next room.

The Scout Relay was one of the two frequencies using the network. The other was for Systems communications which held together the web of worlds.

The Control people received the acknowledgments from the other Scouts about the missing *Nightwatch*, and then they waited.

"According to Billy's last transmission, he was nearing the probable. His estimate was four hours to RP," said Doctor Snorkel.

Maxwell Big-Eyes scanned the plot of the as-yet uncontacted

ship of his great-nephew. Then he sat still, turning his head to study the other sector wherein the *Nightwatch* was lost. He envisaged the growing cone of search needed to find the missing ship. It would expand geometrically with every arithmetic expansion in time.

The place where the ship could be found was at first a funnel with a point at one end, extending outward and widening, .001, .003, .09, .27 light-years across. It would continue to widen and lengthen with the passage of time.

The job of the rescuers was to reach the area, cut it into small sectors and begin their search for the ship or some trace of it.

When the ships came out of their High Acceleration ftl modes, they would drop immediately to the speeds at which the *Nightwatch* disappeared.

There would be a long and tedious search if they did not find it within the first few days. The sectors they covered would be quickly dwarfed by the growing probability cone. At the end of the first day's time it would cover three times the original area. It was widening with every passing hour.

This did not mean that the *Nightwatch* could not be found, only that the probabilities were against it. The ship *could* be only a few thousand kilometers from its last position, at a relative standstill. The Scout could be repairing whatever trouble there was, or be on the way back towards its original course, under radio silence. Some way could be found to signal the searchers. All these things were possible.

Meanwhile the cone of search continued to grow like a chambered nautilus adding room after room to its shell.

Snorkel watched his stocky friend. "You think he'll join the search," he asked, "when we tell him? Even though his position's wrong, his vector's too far off? Even if we don't give him permission?"

"Hmmm?" Max came out of his thoughts. "Yes."

"Here comes Dierdre," said Otto Snorkel, rising.

"She always cheers me up," said Maxwell Big-Eyes. He too rose to meet his great-grandniece.

Billy Big-Eyes was a Scout, one of the Sighted whose job it was to search, to map the stars, reconnoiter space and find usable black bodies. The Systems, the government of mankind's planets, tapped these black holes, harnessing their energies to meet the needs of the worlds. The Scouts, in their great crystal ships, used their visual gifts like interstellar mountain men on Old Earth.

Billy was of the family Big-Eyes, whose honor and fame stretched back to the Secondary Worlds. The name had been bestowed on them by Council for the trait they held in common. The eyes were their fortune and fame, their reason for life, their albatross.

The Big-Eyes had chosen long before to breed for the trait and had submitted themselves and their offspring to operations, changes, mutations. These brought about the enlargement, the expansion of sight into other spectra. It set them apart from the rest of mankind forever.

The mutations had been worked on their eyes for generations. The size was a product of that. The operations, performed from puberty of the individual onward, allowed sight in other spectra while they were being trained for Scouthood. These changes further separated the Sighted from the rest of mankind. The mutations worked on the eyes of the Sighted from generation to generation gradually lost them normal vision; rather, they left eyesight behind. To all the Sighted, there was a gap between the high infrared and the low ultraviolet. This was the only spectrum in which the Scout could see nothing.

The Scouts flew great crystal ships between the stars, leaving jets of radiation half a light-year long. The ships were engineering miracles for their simplicity. They could have been built with systems for the detection of black bodies, complicated equipment with backups, warnings and scanners, but they had not been.

They were simple reflector dishes seventeen kilometers across, powered by engines which pushed them around the starways.

In High Mode, they carried the Scouts faster than light towards the sectors they had been assigned. On station, they could drift leisurely for months, correcting course, barely pushing the great curved mirrors through space. They sailed the night like windows, and not much in the electromagnetic spectrum got by them.

Each dish was made of a crystal tracework, like a perfectly formed spiderweb. Within the limits of the dish were sets of smaller reflectors, and smaller inside these, a reverse Eltonian pyramid of mirrors and accumulators. Their focii were in the control room of the ships, set above the center of the dish. It was here the Scout sat and watched the Universe for signs and portents.

"Hello, Uncle Max," said Dierdre. She was slim of build but gave no hint of fragility. She was in her early teens and had undergone the first two of the operations which would give her complete Sight. She wore the great protective opaque helmet all Scouts wore outside the confines of their Ships or homes. It was transparent to all but visible light. The chrome helmet made her look like an egg atop a doll figure. Maxwell hugged her, and she touched her helmet to the side of her great-granduncle's face.

Only Maxwell Big-Eyes, some of the retired Watchmosts and the men and women who had foregone Scouthood wore only the light protective masks. Some Scouts considered them ostentatious and a sop to the rest of humanity. Maxwell wore his now because he had never been able to let his hair grow in the years he had been a Scout. The idea of a full head of hair had always attracted him.

"Hello, Dierdre," said Doctor Snorkel. "How are the eyes?"

"Just fine," she said, sitting in a small chair in the near center of the room. She looked up at the softly glowing plotboard above them.

"Could you give me the positions of the others?" she asked the technician.

He looked to Snorkel.

"Give her every assistance," said Snorkel. "Act on her requests as you would mine or Max's."

"Very good, sir."

The human eye detects nothing which subtends less than thirteen minutes of arc. The eyes of the Scouts had been altered far beyond the human. At the focus of their ships, the waves moving through the night were shunted and reflected into the Scout's eyes. The Scouts were the human lenses of the gigantic telescopes which were the ships.

In their lives, and in their crystal ships, their work, their mutations, the Sighted were set apart from mankind. They were also honored among them, respected and proud.

The Families of the Systems were not limited to the Sighted; there were many others. Some had varying talents and skills, others had no useful skills at all. These latter had been in the service of the Systems for tremendously long times, and performed about as well as could be expected. They received their name and station among the honored families by longevity.

The Pilemongers, the Dimsdales and the Pierceys could be found in every part of the government.

There were also the three *pongoides* families, the Gumps, the Kongs and the Youngs, whose anthropoid talents were suited to many jobs true humans would find dangerous, difficult or tedious.

It was the Talented Families who were the mainstays of the Systems, the Sighteds, the Naturals, the Speakers, the Quick, the Sleepers, the Unseen and the Aware. Each had some special genetically or somatically produced skill needed in mankind's habitation of the galaxy.

The Naturals came in touch with any planets which bore life.

They read the worlds, discerned the relations between living things and the planet, proscribed the limits of mankind's growth there.

The Sleepers oversaw and controlled those processes for which the human lifetime was not long enough. Their wakings and walkings, measured in decades and centuries, were as days and weeks to them. Some third- and fourth-generation Sleepers were still in the service of the government.

And on through each of the skills needed; for the settlement of worlds, the transfer of materials, the running of the Systems. For each of the talents needed there was a Family or Families. There had been for centuries, there would be for ages.

Most important among these were the Sighted families: the Ocullis, the Watchmosts, the Big-Eyes, the Lemur-Pottis and the Scoutmakers.

The family Big-Eyes was the oldest of them, and the toughest. Maxwell Big-Eyes thought himself the best Scout who had ever served a career. He was now retired. He thought Billy would be a better Scout than he, and that his great-grandniece would be better still.

Dierdre watched the changes on the great screen. It gave three-dimensional overviews of the original path of the *Night-watch*, the location of the other Scout Ships, their courses and probable search patterns.

She turned her head towards Max. "It doesn't look very good, does it?"

"You can tell that? Then it's worse than I thought," he said. Snorkel, standing behind him, looked towards Dierdre and raised his copious gray eyebrows.

"Well, there's Abraham Watchmost, there." Dierdre pointed towards the diagrams. "He's closest, but he's in deceleration mode already, and it'll take him longer to get back up to speed than it will for ... " — she checked a readout on a side display —

"than for Yvonne Oculli to reach the point of last contact." She looked past the display to the ceiling. "That will be sometime day after tomorrow. *Then* the search can start."

Max leaned on one elbow, propping his uncovered chin.

Dierdre turned to him. "Does Billy know yet?"

"No. He's at a critical mission phase, he thinks. I'll let him know as soon as he reports back."

She looked at the plotboard. "He doesn't even show on that sector."

"He's not. He's much too far away to be of any help. And he's on the mission we've been planning for some time, one we don't want aborted."

Dierdre pulled her feet up into the chair, hugged her knees.

"He loved her, you know," she said.

"Yes," said Maxwell Big-Eyes.

Black holes do certain things in one spectrum and others in another. Once within visual range, a Scout can spot one within a few hours. Black bodies themselves have no appearance, but there are associated electromagnetic phenomena which mark them to the trained observer. Most are formed from the remnants of stars. Not all the exploding shells and chromospheres manage to escape the intense gravitational tides which the singularities form.

It is for these signs a Scout looks. The plasma cloud ahead of Billy was a probable in many ways, not in others. It was still opaque in ranges where it should have been translucent. His gravity sensors within the ship still gave indefinite readings, even so close. This made him think there were very unstable conditions inside the cloud. That it surrounded a black hole.

Billy watched in the infrared, then shifted his mind up to the ultraviolet. The cloud did not resolve, it simply became opaque in other interesting ways.

He broadcast on the Scout Relay frequency. As he did, he

watched his own message speed away like a giant forked cactus. That was always disconcerting, no matter how many times he did it.

"I'm punching in readings," he said. "The shipboard pickups can't do much more than approximate what's going on."

Billy studied the console. It glowed softly in the UV and IR. Warning lights in the ship were visible in seven spectra; should an emergency occur, the Scout would have warning no matter what frequency he happened to be looking at. None of the trouble lights were on now. The ship was quietly doing its job of transporting its lone human occupant on his mission.

Behind and above Billy lay another great spattered gas cloud, a few solitary young stars, all the apparatus of creation. He kept glancing to the burnt old stars spread to the sides. They looked like tarnished fishbowls hung in a room full of moss.

The plasma ahead intrigued him. Its shape and size were like nothing he had seen. It should have already been transparent in the X ray, but showed detail in small depth. Billy sometimes wished for the ability to see through a light-year of lead. Scouting would be much simpler if he could. His vision in the X ray depended on the amount of radiation leakage in that form. Something bright enough for him to see through in that depth would have crystallized all the metal in the *Argus* and left him a dead man.

He set a tangential course for the heavy edge of the cloud. It would be like slipping through the wall of a hurricane except that chances were small for a calm windless eye inside. It would be like sailing into the target end of a cyclotron as big as the sun.

"He's not still in love with her, is he?" asked Max.

"He says he isn't." Dierdre scratched at her knees with her short-clipped fingernails. She wore shorts, boots and a red halter. Her great chrome helmet bent towards her knee.

"You'd better have that checked by the medic this afternoon," said Doctor Snorkel, reentering the room.

"What is it?"

"A rash. Side effect of some of the drugs we used in the last operation. Billy had it for months. Mostly nerves, not much we can do except give tranquilizers."

"I don't want any more tranquilizers," said Dierdre to Snorkel. "I'm wonky enough anyway, early in the mornings, and I feel *blah* by nighttime. *And* I get edgy."

"That's the way it's always been," said Snorkel. "Except for Wilhelmina Scoutmaker. She became hyperactive. So we had to give her stimulants; then she showed the same tensions as everyone else."

"Is there *anything* about me you don't already know?" asked Dierdre.

Snorkel smiled. "Tell me something, and I'll let you know if we know it or not."

Maxwell Big-Eyes had been listening, his hands cupped together in a cone, teeth touching fingertips. He sat slumped in his chair. He always slumped. He'd had to sit upright in the focus rooms of ships for many years, and was in rebellion against all parts of his past.

"Dierdre, they knew everything about *me* when I was going through the operations and training. I think on their deathbeds the directors tell *everyone* about us. It's passed down like shamanlore. A secret cabal of personal information."

"Not quite that bad," said Snorkel, drawing himself to his full height. "The more we know, the better we can gauge your progress, the smoother we can make the treatments, the sooner you'll get away from us."

"You're talking a little like we're cattle again," said Dierdre.

Snorkel winced. "This is an inexact science. The development of unknown quantities such as yourself. Some of the nomenclature from earlier times has carried over. I'm terribly sorry."

"Oh, fuck it all! I'm sorry, Otto. All this boredom, all these tests, I just don't feel like ..."

"You're also growing," said Snorkel. "One of the problems is that we have to wait until puberty before we begin the larger alterations. It would be better if we developed a technique for genetic manipulation for the Sighted. We've tried and failed, so far. Puberty is the worst time to undergo a major change. You haven't learned to live with your body, the one you grew up with, and we change it."

"In my time ..." began Maxwell Big-Eyes.

"We know," said his great-grandniece, "you walked twelve kilometers a day through a photon accelerator, just to keep in shape."

Maxwell smiled. "You're right. I'm getting old. I'd like to move back into the past and live there, instead of worrying about the future.

"Dierdre, a Scout spends all the adult life worrying about the present and future. From adolescence on is the training, then the work of looking out for the rest of mankind. All too soon that's over, and you're left with nothing but the past, when things were exciting. Even though you thought it only a job.

"But I could grow maudlin."

"You could, easily," said Dierdre. Then she looked at the plotboard. "I see Watchmost has abandoned his other mission. The search is starting." She turned the chrome reflector of her helmet towards her great-granduncle. "You're going to direct it from here?"

"I'm going to try."

"With all the search ships arriving so far apart? Are you up to it?"

"Yes. But I'll have to depend on you for help. Your mind is much quicker than mine has been in a long time. And you know Billy better than I do. Unusual, but you do."

"We get along okay," said Dierdre.

They were all three silent for a moment. The technician above them on his platform stretched his arms and legs.

"Jiminez," said Doctor Snorkel, "I want the three best plotters here, on duty."

"They're already on the way. We're going to work four-hour shifts."

Doctor Snorkel raised his eyebrows. "You should be checked for psi powers."

"Doc, you work at a job twelve years, you gotta know what's going on."

Max noticed the change in tone between the two. They did not stand on the formalities during a crisis.

Dierdre sat still, her head up.

"What are you thinking?" asked Maxwell.

She turned to him. "You've got regular beacons broadcasting towards where she disappeared?"

"Certainly," said Snorkel.

"Of course, we can barely see the messages ..."

"What?"

"Morbid thoughts, Uncle Max. About what it would be like to be out there with no way of making contact, watching the messages come by and knowing there's nothing you can do but wait."

Maxwell Big-Eyes looked at his great-grandniece. "You're certainly not very much like your brother," he said.

It was like moving at high speed next to a great looming wall. There was a feeling of impending collision, of the end coming quickly at any time.

Billy swung the *Argus* to face the plasma cloud on a tangential course. All his concentration and vision were directed towards the opaque object; he still did not know what went on inside. There was confusion there, even in the X ray. It was the damnedest thing Billy Big-Eyes had ever seen. Even the *Argus*'s instrumentation did little. He depended on the gravity sensors to tell him what was inside the plasma sheet.

All they told him was that something was inside. There were gravity wells of some sort. They seemed to be in constant motion and followed no set pattern.

He broadcast on the Scout Relay. He sent out diagrams which looked like wingtip vortices on old aerodynamic bodies. He waited for the data returns.

But he knew before the answer came that he needed to enter the plasma cloud to get any more information. Tension and anxiety rose in him. What he did could be very dangerous and very important. Or perhaps it could just be dangerous.

"I'm going in now," he broadcast, and set course to swing the *Argus* in, then out, of the cloud.

The crystal latticework gleamed dully in the various spectra, like an icicled geodesic dome. Billy looked out through the mirrors of the low-spectra reflectors to the dull-orbed stars around him, to the glowing curtains of dust in the soft night, the zip of interstellar garbage.

The cloud moved slowly to the side, then loomed ahead. He intended to skirt the edges of the central mass, dip in, skim out again. He would use himself and his ship to the utmost on the first penetration. It would be blinding in there in many of the frequencies. Unless he or his instruments were very sharp on the initial skim, he would have to repeat the maneuver several times until he found the answer or until it became too dangerous, too much a gamble with the Big Sleep.

In which case the cloud would have to be marked "unknown" and put on the charts.

That would be the first time those words would appear in any sector explored by Billy Big-Eyes. In the three years he had been a Scout, he had found more of lasting value than any other. He had never failed to determine exactly the nature of objects in his path. No subsequent black holes had been found, even after secondary colonization had begun.

Billy did not want this to be his first professional failure, either of his nerves or his limitations.

He sighed, and swung the lacework ship over like a shark.

Maxwell worked quickly with the readouts of the plotboard.

Snorkel and Dierdre were talking in a corner of the room. In deference to the Scouts, Snorkel and the other technicians were wearing bifocal infrared goggles. The room was now lighted totally on that wavelength.

Words drifted down to Maxwell. "... more surgery ... upside down ... way it used to be ..." Then Dierdre's laughter started, joined by Snorkel's.

"Private joke?" asked Maxwell.

"No," said Dierdre, moving towards him, her shoulders still shaking with laughter. Max looked through her helmet to her smiling face with its eyes the size of large hen eggs. She could not as yet see in the X ray, like he, but he knew she could see his face in the infrared, where his eyes absorbed the light. "We were talking about Nelson Watchmost and Gini Oculli. High school romances. I didn't think you'd be very interested."

"I shouldn't be. But everything about the Sighted families interests me sooner or later. I might as well try to think of the future a while, as well as the past. Does it look as if the two of them will choose each other? Or be donor parents?"

Dierdre looked at Snorkel. "That's what we were talking about. No, I don't think so. They're just having fun. But the Ocullis are watching very closely. They're upset. They want Gini to mate with a Scoutmaker. Some of the Ocullis think it would be a gesture of goodwill towards the newest of the Scout Families."

"The Ocullis have their hearts in the right places," said Maxwell, "though some of them have their heads up their anii."

"That is the image they're fighting," said Doctor Snorkel.

"Yes," said Max. "But you and I know that's why, rather than out of the democratic goodness of their hearts. They want to fight the nouveau riche image they've acquired. The easiest way is to be nice to a family even more nouveau than they."

"Reverse snobbery," said Snorkel.

"Perhaps," said Dierdre, looking at Snorkel, "the Service would like it better if they could choose *who* mates with *whom*?"

"No," he said. "That's individual prerogative. All the families have the abilities we need, all the right genes, few recessive traits. It would only work if we knew exactly how each individual would turn out beforehand. Or work the genetic changes to bring about Sight. But we can't. All we can do is use amniocentesis, determine which traits are most pronounced, which ones we'll have to concentrate on later.

"And the Sighted Families know more about their own lines than they claim. Most heads of the families get the gene data on the offspring as soon as it's available.

"Max thinks we have a cabal about the chaos you go through in training. I think the Families have a session every generation or so in which they decide who will be with whom, so far as genetics go. It works both ways."

Dierdre moved her arms up to wrap them around her bare shoulders. "Then someone like Sally comes along," she said, "and doesn't go along with anybody's wishes, not even her own. Not Billy's, her family's, nobody's. I don't think she knew what she wanted, or how to get it."

"You're wrong, Dierdre," said Snorkel. "She knew too well what she wanted. That's why she's lost, right now."

"Whatever it was," said Dierdre, "it wasn't Billy."

The *Argus* entered the plasma wall. It had run beside it like a boat along the length of a long breakwater. There was no shock as it entered.

Billy Big-Eyes watched his instruments, saw them adjust to the plasma flow, the changed environment outside the ship. The gravity sensors did not define the stress within the cloud. The indicators moved and swayed but would not settle.

Billy was busy. He looked about him. The reflectors of the ship shone into his eyes, pushing all the spectra in, letting him see what was there. Half his attention was on his instruments, half on what his eyes told him.

In the X ray were huge swaying masses of gas, thick and opaque, like tarpaulins thrown over his vision. They swirled, they cleared, yet he still could not see through them.

They rotated like a cosmic maelstrom with no regular rhythm or order.

The ship hove closer, slowly, moving through plasma roils without effort. Too easily for Billy's liking, too effortlessly for him not to be nervous ...

The instruments swung over, gave definite readings, settled in a regular gentle pulse.

His printouts showed two steadily rolling masses, tumbling around each other like millstones, gravity wells spinning away from them like swirls of mist. They twisted and pulled, broke away from the masses like smoke.

At the same time his vision penetrated the rolling swells of gas and plasma, and he saw into the heart of the great mystery he had been trailing across the skies like a wounded bear.

Shivers ran up Billy's spine as he realized what he had found. Then he laughed and turned his crystal ship out of the great pulsing cloud.

He broadcast his findings back to control.

He had found binary black holes. Two rotating masses locked in a double-system. The find would raise great questions about the physics involved. It was impossible that they had formed from a single stellar mass, even more unlikely that they formed from a binary system at the same instant. The possibility of the capture of a secondary black body by another was remote; even then something besides a stable binary should have been formed. Billy's find would question the theories behind the formation of rotating black holes.

In the end, they would be academic curiosities. For, as power sources, a binary system with its tides, fluctuating gravity wells and plasma field would be useless as teats on a boar shoat.

The questioning and theory would come later, by others less interested in exploration itself. As soon as Billy Big-Eyes brought the *Argus* out of the plasma cloud and was safely away, his granduncle Maxwell told him that Sally Lemur-Potti was missing and presumed lost.

"Of course I'm going," said Billy.

"I can order you not to."

"I'd rather you wouldn't."

"I know that. But it would be foolish for you to try. The search is under way. You're much too far from the sector. We'll find her by the time you get turned around."

"I'm already turning around."

There was a pause. "So I see. You leave me very little choice, Billy. I'm ordering you to proceed with your planned mission. *Before* you reach that slingshot point you've plotted. I'll have that backed by a directive in a few moments."

Silence.

"Billy, give me your answer."

The silence broke.

"Don't do this to me, Uncle Max. Don't send a directive I'll have to ignore."

Maxwell ran his hands through his hair. "I'm telling you not to do it, Billy. It'll be a big mistake. We can find her before you get there. We'll know what happened to the *Nightwatch* before you get out of your assigned sector."

"What if you don't? No, that's not what I want to ask. The real question is whether she's dead or not, isn't it?"

Maxwell's lips turned down as he paced back and forth across the center of the plotroom.

"All right, Billy, listen to this: I'm ordering you not to leave your assigned sector, or abort your present mission. That is that."

Dierdre, from her chair in the corner, said, "Orders never stopped you on the Wilson thing."

"Oh, be quiet, Dierdre!" Maxwell glared at his great-grandniece. "That's why I'm doing this, so he won't make the same mistake!"

"Then I'm going to refuse your orders," said Billy Big-Eyes, over the Scout Relay.

"I'm not going to let you do that!"

"Max!" said Snorkel, holding out his hand. "Calm yourself down."

"I have her last position and speed," Billy's voice came over the speaker. "I don't need anything else. What if I'm the only one who *can* find her, Max?"

"Wait," sighed Maxwell Big-Eyes. He slumped his shoulders, sat heavily in his chair. "Just wait." He rubbed the tip of his nose with his fingers. "It's Systems' policy. You know you'll be wasting your mission, mismanaging the ship. You'll be late. You'll come into the sector ass-backwards. Chances are, you'll pass her position ..."

"Max, I had the same training as you. Only I had all *your* experiences in the classes, and you didn't. I know all that. I know how to search frontwards, backwards, upside-down. I knew how *you* found Wilson and Termire, which is more than you did at the time. This argument is a waste. Are you going to help me, Uncle Max, or do I have to do it all myself?"

The only sound for a long time was that of the relays transferring information to the plotboard. Snorkel stood with one of his thumbs in his mouth, chewing at the nail. Dierdre scratched her arm.

"Okay. I'll help you, Billy," said Max. "I don't know how long we can keep the Council off you. But we'll try, we'll try."

Dierdre and Snorkel kept their eyes off Maxwell. They studied the intricate path trajectories on the plotboard.

"Thanks, Uncle Max."

"Dierdre's here, Billy. She's going to help."

"Fine."

"I'll get back to you. Take it easy for a while."

He signed off. He sat with the speaker held idly in his hand. His foot tapped some unknown rhythm on the floor

Dierdre came to him and hugged him. "Thank you, Uncle Max. I'm proud of you."

"You shouldn't be," said the Chief of Scouts. "I'm doing a stupid thing. I'm letting him do worse. He'll repeat the mistake I made years ago." Maxwell brightened a little. "Well, Otto, let's go see the Director. While we're on our way there, we'll figure out some way *not* to tell her why we're letting Billy do this. For the moment, I can't think of a single reason."

"Let's eat, too," said Dierdre. "I'm hungry."

"Only if Otto promises to find us some place where the music won't hurt my eyes," said Max.

Sleep was not easy for Scouts at any time. Billy knew that he would have to get rest. He had not had a sleep shift in the nineteen hours he had been pursuing the plasma cloud. He could not afford to be without sleep in the ordeal ahead.

He traveled down the long tubeway from the focus room to his crew compartment. Both the tubeway and the room below were walled with reflectors which turned aside many of the wavelengths and frequencies coming through. The inner workings of the walls also gave off pleasing white noises on wavelengths designed to soothe the Scouts.

Billy undressed and climbed onto the couch. Gentle wafts of air blew through the room. He took off his large chrome helmet, leaving only his light protective harness. Opening this, he placed the sleep headgear over his face. This covering bathed his grapefruit-sized eyes in gentle solutions which washed, cleaned and massaged them. The Scouts had no eyelids, and the blinking reflex had been bred out of them.

Shielded speakers, which were not magnetic, played music to Billy, usually, but not always Pre-Systems "classical," the music of abandoned Earth. The walls poured out their white noise under this.

Billy reached out, while the bed began to massage him, while his eyes and ears were bathed in liquids and sounds, and moved his fingers and toes over the tactile surfaces at the edge of the couch. They turned now smooth or rough, soft or hard, in random patterns.

Massaged and lifted, hushed and cooed, he looked into the visible spectrum where all was dark and slept.

The great crystal ship *Argus* flew through the night, watching over Billy and its course, rounding the sector in a long, slow curve up into its Acceleration Mode which would take them towards the lost Sally Lemur-Potti. She would be an infinitely small dot on the large black night of the galaxy.

The only lights in the ship glowed in the soft infrared and ultraviolet. Like its namesake, the *Argus* watched and flew and waited dutifully for Billy to awake.

After they had napped and eaten and been to their homes, Max, Snorkel and Dierdre returned to the plotroom.

Nothing had happened. Only routine reports on the search had come in. The Watchmost Scout had begun pie-slicing his sector into usable cones. One of the Scoutmakers would take a portion of it in a few hours, as soon as she entered the coordinates. It looked to be a long and monotonous search unless something turned up unexpectedly. The chance of finding Sally Lemur-Potti diminished with each hour.

Billy was still asleep; he would be on sleep-shift a while. He was nowhere close to the search patterns of the other ships. He would enter the probability cone long after the others had gone through the most likely portions.

Dierdre was working with a pocket printout. Her fingers moved over the keys. She wrote figures on a memory pad, coding them with letters before they disappeared to be replaced by others. Occasionally, she would key one back and add it to the figures she worked on.

Maxwell watched with some amusement.

"You haven't memorized them yet?" he asked when she stopped.

"Everybody knows only you and Gilmore Oculli commit things like that to memory. No, I use the safe way, pad and stylus. If I do something wrong, I can find where I messed up. Hey!" She looked at her great-granduncle. "Why did you send Scoutmaker on that trajectory? By the book, that shouldn't start until they have a twenty-five-loop grid."

"I'm hoping we'll have a lot of luck. The two inmost ships can start sweeps and cover about as much as three. I'm hoping the *Nightwatch* will be in one of the most probable areas. But I'd really like to have five ships there already, instead of three ... "

"You'll have, soon," said Dierdre, "but I'd advise using the standard pattern. Really, and you might have to get through it more than once, if something really bad's happened. There's an *awful* lot of territory out there. You were right, it'll be a miracle if she's found on the first sweep."

"It's always that way," said Maxwell Big-Eyes. "You haven't been out yet, haven't seen the Deeps. Where this place is nothing more than a coordinate, because there are so many better places to use as reference points."

"All we know is that something happened out there. Communication cut off in mid-sentence. She was chasing a probable. Her data looked perfectly normal, nothing dangerous. She was too far from the probable for any known forces to affect her ship.

Unlikely, I know, but I'm working on the assumption of massive shipboard failure."

Dierdre looked at the pad held in one of her thin hands, held it up.

"If only it didn't come down to a bunch of numbers," she said.

"It always does, Dierdre. Much as we don't want it to."

"I mean," she said, "there's a person out there, so important to someone he's willing to stand up to you, the Council and everybody to get to her. But finding her comes down to a bunch of numbers that get bigger and bigger every hour."

Maxwell shook his wrists, ran thick fingers across his neck. "Numbers are tools, Dierdre. Men and women made them, based their sciences on them, their technology. When science fails, they have to fall back on the numbers."

He expected her to say more, be upset, to bring up the words "not fair." She didn't. She sat silently a moment, then went back to work.

Maxwell found himself nodding. There was nothing anyone could do right now that wasn't being done.

Sleep did Billy no good.

He had had only vague, disturbing dreams which he could not remember on waking. It would be the hours that he was conscious now that would hurt him, rather than those he spent sleeping,

He cleaned and relieved himself, ate and put his chrome helmet on. He climbed up the long tubeway to the focus and took his place at the controls. He punched in his course evaluations and changes, all the data he had on the lost ship, and the probable search patterns the other Scout ships would take.

He did not call Max yet. He wanted to think. He also wanted to get away from thinking for a while.

He sat back in his chair and watched the stars go by in exceptionally long waves at the very edge of the ship's capacity. These were the only frequencies in which he could see out when the *Argus* was in High Acceleration mode. Here the stars were black mats on a gray background. All he could see of his environment was the ship itself, ghostlike, and the pulse of the engines behind him. The rest was gray restlessness and lumpy stars where gravity itself bent around them in long waves.

Was it just a few hours ago he had chased down the binary black holes? Already it seemed half a lifetime away, something he had done in childhood, or which he had read about and remembered.

That had been his job, though; this was something else.

He did not know what he would find at the end of the search, or whether he wanted to be there when the end was known. It was something he had to do, out of a host of old allegiances and feelings, and the bitter remembrance of love.

He sat in the control room and did not know, once again, if he were still in love with Sally Lemur-Potti.

It had begun four years ago, when he was recovering from his fifth major operation. Sally, a year older than he, had already soloed. She had been in the hospital for a minor surgical correction. They had met there.

He remembered the first night they had walked under the stars, under the soft infrared glow from the star cluster, across the soft sands and mosses of Fremont, home world of the Scouts.

It had been warm and fragrant. Billy was outside at night for the first time since his operation. Night and day had little meaning for Scouts; in the daytime there was a rather large, harsh ultraviolet source point above the horizon. It moved from east to west. Billy's operation was the most major one, where recovery was longest, where the patient could do little but study and listen.

Both he and Sally wore their light protective head harnesses, form-fitting and much more comfortable than the chrome Scout helmets they would later take up.

To each other, they were soft-glowing red outlines, human shapes walking on a smooth background.

"Don't worry about it," said Sally Lemur-Potti.

Her face was turned towards his. It showed the two dark centers of her large eyes where they absorbed the infrared. He knew he looked the same to her.

The Sighted Families preferred infrared and ultraviolet for their usual vision. It had become habit; perhaps it had started with the desire, long ago, to stay as near human sight as possible. No one was sure.

"But I'm so sick of doing nothing," said Billy. "Of listening to tapes, studying. I don't feel like I'm doing anything. I'm standing still."

"I felt that way too," she said, "really I did, I'm not just saying that. I thought I'd never get into the Deeps, or fly, or anything. But I have."

"Snorkel keeps telling me that. He's seen them all come and go, but he can't know what it's like to be Sighted and then have to wait. He says we all go through the despondency just about now. We've been in the program too long without anything really happening, just alteration after alteration, study after study, nothing on top of nothing else."

They sat on a soft moss hillock under the glow of the Shitpot Nebula. Sally took his hand so naturally that he did not notice it.

"He's right." Sally turned her head toward the zenith. "See up there? What do you see, the nebula in IR and UV, the long flickers of the short radio waves? Right? Well, to me, in the X ray, the thing is a bunch of haloes, like water on a screen, with dots rising and falling all along it.

"And ..." She turned her head toward the southern horizon. "You know what? You squint your eyes, you get lucky, you know what you see? Sometimes, walking, you see little spots. You switch to X ray. It's hard on a planet, you can't see the horizon, you have to stand still.

"Anyway, you look at the dots. They come down all the time, secondary particles. But every once in a while you see a primary, bright like a drop of burning lead. And sometimes ... sometimes they come up out of the ground. They really do. They've hit kilometers away, and get deflected; they come up out of the ground like a spent bullet, getting slower all the time. They break apart.

"There're fireworks everywhere, Billy. Little pieces of light, and particles always moving, zipping around. There's nothing like it."

He watched her. She was sitting up, moving her small hand-blobs around, taking in all the sky above them with motions of her softly glowing arms.

"And long radio! Wait till you see that! Big loops in the night, like giant moving fingerprints, with lines and whorls. You need the ship for that, with the reflectors, but wait till you see it. They're tremendous. And the ships themselves.

"They bring in everything out there so clear and sharp. You think you're ready for the first views, after the trials with the small reflectors, but you're not. You're sitting out there in the Deeps by yourself, with no planet under you, no horizon. The ship itself is the only thing that matters, and the seeing is good, there's something to look at everywhere you point the ship. You can live a lifetime out there in a few moments. Billy, you don't know how good it feels, how ... "

Billy had become tense, tight with the sound of her words, so moved he wanted to reach out, touch her, hold her, make her be quiet while the wonder of her speech settled in him; he wanted to keep her quiet so the thrill inside him would stay.

He put his arms around her and she was still and very quiet.

"Nobody ever talked about the Deeps like that," he finally said. His despondence had passed. He felt some kind of new hope inside himself. Uncle Maxwell and the others only told him he would like it once he got out there. That had grown thin in the months he was in surgery and recovery, during the drug treatments and training. Now it didn't seem such a dead end. He was more anxious than ever to get out there. Now he *believed.*

Sally extended one of her soft-glowing hands on the end of her shining arm from her shimmering body and touched his face. "You'll see when you get out there," she said. "You'll see what it's like."

They stared up at the cluster overhead.

The ship warned him that it was coming out of Acceleration Mode. His reverie ended.

He called on the Scout Relay frequency. The overlag would keep his message suspended until the moment he dropped below light-speeds. The *Argus* would file its own stress reports automatically and put the information in its flight recorder. The recorder also monitored its position constantly and held as much data on a flight as the Scout programmed it to take. It served a function of which most Scouts were incapable; it remembered everything about a mission, stresses, where it had been, anything which affected it. The recorder, Billy knew, would have a huge load of information on the binary black holes he had found. So his mission had been important. He knew his Uncle Maxwell was against his search-and-rescue mission for good and valid reasons.

It still did not help his feelings. His emotions were compounded of many hurts. There was the possibility that he was still in love with Sally, after three years, after her indifferences and the pain she had caused him.

The front part of his mind told him he was feeling concern any Scout would feel when another was missing. He would expect the same from the others. The Sighted Families held together. That he would go out of his way was expected by Scouts, if not by the Control people. Uncle Max was in the unenviable position of being Chief of Scouts and still responsible to Control.

When Maxwell Big-Eyes had taken up the search for a mission colony ship, long after others had given up, he had been on more solid ground from the view of Control, but still irresponsible. The only thing that had saved him was success.

Billy assumed the *Argus* would bring him out where he wanted. His search would begin soon, and he set to work on patterns and the castings he would make when he dropped from High Acceleration.

It was quiet in the unknown gray space, with not much showing outside, and Billy worked for a long time on time on his calculations.

"He's out," said Jiminez.

Nine days after the search began, Billy came out of High Acceleration. In that time none of the other Scouts had picked up the slightest hint of what happened to the *Nightwatch.* There were no beacons, signals of any kind, no sporadic interference in those sectors the ship was most likely to appear.

Unlike the sea, sudden catastrophe leaves no signs in space. On water many things by their nature float; wood, plastics, heavy objects with air trapped inside, oil, wastes. In the Deeps, accidents happen, and the powers that propel the ships are so great that everything can be obliterated. Things not vaporized are broken to tiny pieces and flung to all directions. This debris moves out with the force of the initial blast and quickly disperses.

Or in the case of some quick and total power failure, the ship becomes a dead piece of metal and crystal, on whatever path it was following, with no sign except the residual radiations from its engines. Even a Scout would have to be very close to see or detect that, on the immensity of the Night.

Billy's ship came out exactly where he planned. Others in the search had begun much more towards the homeward direction, near the point of last contact. Two of the ships, the *Many-Orbed* and the *Lookmeover*, had been as far in as Billy Big-Eyes, but in other directions.

Dierdre talked to her brother a few minutes after the ship slowed enough to allow communications.

"I've checked your figures."

"And?"

"I think you should move on closer courses. Intersect the probables as often as you can. You've got these open circles planned."

"Max?"

"Yes?"

"Max, is Dierdre right?"

"I don't know. It makes sense, by the book. But we've run this one by the book since the second day, and we've had no results. Yvonne Mustafa ... er, Oculli, we've got her on a simulated power loss run. You'll pick her up in a day or two, she's got a beeper going so you won't mistake her. Ignore it if you can. Control wanted the solidstates to run the simulation, but I told them I haven't come up with anything so far. Not their fault.

"Billy, something bad must have happened to the ship out there. I hope you realize that?"

"Max ..."

"I know, I know. Look, I'm beginning to think we're *not* going to find anything out there. Maybe some debris ..."

"It's possible that it is only the ship which is in trouble," said Dierdre.

"That *was* possible," said Max. "I had great hopes, in the first week. Unless she's dead, she would have tried some way of signaling by now, anything. Radio, spark-gap transmitter, anything. Flares — even if you couldn't see them, you'd pick up the bursts, the ship would squawk.

"This is something I didn't want to say. Either everything — the ship, Sally — is gone, or it's still there and Sally's dead. And if so, the ship's somewhere we're not looking. We won't find them, either way."

"If she's there, I'll find her," said Billy.

"I know you believe that, so I won't say anything."

"I'll run the search like I planned, Max."

"Okay." Max paused. "Something else, Billy. Control's given us seventy-eight more hours. Then the search stops, except for passive beacons. You'll all be on Recall."

"Max, I just got here."

"You knew it would be like that when you started, Billy. I haven't told them you're there yet. Don't compromise this order. The Recall will include you. That's all."

"Max ..."

"Billy, I'll be here in the search control, so will Dierdre. When the Recall goes out, I want to see you in an Acceleration Mode. Until then, anything you need from us, let us know."

"All right."

Billy contacted the nearest Scouts, watched his and their relay beams lock instantly, once again in the giant cactus designs peculiar to their frequency.

The Scouts could not see each other, except as directions in which their beams originated. Both the *Many-Orbed* and the *Lookmeover* were finishing large sweeps of search. Billy fed data to them, turned on his identifying beacon and entered his initial pattern. He would intersect those of the two ships and the probable path of the *Nightwatch* at many points, but also swing away in open arcs from the others. His search path was also separated in time; sometimes he would cross ahead of the other two ships, sometimes behind.

There was noise and movement on every frequency. No matter where he looked, Billy's attention was distracted by something.

He kept himself mostly in the infrared. This was a region of younger stars, where the soft, dull background was broken by brilliant splotches. He occasionally searched the X ray, looking into stars and their photospheres. It was possible her ship had been captured like a moon by one, its noise and stellar wind interfering with communication. Shielded in her rest compartment, Sally could live through the ordeal, though the *Nightwatch* would begin to crystallize and fall apart.

There were no foreign dots on the shells of the suns, no tiny traces of garbage like flour dropped from a leaking sack.

There were no softly glowing dots signaling the burned engines of a ship coasting through the night, no matter how long or hard he looked, no matter what wavelength.

His crystal-work ship picked up no unknown beacons, no sparks; his eyes saw no lights, flares or reflections he could not name.

Billy's responses were mechanical. He was paying attention to things around him; the view, his instruments, the chatter on the frequencies, the dip of his gauges as the long cycle of gravity waves passed through his ship each hour.

But there was nothing he was looking for, anywhere. He would know something amiss as soon as he saw or heard it. *Nothing wrong out there*, nothing he *wanted* to see.

Where was she, where was her ship, where?

Billy remembered things:

They had become lovers soon after the night under the stars. It surprised neither of them. At first they were happy for days, then weeks, then months. They talked, they studied, they worked, they slept, they made love, they wasted time together.

Billy fell in love with Sally Lemur-Potti.

She never said she was in love with him.

But she was happy with him, they had good times, and Billy did not push her about it, after the first. He thought whatever she felt for him would turn to love, and that with her it was a slow, growing process. He could wait.

He lost his despondency, threw himself into his studies and the adaptations he would have to make. He became *nice* again, after months of quiet anger. He got his confidence back.

It was the best time to be in love in the history of mankind. The worlds were rich in both people and resources. Each of the Talented families had its own homeworld, with a diverse gene pool, with many accommodations to the needs of the talents.

The government of the Systems was a benevolent one. It had been compared with the Byzantine Empire on old Earth, but without the religions and the wars. It was a true commonwealth of worlds; its job was to portion out the resources, the manufactury, the exchange of culture and ideas among the planets of the settled stars.

There were more than a thousand worlds which were the abode of man. These stretched from the Secondary Worlds, within ten light-years of old Earth, to those scattered far away from them.

Among the homes of man, abandoned Earth was not numbered. It had been left to the dolphin, the whale and those pongoides who had chosen not to leave four thousand years before.

It was the best time in the history of man to be in love.

Five months after they had begun living together in his home, Sally received her first station assignment. She had recovered from the minor surgery which opened the longest of the radio waves to the Scouts. It was time for her to leave.

They lay in bed, two soft-glowing forms in the dim UV light from the shielded walls of the house. They were naked except for the lightest headpieces which supported their eyes. The night outside was quiet. Billy had not shut the shielded windows which kept out chance radiations, spectra garbage from engines, tools and lights that might disturb their sleep.

"I love you," said Billy Big-Eyes.

"Mmmmm. That's nice," said Sally Lemur-Potti.

"You won't say you love me?"

"It won't make any difference, will it?"

No. "I suppose not."

"Then why ask?"

"I don't know."

They lay quietly for a while. It would have been a beautiful night outside if they had been able to see it. The Shitpot would have been glowing quietly overhead, silently roaring. Streaks of cosmic ray would have danced in Sally's sight. Billy would be altered for X ray next month.

She put her head across his chest.

"Your heart beats very slowly," she said.

"It always has. I was born that way."

"I sometimes listen to it while you sleep."

"Do you?"

"Yes."

"You'll meet new people on Complex."

"I suppose so."

"Lovers, and everything."

"I suppose so."

"I love you, Sally."

"That's good."

They kissed.

He was in the transit tunnel above Fremont when she left. The place was lit with visible light which gave off scratchy X rays. Billy was there with Sally's family.

They all made small talk. She would be back in eleven months.

Her flight was ready.

"It'll be the last time somebody else does the piloting for a while," she said.

She embraced each member of her family. Billy grabbed her and hugged her.

"Hurry back," he said. "I'll miss you."

"I'll miss you, too," she said. He could see the dark pulses of her eyes under the helmet, but nothing of her expression, her features.

His chest hurt.

He held her close, as if no one had ever been parted from one they loved in the whole history of the Universe.

"I love you, Sally."

"That's good," she said. Then she laughed, to show it was the response he expected of her. Then she held him very tight while the last call was made for her flight.

She left.

Billy wished that the Sighted Families still had the physical ability to cry.

Their messages across the worlds were at first both frequent and full of emotion. Then her answers were shorter and took longer in coming.

He was in the hospital the first few months and looked forward to nothing more than the daily message deliveries.

She told of her life there, her adaptations, her first mission, purely routine, and the people, both Sighted and unsighted, whom she met there.

He was in emotional stasis, waiting for the effects of his new vision to sharpen. He knew she was far away, and could not relate to what it was like to be in training, in the surgical rooms.

Seven months after she left, she sent word that she had fallen in love, for the first time in her life, with Emory Quardon, the son of a Territorial Governor, and that he was in love with her.

Billy's last four months of training passed in a haze of dull, routine days and endless insomniac nights. They were broken by brief periods of happiness when he became the lover of one woman or another. But it was not the same.

Snorkel had come to see him one night. They talked.

"I *can't* hate her," he said.

"Sure you can. You've been hurt," said Snorkel.

"But I *can't* hate Sally. I loved her too much to ever be able to do that."

"Right now, you don't think you can be hurt anymore. Wait till she comes back, Billy. You think you're ready for it, but it's not true. You'll see her, and all of it will come back to you in a rush. It'll be like somebody stepped on your chest."

"Oh, fuck you, Snorkel!"

"Right now you mean that," said Snorkel, rising to leave. "Tomorrow morning you won't." He left.

He was right.

About what would happen when Sally came back, and about not meaning what he said to Snorkel.

The first sight of her made him know the meaning of pain all over again.

They spoke a few times. Then he did one of those things people always do. He went to her one night and tried to make her understand how much he loved her, how much she had hurt him. At the center of it was his love for her.

She would not listen, and gave him a speech she must have rehearsed for six months before her return: I never loved you. I never said I loved you.

Billy knew she meant it.

Three months later, Emory Quardon came to visit her.

Billy never saw them together because he did not want to see them together.

Quardon left one day soon after he arrived. Billy heard that Sally Lemur-Potti gave him a speech much like the one she had given Billy.

By then Billy had toughened enough to leave her alone. He found himself worrying about her sometimes, but he never saw her unless it was a social occasion in the company of others.

In the three years since, both Billy and Sally had distinguished themselves. For a while Sally threw herself totally into her work. She was a woman not quite sure of what she wanted, so she tried all the things she might possibly like. One by one she eliminated them, until she was left with her career, her few lovers, parties, some friends.

She was not vindictive in her whims, her attachments and disengagements. It was that she was slowly finding her way to what she wanted. Those things and people which did not change as she did were left behind like so many cicada shells.

She did not turn against old lovers, friends or co-workers so much as she outgrew them.

Billy did somewhat the same; he had fewer lovers, no real love. He still hurt. He wanted to find another who had been as good for him as Sally. It was impossible.

They had lived separate lives, and time had passed.

Time passed.

Billy came to himself in the focus room of the *Argus*, his mind catching up with his actions. He was watching, and ignoring a piece of natural debris far away.

Time passed.

So much debris, so much garbage. Even the unsighted would have a hard time imagining this space as empty. To the Sighted, it was a cluttered circus. Plasma, gas clouds, breeding grounds for comets, solar tides and winds, radio messages, radio noise, particles and monopoles zipped by. Everything had to be watched.

Everything.

The search was drawing to its last scheduled hours. Billy had not slept in a long time, but he would not leave the focus room for any reason.

Yvonne Oculli came on the main Scout frequency.

"I have a radiation source," she said.

The words fell like rocks onto Billy's ears. He punched in. The ship console showed him several curves and courses enlarged until the plot followed the dot on the immense night that was the Oculli ship.

"I'm in pursuit," she said. Her ship broadcast data. The *Argus* and two other Scout ships triangulated her. Their own plotboards glowed softly, getting a true fix on her position.

Billy found the Oculli ship was several times too far away for him to reach it by the end of the scheduled search time. They would extend it, of course, even though the Oculli ship would reach the object long before then.

"I'm having trouble keeping a fix on it," said Yvonne Oculli. "Anyone got it?"

The plotboards remained clear of all data except that her ship broadcast.

Billy looked back over his shoulder; there was nothing there but the great crystal reflectors of the Argus. He wished that even for a millionth of a second he could see through the light-year of lead, see the object the other Scout ships were chasing, know what it was.

If only he could see it.

"Tighten your patterns towards the search area," said Maxwell Big-Eyes, "but don't break them off until we know for sure what Yvonne's after."

On the plotroom wall ships broke off their predicted courses and moved like a pod of whales forming up slowly.

Dierdre and Max scanned the charts.

"A cone. In the middle. A ship *could* have gotten through undetected so far. It was Oculli's good luck to catch it. She under power?" he asked Jiminez. "Good."

"I've got a definite fix. I'm starting an intercept now," said Yvonne.

"Don't let your safeguards down," Max spoke. Yvonne was

only on her third mission but had acted commendably so far. He did not want her to get overanxious.

"Let me handle the ship, Chief," she said.

"Sorry."

"I'm doing this by the book. It'll take a while. I'm not in *any* kind of visual range, I'm on instruments, and all they tell me is how far away, and how weak, the source is. I'll have it in an hour or so. A visual maybe before then. It's ... it looks very small on the detectors. Don't get your hopes up."

"Jiminez," Max turned to him, "run a lost-probe check on the adjoining sectors, see if anything was heading that way, say ..."

"... two centuries ago," said Dierdre.

"... two hundred years ..." Max's voice trailed off.

"Will do," Jiminez said, his hands running over buttons, displays.

Occasionally, Scouts ran across probes sent out centuries before light-speeds had been achieved. These had been launched when man first reached across space in rams and photon ships. Most probes had ceased functioning long ago. Many arrived at worlds to find men already waiting for them.

Sometimes their power sources were still active, only their systems broken down, crystallized or pitted away. Sometimes these probes fell as meteors on mankind's worlds, sometimes they were spotted by normal craft. Usually they passed silent, inert, of only archaeological interest.

Max wondered at the tenacity of his ancestors. With nothing but the bodies and simple talents evolution had given them, and desire, they made beachheads on the night with small, slow craft which had long outlived their purposes.

Perhaps Yvonne was chasing one of these, a probe forgotten by even the few ships which had encountered it across the years. Max hoped not. He hoped her estimates were wrong, and that she was following the ship *Nightwatch.* They would soon know.

Billy listened to the hour unravel like a garment; he hung on each word, watched the intricate play of paths on the location grids. But with his mind and eyes and senses he was watching around him for a sign, anything out of the ordinary. He would not rest; he was tired, the tension made him hurt through his shoulders and back.

Sally used to rub his back.

He slammed his fist on the control console.

Sally.

Did it come down, after all, to love? He had thought for three years now that he was beyond it, that the emotional scars had healed, not well, raggedly, but healed nonetheless.

He stared at the night, the Deeps he shared with the other Scouts, perhaps with Sally. It was not hostile, it was a giant indifference filled with electromagnetic phenomena. It was immense, and you got lost quickly if something went wrong. But it did not hurt people.

Only people hurt people. His chest tightened, his head ached. He wanted to cry for the first time in three years, to relieve his frustration with sobs. But he couldn't. His job was to watch and wait and use his abilities as best he could. To find the lost Scout.

The least he could do was not cry about it.

"An engine. Torn off all raggedy. Maybe some port tubes attached. No sign of webwork, focus or crew compartment. Scans show nothing else. I'm checking it visually. All I get is inert equipment."

"Take your time," said Max.

"I'm sorry, Chief. I hoped there'd be more here than this."

"It's okay. Remember to beacon-mark it."

"By the book. Uh, Chief, you could run a backward ..."

"We're already doing it."

The SSI's were busily plotting the backward trajectory of the engine remnants from the *Nightwatch*, its mass, its probable future path.

Dierdre watched while it ran through the program on screen. She turned to her uncle.

"That's what I was afraid of," he said. He broadcast the program onto the Scout frequency, let it run into each ship's console. "Here's what we get on a backward trajectory."

Billy Big-Eyes watched.

It was as good a simulation of an explosion in reverse as Billy had ever seen. In reverse, it would be an explosion, with only the engine remnant's path able to be followed out of all the infinite possible trajectories of debris.

The engine had been flung away from the ship by an explosion of some sort which ripped through the *Nightwatch*. The rest of the ship could be an ever-widening globule of debris moving somewhat along the initial path of the ship.

Sally could be anywhere, moving in any direction. Or there could be no more Sally, no more *Nightwatch*.

"Make one more sweep of your sectors," said Max, "then get ready to bring them home. Put out the beacons and mark them."

That was all in the book, he didn't need to tell them. He felt old and useless and empty. "We'll still be here until we get a Recall check on all of you. Keep looking, but have your Acceleration programs ready."

He signed off.

"Christ!"

"Odd," said Dierdre. "I've never heard anybody but Chester say that."

"It comes easy," Max said. "It's about the last good curse we had. We've lost most of our gods, and all the good curses with them."

Doctor Snorkel came in, his mustache unkempt, his hair kinky. He carried food from the commissary for himself, Max and Jiminez, and a drink for Dierdre. Her helmet would open, but the harness she wore after the operation allowed only straws to enter the mouthpiece.

"I heard," he said, before he sat.

Dierdre opened the hinged front of the egg-shaped helmet. The room glowed redly in the IR. She looked around.

"How are the eyes?" asked Snorkel.

"Itchy."

"You need lots of rest."

Max spoke. "We all need rest, none of us more than those out there." He indicated the board. "They'll be glad to get rest, let the ships do all the work for a while."

Snorkel was looking at the plotboard along with Dierdre.

Max looked from one to the other.

"I don't think he's going to come on Recall, you know?" said Dierdre.

"I know."

"I didn't want to bring it up," Snorkel put in.

"Nothing has to be said until after the Recall. It's not official until then."

"You may as well get ready for it," said Dierdre.

Max sighed. His age and experience were leaning on him like an overturned bookshelf.

"She's dead," he said. "She's got to be."

"It's not us you have to convince."

"I'm trying to convince myself."

"It's like artificial respiration," said Dierdre. "You're not supposed to quit trying to revive someone until you're sure they're dead. And the only time you're sure they're dead is the minute you decide to quit trying. That's the only time."

"He loves her that much?"

"I don't know if it's love or the idea of love," said Snorkel.

"Billy was the closest thing to the classic case of someone trying to die of a broken heart, or acting like it, anyway. He was tough, though, and didn't. He kept at it, kept working, got better. Somewhere in there he realized what he was doing to himself. So he quit it, quit the posing. But he kept the real feeling inside."

"That's the longest I've ever heard you talk about one person, Otto," said Max.

"That's the longest I ever want to talk about one person."

"He won't come back until he's sure," said Dierdre.

"When will he be sure?"

"When he comes back," said Snorkel.

The Recall came. Billy watched the other ships go into Acceleration Modes and become probability lines on his plots.

So much to do, so much to cover out there. So much noise, so much light.

The great crystal ship *Argus* swung in closer towards the beacon marking the engine remnant, though it was still a day away at this speed.

"Billy, this is Dierdre."

"Hi, kid, how are you?"

"Terrible."

"Eyes hurt?"

"Skin, too. A rash."

"Oh, that. That'll go away."

"So Snorkel tells me. Billy ..."

"How's Uncle Max?"

"He's right here. He's hurt."

"Oh, Dierdre ..."

"Billy, come back please? For me, at least, if you can't for him?"

"Dierdre, I can't. I just can't, not yet."

"I know you don't think you can, Billy, but you can. Just do it.

You can't have slept any, or anything. You couldn't see anything if you found it. I've just started alterations, and I can probably see better than you, right now ... "

"No, you can't. You'll be able to one day, kid. You'll be better than me and Uncle Max and Uncle Chester put together. I'm okay though. I'm taking some stuff, and I can see pretty well, still."

"Oh, Billy, there's no way Sally — "

"William! This is Snorkel. What the hell are you taking?"

"... Uh, Myoptine. Just a few grains. Don't worry, Doc. I know my limits."

"That's great, William, just great! Not only are you going to keep at it till you drop, you're going to burn your eyes out doing it. *Do not* take any more, Billy, I mean that. You want to be blind? Really blind? Imagine it. I hope you can. I hope it makes you shake. Don't play around with that stuff. Put your ship in Acceleration and get to sleep and get back here. You've got me worried now."

"Okay, Doc, no more, no more. I'll leave it alone. Just something to keep me awake, just a little longer. I could figure out something but ... "

"Two milligrams BNK every six hours for ... twelve hours. That's it. No more. Then turn around and head it back home."

"Two BNK. Okay, Snorkel. Put Dierdre back on, will you?"

"Billy?"

"Yeah, kid. 'Come back.' I know."

"Come back."

"Another half-day, like the doctor says. That's all. I'm really getting tired. I know when I'm beat. Kid ... "

"What, Billy?"

"I hope you never have to do anything like this. It tears your heart out. It really does."

Dierdre turned away from the speaker. Billy signed off.

"My god," said Snorkel, shaking his head. "Myoptine, my god.

Letting his head turn off while his eyes keep watching. My god. Save us from love, save us from love."

Dierdre's shoulders were shaking. Maxwell went to her and held her, but the shaking did not stop for some time.

Billy Big-Eyes was alone now, as alone and more tired than he had ever been. He'd gone past the point of caring. His head was made of dough, his arms and legs lead. His face belonged to someone else. The drug had made his eyes burn. Snorkel had been right. It was just that the tiredness and the immensity and the activity around him had begun to get to him for the first time. He realized he was out in the Deeps and that it was bigger and more full of movement and noise than man could really imagine. On the surface of a planet it was impossible to believe, you were bounded by the stars above you, the ground at your feet, the hori —

Out of the corner of his eye he saw an instrument gauge *move.*

He looked at the console. He stared at it, trying to make something move again by force of will. The gauges remained steady.

Myoptine was not a hallucinogen. The BNK was supposed to cut down fatigue poisons, the ones which caused visions, at the expense of the body's insulin. He knew a gauge had moved.

He cleared the console and punched through the instruments one by one. He studied them. He moved sections, working one at a time until he memorized them all. Then he quick-patched a program to make all the gauges line up at their optimum readings. He watched. His hands gripped the chair arms.

"Move, damn you!"

Several of the beacon receivers pulsed regularly, normally. They distracted him. He moved uprange, but it was useless. The warning light spectra made them glow, and they impinged on his consciousness.

"Max! Max!" he called. "Who's there?" still watching the corner console.

"This is Max, Billy. What is it?"

"Max, kill the beacons, kill everything. One of my detectors moved."

"We can't kill the beacons, not this second. You know that."

"Damn it, Max, kill something!"

"Billy, this is Snorkel here too. What is it?"

"Get Max on, Snorkel, Goddamn it!"

"I'm still here, Billy. What did you see?"

"A detector. It moved once. I can't get a reading."

"Was it a beacon?"

"No, Max. No! Something else, some other frequency. Too much noise and garbage out here. The beacons are bothering me. Kill 'em. I'll damp the hydrogen and oxygen emissions. But kill the beacons, Max, for just a while."

A few moments later, they did.

It was quiet in the focus room, really quiet. There was no stellar noise, no flicker of solar winds, no crackle of ionized matter. Billy killed his engines, drifted on a curved path. He listened and looked and watched his detectors.

"Is he breaking up out there?"

"I don't know. The drug may have something to do with it, or fatigue. He could have taken something he didn't tell me about. I doubt that. If we had biotelemetering, like in the old days, I might know more. But he's so tense up there I couldn't get good readings anyway."

"Dierdre asleep?"

"Yes."

"Wake her. We may need her to talk to him." Max looked at his friend of thirty years. "I'm afraid right now for him, Otto."

"So am I."

The needle flickered *once* again.

There were many people in the plotroom a few hours later, including the Assistant Director. Her name was Smedd. She was pleasant but businesslike.

"The crew compartment?" she asked.

"Either that," said Snorkel, "or the low-pulse generator in one of the maneuvering engines. Nothing else aboard puts out waves on that frequency."

"The crew compartment wave is a shield against low-frequency which might disturb sleep," said Max. "They've been in ships as long as there have been Scouts. We're hoping she was able to get to that part of the ship after the explosion."

Smedd placed her knuckles together. "That still doesn't explain why Big-Eyes didn't answer the Recall."

"We're checking on that now," Max said. "It's possible he was near interference when Recall came, and he never got it."

"I know nothing can stop the Scout frequency, Maxwell," she said.

He looked to Snorkel for help. He started to speak.

"Don't implicate yourself in this ruse, Otto," she said. She turned to her assistant. "Big-Eyes, in the ship *Argus*, is chasing possible remains of the ship *Nightwatch*. Big-Eyes did not answer Recall and is therefore in violation of his directives." She looked up. "That's the official message." She looked at her assistant. "Now hold it, and wander around the building for a while so you can't be found. Be back here in an hour."

She turned to Max. "You shouldn't wear your small mask, Maxwell. It shows too much of your face. I want an explanation of all this, straight."

"Allow Dierdre to fill you in, Ms. Smedd. I'm very tired. I want to look at that board and listen to Billy and find out where in God's name the *Nightwatch* is."

Smedd walked to Dierdre. They began to talk.

"Billy?"

"Yes, Max?"

"We're running the beacons as fast as we can. We'll get you a fix on it. The pulses still regular?"

"Yes. Every six minutes."

"At least, whatever is making them is still in one piece. If it's the maneuver engine, that means it's a big hunk of metal. If it's the crew pulser, it may be the whole section or just the source, which is about as big as your hand. And it's not a frequency you'll be able to see head-on when you take the ship towards it. You'll have to move in on instruments so you don't overrun. Or hit it."

"I've been trying to think of all that, Uncle Max. It isn't too easy."

"I know. Hang with it a while, Billy." Max realized as soon as he said it how really bitter he could be with himself sometimes.

"We got it, maybe," said Jiminez, excitedly.

It was like doing the pencil thing in the mirror, trying to look at something held in front of you in reverse and drawing a line in a circle.

Billy had to triangulate from the beacons, alter his course, triangulate, try to determine the speed and angle, recheck to see if one or the other were changing. Always, maneuver, recheck, maneuver, check.

He was intent on the intercept and ignored the space around him as much as possible. It was only a backdrop to the thing he was doing. Occasionally he scanned it up and down the spectra, watched a star or a gas cloud and dust particles.

Somewhere ahead was what he *knew* was the crew compartment. He had been broadcasting since the moment he located it, his relays racing ahead of him. He watched them go, telling the *Nightwatch*: help is on the way hold tight please answer if you can help is on the way ...

There had been no answer.

There had been no answer for the thirteen days of the search. He kept imagining this as a maneuver, a challenge; he kept backing his ship down into parking orbit with it, talking to it, his beacons telling the object who he was and when he would get there and that it was all right.

There was no answer.

Billy was tired, he had to remember when he started to do things in the wrong sequence, or too quickly, or forgot to check steps.

By rote, by care, he moved his ship in.

It was more than the shielded crew compartment hanging twenty kilometers away from him. There was the focus room, the tubeway and three square kilometers of wrecked lacework reflectors.

He had known this from hundreds of kilometers back, when he determined and finally saw what was there.

He sat and watched the wreckage for a few seconds while his ship told him over and over that it was docked in orbit with the object.

Then he got up out of his seat and went down the tubeway to the work section.

Scouts were never meant to leave ships in the Deeps. That they could was a safeguard men like Chester Big-Eyes had had built into the ships, whether needed or not.

Billy came out the small access port in a shielded pressurized suit, its helmet transparent and huge to allow his chrome helmet room inside. He carried with him an empty suit, tools, a small propellant unit, communications gear.

He had never seen the outside of a ship in the Deeps. No living Scout ever had.

He moved to the area outside the focus room and kicked off,

moving slowly across the great expanse of the reflector network. From the focus room, you never noticed how big it was. It was mostly behind you. Here, it was like sailing above the surface of an ocean, the surface of a moon built by spiders who worked with wire and ice.

He talked to the object hanging off the dully glowing horizon of his ship. It floated like an island, so close to the big metal Archipelago of the *Argus*. It was unrecognizable as the *Nightwatch*. As any ship.

One section of the side glowed very deeply in the infrared. The metal must have been slagged there.

Sally he said Sally it's me.

There was no answer and had been none for thirteen days.

He looked at the ship in the infrared. He could not bring himself to look in the X ray.

His duty as a Scout was to get the other Scout safely back to Fremont.

He talked, amplified by his ship, to the wreckage, to Sally.

I've made it all this way, I'll get you back home.

Us Scouts have to stick together.

He reached the access door of the *Nightwatch*.

Now it was this wreckage which was the island, dwarfed by the continent of the *Argus* overhead, glowing bloodily in the IR, like wicker in a pool of magma.

The door opened easily when he pulled. What he really noticed was the crystallized scorch along the right side of the ship where the starboard engine must have exploded like a burst paper bag.

Millions of roentgens loosed in the night and the ship.

Sally he said up the dark tubeway as he cycled the lock and all kinds of waves shone around him from the focus room above, Sally I love you I love you I love you.

Sitting in her chair so small so beautiful so lovely where she was when the ship blew up, the woman he still loved with all his heart.

He crossed back through the boiling purple ultraviolet night around the *Argus*, across the immensity of the crystal lacework of his ship.

In one hand, he held the arm of the filled, but still unpressurized extra suit, guiding it gently.

In the other, he carried the flight recorder from the *Nightwatch*. The instrument was the second most important piece of equipment on a Scout ship.

Overhead, the music of the spheres hurt his eyes.

UNSLEEPING BEAUTY AND THE BEAST

In the year 2431, Gini-in-the-machine appeared at the center of the old bomb room with a flash of thunder and light.

The machine appeared when no one was nearby. It sent a small, wheeled robot to find people and bring them to her. The robot rolled down a hallway and found a nurse. It tugged her tights and announced in a loud voice, in slurred World English, "Hey!"

The nurse jumped.

"I've got something to show you," said the robot. "A human is in danger."

The wheeled robot turned. The nurse followed it hesitantly, waved for an orderly to accompany her. The robot was strange. It had no clear parts to its eye membranes. It was without legs, squat, not anthropomorphic.

They followed it through several subbasements to the open door of the long-unused room. At the center was a polished machine with many parts, and lying on a table in the center, a girl dressed in white: still, sleeping.

They found through tapes and with the help of the robot that this was Gini, that she was sent from four hundred years in the future, that she was suffering from an incurable disease. Incurable not from lack of technology, but from lack of people. She had been one of the last on Earth. Her uncle had sent her back. The crash of thunder throughout the building before the robot appeared had been her uncle.

He was coming back with Gini to the past, to prepare them for her, to enlist the aid of the Station. He was unsuccessful. He had been dying when he entered the machine. His atoms must have been scattered across several minutes or hours each side of the time at which he meant to stop.

She was pale. She was dying. She was Gini-in the-machine.

Bobby-from-the-freezer sat up in bed. He was disoriented. He thought he remembered being revived a day or two before: he had vague impressions of an operating room, of people, of machines. These were his first thoughts in four hundred years.

He had actually been awakened over a period of months while technicians watched him along the way, checking the functions of his organs, his systems, his body's adjustment to the long waking process. If anything had gone wrong, they would have stopped the wake-up, kept him in a suspended state. The operation he remembered, the floating faces, the lights; this was the last step in his awakening and the cure for the disease. To him, the last days seemed only a few seconds.

They were talking of Gini-in-the-machine, the girl from the future who had appeared at the hospital two weeks before. Of her robot servant, her sleep-death, and the tapes and tools for learning of her time, her illness, her predicament.

It was not easy to hear her name: the patients were restricted to certain areas, particular rehabilitation programs, narrow channels of communication to the outside. But as long as humans have to carry out such orders, the barriers will be circumvented. By rumors, soft-spoken words in the wrong places, wrong times.

Gini, Gini, Gini-in-the-machine, Gini from the future. The sleeping beauty, the frail girl in the tube like a pre-packaged angel for the Old Christmas trees. Gini was the word doctors said, making their rounds between rooms. Sometimes it was the word nurses said in passing. Gini-in-the-machine.

Compared to the elaborate preparations for her wake-up, those of Bobby-from-the-freezer's were commonplace, ordinary, routine.

Bobby-from-the-freezer was once named Robert van Patten,

of the New York van Pattens. Not that he lived long enough the first time to appreciate the wealth, the ease of life, the lack of responsibilities. He had been interested in space travel as a boy; his hobbies had never been put to practical use. His interest came easily, went easily. He learned few social graces. He lived only seventeen years before they found his disease. He would not have lived more than twenty.

They made the decision for him one cold day in November in the year 2004. It had rained. Robert van Patten was in the hospital, watching crystalline raindrops on the glass panes dry and leave greasy circles.

The nurse brought him what he thought to be his usual pain-killer. The disease had started to hurt, and hurt badly. After he'd taken the injection, the doctor came and told him that when he awoke, it would be sometime in the future and that he would have a new life. Or that this would be the last few minutes of his life forever.

And then he had gone away from there in gray falling-doppler sound and awakened on the table four hundred years later.

Now he was conscious and scanning the tapes each day, had met a few of the other Returnees, though none of them had attended the first formal gathering, the social events, the accidental meetings planned by the staff of the institution. He had had visitors from the outside. Two great (8) nephews from the line of his sister. They had stayed a few minutes, presenting him formal recognitions of kinship and invitations to visit once he gained the large world outside the fences of Returnee Station.

Besides all this, he was ugly. He had not been nice to look at from the start. The early ravage of the disease had lined his face, frown lines, pain lines deep-cut in less than a year. He was short, pudgy, though that could be taken care of. He had stiff hands like blocks of wood and a head (still fresh from a four-hundred-year-old head-shave) slightly misshapen on the left side.

His teeth had come in crooked, though braces had partially restraightened them. He moved, in life, like a toad on wheels. He had looked the same in death, with the rollers taken off. He was moving about again, though now his every move was closely watched.

He was not the man to build stories upon, songs, legends, the last faint glimmer of high romance in a world given to the ordinary, the commonplace. Not from appearance. But from the heart.

Gini-in-the-machine was awakened during the second week of Bobby-from-the-freezer's new life. Her wake-up had been simple, after all. They followed the machine's direction for revivication. All the preparation had been done for them four hundred years in the future. Their real work was restoring the body, ridding it of the disease.

Gini was alarmed on her first waking. She could not see her robot; it stood at the foot of the machine below her line of vision. It stepped around the side and hummed until she noticed it. They gave her another sedative, and she went to sleep smiling.

The next day she was better and nicer. All the nurses liked working with her. The information services had been told the story as it developed. They wanted to get to her, not like the old *paparazzi*, but to inform the people about her.

For Bobby-from-the-freezer and Gini-in-the-machine had been revived in the Golden Age. It was another Byzantium, without the Christianity, the wars, the political feuding, the statesmanship. It was the highest civilization man would achieve for another 18,000 years, until mankind reached the fruition of ideas set in motion by Bobby and Gini. Until a future which did not exist was created by those two people, two humans whose minds and bodies crossed time as animals pass from place to place on earth.

Because of a small fish in a pond.

The fish was a golden carplet of the kind once grown for the amusement of people in their homes. It was feeding on a bug which had fallen into the water from the whispering fountain above.

Gini-in-the-machine was being wheeled about in a robot nurse-teacher. The nurse was telling her a little history of the Returnee Station. Gini's small robot tooled along noiselessly.

She asked the nurse-teacher to stop so that she might watch the fish and the insect.

The teacher did, though it continued to give its oral history lesson for the day.

Bobby-from-the-freezer was walking alone, across much the same place. He would not have noticed had not the splashing drops from the fountain in the carefully landscaped garden reminded him of the last few minutes of his life before, of the raindrops on the window.

They saw each other at the same time the fish swallowed the bug.

They did not look at each other long, and the nurse robot soon wheeled Gini-in-the-machine away. Bobby-from-the-freezer left, too, and thought he had forgotten about her.

He awoke in the middle of that night and thought of the girl in the nurse-teacher with the small wheeled robot beside her.

Gini-in-the-machine had gone to sleep long before, and was not thinking of the ugly man by the fountain.

The dance was formal, or as formal as possible. Some Returnees were still recovering from operations. The turnover at the Station was constant. Patients stayed from one to three months, depending upon whether they had been frozen alive or returned from the dead.

Bobby likened it to a dance on an ocean liner full of sick or recovering patients. Those who were still too bemused or weak or bewildered to dance sat and watched. Some, upon whom new legs had been grafted, were trying them out and looked as if they would dance the stars down and the sun up. The choice of music was slightly awry to Robert van Patten's ears. It ranged from waltzes to popular tunes he had known, to those he imagined had come after his time. The Returnees were dressed in their best clothing, their Fourthday suits. In this future, he had learned, clothes were functional. They fit the body.

The music seeped from the corners of the room, from the air above and behind his head, no matter where he stood. He sipped some delicate, very light wine and wondered how much of his insides had been removed.

Only now was he becoming curious about himself; all curiosity had been directed towards the outer world. It was carefully planned that way. He recognized the Returnee Station as an efficient organization.

He imagined it as what he'd heard about the old U.S. Army Reception Centers, only turned upside down and inside out.

It would be a tough place to run.

A waltz started. The two or three hundred Returnees who'd lived after him did not waltz, but began a dance he didn't recognize. He found it interesting, but unaesthetic. Another two dozen people waltzed. Then his eye went to a far corner.

A girl was dancing without a partner — no, he had not seen the robot at first.

They had bowed to each other upon entering the floor, the girl curtseying, the robot dipping its plating skirt to the tiles.

Robert van Patten found himself walking towards them.

The robot did not have arms which could reach to the girl's waist and arms at the same time. Its appendages were useful only for picking up objects and raising them to waist level, where they could be taken by humans. The robot and the girl waltzed without touching.

He came closer, and others were watching. They had all been rich or well-to-do in their former lives, and they still suffered from the superstitions and prejudices of the moneyed.

The girl spun, whirled. But the robot was leading; they moved around the floor. Robert recognized the tune: "The Emperor Waltz." He watched them wheel about through the quiet, staring crowd like runaway planets through a slow galaxy.

As they came near him, he heard himself say: "May I cut in?"

The robot stopped in mid-swirl. "Sure," it said. The girl looked at Robert, his ugliness, as if he were a new baby animal, with curiosity. The robot waited until Robert took the girl's hand, then turned away, moving through the dancers without touching or being touched.

Robert said, "I doubt I dance as well as your robot."

"Oh," said the girl, "I'm sure you do."

The waltz surged above them, and they danced.

They talked.

"I'm the girl from the future," she said.

"Yes," he answered. "And I am Robert van Patten, from the past."

"My name is Gini. They are calling me Gini-in-the-machine. Or Gini-from-the-future."

They danced, and the waltz ended.

The lights lowered with the passing of a few minutes while other songs played, and they danced to them.

"Let's go out onto the patio," she said.

They walked through the soft-glowing room of moving shapes, out into the world of stars and flowers. As they passed through the door, the robot hummed after them.

"The garden is lovely," she said. The staff of Returnee Station had not let any of the revived into this portion of the grounds before tonight. It was to be a new thing in a world full of surprises. The air smelled of twenty, thirty species of flowers, though men could distinguish only a few when near them. Other people moved through the garden on the walks, dark shapes in dim light. The music floated through the doors from the ballroom.

There were two fountains, near the entrances. Cedars of Lebanon stood high around the outside garden wall. The stars blazed overhead, and the moon had not yet risen.

The only sound was of their walking and the pulsing of the robot following a few steps behind.

"I never imagined this," Robert said.

"I should think not," answered Gini. "You have no history of it."

"And you do?"

"Dimly. We were not a world which lived on our past. But it was quiet," said Gini. "Until the last year and the plague from the stars. Then we had to learn our history all over again, because there was no future for Earth."

She was beautiful.

"Would you like a dr— some refreshments?" asked Robert van Patten.

"Yes," she said. Immediately the robot turned to go inside.

"Allow me," said Robert.

"Very well," said Gini.

Robert turned to go.

"Do they ever call you Bobby?" she asked.

"They did. Why?"

"I was wondering. Please get the drinks."

He went inside.

She trembled slightly in the garden breeze.

"Robot," she said. "I think he is Bobby-from-the-freezer."

"Yeah."

"Robot, I'm so afraid."

"Yeah."

Robert found the workings of the Station fascinating. During the next day after the dance, he studied everything the staff did. He caught the pattern from the comments of the workers, from the instructional tapes and shows, from the oral history which his room insisted he listen to. He heard, not the tapes themselves, but the direction of the tapes, the way they were put together.

Here is what he realized.

Returnee Station was one of many on the continent. The returnees like himself were rich, or had been rich in previous lives. Some would leave here not rich at all, but comfortable. Sometimes the trusts had been used up before a cure for the particular discomfort had been discovered. Not poor, though. No one left poor. It was a changed world. A poor man would not make it, not be allowed to make it.

Rather, some would not leave rich.

There had been disasters in the years between Robert's encryptment and revival. The world population had gone down, at last, from birth control, from disease, from famine.

The Returnees faced a future which stretched before them in a golden horizon. It was the best possible time to live, in many ways. In others, it was not. Man had colonized Mars early in the century Bobby died. But that was about all. And the colonies slowly dwindled, until very few were left. Man had not set out for the stars in the four hundred years Robert van Patten had slept. It seemed a shame to him.

But why go to Mars, humans had reasoned, when whole areas of their nice Earth had been eased of their population burden? When whole countries which had been choked under people and farmed-out lands were recovering from centuries-old barrenness? When deserts were opened?

So man has lost the urge for space, thought Bobby. He had been young in his first life, and had not had a chance to do anything. Perhaps in this one ... he had money. His family had used the right trusts for him, the kinship ties were strong. There would be many things a rich man, with a new life, could do in this world, as soon as he got used to it.

He listened to the teacher-robot explain the uses of credit and international exchange on the New Asian continent, and found his mind wandering, back to the dance; the girl Gini-in-the-machine, her robot. He wondered why she looked at him so when he told her they sometimes called him Bobby. *She* had asked. Hadn't she?

And why, when she was beautiful, and young, did she dance with him all night? And why had he not seen her all day, though he had called?

His heart clutched there. It was the ugliness again. He had almost forgotten it in his new life. He was not nice to look at. He had never developed other than a sexual interest in women. He had been young, rich, busy. And he had been ugly.

He had not been shy with women. Ugly people can afford to be forthright, brash. The worst they can be called for it is ugly.

He got up from the bed, went to the mirror. He looked at himself closely, for the first time. His hands on the desk looked like naked sea urchins, stripped of spines. His skin was white, with lighter marbling. He could sun himself. But then he would only be dark and ugly. Quasimodo, he thought. Richard III. Ugly.

She came to the room an hour later, crying. Her robot came into the room and stood by the door behind her.

He had been asleep, and when she knocked, he awakened and opened the door. And she came in.

"What is it? May I help you?"

"I need to talk to you, Bobby-fr— "

"Would you like to talk here?" he asked. "The staff will not like you being out of your room. Especially here. They certainly know you are here and will come soon."

"I know. No. Let's go down to the beach."

"Very well."

They left his room, and Dr. Samond met them in the hallway.

"Well, hello," he said. "Up late, aren't you? You've both got busy days ahead of you. I suggest you get rest."

"We — " said Robert. "We're going down to the lake for a walk."

Doctor Samond, who treated them both once a week, looked at him. "Well, I'm sure it would be all right for you to go, Mr. van Patten. But Gini is under orders to get rest and have regular medications."

"I want to go for a walk," said Gini. "I have my robot. If anything goes wrong, I shall send for you."

The doctor looked from one to the other.

"Gini. You present us with a special case. You are not like other Returnees. We do not want anything happening to you."

He looked at Robert.

"Nevertheless," said Robert, "we are going for a walk."

The doctor stepped aside. "Have a pleasant evening," he said.

The beach was a kilometer away. The sand ringed a bay that had once been part of an ocean, but which was now landlocked, and for a century. The wind was cool.

"Why don't they leave me alone," said Gini, between her teeth.

"Do they bother you?"

"All the time. I'm a person, like them, just like you!"

"They haven't especially bothered me," he said, then quickly added, "but you're special to them. You came from the future. You know the history of our future. They need you."

"To find out what they'll do wrong?" She looked at him.

"Well, perhaps," he said. Why me?

"I haven't told them much of anything, yet."

"Why?"

"Because I'm afraid they'll change things."

"What things?"

They stopped then, and sat on a ramp overlooking the bay. Far off were the lights of the city which they had not yet visited, but which looked very pretty at night. There was a high dome there, and a low skyline.

The robot whirred to stop behind them.

Robert held Gini's hand.

She looked at him. "The things which happened. The story of you and I. The story of Bobby-from-the-freezer and Gini-in-the-machine."

He looked at her, her shining hair the wind blew, her pale hands, her face.

"You and I?"

She laid her head on his hand where it rested on the rail. He felt a tear go down his fingers.

"You are Bobby-from-the-freezer," she said. "And I'm — I've got to be Gini-in-the-machine. We will kill the Earth."

"What do you mean?" *He thought he knew then didn't.*

"We, we had a legend in our time," she said. "Of the man from the far past who had been revived. Bobby-from-the-freezer. You. And I. Gini."

She quit crying. She looked at him, and in the light her eyes shone like oil.

"We will be together. We will leave the Station together. We will restart colonization of the planets. We'll reach the stars. Because of you, your wealth, your riches. And we'll die together out in the stars. That will happen."

"But ... but what's wrong with that?" He couldn't think. His mind refused to work in webs, in nets, growing outward.

"The plague. The plague, Bobby-from-the-freezer. We start the colonies, we give humanity the stars. We die, but the planets live on, the settled places grow, expand. One of the ships brings back the plague, in the time I came from. Man will live on among the stars. But everyone on Earth dies. Everyone. And I come back here, just before the end ... and this is where it starts again."

"I don't understand," he said finally.

"Oh, I don't either." She began to cry.

"What if we don't do it?" he asked.

She looked at him. "All the time I was growing up, I lived with the name Gini. Like in the legend. I never thought much of it — the story of Bobby-from-the-freezer and Gini-in-the-machine. It was old. Like a fairy tale, it was made into shows. They'll love us. They will admire us. This generation will pass on, not knowing we'll kill all life on Earth in four hundred years. We ..."

"You want something?" asked the robot.

"No, thank you." She patted the smooth metal of its side. "He's been my only help," she said to Robert. "I couldn't have made it without him. I wouldn't have known what to do."

Robert looked at the small robot. "What did he tell you to do?"

"He told me to do what I had to. He knew all this was upsetting me. He only wants me happy."

Robert looked up at the stars in the cold bright sky. He held Gini close to him. What should he do? Why should he be the one, *they* be the ones, to act out this playlet written in the future? What if he walked away? What if they left, but went somewhere else, if they never went towards the stars?

"It wasn't easy," said Gini. "It wasn't easy to come back here. When my uncle started to send me ... I — I think I knew. I think he realized he was sending back the doom of the Earth. He ... he never let it bother him. He wanted me to live. He knew this was the one time, the one place that could surely save me. It ... it wasn't easy, Robert."

She had her head on his hand again. The wind was making him shiver. He kissed her quickly. It surprised him. It surprised her.

"Do you know what I'm thinking?" he asked.

"Yes," she said, with conviction.

He stared at her a moment. "What, then?"

"That you will go to the doctors and have them make you handsome," she said, as if by rote.

"Was that part of the legend?"

"Yes."

"Will I do it?"

"No."

"Why?"

"Because I will love you as you are."

He stood and kissed her again, silhouetted against the bay and the city. The wind was cold. The robot lifted itself to its wheeled position.

"Let's go," he said.

She took his hand.

The stars were waiting, and death among them. Earth would die, but mankind would live on throughout the galaxy. He was Bobby-from-the-freezer. She was Gini-in-the-machine.

MY SWEET LADY JO

His name, according to the birth certificate, was Edward Smith. He was left at the hospital by "Mrs. Smith" when she left for parts unknown. He was raised in the Sylacauga Home on 12th Street in Birmingham, Alabama.

The child was precocious, else he wouldn't have been noticed. Psychologists were led to believe that his mother and father were both of genius level. He hadn't gotten brains behind a truck-stop café. What led "Mrs. Smith" to leave a newborn child alone in the maternity ward of a great metropolitan hospital was unknown.

Suffice it to say that by the age of twenty-seven, Edward NMI Smith was appointed director of public information of the Space Science Services Administration. The youngest, and brightest, man ever placed so high within the government. At the time, he was unhappily married, the father of one child; a very lonely man.

The year he took the directorate, the first men came back from the stars. They had gone to Alpha Centauri twenty-six years before, accelerating to near-light speeds for the middle third of their journey. They got there in twelve years. Sixteen years after the first ships left, a message dropped out of the clear sky one night.

Seven of the original nine ships made the trip. For the duration, the crews remained awake like any other spacecraft crew. They guided the great craft through the darkness, monitoring those colonists they carried frozen in hopes of finding a new world orbiting the nearest star.

Alpha Centauri IV, named Nova Terra (of course), had been found in short order. Less gravity, more sunlight, less oxygen, more nitrogen. A good world.

The message came from the new transmitter on Nova Terra. The radio station had been broadcasting four years when its first message reached the Earth, and it would be another four before they knew whether Earth had received it. The distances immense, the blackness deep, the stars bright.

Meanwhile, two and a half years after the settlement of Nova Terra, an expedition headed back. Due to the time lag between broadcast and reception, the message of their departure from Nova Terra was received eighteen and a half years after the ships left Earth. Someone quickly figured that the ships had been on their way back four years already, and would arrive in another eight.

The message said, "Two ships to return to Earth. Methods developed here allow crews to sleep in shifts. Some colonists returning. See you in twelve years."

Eight years later the ships coasted into solar orbit a few hundred miles above the Earth. At night, they were brighter than Venus, brighter than the space stations wheeling near them; two new stars on the zenith.

Ed Smith, the new director of information of the Space Science Services Administration, and his team were on Station No. 3 to meet the first men and women to return from the stars.

"Mom Church! Any time now," said Newton Thornton, looking at the clock on the wall.

"Easy, Newton," I said. "This is the Station's moment of glory. First they've had since the starships left almost three decades ago. You can't blame them for taking a little longer in decompression than they have to."

"I know that, Mr. Smith," he said, "but damn, they're sure taking their time."

"Well, we'll have them long enough," I said.

The doors opened and out they came, the station's director striding before them like head lion of the pride.

His glad hand came out almost automatically. "Mr. Smith, the head of Space Services information, ladies and gentlemen. Mr. Smith, the crew and colonists from Nova Terra."

I made an impatient little bow. Several of the crewmen returned the bow, stiffly, formally. Two of the women curtsied.

We all broke into smiles.

Commander Gunderson was breathing smoke from the cigar as if it were air. "You'd be surprised to know," he said, "that tobacco will not grow well on the areas of Nova Terra we settled. Most of the soil is too acid. Of course, that was ... what? twelve years ago. Place may have more tobacco than North Carolina by now." He breathed more of the cigar smoke.

"I hope so," said Newton. "Carolina doesn't have any."

"What?"

"Virginia, the Carolinas, Georgia, lost more than three quarters of their crops eleven years ago. New fungal disease. Spread quickly. Spores in the ground so thick the land still can't be used for years. What tobacco is raised is now done in Arizona, New Mexico and parts of the California plains ... still partly desert land when you left," said Newton.

"I'll be damned," said Gunderson. Weariness crossed his face. "It'll take a while to get used to things ... you know." He stared at the burning ash of his cigar. "I went out as a colonist. Twenty-six years ago. That's a long time. Decided that, even with my Services training, it'd be better for me to go out asleep. Just in case they ever wanted to come back, and the crews didn't want to make another twelve-year trip." He rubbed his graying hair.

"The crewmen who went out ... they aged. I didn't. I thought I'd be like them on this trip back. That was before we developed the rapid cryogenics that allowed the crew to sleep in shifts. I've only been up seven months, since we left Nova Terra.

"I knew there'd be people who'd want to come back. It's not adventure out there, you know. It's hard work."

He put out the stub of the cigar very carefully.

"Hell, I've only aged three years and seven months since I left Earth twenty-six years ago. Course, I was old when I left."

Thornton laughed.

Commander Gunderson became serious. "There are some people who only aged three years," he said. "Some of the colonists went out asleep. They've come back asleep. They were only up three years. They didn't like what they found there any more than they liked what they left."

He sighed and leaned back in his chair.

"I guess that's why I went out asleep, rather than as a crew member. I knew there'd be people like that who'd need to get back more than they needed to leave. I guess that's why."

After he left, Newton Thornton looked at me. "How are they ever going to make it?" he asked.

"Like everybody else does," I said, remembering. "They just get along, one way or another."

The debriefings lagged. The reports occupied a small room. Births and deaths, arability, mineral deficiencies; all the things that tell you what a planet is so you can decide how to make it what you want it to be. We still had twelve returning colonists to interview, and Captain Welkins had gone out as a crewman and had come back as one. Remaining awake the whole time. The psychologists were questioning him first. We would talk to him later. The colonists and crewmen were anxious to get down to the planet that they had left twenty-six years before. We were going as fast as we could and still get all the information we needed. And we were as tired as they were. We could use a rest.

Sometime that second week I called my wife and boy.

Me: Hello, Angie.

AN: Is that you? Ed?

Me: Yes. How're you? How's Billy?

AN: Oh. We're fine. Just fine.

Me: Tell him I don't know when I'll be back. But it shouldn't be too long. A week at most.

AN: He misses you. He asks about you all the time.

Me: Well, I miss both of you, I guess.

AN: You guess?

Me: Hell, you know what I mean.

AN: Well, I guess I hope you get home soon.

Me: Dammit, Angie. It's just that I need a rest. I'm beat. I've got a lot of work here.

AN: Then maybe you can take Billy to the mountains in a couple of weeks.

Me: I don't want to take Billy anywhere. I just want to rest.

AN: Pardon me.

Me: Look, Angie. Just tell Billy I'll see him soon.

AN: What about me?

Me: What about you?

AN: Can't you even try to be nice sometime?

Me: I quit a long time ago. I'll see you soon.

AN: Are you sure it won't cut into your valuable time?

I hung up. Damn. Damn.

Her name was Jo Ellen Singletary. She was one of the people Commander Gunderson had spoken about. She was very pretty. Sometimes, as she talked, small lines formed around her mouth. Tiny lines. She looked twenty, maybe twenty-five.

I had her partial records out. I never looked at anybody's until I had to write up the finished reports. I worked from the bio Newton wrote on each person. I still hadn't interviewed Welkins. The psychologists were holding us up.

"You're one of the special cases," I said.

"Special? Oh. You mean turnaround."

"Yes. Turnaround."

"I suppose I am, then. Special," she said.

"What made you decide to come back?" I asked.

"I ... I didn't especially like it out there." She shifted her weight in the chair. Newton had gone to get us some sandwiches. She looked around the room. "So I came back. I want to start over again, here. On Earth."

"You realize that things have changed in the twenty-six years you've been gone," I said.

For an answer, her eyes started to water up. I didn't like women crying. I started to get up out of my chair, then decided against it. "I'm sorry if I've upset you," I said. "I only meant it as a question."

"No. No, you didn't." Her face tensed. "You meant it won't be any easier living here now than it was when I left. Didn't you?"

I looked down at the papers on my desk. "No. It's been a busy week. I'm sorry if I've upset you. There is no excuse."

"I know you've been busy," she said, still staring at me. She started to cry again. "There's no excuse for me crying, either."

She really began crying now.

I put my pen down, walked around the desk, then stood like a dummy beside her while she cried. Her hair smelled musky. She wore a new perfume which she must have bought at the station. Angie had some of the same at home.

It was then I realized what she faced. She returned to Earth, aged only three years more than when she left. She came back to an entirely different world. What she must have seen outside the station windows was not the familiar Earth, but another blue planet where they happened to speak the same language. Culture shock waited with trapjaw mouth. Technological shock lurked behind every street corner, in every new sound. And she had not touched down yet.

I put my hand on the back of her head. I patted it. "I can get one of the doctors to get you something," I said.

She shook her head No.

She leaned towards my hand. "I'm so afraid," she said.

"I know. I know," I said.

I lied.

You never mean for it to happen. It just does, like marriages turning bad, and it is such an easy thing that you do not notice it for days, or hours, until you see what has happened. And then there is nothing you can do, because it has you by the guts and heart.

There are no bells ringing, no birds singing. I know that I shouldn't have helped her as much as I did the next few days. But I know too that it couldn't have happened to me with anyone else, anywhere.

The interviews were finished, even with Welkins. Welkins we would keep in touch with. Some of the crew and all the returned colonists wanted to leave the Space Services. That was a legal tangle decided by the courts. If a man had been in the service thirty years, he got his retirement pay, plus the hazardous duty pay accruing, even though he had been in deep cryogenic sleep twelve or more of those thirty years.

I could leave those problems to lawyers. There were the usual jokes about sleeping on duty, and getting promoted in your sleep, and all those other things I could do without.

It wasn't just the last two and a half weeks that made me tired. I was really tired. Tired of work. Tired of living at the very sharp edge I had for the last five years, pushing myself. I was as far as I wanted to go in the Service. They could try to promote me to some admin slot in the labs, but I didn't want it. My life had been writing, working with words. I didn't want a job where the only words I'd use would be in the Annual Report to the Nation. I didn't want out; I just didn't want up.

Jo Ellen, the tiredness, the loneliness, the work; all got to me at the same time.

I couldn't just let her go away, get lost in the masses, with only a letter every three weeks or so.

She had been to Accounting to get her separation pay. With that last payroll signature, our relationship was no longer official. The sun was bright in the blue morning sky above the Space Services building. No rockets shining in the sun. No aircraft whizzing overhead. All the launchings took place Out There, except for the shuttle runs from Florida.

She was dressed in a new pantsuit set. She was beautiful, her bronze hair shining in the light. Heat waves had begun to shimmer off the concrete of the mall.

"Well," she said.

"Yeah. This is where it all ends," I said.

She looked at me. I looked at her. Visions of doom and stardust.

"I don't guess it is," she whispered. In front of God and everybody.

Hand in hand, across the mall.

The PACV we'd rented sluffed to a stop as I killed the engines.

The stars, one of them the same star she'd been to and returned from, glowed overhead.

Angie and Billy and thoughts of Angie and Billy a thousand miles away. Frogs from Florida in the background. A girl from the stars at my elbow. Beer from Milwaukee in the cooler. Hell of a note.

We listened to the frogs.

"There aren't any," she said.

"What?"

"Frogs."

"What?"

"There aren't any frogs there. On Nova Terra. No frogs."

"Oh."

Later, after a silence: "What will your wife say? You have children, don't you?"

"One," I said. "A boy. Five. Name is — "

"I don't want to know," she said. "I don't."

"All right. Don't worry."

"I am. You are."

"Jesus," I said. "Jesus."

She kissed me. "Am I worth it? I can't be."

"Yes," I said.

A neighbor lady called the hotel five days later. She was upset. Angie had found out all about it, and was crying all the time. The neighbor lady said the least I could do was have the decency to call. The photostats of the colonists' records had arrived at the house. The least I could do was tell what I wanted done with them. And so on and so on and so on.

I told her to tell Angie I'd be there tomorrow.

Jo Ellen packed for me next morning. She was crying, and trying not to.

I hadn't told her. I woke up and watched her finish putting the last of my clothes into the suitcase.

"There's a bath run. Your suit is hanging by the tub. I've got a flight for you at eleven forty. You'll have to hurry just a little bit."

"How did you find out?" I asked.

"I can tell. This isn't a new thing with me. It's one of the reasons I left in the first place. It wasn't any better out there."

"I'll be back in a few days."

"I know," she said, crying.

I shaved, bathed and showered. When I came out of the bathroom, she was gone. Leaving no note.

The weather calm, the flight uneventful.

"You didn't bring Jo Ellen?" she asked when I came in the door.

I got a case of the ass that lasted till I left. There was no compromise, no hope, no use arguing or pleading. She had taken Billy to her mother's. She already had a lawyer. She didn't want anything but out and Billy. I told her she could have it all. To leave the records where they were. I'd have the Agency come and get them. And goodbye.

Bad moods. Hate. All that.

There are only so many places you can run when your world has changed completely. I found her at one of them.

I came up very quietly and sat down beside where she sunbathed. It was a few minutes before she turned her head to where I sat.

"Hi," I said.

She jumped, then laid her head back down on the sand. "I didn't think you'd come back, Ed. The last one didn't."

"It doesn't matter," I said. "I did."

She continued to stare at the sand awhile.

I doodled in the glistening beach. "Tell me," I said. "What's it like out there?"

She laughed and cried and pulled me to her.

The waves moved and susurrated against the shore. The tide was coming in.

We first noticed the private detective about three days later. He was a fat little man who went to two of the same places we did. Jo Ellen saw him first.

What with the resurgence of Mom Church, there are some new archaic laws on the books. Some require you to be gone for six months and a day before desertion is declared. Or you have to sign mental cruelty affidavits that make you look like a real sonofabitch. There's still one way for a divorce to be granted in a few weeks.

I tried to kill the bastard before he and his buddy popped the flashbulb that night. There were still people who made their livings getting divorce evidence. I don't know what'll happen when man gets enlightened enough to dissolve a marriage when two people don't get along any more.

The lamp I threw bounced off the doorsill beside the photographer. The big one, the muscle, stepped towards me as I climbed out of bed. I kicked at him hard as I could. He grabbed my foot and dumped me on my ass. My head smacked the bed. Pain shot through me. I lay there with my head buzzing

"You get up again, I'll hurt you," the big one said. The little fat one popped another snapshot, waved the big one out the door.

Jo Ellen was crying as she helped me up. The fat one left. I was crying too. At least it would be over, soon.

After I got my head cleared, I began writing my resignation.

We thought it would be over. Angie wouldn't let go, though. She called me that night. She wanted to see me. She wanted us to have one more go at it. Think of Billy.

"After your hoods did what they did?"

"I'm sorry, honey. I didn't know they'd do it that way. You know I had to have those pictures."

"Sure."

"Honey, come back to me. I'll forget. I'll forget if you will. I'll tear up the pictures. We'll pretend this never happened. Please, honey, please."

"Give your pictures to the judge. And to the papers if you want. I'm quitting the Service. There'll be a scandal anyway; might as well be a big one. Do it up right."

"I don't want to hurt you, honey. I'd ... I don't want to."

"You're a bitch, Angie."

"Don't say that. Don't."

"Get out of my life." I slammed down the receiver.

The morning before I turned in my resignation, we lay in bed.

I looked at Jo Ellen's stomach. Tiny stretch marks ran in a fine net up her abdomen. Funny the things you don't notice for a long time.

She wasn't married. I looked at the marks. I didn't say anything.

She rubbed her hands through my hair. "What are we going to do?" she asked. "They'll follow us anywhere we go."

"Not anywhere." In that instant, I made up my mind.

"Where?"

"Out there," I said.

"Oh. Ed, No. I couldn't do it. I don't think I could. Not again."

"There's nothing to it, you said. Just going to sleep and waking up somewhere else."

"No. Not that. What if something happens? What if one of us ... doesn't ... doesn't wake up? Or either of us? Or the ship doesn't make it? Two of ours didn't," she said.

"We can't stay here. I don't want to. Too many memories, all bad. Except you." I kissed her wet eyelids.

"When?" she asked.

"Next month. The twelve ships. We could forget it all, all of it. Your troubles, my troubles."

"Yes," she said. "Yes."

SPACE OFFICIAL QUITS
WIFE OF SPACE DIRECTOR SEEKS DIVORCE
LOVE STORY FROM THE STARS

It was very quiet in the Cryogenics section. The papers had lost us; we were safe until after the ships left. I still had some friends in the Service.

Preparation Room No. 3. White-smocked technicians left us alone.

"You'll be all right," I said. "You've done it twice before. You'll go right under. Me, they'll have to chain me in."

"No," said my sweet lady Jo. "You'll go right under too. Next thing you know, we'll be on a new planet, starting over."

She was crying. She was beautiful. She was mine.

"Go ahead. I love you. I'll see you later," I said. I kissed her. I had given her a rose, and she held it like a butterfly and cried on it.

"I love you," she said. She kissed me. A technician took her away. She was light and air and I loved her.

I waited for the needle.

Someone was in the room. I looked.

A month had changed Angie. She looked twice as old. Her face was drawn, her eyes red. She had a wild look on her face, an animal hid beneath the skin, waiting to pounce out. I was afraid.

There was no one else with her.

"You didn't bring the newsmen?" I asked. "Can't let go, can you? Are you going to watch, make sure I'm going through with this?"

"No," she said. "I wanted you to read this. I just got it from the detectives. I just wanted you to know what you're doing. I couldn't let you go through with it."

"You think you can stop us?"

"No. Not me. You'll stop yourself."

She turned and was gone. I couldn't believe it. No pleas, no threats. I tore open the envelope.

The top page was a message from the head of the detective agency. The following information, etc., etc. There were tearstains on the page.

The second page was Jo Ellen's records, one of the copies which had been at the house. I read it. Then I turned the page.

Angie, you couldn't let go, could you?

Can you forgive me, Jo Ellen? I love you so much.

Angie couldn't let go. Had to pry. Had to. Down the long trail reaching back twenty-seven years.

Angie's life. My life. Your life.

Cool cool the needle going into the vein. Hot the drug. Quick the rush of sleep.

Angie didn't think I could still go through with it.

Heavy my eyelids, dark the night in my brain. Sleep, like a stone.

Jo Ellen, I love you, no matter what. Years will go by in quick darkness. There'll be a green planet there, maybe.

A cool green planet. The perfect place for a boy to take his mother on their honeymoon.

Hopefully, not another Earth.

Because Earth really messes some people up.

3. Con Man

CON REPORTS, MEMOIRS, AND PARODIES

"The Droog in the Green Flannel Blanket"
"The Great AmeriCon Novel"
"Cthu'lablanca and Other Lost Screenplays"
"Chili from Yuggoth"

INTERVIEW, PART THREE

1. "The Droog in the Green Flannel Blanket"

BRAD: We've talked about "The Droog in the Green Flannel Blanket" before, but we didn't record that conversation. The piece itself was "lost" for a while, but George finally tracked it down, along with "The Great AmeriCon Novel."

Now, "The Droog in the Green Flannel Blanket" was a convention report about the 1972 "Little Mac" in Kansas City —

HOWARD: See, when we talked before, I was thinking that the "Droog" report was for a convention in Oklahoma City.

BRAD: Right. But then we figured out from talking to Ken (Keller) and, I think, George, that it was actually Little Mac. Which, of course, is what it also says in the piece itself, now that we finally have it. [*BD Note: The convention in question became known as "Little Mac" in retrospect, following the 1976 MidAmeriCon, which was "Big Mac." In 1972, the actual name of "Little Mac" was "the Mid-America Science Fiction Convention," or "Mid-America Con." It took place June 16–18, 1972.*]

That convention was the first time you actually met George R.R. Martin in the flesh, right? And there's a legendary story about sleeping arrangements. [*BD Note: Howard wonders if this incident might have occurred at D-Con in Dallas in 1973. But previous iterations of the story, both from Howard and from George, place it in Kansas City at Little Mac.*]

HOWARD: See, George thought he was gonna share a room with me and Buddy (Saunders). And Buddy was the only one who could pay for the room. So Buddy was asleep in the bed. There were, like, six people right around the bed on any flat surface they could find. And ten or twelve other people were scattered around the room, too. There was a hi-boy dresser with a space under it, and I said, "That's *my* spot!" and slid underneath. That way I wouldn't get stepped on or anything.

So George had to sleep across the bathroom doorway, which was the only space left. And I was woken up by a lot of noise at, like, 2:00 or 3:00 in the morning. Then somebody went back to the sofa, where two of 'em had been sleeping, and one had gotten up to go to the bathroom. At which point there was all this cussing and stuff. The person who had stayed on the sofa says, "What happened?" And the guy says, "I stepped on some pasty-faced bastard lying across the bathroom door!"

And that was George, of course.

See, this is why I think it might have been in Dallas — because this was George's introduction to Texas fandom.

BRAD: But it was still in '72?

HOWARD: Yeah, it was the same year as Little Mac. [*BD Note: D-Con '73 was actually June 28–July 1, 1973.*]

See, Little Mac was at the Continental, near the Muehlebach, where MidAmeriCon was gonna be four years later. And another hotel, the Pioneer House, was across the street. But it had a better café that was open twenty-four hours a day, and I ate every meal there. And no matter which meal it was, I had a hamburger and french fries. Breakfast, lunch, dinner, 3:00 o'clock in the morning, whatever.

But as for "Droog in the Green Flannel Blanket" ... It was just like I said in the article. I did not know, when I did my costume, that the movie version of *A Clockwork Orange* had not opened in Kansas City yet.

But I had seen it. I had just left the Army, and I had seen it in Raleigh, North Carolina, on a Saturday morning the weekend it opened. My wife and I had driven there with my friend Lockridge, Sergeant Lockridge. We get out of the car — we had driven about seventy-five miles to get there, and it was about 10:00 in the morning, because the first showing was at 11:00 AM or whatever — and Sergeant Lockridge steps out of the car and says, "I smell a hamburger. Wrapped in wax paper." He says, "With a toothpick in the top with a pickle on it."

We followed him down the street, and we walked in this place — and at the counter, a waitress was putting a hamburger in front of somebody. And it was wrapped in wax paper and had a toothpick in it with a pickle on it. It was the goddamnedest thing I had ever seen. But he had known *exactly* what he was smelling, you know?

And then, of course, we watched *A Clockwork Orange.*

But I thought *A Clockwork Orange* had opened everywhere in America by the time of Little Mac, which was like two months later. But it turned out it was on a limited release. They had opened it in big cities and on the East Coast, but not Kansas City. So I did the whole thing, the droog costume, and Ken Keller thought I was doing Dum Dum Dugan (from *Sgt. Fury and the Howling Commandos*) because he wore a derby hat and stuff.

Everybody was mystified and staring at me. I had a jockstrap with four pounds of shredded foam rubber stuffed into it for the codpiece, you know?

BRAD: So you did this painstaking costume from *A Clockwork Orange* — and nobody had seen the movie.

HOWARD: I was singing "Singing in the Rain," too, of course.

BRAD: Yeah, they just thought you were off your nut.

HOWARD: And not a lot of 'em knew me at the time. Ken knew me, and a few other people.

BRAD: I'm guessing that because you and George had been corresponding for ten years at the time, you knew he was going to be there.

HOWARD: Oh, yeah.

While we were there, George and I went up to the Playboy Club, which was in the penthouse at the Continental. First time I ever paid a dollar and a quarter for a beer. Anywhere else in America, you walked in and it was sixty cents or seventy-five cents for a beer.

Anyway, that's where George and I discussed "Men of Greywater Station." And we were able to get a typewriter, because Harlan was there.

BRAD: Harlan Ellison was at Little Mac?

HOWARD: If I'm not confusing it with the Dallas convention again. [*BD Note: In fact, Harlan Ellison was not at Little Mac, but was a guest at D-Con in 1973 — as described in "The Great AmeriCon Novel."*] Anyway, George and I got a typewriter somewhere and started writing the story, and we got four pages done that weekend. George took it home, and then we each did alternate sections much like Buddy Saunders and I did in *Texas-Israeli War.*

BRAD: You went to Little Mac fresh on the heels of getting out of the Army, didn't you?

HOWARD: I'd been out about a month. I got out on the first of May, or maybe the second of May.

I'd just gotten back to Texas. And then me and Buddy drove up to Kansas City. And the rest is history.

2. "The Great AmeriCon Novel"

BRAD: Let's talk a bit more about Little Mac in 1972 and D-Con '73 in 1973. For obvious reasons, you remember some of the incidents at one as being at the other, because they both involved a lot of the same people, and were a long time ago.

HOWARD: And I had just gotten out of the Army, and everything was fresh and new again. And it all seemed to be happening right at the same time.

BRAD: Those two conventions were almost exactly a year apart. Little Mac was June 16-18 of '72, and D-Con '73 was June 28-July 1 of '73. And in the case of Little Mac, you had only been out of the Army a month.

Now, in "The Great AmeriCon Novel," about the Dallas convention, it's clear that you're working the convention. You're hauling stuff, you're putting stuff together, you're setting up tables, and all of that. Were you actually on the con committee?

HOWARD: Oh, yeah. I was in charge of, whatchacallit, advertising around town. Which essentially meant going to different stores and putting up posters in their windows. Some stores had a bulletin board, too. "In-Store Advertising," I believe was my official duty.

BRAD: So, "Howard Waldrop, Public Relations."

HOWARD: Well, part of the public relations. There were several people doing that. But that was when it was gonna be "Big D in '73" (the famous, but failed, Dallas Worldcon bid), of course. Then they downscaled it. And then [Name Redacted #1] and [Name Redacted #2] hijacked it.

BRAD: Yeah, you told me about that. I guess you were present when that happened.

HOWARD: Oh, yes. I was present when the settling-up happened, see? Because we kept asking them for months, "How'd we do?" and "How much did we make at the convention?" and all this stuff. And they kept saying, "We're gonna have a meeting and tell everybody that." But they kept postponing it, because they didn't want to tell everyone they had trademarked "Big D in '73," and had put the money in their pockets. When the meeting finally happened, they started it by saying, "Thank you all for working on *our* convention."

And there was dead silence in the place. Then everyone started going "mmmMMMMmmnnnn" and muttering and stuff, and so those two guys knew they were in trouble.

BRAD: They were trying to brazen it out.

HOWARD: Exactly, but that wasn't gonna happen. We met at a Howard Johnson's, and everybody had clams and stuff. Then we went to the meeting room, and they started the meeting by saying "Thanks for working on *our* convention" to, like, forty people. One of the forty, [Name Redacted #3], started moving around in his chair, and then he just jumped up and took off across the top of the tables for [Name Redacted #1]. And [Name Redacted #1] goes out the door.

See, everybody had been so let down when the Big D in '73 bid fell apart the year before. But we thought, "Well, we'll do this convention (D-Con '73) and then be set for the next few years. And then maybe try again." But what happened was that

Big D in '73 really became MidAmeriCon in '76, after Tom Reamy took off for Kansas City.

BRAD: So the meeting at the Howard Johnson's where everything blew up — it would have happened *after* the convention we're talking about now. After D-Con '73.

HOWARD: Right. The convention happened in the summer, and I want to say this meeting happened in September or October. That's when the Dallas science fiction club fell apart, because nobody could stand being around each other anymore.

And then [Name Redacted #1] went through a divorce, and his wife got half his stuff. So there is some justice.

It was a bad thing they did, you know?

3. "Cthu'lablanca and Other Lost Screenplays"

BRAD: That brings us to 1976, and the MidAmeriCon Program Book.

Now, MidAmeriCon (the 1976 World Science Fiction Convention in Kansas City) has passed into legendary status at this point, because if you talk with people about it now, it was maybe the first *modern* Worldcon — in the way that Worldcons were going to be from then on.

HOWARD: Right. Tom Reamy had anticipated *everything.* Everything that he was gonna do in "Big D in '73" just moved to Kansas City in '76.

BRAD: So you're saying it was sort of Tom Reamy's brainchild, and then Ken Keller and others worked with him on it to make that vision happen.

HOWARD: Well, they wanted to have the Worldcon, and Tom incidentally happened to move up to Kansas City to work freelance for Hallmark and places. And Ken and the Kansas City crew adopted as many of the "Big D in '73" things as they could get away with. It was the first Worldcon that cost fifty dollars for five days!

BRAD: Which I'm sure was shocking at the time.

HOWARD: It *was* shocking. But see, Tom Reamy had said, on paper in 1971, that "Complete amateurs will be handling half a million dollars on a weekend." And nobody believed him.

MidAmeriCon was also the first Worldcon to have three-track programming. 'Cause in the old days, people just went from one thing to another, right? That was the only thing there was.

BRAD: And now at a Worldcon, of course, there can be five or six things happening at the same time.

HOWARD: Exactly. For the first time, Kansas City had three-track programming, plus the film room. And the dealer's room.

BRAD: And they had Heinlein as Guest of Honor.

You've already almost answered my next question, which was about Tom Reamy. He's kind of a legendary figure now, but at the time — I guess at the time, you realized he was something special, at least in terms of his vision for what the Worldcon was going to be. But of course now he's also legendary as a writer, too.

HOWARD: He was a tremendous writer. He was the best writer of all the people who were selling in Texas at the time, I can guarantee. And of course his career was only eighteen months long.

BRAD: He didn't live too long after MidAmeriCon, did he?

HOWARD: He died in November of the next year. You know, he and Elvis were exact contemporaries. They were born within a couple of months of each other, and they died within a couple of months of each other.

BRAD: You know who I was an exact contemporary of? Prince. We were born on the same day.

HOWARD: You know who *I'm* a contemporary with? Oliver Stone and Tommy Lee Jones. *We* were all born on the same day in 1946. (September 15.)

But Tom Reamy really was the best writer among us back then. He was up for the Campbell Award for Best New Writer, and he had been up for the Nebula for "San Diego Lightfoot Sue." And he was up for the Hugo for something else. And that was all in the first six months of his career, right?

He sold his first two stories on the same day. He had one out to Damon Knight, and one out to Harry Harrison. And they were both accepted on the same day. He had these envelopes with a shoe on them, and a bug on top of the shoe. And I got a letter from him, and the bug was saying, "Whoopee!" I opened it up, and he told me about making those first two sales on the same day. He had closed his previous letter by saying, "My problem now is to convince Damon Knight that angels have assholes." That was because he was revising the story for Damon. So he probably knew he had the sale to Damon, but then the one from Harrison came on the same day.

BRAD: Now I need to ask you about the piece itself, the piece you wrote for Tom for that Worldcon program book: "Cthu'lablanca and Other Lost Screenplays." It's part of the "M.M. Moamrath" cycle, which several people wrote for.

HOWARD: It was created by Bill Wallace and Joe Pumilia, with help from Sally Wallace. In the original articles they published, Sally always appeared in photographs as Moamrath, with a scarf and hat covering her face so you couldn't see any features. The idea was that there was a pulp writer in the 1930s, equal to H.P. Lovecraft, a recluse and everything. He was an admirer of the "Marquis de Hacque." They thought of everything!

BRAD: The Moamrath stuff was so much fun, and what you did in "Cthu'lablanca" was really funny. It hearkens back to your old "Cosh Comics" spoof, and the idea that "We're gonna take the notion that this thing existed, and treat it completely seriously."

HOWARD: That was the idea. There was supposed to be a Moamrath collection. Mike Bishop, Steve Utley, and other people contributed to the "Moamrath Bibliography," you know? It was gonna contain like 300 pieces, all spurious. Utley came up with "Suspenders of Doom," and I said the working title was "The Gaiter People." Everybody was doing stuff like that, just trying to top each other. And Robert Heinlein, while he was alive, offered to write the introduction to the Moamrath collection.

BRAD: You're kidding!

HOWARD: Ken Keller still has that letter. Because Ken, of course, was gonna publish it at one time.

BRAD: You know what this reminds me of ... And of course, this was science fiction writers doing it about ten years before ... But it reminds me of *This Is Spinal Tap.* Which was the same kind of thing: We're gonna create this fake rock and roll band and treat it completely seriously. McKean, Shearer, and Guest came on *Saturday Night Live* as the musical guest, as Spinal Tap, and people believed it. They believed that this was a real band that had been around for twenty years. And I think today that somebody who came across that MidAmeriCon program book might think, "Who's this M.M. Moamrath guy? I should look him up."

HOWARD: Exactly! See, Tom asked me to write it because he had some stills of Bogart and Bergman, and some others. And he doctored them so they would appear like Elder-God-looking things, with tentacles and all this kind of crap, right? He wanted to use those photos, so I came up with the article to go with 'em. And he published it in the program book.

BRAD: That's terrific. And I do wonder how many people saw that in Kansas City, and wondered if M.M. Moamrath was a real writer.

HOWARD: The best part in it, I thought, was the *Wizard of Oz* stuff.

BRAD: I liked that, too. That was very funny.

HOWARD: I just parodied everything I could think of before 1940. Of course, *Casablanca* (1942) is out of that range. But that's okay, nobody noticed. And it was great fun writing it.

4. "Chili from Yuggoth"

BRAD: Now we're going to talk about "Chili from Yuggoth." I don't know if George is going to use this one or not. But it's different. And unlike some of the things we've talked about so far, it's autobiographical.

HOWARD: And every word is true! I'm not kidding.

BRAD: I believe it. And that's one reason I hope George includes it, because I think it'll give people some insight into where you were in your life at the time.

HOWARD: In the wrong town at the wrong time, you know?

BRAD: And because it's so autobiographical, and every word is true, there aren't many questions I can ask you that aren't answered in the piece itself. But I will say that you were writing this piece in 1983, remembering events from nine years before. With that perspective, and especially considering what you wrote in the first part of the piece, it's clear that 1974 was a crucial year for you.

HOWARD: Like I said, of everything I wrote that year at the Monkey House in Bryan/College Station, not a single thing sold for six months. [*BD Note: The Monkey House was a "Slan Shack," where various science fiction fans lived together. Sort of like a continuous small sf/f convention.*] So when I had the opportunity — I had a girlfriend — to move to Austin with my dog, I took it. And then once I got to Austin, everything I had sent out in the past six months started selling. Just overnight, almost. It was unbelievable. Nothing had changed but my address, right?

BRAD: "Chili from Yuggoth" lists some of the stories you wrote while you were at the Monkey House, and what jumped out at me was "Mary Margaret Road-Grader," which seems to me to be a watershed story for you. I don't know if you knew that at the time, so I guess that's the question I should ask. But it seems clear in retrospect that it was.

HOWARD: It probably was. The thing was, I was living in the Monkey House, but I had gone to a party in Austin. And I actually wrote "Mary Margaret Road-Grader" in Austin. Which should have given me a hint. And when I got back to College Station, I rewrote it and sent it out. But it didn't sell until I came back to Austin again.

BRAD: What I've written here is, "You were writing stories like 'Mary Margaret Road-Grader' that would begin to define who Howard Waldrop really was as a fiction writer." I don't know if you feel that's true or not, but just as a reader, I do.

HOWARD: Well, like I said, I was at the party in Austin, and everybody was sacked out the morning after. People had kind of paired off, but I was sleeping downstairs on the couch by myself. I got up to go make coffee, and dropped the needle on "Bridge Over Troubled Water" by Simon and Garfunkel. And between the time the intro started and Garfunkel started singing, the plot to "Mary Margaret Road-Grader" came to me. So I sat down to write it, and by the time everybody else got up in the afternoon, the first draft of the story was finished.

I've had that happen maybe three times in my fifty-two-year career, right?

THE DROOG IN THE GREEN FLANNEL BLANKET

... I am sitting in the N3F hospitality room. It is 11:30 p.m. on Thursday night before the Mid-America science fiction convention opens. I have been waiting since my arrival at three p.m. I am reading the May, 1952 issue of *Startling Stories* I bought that afternoon. I am waiting. Everybody I drove up with is asleep: Buddy Saunders, Bill Kostura, George and Lana Proctor. I wait for George R.R. Martin, and the hotel is asleep.

George R.R. Martin and I have been corresponding since 1963, when we were both in high school. We have never met. We are writers, and through our letters we've shared rejection slips, frustrations and all the kind words from people like Damon Knight, Robert Silverberg and Terry Carr which keep us writing. I have been in the Army the past eighteen months. George is doing alternative service as director of information for the Cook County Legal Aid Fund. He has suddenly sold nearly all the stories he has written in the last year. George is two years younger than I am. George is probably a better writer than I am. I am afraid of George R.R. Martin.

Suddenly, the elevator door swings open and this short person in a bush jacket wearing an SFWA button walks up to me.

We look at each other.

"George," I say.

"Well. Howard," he says.

We shake hands like twin brothers meeting in the womb. Meanwhile ...

Down at the banquet, one of the guests of honor, Philip José Farmer, is reading a short story he just wrote about King Kong to the banqueters feasting on plastic steak and rubber potatoes. The story is dynamite. Farmer has written such things as *Wind Whales of Ishmael*, *Time's Last Gift*, *The Fabulous Riverboat*, the Hugo-winning "Riders of the Purple Wage" in Harlan Ellison's *Dangerous Visions*, and the story, "The Lovers," in 1952, which dropped like a nuke and made sex something you could write about in the sf magazines. Meanwhile ...

... George R.R. Martin says, "And we send it off to Ben Bova and wait for the check."

"Dynamite story idea, George," I say. "Let's do it." So in the middle of the convention we hole up in the hotel room and write the first 5,000 words of this 12,000 word novelette I want to call "Journey into the Fungus" and George wants to call "The Men of Greywater Station." I don't like the title he wants, but then again, George has sold three stories in a row to *Analog*. Meanwhile ...

Back at the banquet, James Gunn, past president of the Science Fiction Writers of America, is reading the last chapter of his history of science fiction due out soon from Prentice-Hall. The chapter is entitled "The Future of Science Fiction" and says that when the five-year-old hassle over the New Wave and Old Wave elements of science fiction finally, really dies, there's going to be a synthesis that'll knock everybody cold. The speech is dynamite. Meanwhile ...

I run into David Anthony Kraft. David Anthony Kraft has just sold a couple of things to the sf magazines. I have sold a couple of things to the sf magazines. In my hand is a copy of the fanzine DJ #4. DJs 1, 2, and 3 were put out in 1969. DJ 4 has come out with three-year-old material apologies. Part of this material is a story about two mountain-gods who mate every century or so, by David A. Kraft. Part of the material is the fourth installment of my review column *Black Vista.* Fine, good. In the letters to the editor section, though, was a letter written by David A. Kraft. He asked, "Does DJ need nowhere people like Waldrop?" I read it, turned my Mid-America Con name tag around, wrote "Nowhere Person from DJ" on it, and turned to Buddy Saunders and George R.R. Martin and said, "Let's go."

"Where?" asked George.

"Where?" asked Buddy.

"To see David Anthony Kraft. I'm going to punch both his eyes shut," I said. We went.

On the way down, I said, "Maybe I'll punch one of his eyes out, show him the DJ, then punch the other shut so he'll know what it's for."

David A. Kraft is in the dealer's room, looking at old *Startling Stories.* He's got a copy of the DJ under his arm. He sees me. I see him.

"Oh, you've got your copy too?" he asks. Then he sees my name tag. Then he says, "I see you read the letter column ..."

I smile. I make a noise like the charging handle of an M-16 sliding back. "We were all three years younger, weren't we, David?" I ask.

And David starts telling me about the story. How he tried to get it back once he found it didn't look there'd been an issue of DJ after #3. Then we got to talking about lost stories we did years ago, and how if anyone ever prints them we are ruined.

It ended with David Kraft and I holding our arms around each other, with a copy of DJ between us. George Proctor captures the shot forever on film. David Kraft is a good guy. Meanwhile ...

I am wrapped in a green flannel blanket. Dracula grins at me and takes his teeth out. Airboy and Captain Midnight keep coming over to talk. Nyoka the Jungle Girl is posing, for photographers are everywhere. I have only one eye sticking out from under the blanket. I am sweating profusely. We are waiting for the masquerade contest to start. The first prize is an acrylic painting by Richard Corben of *Up from the Deep*, *Rowlf*, and *Slow Death Funnies* fame. I want to win that painting.

Underneath the blanket I am a Droog. White long underwear and black combat boots. Suspenders made from the headstraps of an M17A1 gas mask. Belt made of a .30 cal. ammo belt. Eyeballs on the sleeves of the underwear shirt made from ping-pong balls. A cane and derby hat are under the blanket. Around my waist is the world's most obscene codpiece made from a size 32 jock strap stuffed with about 2 pounds of shredded foam rubber. I am magnificent.

The contestants walk out one at a time, handing name cards to the announcer.

Ken Keller, who is putting on the convention, walks by, sees the blanket, says, "Waldrop, if you take that blanket off and there's nothing under there, I don't know what I'll do."

I wink the one eye he can see. "Why do you think they call me Flash Waldrop?" I ask. He moans and runs away.

It's my turn. I throw the blanket off. Lana Proctor hands me my name card. I put on the hat, put the cane across my shoulders. I walk out into the spotlight. There are oohs and ahhs before the light hits me. Most people know already. A lot don't because *Clockwork Orange* only opened the night before in Kansas City. Applause filters. Moans and groans begin as people take in the totality of the Droogfit, including the codpiece. I *am* Malcom McDowell and Alex Burgess. I swagger to the stage, give an unconcerned leap up three steps, throw my card to the announcer, and continue to march.

Dracula wins. He takes his teeth out and smiles at me. I want to practice a little of the old Ultraviolence on him. His costume is good, though. So I think of practicing a little Ultraviolence on the judges, Farmer, Gunn, and Russell Myers, the cartoonist.

Meanwhile ...

Mid-America Con was held in Kansas City, Missouri, June 16 through 18, 1972. The attendance wasn't as expected: Dealers complained because people weren't buying all that much, but the convention was something else again.

There were the Kansas University documentaries on science fiction; movies like *Seventh Voyage of Sinbad*, *Destination Moon*, *Forbidden Planet*, and *Rocketship XM*, most of which I had to miss. There was the Saturday night party in 1104 thrown by the Utleys which roared on and on and on. And on.

I came from Mid-AmericaCon with a greater feeling for science fiction, where it's going and what it's doing than I've ever had before. There were five new authors there whose first works appeared last year or will appear this year, 1972. They and I haven't even learned the trade yet. But you could feel and hear the enthusiasm there. Talk about talk and bullshit. Madness and seriousness. Childish things. Ways to gross everyone out. Constant reminders that science fiction is changing, is becoming totally different from its past. Meanwhile ...

Buddy Saunders is driving beneath an Oklahoma half-moon, back to Texas. I am talking in the last minutes of twilight about science fiction, about where it's going, about the convention, about George Martin, about Philip José Farmer, about James Gunn, about America.

"Carl van Vechten once said there couldn't be a Great American Novel, because there was nothing that could be called the American thing, the common experience, the basis of American epics," I said. "I don't think so. I think he was sort of wrong."

"How?" asked Buddy.

"I think science fiction, fantasy, that sort of thing, will someday find it. The American thing. The common experience."

I watched the rolling hills creep by in the dying light. For a few minutes.

"We're searching our past. Philip Farmer is. George Martin is looking at it. To see what can be said about it. Lots of sf writers are. Seeing what makes us go. Putting it down on paper. Selling it. Moving on to something else."

"Like Gunn said," said Buddy.

"Yeah. Like Gunn said. Once the old and new waves settle down, reach a midpoint, we'll be on our way. What comes out of that will knock everyone on his ass. Five years, Buddy. Sometime in the next five years some sf writer is gonna do it. Write what may be the American thing, the Great American Novel. Maybe Philip Farmer. Maybe Harlan Ellison. Who knows?"

"Who knows?" said Buddy.

Kansas City, I love you.

THE GREAT AMERICON NOVEL

This con report contains at least three Harlan Ellison stories.

D-Con 73 was held in the Sheraton Dallas Hotel June 28-July 1. A grand time was had by all.

Now that that's out of the way I want to tell you about D-Con 73. It began for the con committee in 1971. It got hairy two weeks before the con, what with running around, putting up posters, answering the phone, and screaming at each other.

Tuesday the 26th, Buddy Saunders and I went to the Amtrak station in Ft. Worth to pick up George R.R. Martin. George had been to Midwescon and then hopped the freight for Texas.

Going into the Amtrak station in Ft. Worth is like stepping into the past. I expected a troop train to pull in any minute, full of guys singing "Don't Sit Under the Apple Tree." No luck. A really smarmy place. Ft. Worth has three Amtrak trains a day (the same three). We arrived about ten minutes before George. We waited on the tracks with thirty others, watching truck drivers try to turn over piggyback loads in the Santa Fe docking area.

The train arrived with, I'll swear, a gush of steam. There were more people on it than we thought possible, and they were in a hurry to get away. We were running up and down the tracks trying to find George when he tapped us on the shoulder.

George was shorter than I remembered.

"Dynamite, George," I said, grabbing his (kit bags) suitcases away from him.

"You may have to bear with us," said Buddy. "We're gonna

have to do some running around before we get settled."

"Fine," said George. George is up for the Campbell Award this year ((This was written before Worldcon — he didn't make it — H.W.)) and he had just come back from Milford. He told us gossip, and told me Ted White did too think he had a couple of stories of mine I'd sent two years ago. So we passed the time cheerfully while Buddy a) delivered some posters b) got some material for the con c) dodged traffic.

We got back to Grand Prairie by four. George met my wife Linda and the baby, while Buddy and I packed up (our troubles) con materials into the car. Ray Files, the art show chairman, Steve and Darrel Schleef all dropped over and got in the way while we worked. Linda fixed dinner, we ate and jumped into Buddy's car. Files and the others would be over to the hotel tomorrow morning.

We get to Joe Bob Williams' house at six. We meet him roaring down the road with a borrowed pickup. "Go on to the house," says Joe Bob. "You can start loading the con stuff out into the yard if you want to."

So we go to Joe Bob's house. We get inside.

There are nineteen tons of boxes waiting to be loaded out into the front yard, and it's all supposed to go into the pickup. "No way," we say.

"Hey!" yells George, as we're carrying all these immense boxes out into the yard. "*Star-Studded* #17, the only one I don't have." He pulls one of the fanzines out, puts it under his arm.

When Joe Bob gets back fifteen minutes later, all the nineteen tons of stuff are in the front yard.

"No no no," says Joe Bob. "All that didn't have to go."

"Thanks a heap, Joe Bob," we say, "and the same to your mother."

So we load seven of the tons of stuff back into the house

While we're breaking our backs, Steve and Lana Utley pull up.

Hoots of derision greet his arrival.

"Hi, guys," says Steve. "Looks like you've got it just about loaded."

"Okay, wiseass," we say. "You get to ride on top of the pickup." By this time, the pickup looks like Pike's Peak with wheels under it. "Gah!" says Steve.

The caravan pulls out. But not to the con. Not yet. We gotta go to Paul Adair's house. Paul Adair is the film chairman. We're showing films in 3D at the con. Now, showing films in 3D means you gotta have two projectors, two heads, two stands, two motors, etc. We get to Adair's. We find that there is at least eleven tons of movie equipment there. Quick mental arithmetic tells us this ain't gonna fit the pickup. So what do we do?

Right.

We unload all the stuff we loaded on at Joe Bob's. Then we load on the film equipment while Joe Bob's wife Peggy and Lana Utley go back for another car. To load on the stuff we unloaded from loading on at Joe Bob's.

What follows is a scene from *Bill, The Galactic Hero.* As we enter the fuseroom, George is saying to Howard, as they lift a projector head:

"Yeah (OOOMPH) ask me to come to D-Con (Arrgggk) free booze, lotsa wimmen (Ooork) (arpfff) (oomph) rub elbows with pros (erk) and whatta I end up doing (ooooommmmphph) slavvy labor."

Lift that barge, George.

Slowly, slowly the stuff is loaded. We gotta take the stuff up these stairs, around a turn, out, down the porch steps, up onto the pickup. Not only does this equipment have sharp edges, it is oily. And the stairs have sharp edges. We are not without casualties.

Utley and Waldrop pick up a sharp thing which weighs hundreds of pounds:

Utley: look out for my (SHRIIEKK!!)

Waldrop: your what???

We get the stuff loaded. Projectors, films, sound systems. We look like seven soldiers from *Bataan.* Utley is bleeding with a cut running from eyebrow to elbow. We lie on the truck and porch, wheezing. Joe Bob finds the beer. He, Buddy, George, Steve, and I have eyes which look like poached oysters. It has Not Been Fun so far. And the con doesn't start for two days.

We get to the hotel, Steve riding the Mt. McKinley made of old movie cans. It takes approximately one hour and twenty-five minutes to take the stuff up the freight elevator, down the long hall, and out to the wonderful Prairie Room. I am not enthusiastic about the Prairie Room.

It will be my Home For The Night.

See, we've got $10,000 worth of goodies in that room: the movie stuff, funny books, Frazetta artwork, all the art show, and various and sundry oddments and miscellanies. Someone will have to sleep there for the night.

Me. I'm the only one who's a trained killer. I know seventeen ways to kill a man with a broom. If the man doesn't have a broom ...

So I'm elected. We get settled in about ten p.m. George comes down and we shoot the bull for an hour, while Joe Bob runs home to get still another load of goodies. George gives me his latest bunch of stories to read. The hotel has put a rollaway bed in the Prairie Room.

Joe Bob gets set for the night about twelve. I lie down on the bunk. There's the 105th class reunion of Raucous College or somesuch winding down in the next room. There are drunks stumbling down the halls, opening doors, looking for a place to barf. I relock the door, which people keep unlocking. I drift off about two ayem with the umpty-ninth chorus of Dixie ringing in my cars.

Bam Bam Bam. I jerk awake, looking at my watch. Three-thirty a.m.? I open the door, all my training ready to kill the international funny book thieves outside the door.

These two zombies stand there.

"Hey man. Tell us about D-Con," says one.

"Whozzat?" I ask.

"When's D-Con start?"

"To-mor-row. Six p.m. We'll be getting set up all day to-mor-row."

"Dynamite, man."

"Yeah. Real fine," I say. "Get out of my sight."

I lift my hands to the heavens. I tear out handfuls of hair. "Why me?" I shout. "Why me?"

Bam Bam Bam.

"I'll kill you all!" I scream.

Buddy unlocks the door and comes in. He had gone home the night before to paint his dinosaur. He has hurried back. It is 6:30 a.m.

"Jeez. Mumble," I say.

He guards the room while I go up to shave, shower, ka-ka, and shine. This I do in a quondam blur. "Hi, George!" I yell, shaking de Joisy Bum awake. "I'm up, nobody sleeps."

"Arrgh," says George. "What time is it?"

"Almost seven. Day's almost gone."

"Arrgh," says George. "What's going on?"

"Well, if you hurry, you can help us set up tables in the huckster's room."

"Lemme lone. I'll be up later. Snore zzzzz," says George.

"Dynamite, George," I say.

We eat breakfast. Yum yum yum. Buddy, Steve, Joe Bob and I. I might add here that I have ten dollars to last me through the con unless Ballantine comes through with a check on the novel. I am looking at the menu. I get coffee while others hog themselves on groceries. Up in the room, I have a whole cake, and I'm not letting on. Peasants.

"Dynamite coffee," I say.

Hustle hustle hustle to the dealer's room. We begin setting

up tables. There's the usual hassle. We wanted six-foot tables. The hotel gave us mixed sixes and eights. So we have to put three eights where we wanted to put four sixes. It calls for higher math, and none of us is up to it.

About ten thirty, who appear but Ken Keller and Floyd Johnson of Kansas City. About half the people in the room, including George who is up by this time, scream and go running for them.

Ken gets a look on his face Mussolini must have gotten in the plaza. He covers his head.

"Wow! Ken Keller and Floyd Johnson," we say. "Great!"

See, in 1972 the Kansas City people put on the best con I've ever attended. And so thought a lot of other people. Ken didn't know it, because nobody ever thanked them, and no con reports were written, and the con lost its shirt.

We clapped them on the backs and danced around, and Ken and Floyd threw in with setting up the tables. Lift that barge, Ken and Floyd.

After noon, what to our wondering eyes should appear but Tom Reamy, a surprise to everyone who didn't know he was back in Texas. We went the round of introductions between Ken, Floyd, and Tom. Then Tom threw in with setting up tables. Lift that barge, Tom.

People had started coming in that a.m. And didn't slow up. There was nothing for them to do but help us set up or check into their rooms. Dealers started gathering outside the dealer's room at noon, waiting for it to open.

Guests:

Harlan Ellison, Guest of Honor
Burne Hogarth, Artist
William M. Gaines, Comics
Jerry & Jean Bails, Fan Guests of Honor
andy offutt, Toastmaster

I thought I'd give you the guest lineup here, in case you're wondering. Also: David Gerrold, Kenneth Smith, Neal Barrett, Jr., Don Punchatz, and George Martin got free run of the place with no restrictions on them but those of good taste. Plus three dozen of us Texas nebbish pros.

Noon of the second day: We get our break at 3:00.

Joe Bob and Buddy come to George and I: Would we go pick up the Bails at the airport? Harlan is coming in about twenty minutes before them, but they're bringing tons of fun with them, and one car won't do it. Sure, dynamite, we say. We can help pick up Harlan, then go get the Bails.

George and I both started as comic fans, way back in 1962. We were never really strip writers: we wrote text superhero stories back when comic fanzines published text. So we'd always wanted to meet the Bails.

I took Buddy's car, then I took the wrong turn. It was rush hour, and Dallas streets were built in the fifties and can't handle 1973 traffic. It took two miles before I could turn around and get back. We got to the airport parking lot the same time as Joe Bob though we'd left forty-five minutes earlier. We hotfooted to the lobby. None of us set off the gong in the security line, so we made it about four minutes before Harlan arrived.

Meanwhile, George and I are turning cartwheels and giving off sparks: the Bails' flight was two hours behind schedule. We faced what is known as a long wait.

Joe Bob, Peggy, George, and I waited at the exit ramp. As soon as they opened the door we saw:

A poster with two legs, holding a film can and a typewriter, bouncing up the incline. We grabbed the poster, and sure enough Ellison was behind it.

He shook hands all round. The poster was from the *Starlost* series ((before the incredible hassles)), the film can contained *Demon with a Glass Hand*, and the typewriter was the legendary fourteen-year-old Oliver portable. George had to fight to get it away from him.

While we waited for the baggage, Harlan and George shot the shit about Milford (which they'd attended two weeks before) and Joe Bob ran around trying to find luggage. Harlan was cool, he waited until the baggage came off the truck, leaped the rope, and picked it up. Harlan complained because someone at the studio had ordered a kosher inflight meal for him on the airline.

Harlan spotted a magazine rack and went to buy the new *Hulk*. We trooped to the car and waved goodbye to them.

We decided to eat while waiting for the Bails, so found ourselves in the gourmet airport snackbar, munching on potato chips and burgers. We drifted up, talking about magazines in the racks. The Bails' flight came in two hours late, at 7:20.

Jerry and Jean Bails are these very nice people, much younger than you would expect. Like, in the early sixties when Jerry published *Alter Ego*, people thought he was already an octogenarian. No dice. He shook hands and we were mildly surprised that they knew of us, though neither of us had worked in comics fandom for years.

Getting them back to the hotel: I meet Dave Gerrold.

This very tall dude who looks a lot like David Gerrold's photo comes up to me. He has this portable tape recorder in his hand, and the earphone sticking in his ear.

What will be the first words he says to me? Will he see my name badge and know me? Will we become fast friends? I tremble.

His mouth moves. He speaks.

"How do you get to the Belman Theatre?" he asks.

I mumble directions, he nods and leaves.

We get the Bails settled in about nine, then Steve and I and George go up to the room for some drinking. We may have collected some others along the way.

THURSDAY: A Day Like Other Days

We were up early (we were always up early) and headed down to chow. Nothing was shaking. We rummaged through the dealer's room, which was nothing but people already. I picked up a couple of *Imaginations* from Joanne Burger, and was sore tempted to buy *Startling*s and *Thrilling Wonder Stories*. But my ten $s had gone down to four already, what with meals, etc. (The cake was gone now.)

11:30. Official greetings. Everyone present was introduced, being Harlan, the Bails, and I think, Kenneth Smith. Joe Bob announced when Gaines and Hogarth would arrive. He looked around for more people to introduce. Utley and I started pointing in Gerrold's direction.

George is sitting with Gerrold.

"Don't worry," said Joe Bob. "I'll introduce him."

"Ladeez an gennulmen," he continued, "one of our best new writers, George R.R. Martin!"

Steve and I fell over the backs of our chairs. This was to be the first in a series of slights (unintentional) towards Gerrold. He took them all with Rare Good Graces.

Following was the auction with Harlan auctioneering. In his inimitable style. Which means we were royally entertained. As soon as the auction was over, I heard the first of many gripes.

"Goddam," said a dealer. "We came here to sell stuff, not make jokes."

Another said, "Who does he think he is?"

It was not a Good Portent of Things to come.

Arriving that morning were the Houston-Austin-Aggie bunch, including Joe Pumilia, Bill Wallace, Dianne Kraft, and Lisa Tuttle. Lisa was, like George, up for the Campbell Award. I was not present at the meeting between them, but eyewitnesses tell me there wasn't much enmity. In fact, George and Lisa hit it off like highschool sweethearts.

Comes my time to run the registration desk. Segue to:

D-Con Horror Story #1

I am running the desk. I am also paging people on the PA, trying to keep track of the con officials; the usual hassle.

Up comes (we shall call him Top of the Heap, though the real title he uses involves nobility and comic books) who tells me that he's one of the guests of the con, and that he's the man who sold Michael Mehdy the $1801.26 *Action* No. 1, and that he'd been invited to the HoustonCon the week before but couldn't make it and now he's a guest here.

I know who's supposed to be here and who's not as well as he does. I give him a glassy stare and call Joe Bob. Joe Bob talks to him, and Joe Bob has a lot on his mind. "Go ahead and give him a ticket," he says.

I fill out Top of the Heap's membership badge. Top of the Heap keeps telling me he's Top of the Heap and how he sold the $1801.26 *Action* No. 1. Yeah, yeah, I say, have a good time at the con. He asks, "Aren't you going to give me a guest ribbon? I'm a guest of the con, you know." He reaches for some of the badges which have been made up for Hogarth or offutt, planning, I suppose, to take the "guest" ribbon off. "Keep your hands off those ribbons," says Lana Utley, who is in charge of the desk. Top of the Heap walks away, miffed.

So I get called away for some nitty thing or other, and when I get back, here's Top of the Heap with these two dynamite-looking wimmen.

Top of the Heap is saying, "Miss Smith here is with me. I'd like to get her in free, and if you could, see to it that she gets a free room at the hotel."

He's got his hands in the "guest" ribbons again, and pulls out the one for Kenneth Smith's wife. "See," he says, waving the badge which says "Smith," "here's her badge." He hands it to her. I'm hearing all this out of the side of my ear as I've got a list of ten people to page, the phone is ringing, etc. It ends up that the girl gets the badge and Top of the Heap escorts her off towards the hotel desk.

I'm trying to find out what happened when the girl comes back.

"Look, I'm sorry," she says. "I'm Marc Rains' sister, and I've never seen that guy in my life. He met me at the door, says 'I'm a guest here,' and drug me to the registration desk." She is slightly embarrassed. "I'm used to this," she says, "and I'm sorry you had this trouble."

Marc Rains is probably the best friend the con ever had. He ran a bookstore in Ft. Worth, put up posters, got us phone calls, helped with everything. He's told his sister and sister-in-law how good sf people are, and now they've come to the con and the first thing they meet is Top of the Heap.

"Joe Bob!" I scream. I apologize to Marc's sister for all the trouble. Top of the Heap is hovering around in the corner, like a hyena waiting for a lion to leave its kill. You know the kind.

Marc's sister leaves, Top of the Heap following. He walks past, rebuffed, in a few seconds, no doubt looking for new targets.

Joe Bob comes up. I tell him the whole story. "Joe Bob," I say, "you better talk to him or I'm going over and punching him out. I mean it."

"Calm down, Howard," says Joe Bob. "He's been here two hours, and I've already had to talk to him twice. First he tried to get the hotel to give him a free room and gave them my name. They took his word for it until they could check with me. When they found out he wasn't, they told him no freebies.

"When Channel Four interviewed Harlan, he walks right into the camera and says, 'Hi. You're the press, aren't you? I'm the Top of the Heap. I sold the *Action* No. 1 ...'"

"Why didn't Harlan kill him?" I asked.

"He didn't. He was very nice," said Joe Bob. "Some of Heap's friends came to apologize, say he's not really like that. But I'm going to tell him if there's one more complaint about him, he's going out on his ass."

Joe Bob went off to have a heart-to-Heap talk, and it worked a little. He didn't give us too much trouble for the rest of the con.

Top of the Heap: I ever meet you at another con, you better be nice.

(end of first D-Con Horror Story)

Thursday afternoon finds our heroes at the Amateur Film Festival, wherein a thing called *Pipes of Pan* blows our minds. An animated three-minute short, and it is good. Plus several other films, some very well done and entertaining, some well done and not entertaining, and some neither. Reamy was one of the judges.

We ate. Eating at con consists of finding the three or four people you want to eat with, then waiting while they find all the people they wanted to eat with, *ad infinitum*. When you leave, there are fifty-seven people with you, most of whom you don't know. We tried to find a place in downtown Dallas that wasn't a) expensive b) closed at six p.m. The only place I knew was the Eatwell Café, and it was twenty blocks the other way. So we spent an aimless thirty minutes going from one closed place to another. We consisted of George, Tom, Steve & Lana, Lisa Tuttle, Ken Keller, and me. We had No Luck.

I forgot how we drifted back to the hotel, but I remember eating at the Majestic Steak House. Steve and I went down to the film room to see the last thirty minutes of *Catwomen of the Moon*. Steve and I, battle-hardened veterans of *Robot Monster*, *Plan 9 from Outer Space*, *The Leech Woman*, *Invasion of the Star Creatures*, and *Zontar, Thing from Venus*, couldn't take it. Even with the 3-D effects. We left.

Sometime during the day I met Judith Weiss, world's smallest artist. She is three feet tall and beautiful. She draws like a maniac. She would have to stand on tiptoe to kiss Billy Barty in the knee. She used to live in Dallas and now lives in Philadelphia (on the whole.)

Anyway, she was doing these sketches, and I looked at them and said, "Dynamite." George knew her from Discons and Pghlanges and whatever, and before long we were blood (brothers) persons.

Everybody was waiting for the Con Bheer Party at ten. We waited and the longer we waited, the more people stood in the lobby, around the dealer's room and film room. Ah, tension was in the air.

The electricity fairly crackled. I was talking with Jodie and andy offutt, along with about forty other people. This was the first time I'd really looked at the wimmen at the convention. I had never seen so many wimmen hanging out of their dresses at (two times) one time. My goodness gracious.

At eight, I went to check the mail/messages at the desk. There was a note from Linda for George to call her. George and I went up to the room. I called home, put George on.

The father of George's girlfriend had died. George was on the phone when I left to go up to the party. Tom and I arrived at the same time at the film room before the party began upstairs.

The starting gun had sounded, and the lobby was deserted. I stopped out of the film room where Victor Mature was getting shot in 3-D. I floated up to the London Room on the second floor. The London Room is built like a pub. At one end was approximately four hundred people. At the other was 200 gallons of bheer. The two met, like the Blob ingesting the farmer's arm.

What a party. (Chairs were flying around like rockets. Furniture was coming in the door and going out the windows. It quieted down, then someone hit Jones with a bottle and it started all over again.)

There was an immense amount of people in the room. Harlan was ever-present. andy offutt was over in the corner. Jodie was with Jerry Mayes, Barbara was with offutt. The Proctors came in. Keller was talking with Lisa Tuttle, Gerrold was wandering around with the Texas A&M fans.

I went over to andy, who was with this mature gentleman I'd never seen before. I looked at his nametag.

"andy," I said, "introduce me to Neal Barrett, Jr."

Sure as hell, he did. We were talking, andy was telling jokes. Finally, Neal said, "I only know one joke. I might as well tell it now."

"Sure," said andy.

And Neal did.

The Neal Barrett, Jr. Joke

Neal: (Holding up his fingers in a V) You know what this is?
andy: What?
Neal: A Roman centurion ordering five beers.

The joke swept the room. I heard it four more times that night.

The party went on, but did not wear. Nobody got drunk, but nobody felt pain, either. It was a ghood party. The beer ran out in about forty-five minutes. Floyd Johnson was everywhere, taking photos. There was no lack of conviviality.

Then came the parties. I do not know here if I am confusing Thursday and Saturday nights, but I think this party was in Bob Stahl's room. Whatever, it roared on. Then about two, we went back to the room. Buddy was there, asleep like a ton of bricks. Buddy has to get his kibby-bye. Remember this. This will be very important.

Judith Weiss was with us, looking for a place to crash. Dynamite, Judith, said George and I, you take the couch, Judy. I had been planning to sleep on the floor near the couch (heeheehee). George was going to bed, Judith may have already been asleep, when the Door Bammed.

Then I remembered Buddy was letting Steve Morrell use the floor. He lay down. That left Howard with two choices: a) bathtub b) film room.

When we put this con together, one of the things we said was NO SLEEPING IN THE FILM ROOM.

This is about like Cnut telling the ocean to stop rolling.

Since other people were going to do it, I would too.

Now is time for:

D-Con Horror Story #2

It is now 3:50 a.m. I have been up twenty-one hours, and I had that incredible hassle on the desk, and I'm not Feeling My Best.

I am halfway down the hall to the movie room when I hear what I take to be Alarums & Excursions from that direction. The doors burst open, and out comes Mr. Spleen.

(I might add here that Mr. Spleen later apologized, in a half-hearted way, for his behavior, so I shan't go too hard on him in this account. Mr. Spleen is not his real name, either.)

Roar. "Where's some goddam con people." Roar. "Look, you!" he says, seeing my committee ribbon, "I've helped Sueling run the New York Con and I can get all the free space in *Rocket's Blast* I want and I'll make this con smell like shit."

You must remember it is four a.m. I am tired. I have not got my second wind. My eyes are burning. I am not, as I have said, Feeling My Best.

"What seems to be the trouble?" I ask, politely as possible.

Roar. "Goddam, all you people would have to do would be to announce that you weren't going to show a film. I've stayed up all night, there are fifty other people in there who've stayed up all night to see *Planet Outlaws*, and we're mad."

"Well, as you can see," I say, holding up my ribbon which says POSTER ADVERTISING, "I'm not in charge of the movie room. If ..."

"Where's Williams? I'm sure he's not losing any sleep."

"I'm sure Joe Bob is asleep," I say. "What happened?"

"They're showing *Dr. Phibes*," he says. Roar. "I've helped Sueling run the New York Con, and any time there's a change, we always announce it." Roar.

Before I can answer, he uses The Killer Line. I have heard it before; if I stay in fandom, I'll no doubt hear it again. It goes like this:

"You may not know who I am now, but you will after I get through with this con."

This leaves me Not Impressed.

He tries another. "I've been a newspaper reporter for ten years ..."

"Haven't we all?" I ask. And smile.

He tries another. I wave him off. "If there's an explanation for this, I'm sure our film chairman Paul Adair can straighten it. He left about two, because he has to be at work at six. I'm sure there's some explanation, because if the film wasn't here, we'd have announced it."

Roar.

"Well, there's that, too," I said. "I will bring the film chairman to you, and we'll get to the bottom of this."

Roar. Then: "I can make this con look really bad if he doesn't come up with good excuse ..."

"He won't come up with an excuse," I say. I am now getting p.o.'d. "He'll tell you what happened. He'll be in at nine-thirty. I'll bring him to you."

"Well, I won't be up till noon."

"Alright," I say. "I'll bring him to you at noon. Goodnight."

(end of D-Con Horror Story #2)

Friday. Dynamite Day.

George gets up with the rest of us. (I have slept in the bathroom for two-and-a-half hours.) His girlfriend has not asked him to come to Indiana, but George is very, very down. Okay, I say, let's go eat up all the food.

Halfway downstairs we remember Harlan is supposed to be on tv that morning. We go back up to the room and watch the last forty minutes of the morning show. No Harlan. Hmmmm.

When we get to the café, there sit Harlan, Joe Bob and Peggy, Lisa Tuttle, and Leslie Swigart. Leslie had put together *The Harlan Ellison Bibliography*, which lists everything, and I mean everything, Harlan has written up until June 17, 1973. Joe Bob has been putting Harlan off, telling him the bibliography won't be ready til Saturday morning. When Harlan went to answer the phone, Joe Bob slipped a copy under his casaba melon. Harlan is doing back flips all over the breakfast table. "Wow," he's saying, "this is really great. Leslie, you're fantastic. Joe Bob, I love you. Etc."

"Well," says George as we sit down, "you'll have to quit writing, Harlan, so it'll be complete."

Harlan shrieks.

Next, we go to the Huckster's Room for:

D-Con Horror Story #3

This one's Harlan's.

He bought a *Buck Rogers* Big Little Book from a guy running this table. Harlan wanted one to see what they were like. He didn't know what they were worth. The guy at the table said, "$8.00."

Harlan bought the book.

In five minutes there are Alarums & Excursions in the direction of the guy who'd sold him the BLB.

Seems the guy who sold him the book was hired by the dealer to run the table, and had sold the BLB for $10 less than the dealer was asking.

The dealer comes to Harlan, demanding ten more dollars.

Harlan politely says No. The dealer goes back and shakes down the guy he'd hired to run the table. The guy who'd been hired to run the table comes over and asks Harlan real nice for the ten bucks.

Harlan says, "Don't look now, but you're being used."

The guy goes back. Harlan walks over and tells the dealer, "Look, don't get mad at him. He was selling stuff like you told him. Didn't you give him a price list or anything?"

The dealer sulks. Harlan turns to leave.

The word "prick" floats on the air.

Harlan turns and leans Way Down into the dealer's face.

"Don't ever say that where I can hear it," he says. And leaves.

Alarums & Excursions continue to float through the dealer's room for some minutes. The dealer's room is in a nasty mood.

(end of D-Con Horror Story #3)

I call home at ten a.m. Either I've been calling home, or Linda has been calling the hotel to tell me if anything came in the mail, each day.

Ballantine has come through. The money on the contract for the novel Buddy and I are writing came through. Eureka.

We tell George and hurry home to grab the loot.

We get back in time for the auction, which is much better, and get to eat, but miss Harlan's reading of "Cold Friend." We return at the time *Gone Fishin'*, a film lifted from an EC comics story, is shown. Gaines has arrived and entertains the fans.

I have in the meantime taken Mr. Spleen to meet Adair.

We hunk around the dealer's room until it is time to eat again.

We play the "let's go out to eat" game, wherein you waitnwait for everybody to get everybody else. We start at 4:50. We leave the hotel at 6:10.

The party consists of Harlan, Lynda, Tom Reamy, George, Joe Bob and Peggy, Joe Pumilia, Lisa Tuttle, Bill Wallace and Dianne Kraft, Bob Stahl and girlfriend (forgive an old man's memory), Judith Weiss, Bill Kostura, me, and two others. I know there were seventeen in all.

We get to this place called The Rib.

"Let me tell you how we serve," says the maître d'. "5.75, all you can eat."

"Dutch treat," yells Harlan.

"Oh, boy, food!" yells someone else.

We sit down. The waiter comes with all these goodies as we push three tables together. The place has what might be called a Subdued Atmosphere.

"You don't mind if we get little rowdy?" asks Harlan.

We are the only people in the place, though others will come in before we're through.

We order our drinks and Harlan regales us with stories of Clowntown. George orders a beer. They bring him about a gallon and a half in a schooner. George looks at it.

"Welcome to Texas, George," says Stahl.

"Hey," says Harlan. "Can I have one of those full of tea?"

They bring Harlan a schooner full of tea.

We eataneataneat. And there's still food piled up on the table.

"Want some more?" asks the waiter.

"How about coffee?" asks Harlan.

Which leads us to:

Putting Down Harlan #1

Harlan: Does coffee come free with this meal?

Waiter: No, sir.

Harlan: We give you $80 worth of business, and we gotta pay for coffee?

Waiter: Yessir. (smiling) And we especially charge extra for those giant-size glasses of tea.

Harlan suddenly realizes he's being put on. The waiter brings coffee. Ellison puts too much sugar in it. "Bleh!!" he says.

He passes it to Lynda. Who passes it to Joe Bob. Everybody takes a hit off it. Visions of Manson run through my head.

Pumilia gets it.

He makes the sign of the cross: "This is the blood and body of Ellison ... " he says.

It gets to me.

"I never drink ... *coffee*," I say.

We leave the place in good high spirits. Ready to hear Harlan read a story at seven-thirty.

George goes up to the room, calls his girlfriend. He comes back. "I think I'm going to have to go up there, Howard," he says. It seems some Indiana official has used his girlfriend's father's death as an example of not wearing seat belts, and is shooting his mouth off all over the state about it. George is extremely upset, phones around, gets reservations on a flight out at eight the next morning. Utley makes arrangements to take him. We go to hear Harlan.

Harlan comes to the podium. I turn the dimmers down until we've got this fine pale glow behind him, with his face lit by the rostrum light.

This leads us to:

Putting Down Harlan # 2

Harlan: I'm going to read this story called "Cat Man," it's sort of long, about 15,000 words. The one I read this afternoon was only 7,000. How long did it take me to read that?

Girl in audience: Two years.

It was so well done there was no possible comeback. But it immediately gave someone else the idea to test his mettle.

Harlan Puts Down #1

Harlan: You all want to be here to hear this story, right?

Long-hair in audience: There's nothing else to do.

Harlan: You could get a haircut.

Long-hair in audience: But ...

Harlan: Or you could try unsuccessfully several times to wash your feet.

No more potshots were forthcoming. Harlan read "Cat Man," which is an interesting story, containing several things even Harlan hadn't tried before.

After that was over, it was time for the con edition of the Turkey City Neo-Pro writer's conference, up in this room without air conditioning. We tried, people, to talk shop and stuff, but we all died (at Breakaway Station) after thirty minutes. We gave Harlan a plaque for teaching us how to write good.

Party-Party

Here's how it started: We went to the parties, first at Bails' room, then down the hall somewhere (to Stahl's?). There were soon entirely too many people to fit, so Reamy, George, Ken Keller, Steve and I went to the room to read some stories.

We asked the Proctors to come down.

We were reading when a couple more people looking for somebody else drifted in. When they left, someone else came.

I suddenly noticed the room was very close. There were more

people in it than had been in Stahl's room upstairs. And they kept coming.

I looked about me. There were: Gerrold, the offutts, Joe Bob and Peggy, Barbara and Jerry Mayes, the Proctors, Lana Utley, Lisa Tuttle, Judith Weiss, Bob Stahl and girlfriend, Bill Wallace and Dianne Kraft, Don and Barbara Punchatz, Mike Presley and girl, the Aggie bunch, Pumilia, Tom, Ken, and George, several people I knew by nod, and twelve to fourteen total strangers.

Tom and Ken Keller gave up early (this is one a.m. we're talking about) and went down to Tom's room. George and Lisa somehow ended up in sole possession of one bed, and were talking shop. Judith turned her head to the conversation awhile, looked at me, and said, "Heavy stuff," and started sketching things. Some girl, whom I do not know, was lying on my back. "You have a soft back," she said. I nodded. Close personal contact was giving me terrible thoughts, what with half the wimmen in the room hanging out of their bodices. So I moved around. I ended up in the narrow hallway, or foyer, crunched between Mike Presley on one side, an unnamed person on the other. Jodie Offutt was in much the same position across from me.

So Jodie and I talked for an hour. We had this marvellous time.

When the offutts left, I went back to my niche crushed between the bed and the nightstand.

At two-thirty Buddy arrived, ready for beddy-poo, and found a roaring party in progress. I waved, shrugged, and thumbed my nose at him. It was the Wrong Thing to do. He left.

I learned later that he spent the night in the lovely Prairie Room, and was wroth.

At four-thirty, with twenty people left in the room, the Hotel Detective came to the door.

Which someone had left open, meaning all the noise was going out into the hall. I apologized.

"Okay, folk. Keep it down. We get loud again and the party's over."

In ten minutes there were nine people still sitting in the middle of the floor. None of whom I knew.

They got the hint after I gathered up all the beer cans and put them in the trash.

Everyone was gone by five a.m. George climbed on top of his bed. Judith crawled to the couch. I lay on Buddy's bed and placed a call for wake-up at seven a.m. Judith and I carried on a conversation across the room.

George whimpered.

We went to sleep.

Saturday: Partings and Wowsa Boom

We did get up at seven. Utley crawled down to get his car while George packed.

We drove to the airport. I felt like a side of beef.

George R.R. Martin is one of the finest people I know. He had planned to spend the week with us, working on a collaboration, reading all the mss we had around. He wanted to fly up to Indiana for the funeral and then fly back, but we told him No. We were all feeling very crummy, and this farewell business didn't help. George had not really had much of a chance to do anything, helping with the con as he did. I promised to make it to Torcon. ((Lies! I didn't!))

Steve and I got him on the plane at eight, then went back to the gourmet airport café to eat up hash browns and eggs.

We returned to the con to see Gerrold's *Star Trek* show and wait for the panel with Gaines, Hogarth, offutt, and Ellison to start. It was an interesting panel, and Harlan was slightly upset at the turnout, not because of its lack of enthusiasm, but because of the low number.

"Look," he said to the audience, "here are two of the finest men the comics field has produced, Bill Gaines and Burne Hogarth, and all those people down there want to do is buy funny books."

He was talking about the dealer's room, which was full. The panel was very, very good: You learn that Hogarth has done some fantastic research for his strips, that Gaines is really *funny*, that offutt was a closet *Phantom Lady* freak, and more. The people down there didn't know what they missed.

Steve and I slipped out to get a pile of the Ellison bibliographies to hawk after the panel. Ellison saw us, said, "If it works, do it." Leslie Swigart, the bibliographer (probably the best-looking bibliographer in the world), said, "I don't want to watch," and left.

"Read all about it!" said Utley. "Lindy makes it."

"Oyez, oyez. Find de real troot about Harln Elson. See all de photos right here." Me.

"Martian tripods invade Noo Joisy," said Utley.

"Open beavers inside," I yell.

We look at each other, said "Cigars!" and ran to the smoke store, bought the most evil-looking ones they had. We came back to the lobby, did the Groucho-Harpo mirror bit to draw a crowd, then hawked some more.

In two hours, we sold three.

I was to go home to pick up Linda and leave Teri Ann with granma. Linda called at eleven. Her father had broken his leg stepping off the porch to turn on a water hose. She had to go take care of everybody.

Murphy's Law was quickly taking over the con.

Tom and I went to the auction. Al Jackson had shown up in this dynamite pair of shorts. He drew appreciative glances everywhere he went. The auction was one of those kind where all the excitement generated was somebody else's.

Just after the auction I got my second wind. There's this feeling which comes near the end of cons: You know the feeling if you've been there. You're familiar with all the rooms, you've met most of the people, you've moved into this different pace of life the con embodies. You're totally divorced from affairs outside the convention; sort of a breakaway phenomenon, and you get the feeling that if you were to go into the sunlight, your skin would blacken and fall off. It's a good sensation, one of those pleasant emotions you experience on the edge of sleeplessness.

I'd reached that point; most of the people around me seemed to perk up. Subjective feeling, no doubt.

Al Jackson and Bob Vardeman were sitting in the lobby on this coffee table. They remained there for hours, talking, moving their hands like oil-encased birds trying to fly. I never did learn what they were discussing.

D-Con Horror Story #4

This one is Joe Bob's.

At one p.m. a contingent of eight of the biggest dealers in comics fandom came to him. Not with a question, or suggestion, but with a demand.

Since the first progress report in January, we'd said "The dealer's room will be open at eight each morning and close when the dealers decide to close, but never earlier than midnight." Except: "The dealer's room will close during the masquerade ball and the banquet. From three to four-thirty and six to nine p.m."

We've been saying that for six months. It's in the program booklet and the daily schedule.

These dealers come on with the same line as Mr. Spleen:

If you don't keep the dealer's room open all this afternoon and tonight, we're going to pack up our stuff and go home. And we're going to tell everyone we know how shitty you are.

Joe Bob says alright.

He then tells the guests about the decision. His reasoning is sound. The banquet tickets have been sold, anyone who wants to sell funny books won't be there anyway, and we've got enough hardcore people already there. Okay, this is fine.

It's just that these money-hungry dudes have put Joe Bob on the spot making him refute a decision we'd reached months before, and now they'll tell all the other money-hungry dudes that you can pressure Joe Bob Williams and he'll fall apart like an old wheat-paste map.

This isn't, mind you, a condemnation of all the dealers: There were some very fine people with tables there who didn't know about the hassle 'til it was over.

It's these seven or eight dudes giving dealers a bad name.

I hope you sold lots of funnies, gang. I know you could use the money.

(end of D-Con Horror Story #4)

The masquerade turnout was one of the smallest I've seen for a con this size (1100, by the way) with only about seven costumes showing.

Comes time for the banquet: Judith and I return to the room.

I climb into the wonderful Sky Blue Suit.

Navy pants, pale blue shirt, powder blue coat, blue socks, brown shoes [?], blue polka-dot tie to match the blue polka-dot lining of the coat. Dynamite outfit. Linda made it for me.

Judith gasps. She is in a pantsuit outfit, with bell and collar. We go down the elevator. I Present My Elbow to her. She takes it. We walk through the mezzanine. I imagine Elgar's "Pomp and Circumstance" playing in the background.

Ooohs and ahhhs greet our arrival. Everybody likes the suit. offutt presents a toast to it.

The banquet is superb, buffet style, everyone is seated within thirty minutes and chows down.

We have presentations of plaques, awarding of awards for the masquerade and amateur film festival. The offutt toastmasters.

Toastmastering consists of reading a series of letters between Utley and offutt about Harlan.

"Would you like to toastmaster and introduce Ellison?" asks Steve's letter.

"Sure," says offutt's. "Who's Ellison?"

Utley's: "Harlan Ellison is fifteen years old. He had his first story, called 'Glowworm,' published in *Infinity* in 1956. But he's modest and doesn't talk about that much."

At this point, Utley is praying.

"He has written for tv shows such as *Flying Nun* and *Ralph, King of the Wild Grunion.* He scripted the movie *The Oscar.*"

A cracker sails by the tip of Utley's nose, followed by a napkin. Harlan is shaking his fist.

Steve continues to implore the heavens for surcease.

"But Ellison rejected my first story in three years, and since then I've sold seven, so what does he know?"

Then offutt introduces Ellison to thunderous applause.

Ellison tells us how come he's guest of honor here:

"I was asleep in bed one night around three ayem. The phone rings.

" 'Harln, bwah, how're ya, Harln?'

" 'Hi.'

" 'Harln, bwah, thiz Joebob, Joebob Willyims, in Daylass.'

"'Joe Bob, ain't nobody else talks like you. What can I do for you?'

" 'Harln, bwah, aeenm mnbmbk malka mmbmnbn mnbmbn?'

" 'Why, sure, Joe Bob.'

"Then there was dead silence on the phone for about a minute.

" 'YEW WILL???'

" 'Uh, yeah, Joe Bob.'

" 'I'm a-gonna write you, Harln bwah. I'm a-gonna confirm that, bwah. Thank you, Harln, bwah.' Click. Bzzzzzzz.

"So I go back to sleep. About six in the morning, I sit straight up in bed, screaming 'What have I done????' and here I am."

Harlan told us how he'd worked for the Disney Studios — for four hours; about the tv shows, about the series he's working on, about things in general. Bill Gaines was rolling under the table before Harlan finished.

Harlan got a standing ovation, then happened to spy a program booklet on the table. He then told us about the relative virtues of James Warren as a publisher. Warren had sent an ad for the back of the program booklet. It read: Best wishes to Bill Gaines ... Burne Hogarth ... Jerry Bails.

We gave him another standing ovation and left for the parties.

D-Con Horror Story #5

Mine. All mine.

We're at a party, and I'm feeling better than I have in the whole con. I have been up forty-one hours, minus the one-and-a-half hours sleep this morning before taking George to the airport. The party, in Stahl's room, is shaping up nicely. Pumilia is plying me with questions about the story we were once going to do concerning the Devil's Triangle off Bermuda.

So he convinces me to go get the typewriter, and we'll write up some notes. I do, and we're sitting there writing when Harlan comes in, looks over my shoulder, then sits down.

Brffft brifft brfft bfrtrftf ding zgitch* Brrifgt Brrifftf brrfift brrbfrft ding zgitch* he writes.

"Now finish that," he says, and leaves.

I look at it. Obviously New Wave Garbage, but I'll do it anyway. All these people stand around while I pound off a couple of pages and take them in search of Harlan. He's nowhere to be found.

I find him about an hour later, "You wanna read this?" I ask.

"No."

I hand it to him anyway.

He reads it.

"Pathetic," he says.

(end of D-Con Horror Story #5)

I go back to the party. Pumilia says, let's go down to the room and work on this story.

It's the first thing I've ever plotted in my sleep.

I'm lying on the bed. Joe is typing.

"What comes next?" he asks.

"Archimedes' submarine surfaces, and the Roman fleet is gone," I say. "They're in the Triangle."

type-type type type

"Then what?"

"Then the PBM lands nearby, and the submarine hooks up with them."

typety-type-type type type type

Between each of the sentences, I am asleep. No joke.

I finally whimper. Joe looks at me. "What's wrong?"

"Joe, I'm asleep. I can't even think. I gotta go to sleep."

"Well, okay," says Joe. "We got three pages of outline here already; that's enough."

Three pages? I don't even remember three sentences.

"Joe. *whimper* I gotta get to sleep."

"Okay."

I am asleep before he leaves.

SUNDAY: Be There!

Sunday, like all other con Sundays, goes by in a hurry of baggaging to beat check-out time. We haul stuff to the dealer's room. When George left, he left a jacket (fits, too), tennis shoes, and sox. The day goes by in a blitz of goodbyes. All the new people I've met, all the old friends drop around. Some only think they're leaving. Someone starts a graffiti table, which quickly becomes three, then obscene. It looks like a good bridge abutment before they're through.

A con dies about like a tyrannosaurus, I imagine. The extremities first, then the hardcore fans, *then* the hardcore con-goers. Reamy said he's seen people in hotels two days after cons have ended, walking around like zombies.

It is almost dead by four, closing time.

We tear down movie screens, load the film stuff up, unload it at Adair's. Buddy and I go home, full of the con. Tom will be waiting at my house, where we'll rehash the convention far into the night.

As we arrive home, it is the time of day the Martian fighting machines first attacked from the sand pit.

CTHU'LABLANCA AND OTHER LOST SCREENPLAYS

Mortimer Morbius Moamrath has been most closely associated with the *Depraved Tales* school of weird fiction from the twenties and thirties, and best-known for his inept Lovecraft imitations which graced the pages of a variety of pulp magazines.

It is little known that Moamrath, for a period of six months late in life, turned to screenplay writing and lived in Hollywood, hoping to find his fortune in that medium. It is fitting that this information should come to light for the first time for MidAmeriCon, which has one of the most distinguished film lineups ever attempted by a convention committee.

The only mention Moamrath biographers make of his interest in film is in reference to his one-sided romance with Marsha Moormist during the mid-thirties. Pumilia and Wallace state that, "He sometimes sent her notes under various assumed names, even enclosing photos of movie stars." ("M.M. Moamrath: Notes Toward a Biography," *Nickelodeon* #1, 1975). The photos sent her include those of Andy Devine, "Gabby" Hayes, and Maria Ouspenskaya.

Research and interviews with residents of both Archaic, Mass. (Moamrath's birthplace) and Hatcheck, Conn. (where he composed most of the Moamrath "mythos" tales) turned up the story of the writer's involvement with the film world, and of his western odyssey which matches those of Faulkner, Fitzgerald and Nathanael West, names unknown to most science fiction fans.

1. Puzzlement at First Sight.

Moamrath, contrary to what others would have us believe, was not totally ignorant of the world around him. Though not toilet trained until the age of seven, he soon after developed an insatiable curiosity about his environment, devouring newspapers (for which his mother severely scolded him), reading books, maps and making drawings of things he didn't understand. Those which remain in his earliest notebooks are bizarre, to say the least. (The drawing, scribbled in crayon, entitled "Where I think Babies Come From" shows a piece of cheese, a pair of nylon stockings, a toothbrush, what looks like a large butterfly, and three dishes of the type in which banana splits were once served at Walgreen's drugstores. Arrows connect them in series; unfortunately the young Moamrath did not indicate his starting point.)

Film, however, does not seem to have attracted the future writer at all. We know conclusively that Moamrath saw his first motion picture on June 3, 1935 at the age of thirty-nine. His notebook indicates that he had intended to go into Hilton's Funeral Parlor to see some interesting fungi purportedly growing in the basement. By mistake he entered the theatre next door; seeing people sitting in darkness, he thought a funeral to be in progress, became entranced and stayed through three showings of the film. Its name, unfortunately, is not indicated in the notebook entry which tells of the event.

The episode seems to have left Moamrath in consternation. His personal diary entry for the day consists of the sentence: "I thought they never would get that guy buried."

The next morning, someone in Hatcheck seems to have told him what films were, as his diary entry for the next day, heavily underlined, begins: "It was not until someone informed me that I had been to a motion picture that my mystification over yesterday's events cleared. I could not understand why I had been charged 25c to see a funeral ..."

His confusions past, Moamrath became one of the most rabid movie fans imaginable. Piles of movie fan magazines of the period were found among his effects at the time of his death two years later.

The unnamed first movie Moamrath saw is lost to us, but not the one which sent him forward on his career as screenwriter. That film was *The Life of Emile Zola.* It impressed Moamrath no end. He had long wanted to do a biography of his literary idol, Jean George Marie, Marquis de Hacque, the eighteenth century Basque poet. Moamrath rushed home from the movie and began to make copious notes for his projected screenplay, *The Life of the Marquis de Hacque.* He was so impressed by the biographical film form that he made many enquiries as to where he could contact the actor, Emile Zola, whom he wanted to play the part of the Marquis. Moamrath was understandably upset when told that Monsieur Zola, a Frenchman, had died late in the previous century.

Nonplussed, Mortimer Morbius Moamrath began to read all he could on movies, filmmaking and movie stars. Unfortunately, though he found books on films themselves, he found none on screenplay writing. So he used as his model the guide he found in the 1904 edition of *How to Write Plays for Lots of Money.* This fact in part atones for some of Moamrath's customary lack of craftsmanship, but it does not wholly excuse some of the blatant logic gaps to be found in his screenplays (examples of which follow this introduction).

2. Movie Fan to Cinema Professional.

During the next six months, Moamrath outlined film works and, at the same time, learned as much as he could about films. Where he found some of the revelations about the media contained in his work diary is unknown, but they are interesting in and of themselves:

August 5, 1935: Gabby's real name is George!!!

August 21, 1935: de Mille?

September 19, 1935: Warner Bros.???

It was on December 11 of that year that Moamrath was seized with a transport of rapture and rushed home to labor away at his outlines in a frenzy of work not experienced since he composed the "Young Guy From Fuggoth" poems six years earlier. For the preceding five months he had been, of course, seeing all-talking, all-singing, all-dancing films, the typical product of the day. He had gone far across town that day to catch up on moviegoing. Here is the diary entry for the day:

BREAKTHROUGH!!! I have seen today the most marvellous film of all time, one that heralds new things to come for the moving picture. The film is called Hell's Hinges *(though it is a western and is not about Hell at all). They have done something totally new and exciting with it. THEY HAVE TAKEN OUT ALL THE TALKING AND THE MUSIC!!! Instead of having to listen to all that talk, talk, talk, you get to read what is being said. And you can hum any music you want! Will have to recast all movie work for this form. It is sure to sweep the motion picture industry overnight.*

In time, of course, Moamrath learned the error of his thinking, but not before it cost him many hours of revision on his projects. He had, as yet, written not a single word in the screenplay form, but had amassed notes, drawings, scenes and outlines. Believing film to be the most important medium of the century, and the perfect way to present to an unaware world his "mythos," Moamrath made the decision to go to the filmmaking capital of the world and get a job as a screenplay writer.

On January 3, 1936, Mortimer Morbius Moamrath bid fond adieu to his faithful butler, Abner Skulker Stern, and set out on the Wendigo, Dunwent & Gone R.R.'s 19th Century Limited for Hollywood.

3. This or That Side of Paradise.

Hollywood, Nebraska had a population of 730 hardy souls on the morning M.M. Moamrath set foot on the station platform. That he had taken a wrong connection at Grand Central Station seems never to have occurred to him, then or ever. He had ridden in a sitting car, taking occasional nips at his cod-liver oil bottle, until the conductor announced the arrival at Hollywood.

Moamrath seems to have made contact first with the owner of the town's only drug store, where he went to establish credit for supplies of cod-liver oil, hair marcel cream, and Tootsie Rolls. He inquired as to where he might see someone about getting a job in pictures.

The druggist, a good Rotarian, sent Moamrath to the town's mayor, Mr. Halan Hardy, who also ran the newspaper, mortuary, and portrait studio. Moamrath explained himself, and the mayor, a shrewd transplanted Yankee with some conception of business and finance, hired Moamrath to write a promotional film to be shown industrialists in hopes that they would relocate their factories in the township.

For his work, Moamrath was furnished room, board, and $10 a month cod-liver oil money.

His diary entry for January 5, 1936 shows his concern:

Thought there was more money in this business. Also thought Hollywood was near the ocean. I asked native about this. He said there was a WPA lake not far from here, but that the ocean had left sometime during the late Cretaceous. (Will have to use that as setting for the B'oogym'an stories.) I do get to smell all the fungus in the mayor's darkroom. Hope to be able to flesh out some outlines for other movies while working on this one.

4. Polished Ineptitude.

And work he did, for the next six months, while he struggled with the industrial film. (*Hollywood: Metropolis of the Cornfields*, like all of Moamrath's other screen works, remained unproduced. In the case of this film, it was due to interference of the City Council (Fred and Bob), hassles with the state authorities and the mayor's insistence that a part be written in for his daughter,

Miss Laurel Ann Hardy.) During the days when he was not in the mayor's darkroom or checking locations, he struggled with the promotional movie. At night, Moamrath continued to write the other classics of inept movie scripting for which he is, until now, unknown.

Some words must be given here about Moamrath's lack of finesse at the screenplay form and his subject matter. He had no idea of the technical end of the business and simply described the effects he wanted on the screen, to the best of his not-too-great ability. (See examples of his scene transitions in the script fragments below.)

Also, all the near-classic screenplays he wrote were intended, not for actors, but for actors dressed as the gods of the "Moamrath mythos." For those encountering this body of lore for the first time, some explanation must be given.

Moamrath had written a series of stories with the prevailing idea that a race of elder beings (The Bad Old Ones) once controlled the Earth and solar system, but, through sheer stupidity and forgetfulness, got lost and wandered away. Meanwhile, another race of elder beings (The Good Old Ones) stumbled onto the Earth and decided it would do as well as anyplace. The Good Old Ones then had a billion-year spree and picnic, and then all went to sleep. The Bad Old Ones continue to stumble around in a place beyond time and space (and, we might add, reason and logic).

It was against this background that Moamrath set all his film-scripts, and it was with these elder gods that he peopled them.

It must also be mentioned that Moamrath's screenplays bear a *startling* resemblance to films actually produced by real studios throughout the next decade. It must be assumed that these are sheer coincidences, as no one other than the Moamrath scholars who bought the writer's effects from Sid, the recluse of Pine Barrens, N.J. have ever seen these scripts. Such coincidences *do* happen, and it should not be inferred that later films were plagiarized from the works of Moamrath.

During the spring of 1936, Moamrath saw many movies at the local theatre called the First Street Grand Guignol, and added ideas to his notebooks for movies heavily influenced by current releases. In late January, for instance, he wrote the notes for his series involving two happy-go-lucky elder gods, H'Hope and K'Krozby and their somewhat female companion LL'amo in a series of (for Moamrath) lighthearted adventures called *The Road to Oblivion.* He also thought of a tender view of how one small god can change things through its good works, called *Mr. D'Deeds Goes to Hell.*

He also saw his first Marx Bros. film. He set out to find what was available on the comedy team, and prepared a screenplay of one of the Marx Bros.' best-known works, *Das Kapital,* which Moamrath tentatively titled *Depression Feathers.*

But it was into his mythos screenplays that he poured all his inspiration and some of his talent. The screenplay fragments which follow show some of the many guises with which his near-genius masqueraded itself.

GOODBYE TO ALL THEM.

It was June 3, 1936 that Moamrath, his hopes dashed by making only sixty dollars in his first half-year as screenwriter, left Hollywood, Nebraska with his packing crates full of screenplays, notes, outlines, and story treatments.

It is presumed that he used the backs of most of these many, many pages for his other writings in the two years of life left to him, as all that remains of that deadly half-year of film work are the following fragments, a few scattered notes, and a memory in the minds of the inhabitants of Hollywood, Nebr. (Those who remember him at all refer to him as "that funny writer feller from the East, or somewhere.")

It will be seen that his filmwork, like the rest of his writing, is for the most part wretched and inept, but that the film work especially contains a certain smarmy charm of its own. To the fragments themselves I have appended dates of composition, some technical data, etc. I hope the reader finds them as fascinatingly dreadful as I do.

From GONE WITH THE WENDIGO (Feb. 1936):

(Do the thing where you show R'hett on one side of the door and S'Car'lot on the other side all at the same time.)

R'HETT:
Open this interdimensional gateway, S'Car'lot!

S'CAR'LOT:
Go away! I'm going to have a 106-yard waistline again. I'm never going to have a thousand young at once anymore! Never!

R'HETT:
I can get a divorce for this, S'Car'lot!

S'CAR'LOT:
Go away!

R'HETT:
No non-Euclidian gateway could stop me if I *really* wanted in, S'Car'lot.

S'CAR'LOT:
Go away! I'm fine the way I am!

R'HETT:
Frankly, my dear, I don't give a malediction.

From THE BLACK SLIME OF FALWORTH (March 1936):

(Knights ride up to the slag heap that was the homeland of the noble de Geek family.)

YOUNG SIR GUY DE GEEK:
Yondo is duh Abominations of my faddah.

From THE WIZARD OF OSHKOSH (April 1936):

DUNWITCH OF THE EAST:
Something appealing to the eye, something ... red. Poppies.
Poppies to soothe them to sleep.

(*Camera does the thing where you go to another picture of people but doesn't go black first. Four people come down the road with a little dog. Around the little dog's neck is the Elderly Sign.*)

D'ORTHI:
Oh, look, the Green Slime City. Let's go, hurry!

TIN FINGERMAN:
Hurry!

SCARECOW:
Hurry!

COWARDLY ANTLION:
I'm comin', I'm comin'.

TOJO THE DOG:
Arf! Arf! Tekel-li-li!

(*They run through the poppies. Then D'Orthi begins to slow.*)

D'ORTHI:
Oh, I'm so sleepy!

(*She lies down.*)

COWARDLY ANTLION:
Come to think of it, forty thousand winks wouldn't be bad.

(*He falls. Scarecow does the same. So does dog Tojo.
Only Tin Fingerman is left up.*)

TIN FINGERMAN:
Help! Help!

(*Do the thing where Gimpa, the Good Dunwitch of the North, waves her wand and looks pretty. Snow begins to fall on the poppy field. Tin Fingerman rusts in place. Snow continues to fall, then stops. Nothing moves. Bodies begin to decay. Tojo rots first, then D'Orthi, then Scarecow, then Antlion. Tin Fingerman is still rusted in place. Poppy field withers. Winter comes, then spring again. Bodies are gone. Tin Fingerman has rusted to dark brown. Vines grow up into his leg and out through his head. Seasons pass. Mountains rise in background, then erode away. Tin Fingerman is now only loose collection of rusty parts. His head falls off. Glaciers appear in the background, come forward, recede. Tin Fingerman rusts completely away and disappears. Shallow seas form in background. Huge tentacle rises from the sea, writhes in air, disappears. Southern Cross rises in the night sky. A great arthropod civilization evolves, builds cities near sea, falls into barbarism. Sea dries up. Moon appears in sky, grows larger and nearer. Bad Old Ones return from adjacent dimension and reconquer the Earth. They wander away again. Another sea forms.*

Vast hulk of moon appears on the horizon. Big Dipper rises in the nighttime sky. Stars move apart, become unrecognizable as a constellation (...)*

[*Ellipsis mine. Moamrath's description goes on for six more closely written pages which become very repetitive.]

But it was for none of the above scripts that Moamrath has been forgotten. Nestled among his papers (along with the stirring wartime drama, *Mrs. Minotaur*, and his adaptation of his own story, "The Maltese Trapezohedron") was what is considered to be Moamrath's masterwork in the form, *Cthu'lablanca.*

During Moamrath's sojourn in Hollywood, Nebraska, Italian troops invaded Ethiopia, the Japanese incurred into China and the Spanish Civil War had broken out. Thinking ahead, Moamrath posited a far-larger war in the future, involving most of the nations of the world. Such a situation was unthinkable to him. So he wrote a screenplay, set in a world outside time and space, against which his banished Bad Old Ones moved in their intertheologic dramas, as a warning of what such a bleak future would hold.

Ct'hulablanca, a small settlement in a realm adjacent to ours, but outside the dimensional boundaries, has become a refugee center during the time of the ouster of the Bad Old Ones from Earth. Here, they wait, wait, wait until such time as they can reach the safety of Fuggoth, or gain passage to other dimensions.

The principal characters in Moamrath's screenplay are R'ick Yog, saloon owner ("Everybody Comes to Yog's") who was once the demon-lover of I'lsa Chubby-Nirath (now Mrs. Nigel R. Lathotep). Lathotep himself is the leader of the under-planet movement to regain control of the Earth for the Bad Old Ones, and as such his presence in Cthula'blanca is resented by Major NoDoz, military attaché from the government of the Good Old Ones.

Minor characters are H'Ugar'te Soth, murderer and under-planet figure; F'R'I, leader of all black market transactions in government of C'thulablanca and owner of the Blue Suggoth Café, rival to Yog's; Captain R'eyNoth, temporal authority in the refugee world, and S'am Zann, Nibbian violinist at R'ick's café.

All that remains of Moamrath's film are the following tantalizing fragments and general outline — and one bizarre photograph. I have provided no transitional material or anything else. Everything is just as Moamrath wrote it.

C'THU'LABLANCA

(*F'R'I has come into R'ick's place. F'R'I is a huge corpulent god with many more tentacles than one would think necessary to inspire fear and worship.*)

F'R'I:
Nyhe-nyhe, R'ick. I want to buy S'am.

R'ICK:
I don't buy and sell the souls of people. F'R'I.

F'R'I:
You should. Mad Arabs are Ct'hulablanca's greatest commodity. Nyhe-nyhe.

* * *

(*H'ugar'te comes into R'ick's. He is a thin dry god with a protruding eye. He opens his avuncular fold to reveal shiny objects to the owner of the café.*)

H'UGAR'TE:
Do you know what these are, R'ick? Trapezohedrons.

Trapezohedrons of transit. Free passage to any dimension, cannot be questioned or rescinded. Not even Blazazoth himself can deny them.

* * *

(*A few moments later, Captain R'eyNoth's men drag H'Ugar'te away after he has hidden the trapezohedrons in S'am's violin case. Someone mentions that they hope R'ick will protect them should the Good Old Ones ever come for them.*)

R'ICK:
I stick my hexapodia out for nobody.

* * *

(*Yog's, later the same millennia after R'ick has seen I'lsa for the first time since they were banished from R'ealYeah on Earth. S'am comes in.*)

S'AM:
Ain't you gonna sleep, boss?

R'ICK:
Nah! (*looks to chronomosphere*) What time is it in R'ealYeah? I bet it's the Pleistocene in R'eal Yeah. I bet they're all asleep.

S'AM:
Well, I ain't sleepy either. (*Begins to play screeching howls on his violin which shriek to the nether regions of inter-dimensional space.*)

R'ICK:
What's that you're playing?

S'AM:
Just a little somethin' of my own.

R'ICK:
You know what I want to hear. (*Takes drink of cod-liver oil.*) I want maddening pipings from the dim recesses of pelagic time. If she can take it, so can I. Play it, S'am. Play, "As Aeons Go By."

S'AM:
(*begins to play, singing under his breath*) Pn'nguili mgl'wnafhk
F'nglooie
P'u gngah'nagl Fhtghngnn,
I sing it with a sigh
On the dead you can't rely.
And with weird time even death may die,
As aeons go by.

Hearts full of worship,
N'Glalal sets the date,
Bats got to swim,
Blazazoth must have a mate,
Oh that you can't deny.
When stars move into place
Set table and say grace
The meat is gonna fly.
When the islands rise,
The Good Ones we'll despise.
With weird time even death may die,
As aeons go by.

(*R'ick's eyes brim over. He buries his head in his tentacles.*)

* * *

(I'lsa has come to explain to R'ick why she abandoned him in R'ealYeah when the Good Old Ones took over. R'ick interrupts.)

R'ICK:
Is it a good story? Does it have a zowie finish? I remember a story. A god, standing on the C'chu-C'chu platform with a comical look on his mandibles because his thorax has just been kicked in.

I'LSA:
R'ick, I ...

* * *

(Go to the next scene with one of those things where you just see another picture right through the first one. We are at the gate of transit to other dimensions. A huge coleopterous bug sits in the background while R'ick, I'lsa, Lathotep, R'eyNoth and others move in the foreground, slowly and sluggishly. A glistening ammonia fog drifts slowly over the bugport. Two aphidious creatures in uniforms feed the coleopt raw meat of a disturbingly familiar texture. Lathotep goes towards them. R'ick turns to I'lsa.)

R'ICK:
You're going to get on that beetle!

I'LSA:
But, R'ick ...

R'ICK:
You're going with him. You're part of the things that keep him going. What I'm going to start, you can't be part of. It's easy to see the problems of three gods don't amount to a Hill of Dreams in a crazy non-Euclidian universe like this ...

I'LSA:
I said I'd never leave you ...

R'ICK:
You won't. We lost it in R'ealYeah, but we got it back last aeon. We'll always have that.

(*Lathotep comes back through ammonia fog. Sound: BYYEEE-HHHH!! Beetle's left wing begins to flap. I'lsa looks at R'ick, R'ick looks at I'lsa, Lathotep at both. Sound: BYYEEEH-HHH!! Beetle's right wing begins to flap.*)

R'ICK:
(*to Lathotep*)
Last millennia, your wife came to me. She tried everything to get those trapezohedrons from me, pretending she still loved me. I let her pretend. She said she'd do anything to get them. *Anything!*

LATHOTEP:
And you let her pretend? A god of your stature?

R'ICK:
It was a lot of fun. Anyway, here are the trapezohedrons. Sealed in your names. Mister and Mrs. Nigel R. Lathotep.

LATHOTEP:
Next time, I'm sure our side will win.

* * *

(*R'eyNoth and R'ick stand in the fog. R'ick is holding a smoking suggoth-prod in his hand. Major NoDoz' uniform lies crumpled on the bugport runway. R'eyNoth's men arrive.*)

R'EYNOTH:
Major NoDoz has been transmogrified.
(*pause*)
Round up the most loathesomely unusual suspects.
(*The men leave.*)
I think we should go to the Free Bad Ones garrison
in the Plateau of S'ing, among the C'chu-C'chu people.
*(Sound of beetle flying away into interstitial space overhead.
They watch it go.)*
And the suggoths you owe me should just about
pay our expenses.

R'ICK:
Our expenses? Fnglooie, this could be the start
of a beautiful pantheon.

* * *

Thanks to Moamrath scholars Joe Pumilia and Ray Files for technical assistance.

CHILI FROM YUGGOTH

North of Hempstead, the grass rises wild ...

I lived at the Monkey House from May 15th to October 27, 1974. Writing-wise it was a wonderful time, personally it was delirious, and financially it was a disaster for the other occupants.

According to my work diary, in those months I wrote "Sun Up" and "Pause for Reflection" with Al Jackson, "Black as the Pit, from Pole to Pole ..." with Steve Utley, "Of Death but Once" (and the other outlines of) the Roscoe Heater stories with Joe Pumilia, "Buffalo Bill's Ghost Bison; or the Steam Giant of the Prairies" with Craig Strete, and "Davy Crockett Shoots the Moon," "Save a Place in the Lifeboat for Me," and "Mary Margaret Road-Grader" by myself. I also worked on two unsuccessful starts at novels, one the western *Dig for Old Wooly* and a novelization of "Unsleeping Beauty and the Beast." About 100,000 words of stuff in all.

Most of the stories I wrote in that time sold. One was up for a Nebula, and two accounted for reprints in three *Best Sfs of the Year*. All that is real nice to know. Not *one*, not one *single one*, sold in the six months I was at the Monkey House. I made, I think, about $100 total, off earlier sales, in the entire time I lived there, and I owed everybody money. This eventually caused me to move to Austin to look for honest work, going the David Selig route, reviewing movies, working in an auditory research lab as a guinea pig.

Living in the Monkey House at the time of My Time were Bob and Kathy, Bill Kostura, and Allen Kelly Graham. I lived in the small back bedroom off the bathroom — it was painted whorehouse pink and had red tassled curtains when I moved in. When the four of them drove up to Dallas to get me, my belongings consisted of a sleeping bag, a typewriter, a card table, a tinny record player with the speakers built in the box, a few changes of clothes, all four or five of my published works, some typing paper and notebooks, a fan, and my dog Rat. (All fifty pounds of him; he ate before I did.)

1974 was the hottest summer between the end of the drought in the fifties and 1980. I mean, it was hot. My work schedule was like this — get up at six a.m., work till ten or eleven, go to sleep with Rat taking up the eight or so inches between me and the breeze box, get up at four p.m., wait for everybody to get home from working at the trailer factory in Navasota, eat, work from six p.m. to one or two a.m., go to sleep again.

On any given night, six p.m. till one or two or so, there were anywhere from five to ten extra people around the house, depending on the social calendar and the sleeping arrangements. The only way I could tell there was a party was because twenty or thirty people would come to my room and make me come out and Have Fun.

These people at the time Worshipped at the Shrine of Ganja. We'd get through with supper (there are wonderful things you can do with Top Ramen), they'd go to the living room, I'd go back to work. They'd turn on the stereo (to this day, Emerson Lake and Palmer, Yes, and Tangerine Dream give me the hives). Around one or two in the morning, I'd get up from my desk, go into the living room, pick everyone up and carry them to bed (if they lived there) or to couches (if they didn't, or hadn't made any requests at supper), turn off the stereo, and go to bed.

This all ties in with the night of the Chili from Yuggoth. Not that these people were all doped out of their minds all the time, or anything. They had time to put out *Stanley* and to watch *Captain Harold's Theatre of the Sky* on Saturday nights.

The day of the night of the Chili from Yuggoth dawned clear

and hot. It was, I think, Janie's birthday or something, and everybody was supposed to celebrate by going to the park and eating chili and birthday cake and stuff. Doing the hippie Aggie 1974 stuff. It was a Saturday in June or July.

We went to the park about two. The food showed up about three, in raw form. The basics were three pounds of chili meat and two-and-a-half lids of dope. Brad or somebody started cooking it while we threw frisbees, or tried to play softball, or talked about Alan Dean Foster's new book, or some other hot topic. We all (about fifteen or twenty of us) got hotter and thirstier and hungrier, and the chili cooked on and on, forming first an oily, then black, then a green viscous crust, in which the stems and seeds, stalks and leaves, peppers, beans and tassels floated. They kept adding to it, and transferring it to larger kettles, and a run was made to up the THC content by a factor of 2 or something, around six p.m.

At seven-thirty we all screamed, pushed the cooks aside, made a mad dash, ladled up heaping bowlsfull, and ate, spitting out seeds and stems. I ate three bowls, and I wasn't one of the hogs.

Then we all went off to do whatever it was, which in my and Bob's case was to take the rest of Janie's cake to her via a stop at the Dixie Chicken.

The Dixie Chicken had just opened, and patrons from the Monkey House usually filled anywhere from three to six tables. So they liked us. Tonight, it was just me and Bob, and the place was packed.

We were intent on playing Missile Attack, which was a machine with green missiles flying over that you were supposed to shoot down with your purple anti-missile missiles. It gave off pleasing aural and visual distress signals when you successfully demolished one of the sky-full of rockets.

Halfway through the first game the machine suddenly got much smaller and moved over into a far corner of the room.

I looked at Bob.

He had no pupils.

Neither did I.

We turned around. The room was green and purple.

EVERYONE WAS LOOKING AT US.

All 400 of them. There was no music.

Heeheeeheeeheeeheee I said.

L-e-t-'-s g-e-t o-o-o-u-u-u-t-t-t ofheresqueech said Bob.

We coolly walked to the car.

Heeeheeeheeehee I said, making small talk.

shutupshutupshutup said Bob.

We got to the car. Bob drove over the curb and into the street, found it, used all of it, for about six blocks. Then he drove up over a curb and into a field.

Janie said Bob cake.

We staggered across the field. I knew if we stopped we were dead men. The sky would fall, or Morris Ankrum as a cop with a ruby in the back of his neck would show up or the ground would swallow us.

We knocked on Janie's door. She opened it. Janie said Bob cake.

Heeeheee hee heee I said.

I headed for one couch, Bob the other.

Can I get you something asked Janie.

You just said that we both said heeeheeeheee heee heee.

Then I'll play some music said Janie.

She put on *Pet Sounds.* Brian Wilson was singing just back of my nose. V's of sound flew across the room and into Bob's ears. The shag rug felt like emery cloth. I was in love with the couch.

How about some Pecan Sandies said Janie.

COOKIES we said hee hee hee.

We ate the whole bag, a pound apiece, and we knew what the gods on Mt. Olympus ate. Pecan Sandies.

Meanwhile, across town, everybody else had gone swimming at somebody's apartment pool. At the same time we were in the

Dixie Chicken, they were all horsing around in the water.

Heeeheeeheee they all said suddenly, and curled into fetal balls and sunk towards the bottom of the pool.

Kathy pulled them out, draped them over lawn chairs and towels on the pool edge.

Heeeheeehee thank you hee hee Kathy said someone.

You're welheeeheeeeeheheHeeeHeeeee said Kathy.

hee hee wow said someone.

wow hee hee said someone else.

hee wow hee said Kathy.

Which covers everyone except Allen Kelly Graham, who had driven to Wellborn and was on his way back.

The road sprouted two sets of stripes. Allen continued to drive in the middle lane. Then the road to left and right went off, one to Somerville and one to Tyler, and the center lane ended in a field.

Heee heee hee hee said Allen.

He got out and lay on the hood of his car and watched the millions and billions of bats and chimney swifts glued to the sky.

An ambulance went up the road, lights flashing, siren screaming.

Allen watched it go.

Man, I thought he'd never leave said Allen heee hee hee hee.

Sometime later Bob and I got up and walked unsteadily to the door. Home Janie Monkey House we said.

We found the car in the middle of the field. Geez Bob are you alright hee hee to drive I asked.

Sure heee hee said Bob.

They were all in a car driving home. Kathy didn't remember getting in a car. Hey Brad hee hee are you okay to drive?

I thought hee hee you were driving said Brad hee heee.

Allen Kelly Graham pulled in the driveway. He didn't remember ever leaving. Hee hee he said hee hee.

The Monkey House was dark. Emerson Lake and Palmer were blasting on the stereo, shaking the windows.

Hey Bill are you okay? we all asked hee hee.

Heee heee heee heee sure said Bill with the Altec 750 speakers up against each ear heee heee hee were you worried?

G'night Bob hee hee.
G'night Howard hee hee.
G'night Kathy hee hee.
G'night Allen hee hee.
G'night Bill hee hee.
hee hee.

The next day, the twenty-foot-tall century plant bloomed.

4. The Lost Waldrop

THE LOST STORIES, NEVER BEFORE PUBLISHED

INTERVIEW, PART FOUR

1. "The Pizza"

BRAD: Now for the real oddball in the collection: "The Pizza," a sketch you wrote to submit to Red Skelton. I love the sketch — but as much as I love the sketch, I equally love the rejection letter from CBS.

HOWARD: I'm pretty sure the guy who wrote it realized he was dealing with some young kid. Rather than a demented adult, as someone once said. I'm sure people send stuff in all the time to shows with closed writing staffs.

BRAD: Oh, yeah. When I was in college, I had a professor who sent jokes to Johnny Carson. All of which were sent back, of course.

The date on the rejection letter for "The Pizza" is January 3, 1967. So you must have sent this in the previous fall, in '66, right around the time you turned twenty.

HOWARD: Right, and about the time I sold to Playboy Party Jokes.

BRAD: That's right, you told me that your actual first writing sale was a Playboy Party Joke.

HOWARD: Exactly, in August of 1966.

BRAD: Since I wasn't recording when we talked about this before, I'm gonna ask you to try to reconstruct the joke in your head now so I can put it into the interview.

HOWARD: Oh, great. It was the usual thing. It was a topical joke at the time, because Hugh Hefner had just started the Playboy Foundation, which was essentially like the, whatchacallit, computer freedom thing now. [*BD Note: The Electronic Frontier Foundation.*]

BRAD: Right, it was essentially a "free press" foundation.

HOWARD: Yeah, it was a First Amendment type thing and was gonna fight for First Amendment issues. Because Hefner was accused of being a communist and a pornographer. But for a guy making millions of dollars, he didn't sound much like a communist to me. Anyway, the idea was that he was going to use the Foundation to fight for guys like Lenny Bruce, who had been censored even in nightclubs and stuff, harassed by the cops.

It was called the Playboy Foundation, right? So the joke was, "A friend of ours thinks the Playboy Foundation is an undergarment for Bunnies."

Because foundations were those big girdle-type looking things that they advertised in the fifties and stuff for women, you know? It was one piece, it was the girdle, it was the bra, it was the whole thing.

BRAD: Yes, I remember when I was a kid, they were still calling it "foundation garments."

HOWARD: Anyway, that was the joke. I told you that it came out when I was on my trip to San Francisco, right? In 1966. The issue was out on the stands, and I couldn't buy it because in California you had to be twenty-one to buy a *Playboy*. Whereas in Texas, you only had to be eighteen. So it was before my twenty-first birthday.

BRAD: Basically, you were a guy who made beer, but couldn't buy it.

HOWARD: Exactly! I was the creator, and couldn't buy it. It's like when they told Oppenheimer he couldn't have a security clearance anymore. The guy who invented the A-bomb, and they told him he couldn't have a security clearance anymore.

But that was one of the things that the Playboy Foundation was fighting, that there needs to be a standardized age of consent for people to buy stuff. Because in some states it was one thing, and in some states it was another.

BRAD: Well, that's a basic issue we're still fighting today. Are we one nation, or are we fifty separate fiefdoms?

HOWARD: Exactly. Anyway, like I said, the joke came out in '66, when I was twenty. So I had to wait until I came back to Texas to buy the issue. It was the September or October issue. But I think it was the September issue.

BRAD: I do have a couple of specific questions to ask you about "The Pizza." You obviously didn't wind up going into TV writing, but it seems clear to me from this piece that you *could* have. So I was wondering: At the time, did you have TV writing ambitions in general, or did you just write this because you were a Red Skelton fan?

HOWARD: I was a Red Skelton fan, and I wanted money for my writing. You know? I had no idea what it paid or anything, except that it was probably beyond my wildest dreams of avarice, as we say.

BRAD: Which reminds me — How much did you get paid for the *Playboy* joke?

HOWARD: Twenty-five bucks! They were paying twenty-five bucks at the time. I think *Playboy* eventually made the Party Jokes pay fifty bucks, before they quit carrying them.

But it was twenty-five bucks. And see, that caused me some confusion because I had sent a story off to *Playboy* like a month before, and hadn't gotten it back. And then suddenly, I get the small envelope from *Playboy*. I had never sold anything where you got a contract and all that stuff, so I figured they just bought your story and sent you a check, right? So there was a small envelope from *Playboy* that obviously had a check in it, so I thought "Oh boy, my story sold!" And I opened it up, and of course it was for the Party Joke, which I had forgotten I'd sent 'em, see? I had sent it to 'em like three or four months before. So it caused me a bunch of heart palpitations and confusion, because I thought *Playboy* had bought a story from me. I think at the time they were paying like $1500.00 a story, which was more than anybody else except maybe *The New Yorker*.

But it was twenty-five bucks. And I said, "Aww, jeeez." And then I realized, of course, that I had sold the Party Joke.

Anyway, the Red Skelton thing. I'm sure it was cobbled together from stuff I had read in *Mad* magazine, or *Cracked*, or — you know what I mean. That kind of stuff where you just throw a bunch of situations together.

That was right after I started theater classes, too, so I wasn't thinking so much about TV as about playwriting and, you know, doing stuff for the stage.

2. "Youth" and
3. "The Long Goodnight"

BRAD: Well, that can lead us right into the next things I wanted to ask you about — the two plays that we have: "Youth" and "The Long Goodnight."

Did you write those as projects or assignments for your college class?

HOWARD: No. No, see, the thing was, "Little Theater," it was a one-credit course. Most classes were three credits, right? History class, or an English class or something, you got three credits. "Little Theater" was a one-credit course that you ended up putting about a hundred hours a week into. Because you painted scenery, you did lights, you did everything. You acted. The whole thing.

So while I was doing all that, I was trying to write plays, too — because I was under the influence of Eugene O'Neill, of course. I thought I'd be the next Eugene O'Neill, right? I was going through all his plays and stuff. The operative book is Arthur Gelb and Barbara Gelb's *O'Neill*, which was the first really great biography of O'Neill, and it's like eight hundred pages long. I had a copy that I read to death.

I wrote the plays on my own. But "Youth," I believe, was given a reading at the Little Theater.

BRAD: Where was this? What college?

HOWARD: The University of Texas at Arlington. It was originally called Arlington State College, before the University of Texas got their hands on it. They divided all the state colleges in Texas between UT and Texas A&M. And Arlington State College fortunately got UT to take 'em over. They became part of the UT system.

Anyway, like I said, "Youth" was given a reading in class, but not performed for an audience.

BRAD: You hadn't actually been assigned to write this, though?

HOWARD: No, not at all. I did it on my own, like most things.

BRAD: Okay, so this would have been '66 or '67, about the same time that you wrote "The Pizza," then. So you were thinking very much about stage movement and things like that.

HOWARD: Right, exactly.

BRAD: And obviously, "The Long Goodnight" is about the death of Bogart.

HOWARD: Of course!

BRAD: Which I liked a lot. I like them both. These plays were not anything I expected to see from you.

HOWARD: Well, I was fascinated with the idea. The Bogart cult had just taken hold among college students.

BRAD: Everybody was watching *Casablanca* and *The Big Sleep* and all that.

HOWARD: Right, exactly. And I got a part in a play at the Little Theater because I was the only one in class who could do a Peter Lorre imitation. I got the part of the kid in *A Thousand Clowns* because there's one point where he does a Peter Lorre imitation in the play. In the movie it was Barry Gordon, the kid actor. If you've never seen *A Thousand Clowns*, it's worth seeing. It's Jason Robards as the uncle who raised the kid that his sister left with him.

Anyway, I got the part because I was the only person in class who could do the Peter Lorre imitation.

BRAD: Did you do much other acting at the time, besides that play? Were you in a lot of stuff?

HOWARD: I acted in two or three other plays, but mostly I did the lights and the sound booth stuff, and painted sets and got props. I was the technical guy.

BRAD: I dunno, I just suddenly had a vision of how not only could you have been a TV writer, you could have been a famous actor.

HOWARD: (Sounding dubious.) Right.

If you've ever read "Calling Your Name," in the Janis Ian anthology ... The incident about getting shocked when the light bridge came down with a live male electric plug stuck to the light bridge, and I grabbed the light bridge and it knocked me like fifteen feet across the stage, right? That was a real incident. And I went tearing for the light booth. And everybody had disappeared from it, because they knew somebody had fucked up. It was the first thing I had told them: Live male electric plugs, you have to tie them to the bridge so they can't touch anything. And somebody had just left one dangling so it touched the bridge while it was on the way down. I reached up for it and grabbed the bridge, which was electrified at the time.

You know, you don't forget that.

BRAD: No, I'll bet not.

HOWARD: Anyway, that's based on a Little Theater incident that happened to me.

That's also where I met my ex-wife. She was in the theater and stuff.

BRAD: Oh, she was in that class?

HOWARD: She was in that class. They auditioned us for *Who's Afraid of Virginia Woolf.* They were gonna try to do that before anyone else in little theaters had done it. We auditioned for those parts.

I got Buddy (Saunders) into it because Buddy thought it was a way to meet girls. And he was right. But he ended up doing the set designs for a play about Joan of Arc. He did it very simply with Gothic arches on plywood, and then he had different scenes seen through the Gothic arches. Like before she's called by God to the army, she's a country girl, right? And the Gothic arch drops down, and it's like looking out a barn door onto the countryside that Buddy had painted beyond it. Anyway, he did some really great sets. There were like four different arches and a platform ramp for the whole play. I built the ramp, and Buddy did the Gothic arches.

We also did *Blithe Spirit*, and there's a scene where there's a statue of the first wife who had died. Then the lights take the place of her as she flits around the stage. But Buddy had to do a statue, which he based on another lady in the class. He had to order eighty pounds of beeswax to make the statue from. It came to my house, because Buddy was using my house as a mail drop and to run his comic book business out of the garage. The beeswax arrived from — wherever he had ordered it from, some beeswax manufacturing place — and when it arrived, one of the seals on one of the boxes popped open, and I wrote the Lovecraft line in it. You know, just like in the Lovecraft story: "That is not dead which can eternal lie, yet with strange aeons even death may die."

I carved it into the beeswax, right? Then I closed it back up, and it looked like it had never been opened. And Buddy came home from East Texas State College, where he'd gone because they didn't have a foreign language requirement. So he was driving two hundred miles — he lived in Commerce five days a week, and he would drive back to my house on Friday afternoon and do all his comic book stuff, then drive back to Commerce on Monday morning. He did that for like two years. Anyway, he came back and he opened the box of beeswax, which he was gonna do the statue from, and screamed.

(Laughter.)

Because it had this line from Lovecraft on it, you know?

We did stuff like that.

BRAD: You wacky theater students.

HOWARD: Right!

4. "Davy Crockett Shoots the Moon"

BRAD: Okay, unless something else turns up, this might be the last story we talk about in these interviews — "Davy Crockett Shoots the Moon."

HOWARD: I remember parts of it, but I barely remember writing it. Or the entire story.

When I was doing plays and stuff, I always had the idea of a play based on the Moon Hoax, in 1835. It would have involved Davy Crockett, and Mose the Fire Boy, and people like that. All these mythical people from the period. "Davy Crockett Shoots the Moon" was a precursor to that. I never got around to actually setting down the stuff about the Moon Hoax. There was a part of that in *The Moone World* (an unfinished Waldrop novel). Not the Davy Crockett part or the Mose the Fire Boy part. But the Moon Hoax part would be *real* in *The Moone World*, you know? That was the jumping-off point.

BRAD: You did that sort of thing in other stories later on, too. For example, "The Dynasters" is based on the idea that Piltdown Man was real.

HOWARD: Exactly! And I tried to imagine a world where Piltdown Man could have lived. Britain would have had to have been kept isolated until at least some time during the Roman Empire. Otherwise, Piltdown Man would have been wiped out the first day that invaders had shown up in Britain, you know?

BRAD: Well, the one thing that struck me most about "Davy Crockett Shoots the Moon" ... we've talked about it before. I asked you if you remembered when you'd written it, and you said you weren't exactly sure, but that it was definitely before 1973. So that would make this one of your earliest attempts at doing a real "alternate history" story — which was, of course, a kind of story that would become one of your strengths, with stories like "Custer's Last Jump" and "Ike at the Mike."

You've told me that you've never really thought that this story, "Davy Crockett Shoots the Moon," quite worked. But I thought the *idea* behind it was very cool. Davy Crockett, instead of going to Texas, becomes President of the United States — and how differently things would have turned out for the whole country if that had actually happened.

I'm wondering if you've ever thought about revisiting that idea. Or, once you did stories like "Custer's Last Jump" and "Ike at the Mike," did you just decide that idea wasn't as good as those ideas?

HOWARD: Probably. I probably would have gone back to it if I'd still thought it would have been viable, you knowhaddamean? Obviously I didn't, because otherwise I would have. Because not only "Custer's Last Jump," but "Black as the Pit, from Pole to Pole," was the same type of thing. You know, where incidents that happened in the early 1800s influenced everything afterward.

Anyway, I never went back to "Davy Crockett Shoots the Moon" except as something for the Moon Hoax thing, if I'd ever actually sat down and written that.

BRAD: Well, one thing I told you before, in a conversation we didn't record, was that I liked "Davy Crockett Shoots the Moon" because it shows where your interests were going to go, in terms of what you wanted to do with history and changing history in your fiction. But although it has cool ideas, as a story, it's no "Ike at the Mike."

But I'm looking at the scan of the manuscript now as we're talking, and there are a couple of very brief passages late in the story, after the big historical change has been made ... just very brief one- or two-sentence sections that comment on how things are *different*.

And one that I'm looking at is: "The Canada War lasted three years, and Queen Victoria barely kept the rest of the Empire out of it." And that's all you say about it!

HOWARD: (Laughs.) You know, we had plans to invade Canada *several* times in the 1800s. But cooler heads prevailed. It's a wonder we weren't wiped out by a third war with Britain, you know?

I had forgotten I'd written that line.

BRAD: There's other stuff like that. That's the shortest one. And that's all you say about the Canada War in the story, just that one line.

HOWARD: Neat!

BRAD: Let's see, at the end of the story there's this one: "The first ship touched down on the Moon on July 4, 1957. In command were Colonel Charles Yeager and Major David Simons, USFAF."

HOWARD: I had forgotten I had used Simons and Yeager in that, because I used them again in "Us." You remember? You know, when Lindbergh is the first guy on the Moon. Lindbergh, Junior. Because it's Simons and Yeager, and I think, Colonel Paul Stapp at the time. The head of the aviation and space medicine branch of the Air Force. But I'd forgotten I had used that in "Davy Crockett" before.

BRAD: Like I said, this story prefigures what you went on to do. I mean, that's a specific thing that you used again, but the story as a whole is clearly you figuring out the kinds of stories you were going to write.

HOWARD: I guess so.

BRAD: Well, I think so, at least in terms of your alternate history stories.

HOWARD: I was *thinking* about alternate history all the time, you know? But I'm not sure in "Davy Crockett Shoots the Moon" that I had a real handle on it yet.

BRAD: Certainly your famous alternate history stories — we've already mentioned some of the titles — clearly, you had a stronger handle on what you were doing there. But "Davy Crockett Shoots the Moon" is really interesting, because it does show your early exploration in that direction. And it's got some very cool stuff in it.

I think the ending of the story, which I'm not gonna tell you right now — I'll tell you after I turn off the recorder, because if I do it now, and I transcribe it, that'll ruin the story for whoever reads it.

HOWARD: Ah, of course.

BRAD: Oh, I can go ahead and tell you now. I just won't transcribe it.

They land on the moon, right?

[*BD Note: Here I read a chunk of the end of the story to Howard, and I ask him if he remembers the last line. He doesn't, so I tell him.*]

HOWARD: Right, you're right!

BRAD: So that's a great last line.

The only other comment I'll make about the story is that the copy I have at the moment is a scan of the manuscript that the folks at Texas A&M made. This isn't a transcription, it's the actual manuscript with corrections and everything. And I can see the watermark on the paper, so I can tell you that you typed this story on Eaton's Corrasable Bond.

HOWARD: There you go. Probably that was the only typing paper I had left in the house that day.

BRAD: Well, I remember back when I was in college and having to type papers, you know, this was the good stuff. Eaton's Corrasable Bond was the good stuff!

HOWARD: Right, I ended up with a package of hundred or something from somewhere. Usually, I used the cheapest typing paper you could find. And rarely, I would get the ones with the yellow second sheet. Remember, they came in one piece, and you just stuck a piece of carbon paper between 'em. And as you typed, it would go onto the yellow sheet too, so you'd have a copy of it.

BRAD: Wow. I do remember those things. I remember moving the carbon in and out.

HOWARD: Right, exactly! You had to be sure to line it up with the edges and stuff so you could type all the way to the edge, and the characters would show up. And if you didn't do that, the carbon would end before the page ended.

All the things kids nowadays don't know about, you know? It was a different world back then.

THE PIZZA

Howard Waldrop
904 W. Sanford
Arlington, Texas
76010

THE PIZZA

(A Solo Pantomime for Mr. Red Skelton)

Red is sitting in a chair trying to read a paper.

Narrator: (as wife) Hon-eee. Why don't you go get us a pizza?

Narrator: (as Red mouths words) I'm reading the paper. Besides, it's snowing.

Narrator: (as wife again) I know. I think it would be nice if you got us a warm pizza. Then we could have a nice quiet supper all by ourselves.

Red wrinkles his mouth and sticks out his tongue in disgust.

Narrator: (as wife) (as sweet as arsenic) If-you-don't-go-get-us-a-pizza-I'll-kick-you-out-of-that-chair.

Narrator: (as Red mouths words) Oh yeah?

Sound of kicking. Red flies over the chair onto the floor. Gets up and rubs face.

Narrator: (as Red mouths words) Yes dear.

Narrator: (as wife) Make sure you get a pepperoni. And make sure it's hot. And hurry back. I'll go change into something nice.

Red does bit with the knife, taking it out and starting for her, but then decides not to.

Narrator: (as Red mouths words) Yes dear.

He mumbles to himself while he dresses. Pretends to put coat on, then puts boots on. Stands with one foot pointed one way and one the other to show that he has his shoes on the wrong feet. Changes them, mumbles some more, puts muffler on, then pulls his hat down over his eyes. Opens door to raging blizzard, then walks into door. Pulls hat from over eyes, goes out.

Narrator: (as wife) That pizza better be hot when you get back here!

Red goes over to other chair which represents car. Starts to get in. Door is locked. Snow is coming down and wind is blowing. Red gets out keys and starts trying them in lock. Is getting madder. Then he gets mad and breaks out car window. Gets in and shivers. Tries to start car. Red moves his head from side to side to show he has turned on his windshield wipers. Tries to turn them off, loud radio music comes on. Turns radio off, wipers on, and starts car.

Drives off. Sound of horns as he gets on freeway. Red shakes his fist at someone who just missed his car. Almost is hit again.

Sees pizza parlour ahead.

Tries to stop car. Wrestles with wheel as he steps on brakes. Car slides. Noise of impending crash but no impact. Red gets out of car, dusts hands, and steps towards pizza parlour. Noise of car wreck and of shattering glass. Red shrugs his shoulders, then goes in.

Leans like he is leaning on order counter.

Narrator: (gruff woman's voice) Order, Mac?

Red fans his face like she has halitosis. Looks her up and down, gets expression as if he were sick.

Narrator: (as Red mouths words) One hot pepperoni to go.

Red taps fingers on counter. Watches flies buzz around the room and a roach crawl across the counter.

Narrator: (as waitress) Here's your pepperoni, Bud.

Red takes pizza, gives her money. Gets pained expression on face as he takes pizza; his fingers curl under. Then he smells something rotten, sniffs the air, lifts his shoes. Then he lifts the lid to the pizza box and smells. Nearly passes out.

Goes back out to car. Gets in. Car will not start. Starts walking home with pizza. Sound of traffic as he nears freeway. Gets devilish look on his face.

Starts running across freeway. One car misses him, horns honk.

He yells something at the driver. Sound as if a car missed him by inches. Red stands paralyzed for a second while pants legs and sleeves whip in the car's slipstream. Runs to median in front of more cars.

Starts to climb the median fence. Has to put the pizza box in mouth. Climbs up, gets to top, tears pants on top, jumps down, and runs to the other side of the freeway. He loses one shoe on the freeway. He starts back after it.

Sound of car driving up. Squeal of brakes. Red watches into camera as car door opens, then shuts, and the car drives off. Red takes off his other shoe and throws it at the car, then realizes what he has done.

Cut to Red's face again as car backs up, door opens and closes, and then drives off again. Red starts to cry, then starts hopping and skipping on cold pavement, as snow is still falling.

Does little up-in-the-air step, as he is almost home, then we hear the sound of a huge dog growling. Red tries to calm it, then starts to run. Dog growls and bites pizza box. Red and dog tug-of-war with pizza.

Cut to Red's face. He growls, then bites off-camera. Sound of hurt dog running off. Red spits out fur.

Walks, then starts slipping on ice on the sidewalk. Juggles the pizza around, nearly loses it. Finally gets into the house. Leans against the door and pants.

Narrator: (as wife) Oh, good. You got the pizza. Bring it to the table and cut it, dear.

Red goes through the process of cutting the pizza. Just as he is ready to hand his wife a piece, he wrinkles his nose and sneezes all over the pizza.

We fade as Red points to the pizza and starts crying.

The End

CBS
Columbia Broadcasting System, Inc.
Television City
7800 Beverly Boulevard
Los Angeles, California 90036
(213) OLive 1-2345

Dear Mr. Waldrop:

The enclosed material, which was addressed to Head of the Writing Department, The Red Skelton Television Show, has been referred to me without examination by anyone in the program office.

We have been advised by the producers of "THE RED SKELTON HOUR" that the program is written entirely by its own staff of writers and no submitted material is examined or considered.

While we are very pleased to know of your interest in Mr. Skelton and his program, we suggest that you direct your writing efforts toward material which would be adaptable to a variety of programs. Ideas and scripts submitted to the CBS Television Network will be considered if accompanied by our standard submission agreement. You may obtain this form by writing to:

> Miss Helen Lahm
> Registry Office — CBS, Inc.
> 51 West 52nd Street
> New York, N.Y. 10019

Thank you for thinking of Red Skelton and CBS.

Sincerely,

Barbara Barringer
Registry Office

Mr. Howard Waldrop
904 West Sanford
Arlington, Texas 76010

January 3, 1967

encl-4 pgs.

YOUTH

A play in one act

Cast of Characters

Guitar player, early twenties
Boy's Mother, about 30
Boy's voice
German Youth, 18
Three Boys ...
Two Girls ... 8 or 10
Crippled Boy
David Ashely ...
Bobby Smith ... about 12
Miss Jones' voice
Three Hebrew Children
  Boy, about 15
  Ruth, 15
  Other Girl, about 11
Doctor, about 30
Mr. Johnson, silent part
Mrs. Johnson
Mary Jane Johnson, 16 or 17

(The curtain is opened on a stage bare but for a series of platforms and levels. On one more midstage and higher than the rest, a Guitar Player sits. He is playing "Red River Valley" slowly and mournfully. He is preoccupied with what he is doing for a moment or two, then looks up and notices the audience. He stops playing.)

Guitar Player: Were you ever young once? Pretty dumb question, I guess. Nearly everybody was. You probably had a Teddy bear; you ate tangerines, got spankings and things like that. You ran away from home, stole watermelons, and fought with your brothers and sisters, too, I'll bet. I don't suppose you'd be human if you hadn't.

And you griped. (He waves his hand.) I know, I know. It was good-natured griping, either because you had to take out the garbage or pick up your room. (Mocking a pouting child.) 'Nobody else's mother makes them clean up their room. Aw, gee, I'm the only kid on the block who has to work for an allowance.' (He drops back into character.) You girls probably couldn't go on a trip with your big brother, so you got mad and stuffed beans up your nose, and then got scared and screamed your head off. And that panicked your folks and you got to go to the hospital. For a while you thought they understood you. (He leans closer to the audience.) That means you got all the ice cream you wanted.

That, girls, was a way of griping. Sticking beans up your nose, I mean. But did you really know what you were griping about?

Lots of people have tried to find out.

(Lights go down on the Guitar Player, who begins playing "There's an Old Apple Tree in the Orchard." Light comes up on a woman dressed in a turn of the century dress with an apron. She is at extreme stage right, looking off into the wings. She puts her hands on her hips.)

Woman: Edward Harper Jackson! Get down out of this tree this minute! Do you hear me? Get down now, Edward!

Boy's voice: (from offstage right, up high) Aw, mom, I'm not gonna fall or anything.

Woman: Young man, get down from there before I get a switch to you. Get out of that tree.

Boy's voice: I'll hang on real tight! Honest, I won't fall. Really!

Woman: Edward *Harper* Jackson! Do I have to get a peach limb after you?

Boy's voice: Aw, gee, didn't you ever climb a tree, mom? I won't fall.

Woman: (pauses) Alright, Edward. But don't come crying to me when you fall and break your neck. Do you hear me?

Boy's voice: Sure, mom!

(Woman turns to left as if to walk across the stage.)

Boy's voice: (moving higher as he talks) Watch this, mom. Lookit me!

(Woman continues walking. Then an OOPS! comes from high up, followed by a heavy thud off right.)

Boy's voice: (screams) Mmmmommmaaaa!

(The Woman screams, turns around and runs offstage right. Lights go down on this part of the stage and come up upstage left, on a platform of about medium height. The Guitar Player is playing "Donna, Donna." On the platform stands a young man dressed in an SS uniform. He holds his cap in his left hand.)

German Youth: I was in the Jugend for seven years. They asked me to sign a paper when I was eleven. Just to sign a paper. (He lowers his cap in his hands but keeps his head erect.) I was twelve years old when they changed the teachers on us. Mr. Baum was taken out of the classroom one day by soldiers. I was young and thought the soldiers were the greatest things in the world. I couldn't wait until I was old enough to join the Army. We got a new teacher, but we didn't like him because he was so strict. The next year we were formed into a club. Every day after school we would march and parade until it was so dark we couldn't see. When I was fourteen they began telling us of the glory of our country as it had been. They gave me a copy of the *Nibelungenlied*, and I would read it at night by the firelight until I had it memorized from cover to cover.

(He spreads his hands encompassingly.)

The next year we burned the books of all those who would not see the truth! The books of Brecht and Asch went into the flames, and the fires licked late into the night.

The next year came the war. As the leader of my Corps, I led the cheering for the columns of grey that marched east and west and north. I was seventeen when we turned on those we had befriended the year before.

I became eighteen and went into the army, and was marched to the East along with my friends. Through the cold and frost and snow to Stalingrad.

(He pauses, changes hands with the cap. For a second he bows his head, but then straightens to a soldierly bearing.)

And now I am no age, and can never be again. I will never be lame or sick, or hurt, or ever love a girl. I can only say I did my country's calling and lie frozen and forgotten like the rest.

(Lights go down on the German Youth. The Guitar Player begins playing "Sailing, Sailing Over the Bounding Main." Lights come up near center stage. Two girls are standing, one with a doll and the other with a jumprope. They are watching three boys with wooden swords, eyepatches, and bandanas tied around their heads. Off to the left, barely in the light, a cripple boy on crutches stands watching the whole affair.)

1st Boy: I'll be Blackbeard. Okay you knavy scurves, swab the poopdeck, and main the haulsail. There she blows.

2nd Boy: No. You were Blackbeard yesterday. I'm Captain Hook. (He begins to pull his hand inside his sleeve.)

3rd Boy: No. I'm Cap'n Kidd. I'll board your ship and we'll fight and then I'll make you walk the plank!

1st Boy: Cap'n Kidd couldn't make Blackbeard walk the plank in a million years! Blackbeard'd keelhaul him in a minute, and he could shanghai Captain Hook, too.

2nd Boy: You're crazy! Captain Hook isn't afraid of anything ... well, but the alligator. There isn't any pirate living that could outfight him! Why, he'd take his hook and gouge ...

(Meanwhile, the girls have been watching and laughing and now are whispering together. Keeping time with their feet, they begin singing in a mocking tone.)

Girls:

> Little boy went down to sea
> to see what he could see
> the Pirates of Nod rowed up to shore
> took him away from me

(Here the boys stop arguing, listen, groan. The girls continue.)

> For years I stood upon the shore
> looked away to see
> the little boy come back no more
> who went down to the sea
> And one day he came back home
> Laughed and laughed at me
> he waded_______

(Here the boys start for the girls. The girls squeal and run off, the boys following them, yelling, leaving the lighted part of the stage bare except for the crippled boy. He looks where the others have been, then, crossing through the lights, he goes off, saying:)

Crippled Boy:

> The pirates flew their flags
> and watched the seas go by
> but the wind died on the sailing ships
> and the lonely seagulls cry
>
> raise no more the Jolly Roger
> sing no more of Dead Man's Chest
> watch no more ...

(The lights go down on him as he leaves this area. They come up, stage left, in a cubby cut into one of the platforms. Two boys are crouching down as if in hiding. The Guitar Player is playing "Smoke, Smoke, Smoke That Cigarette.")

David: Where's Miss Jones?

Bobby: (Looking around.) She's over there. Helping the girls jump rope. Now she's going over to referee the baseball game.

David: Good. Here. (Hands Bobby a crumpled cigarette.) She'll be over there a while.

Bobby: (Taking the cigarette and a match.) Yeh. (Excitedly.) Boy, she'd have a fit if she caught us. (He lights the cigarette and looks at it.)

David: Puff on it, stupid. Like this. (He takes a drag and blows it out.)

Bobby: Yeah, sure. (Takes a puff, fills his mouth with smoke, holds it a second, then blows it out.)

David: No, you dope. Like this. (Inhales the smoke, lets it out.) There.

Bobby: Ho-How do you do that? Show me.

David: (Gets a crafty look on his face.) Easy, really. You just get a mouthful and then swallow it. (Inhales, pretends to swallow the smoke, then exhales.)

Bobby: Just swallow it, that's all?

David: Sure, you saw me didn't you? Try it.

Bobby: Alright. Watch me. Here goes. (He takes a mouthful of smoke, then holds it a minute and swallows it. His eyes turn in and start watering. He begins to choke and gag.)

(David is laughing and beating the ground. This goes on a for a few seconds while Bobby coughs his head off. Then David becomes worried.)

David: Hush! Hey, stop it! (Gets up and pounds Bobby on the back.) You want Miss Jones to hear you? Hey!

Bobby: (Half sick, mad and crying) I'll-get-you (coughs) I-will ... (He starts coughing again.)

David: Shhh! Miss Jones'll hear ...

Woman's voice (offstage, shocked and surprised) Bobby Smith! David Ashely! What do you think you're doing?

(Both boys look up. Bobby's face is a mask of very sick little boy. David's face shows fear and sheepishness at once. The lights go down on them.)

(Lights come up stage right. The Guitar Player begins playing "Go Tell It on the Mountain." Three children, a boy and two girls, are walking. They are dressed in ancient Hebrew costumes and are carrying bundles of rags and clothing. The boy has a staff in his hand. They are singing.)

All:

> Come my people, out from Egypt
> Out from Egypt we will go
> Away from Pharaoh, away from Pharaoh
> Follow Moses, follow me.
>
> Walk my people, walk my people
> Leave old Egypt to the sands
> Come, my people, out from Egypt
> Out from Egypt to the Promised Land.

Boy: Look at him up there. (He points with his staff across the stage.) Walking like a hero in front of his army! (The boy jumps to the top of one of the platforms and waves his arms.) We're free, Ruth, free! No more making bricks! No more waiting on the Egyptians. We're going to have our own land to live in and grow up in!

Ruth: I know, I know! Our people are free. And Moses, leading us to a new home. A place in the sun for all of us!

(The boy jumps off the platform, grabs Ruth's hands. They begin a clumsy circular dance. The Other Girl watches then, wishing to join. Then she looks across the stage. A frown crosses her face.)

Other Girl: If we don't hurry, we're going to be left behind. Come on.

(The boy and Ruth quit dancing. The three start off across the stage.)

Boy: A new home!

Ruth: The Promised Land!

Other Girl: A new place to play!

All: Soon! Soon!

(They go off. The lights dim to black.)

(The lights come up, stage left, on a group of three. One is a doctor, holding chart in his hands. The others are a man and woman, Mr. and Mrs. Johnson. The Guitar Player is playing a spiritual of some kind.)

Doctor: Mr. and Mrs. Johnson. We've just got the first tests back. I'm sorry I have to be the one to tell you. There is a growth, and it seems to be malignant. As far as we can determine, the growth is already in the terminal stage. However, there is a new line of drugs that we'd like to ...

(Mrs. Johnson's mouth trembles. She tries to speak but can't. Then she begins to cry. She buries her head on her husband's shoulder. He tries to comfort her. The doctor bows his head. The lights go down on them.)

(Almost immediately, they come up on a girl sitting in a chair, center stage. She is reading a book. As the lights come up, she shifts around in the chair.)

Mrs. Johnson: (offstage) Mary Jane! Would you like some milk and fudge? I'll bring it right up if you do.

Mary Jane: (quietly) Yes ma'am.

Mrs. Johnson: (offstage) What dear?

Mary Jane: (louder) Yes, Mother. (She goes back to reading her book. Then she lowers it to her lap. She looks around dizzily. Then she seems to regain her balance. She stares around her as if seeing a new place for the first time. She closes her eyes and her head slowly lowers to her chest.)

(The lights begin to go down until the stage is very dim. Then Mary Jane gets up and slowly walks up the steps on the platform, crosses the level, and up the steps until she stands behind the Guitar Player.)

(The lights come up on the Guitar Player and Mary Jane, who is looking around at the stage below her. The stage is in dimness but for the spot on them. During the remainder of the upcoming scene, the players come out and begin going through their scenes they have done before, in pantomime. They come out a few at a time during the scene until, at the end, all the characters are onstage doing their routines.)

(The Guitar Player looks at Mary Jane, says something to her, then turns around and faces the audience.)

Guitar Player: So you see, a lot of people have wondered what being young is, and what it's all about. Ever since Time began. (He laughs.)

To some, like the boys playing pirates, it's the time for the best man wins. (The lights come up on the boys playing pirate.)

My dad is bigger than your dad, Captain Hook is better than Blackbeard.

(Lights go down on them, come up on crippled boy.)

To the crippled boy, it's the time to stand still and watch the world go by. He wonders what it's like to run and run till your lungs want to fall out. And deep inside, he knows what being young is. Being young is being able to run.

(Lights go down on him, come up on the two boys smoking.)

And take the two boys who got caught smoking. To them, being young is the time to smoke a cigarette and have it be important. When you're thirty or forty, a cigarette isn't so important anymore. When you're older, no one sends you to the principal.

(Lights go down on them, come up on the mother at extreme right.)

And the boy in the tree. Being young is when you know more than anybody else in the world; it's also the time to learn that fire burns and glass cuts. Being young is a broken arm.

(Lights go down on her, come up on Mary Jane.)

And Mary Jane. Maybe Mary Jane knows more than anybody else about it. To her, youth is the time to die before you get old.

And that's Youth. It's as simple as the sun rising and setting, or grass growing. Maybe it's as simple as the eye of a hurricane, or what makes the lemmings head for the ocean.

But I suppose you know all about that, don't you? After all, most of you were young once.

(He begins playing "Red River Valley" again, very slowly and mournfully, almost as a lament. One by one the lights go off and leave the stage in darkness.)

Curtain

THE LONG GOODNIGHT

A play in one act

CHARACTERS:

Humphrey
Peter

TIME:

11 or 12 years ago.

PLACE:

Los Angeles, California

(The lights come up on an ill-lit set with dark shadows. The set is indistinct, perhaps in a dingy hotel room, perhaps a cave, or a storeroom off a warehouse. The furnishings are a rickety desk with a chair behind it, and another, heavier chair in front of the desk.

In the background is the sound of a slow, steady rain.

At the chair behind the desk sits Humphrey. He is dressed in a blue serge suit, with a light blue shirt and black tie. He is disheveled and needs a shave. On the desk before him is a battered felt hat. Beside it are a bottle, half-full, a shot glass, and a loaded automatic. He is cleaning another automatic with an oily rag.

He stops working on the gun, rubs his eyes, and pours himself a drink. He downs it, then stops as a noise comes from offstage right.

His jaw tightens, and he picks up the other gun from the desk and stands, with the gun ready, facing off and to the right. Peter enters from off right. He is a short dumpy man with large eyes and speaks with a decided foreign accent. He is wearing a light suit and dark tie. He has on a rain coat, which he has begun to take off as he enters.)

HUMPHREY:
Oh. It's you. Did you bring any food?

PETER:
Yes, but I got hungry on the way over and sat down and shared it with a dog I used to know.

HUMPHREY: (laughs)
Hello, Pete.

PETER:
Hello, Humphrey.

HUMPHREY:
What brings you here? At this time of night?

PETER:
A cross-town bus. (smiles) No, I heard how things were on the radio, and thought I'd drop in.

HUMPHREY: (Looks down at guns, then goes and sits down again.)
Hell of a long way to come in the rain. How's business?

PETER: (sitting on other chair)
A job here, a job there. Still around.

HUMPHREY: (Starts to speak, then begins coughing. He overcomes the spell, pours himself a drink, raises the bottle questioningly to Peter, who shakes his head no, drinks, and then continues.)

God. That's better. (to Peter) How's the family?

PETER: (laughs)

I'm not sure. Muriel thinks we're going to have another baby pretty soon.

HUMPHREY:

No kidding? When?

PETER: (leans forward)

Soon as she gets me to bed. (They laugh.) I'm an old man, Humphrey. She's going to have to learn someday. How's your family?

HUMPHREY:

They're fine, Pete. Lizabeth's getting thinner worrying about me. The kids are still running around the house acting like kids.

PETER:

What did you ever do about Bobbie's teeth? They still crooked —

HUMPHREY:

We got him fixed up. He's gonna have better looking teeth than his old man. (He laughs, then looks at Peter.)

I'm glad to see you and all, Peter, but I know you didn't come just to flap your gums. Why don't we quit traipsing around the daisies, okay?

(Peter takes out a cigarette pack, offers Humphrey one. Humphrey shakes his head, pours himself another drink. Peter lights the cigarette, settles back into the chair)

HUMPHREY:

How much longer will it be before they get here? You got any idea?

PETER: (shifts in his chair)

The rain was slowing down when I came in. I don't think anything's going to happen before this storm is over.

HUMPHREY: (picks up the guns)

I never thought I'd be playing like this.

PETER:

You've had enough rehearsals. (laughs)

HUMPHREY: (grinning)

You hit the nail on the head, kid. (He leans back.) You know, it's funny how you can do one thing one time, and do it good, and from then on people expect you to do the same thing again. Only the next time you're supposed to do it better.

But if you keep doing it long enough, you get to be the best there is.

PETER: (looks at the guns)

Are you going to use these?

HUMPHREY: (picks up the other gun)

Seems sort of stupid, doesn't it. I know they're no good and you know they're no good. God knows, *those* out there know they won't even slow them down.

But I figure you gotta do something. You can't just sit and wait for 'em. Some kind of effort oughta chalk up points for you somewhere.

PETER:
I don't know if it works like that or not, Humphrey.

HUMPHREY:
Who the hell does? (pours another drink) But fair is fair, in my book. That's the way I'm going to think about it, anyway. (looks at Peter for a moment)
Did you come by yourself, or did you get sent?

PETER:
Both. I was going to come anyway, and everyone decided to send their blessings with me. (pause)
Their blessings on you, Humphrey. They all mean it.

HUMPHREY:
Don't get mushy, Pete. I can't take it right now. Couldn't they have come anyway? (pause) No, I guess that's a stupid question.

PETER:
They ... I don't think they thought they had enough time to all come. Some of them ...

HUMPHREY:
Not enough time, huh? You think it's that close?

PETER:
I don't know, Humphrey.

HUMPHREY:
Yeah, wouldn't it be hell if those others showed up while all my friends were here. I know some of them couldn't take it. (pause)
You're not afraid, Pete?

PETER:
No, I think they'll let me leave first.

HUMPHREY:
If they do, tell the others not to worry. If you get by them, you'll know the other side plays even-steven.

PETER:
I think I'll get by. Otherwise, they could have gotten you without warning, without even letting you know who you were up against.

HUMPHREY:
Yeah. Even though when you find out who you're up against there's not much you can do but wait. As organized and as thorough as they are, one of them is going to find you, no matter where you hide. (The sound of the rain begins to fade in the background.)
What was that?

PETER: (looks behind him)
The rain just stopped. Pretty soon the traffic will start again.

HUMPHREY:
Don't you think you'd better go, Pete?

PETER: (puts out cigarette)
I probably should. If there was anything I could do, you know —

HUMPHREY:
Don't start worrying now, Pete. I figure this is something I've got to do by myself.

PETER: (stands)
I know. I'm wondering.

HUMPHREY:
What?

PETER:
What's going to happen when they come after me.

HUMPHREY: (smiles)
They'll probably have to drop a bulldozer on you.

(Peter laughs. He puts on his raincoat, shaking his head.)

PETER:
I don't have a beautiful speech, Humphrey.

HUMPHREY:
I didn't expect you would. (holds out his hand)

PETER: (shaking his hand)
See you later, Humphrey.

HUMPHREY:
Goodbye, Peter. See Lizabeth and the kids do alright.

PETER:
I'll try. Goodbye, Humphrey.

HUMPHREY:
Thanks for coming.

(Peter leaves the way he has come. Humphrey stands behind the desk. He has another coughing spell. He sits in the chair until the coughing subsides. For ten seconds there is silence. Then from offstage right comes the sound of footsteps. They are coming straight ahead with a steady pace. Humphrey gets to his feet, holding himself up against the desk with one hand. In the other hand he has one of the automatics, points it towards the footsteps. He pulls the hammer back.)

HUMPHREY: (quietly)
Come on in. The door's open.

(blackout)

DAVY CROCKETT SHOOTS THE MOON

> "Why, with a rifle gun like this, a feller could drill a hole plumb through the Moon. First chance I get, I'll try 'er."
>
> on the presentation of "Ole Betsy"
> by the Young Men of Philadelphia

"But Santa Anna must have more than five thousand men against them, Colonel Crockett. He's sworn to march north and put down the rebellion."

"Well, but, Parfrey, they's a-fightin' for their independence, much like we done. Santy Anna is their King George!"

"Those men went to Texas under false pretenses, Colonel. They agreed to the Mexican terms when they settled there. It's not the same case at all. They knew what they were getting into when they went there. They're a bunch of outlaws now."

Crockett looked around the halls, where another session of Congress was about to begin.

"And," said Parfrey, "there isn't any use you joining up with a bunch of rabble. Hell, nothing will come of that. The nation needs you, Davy, not just a bunch of Texicans spoiling for a fight. No use you throwing away yourself, getting killed over a rebellion by a bunch of hotheads."

"I suppose you're right, Parfrey."

"Hell, Sam," said Crockett, leaning over the desk and handing his visitor a cigar. "The way I heard it, Santy Anna ran you all the way back to Louisiana."

The tall man in the black raincoat looked up, lighting the stogie, stared at Crockett a few seconds, then resumed with an air of fatigue.

"Almost right, Congressman," he said, finally, making David feel slightly uncomfortable.

"Well, ain't nothing you can do about it now," David said, smiling. His boyish grin made Houston think on all the stories he'd heard about Crockett grinning coons down from trees. He looked deceptively healthy for a man fifty years of age.

"We almost had them, Colonel," said Houston. "At San Jacinto. Had them on a point of land, thought we'd caught them asleep. They were play-acting. Had a whole brigade of cavalry and light infantry hid out in the woods, behind our line of march. Cannon, too. We could've gotten them, if it hadn't a-been for the cannon. Lost some of our best men there ... old Deaf Smith, Travis, Fannin. Bowie and I and a few others were lucky to get away. Santa Anna is nobody's fool, believe me."

Crockett thought a moment, then clucked his teeth. "Be-damn me if I know what to tell you, Sam. What are your plans?"

"Get up money and men, try one more time, I suppose. I'm on this like you were on the Land Bill."

"I feel for you then," said Crockett. "Ain't good for any man to be so intolerable *for* something."

"Well, you learned your lesson," said Houston, picking some mud off his boots. It was a rainy June day in the District of Columbia, and the congressional office building was a-track with water.

"True enough, General," said Davy, fidgeting in his chair. He had taken the demise of the Land Bill with good graces, after fighting four years for it. The speculators would get at Western Tennessee now, rather than the squatters who had improved it. But David Crockett, the "gentleman from the cane," had learned a few lessons in his years in Washington.

"You say Jim Bowie made it out with you? He in Washington?"

"Yes. He's recovering from some wounds and the fever."

"I sure would like to meet that feller," said Davy. "Seems me and him got a mite to talk about."

"That you do, that you do," said Houston, standing. "That's why I invited you to the dinner party tomorrow night."

"Well, I'm mighty obliged, and I'll sure be there. You wouldn't be trying to raise money and volunteers so soon, would you, General?"

"Why else?"

"Certainly," said Crockett.

"Tell me, Colonel," asked Houston as he was about to leave, "was it true at one time you were going to come and get in on this fight? We could have used men like you."

"Sure, General, but you know, way I figure it, I'da probably got my head blowed off in one of them little ruckuses I heard about."

"That's for sure," said Houston, "lots of men did. You're probably right."

He went off down the hall, whistling.

Davy Crockett felt real bad.

"... so the man said 'It's like I got a bear by the tail, Davy. I can't afford to let go, and I can't rightly hang on either!' "

The men in the room laughed, puffed their cigars. Their eyes shone with the good food, talk and wine.

Jim Bowie was not as tall as Davy had imagined, and he was not wearing the fabled knife, either. His face was still drawn and a little sallow from his illness, but he held his own in the company. He was much more at home in this society than was Davy. He had lived for ten years, on and off, in Frenchified New Orleans, thought Crockett, and he's just like a fox returned to his favorite henhouse.

"Well, Davy," said Jim, sitting himself more comfortably on the couch, "what do you say about throwing all this politeness over and coming back to Texas with the General and me?"

"Don't rightly know," said the congressman. "Heck if there ain't some talk amongst the Knickerbockers about putting me up for some high office. As a sop to the westerners, you understand? And so I'll lay off'n their man van Buren. I gave him a peck of trouble this last session."

"That's what I heard, too," said Bowie. He was dressed elegantly, even for Washington society; tight pants, calf-high boots, tailed coat, pink ruffled shirt, diamond stickpin in his cravat. Crockett looked at Bowie while he took a sip of his brandy. He saw for the first time beneath that civilized exterior the half-wild man of the bayous who had figured so importantly in the Sandbar Duel, who had fashioned the perfect knife because he knew what a knife was needed for.

"Why would they run a man like you, Colonel?" asked Sam Houston, finished with his talk with the Treasurer.

"Well, hell, Sam," said Crockett. "You know what happened to Tennessee after you left the governor's house to go live with them damn Cherokees. I guess van Buren and his boys don't rightly know what to do with me and figure it's a mite better to have me where they can keep a sorta weather eye on me."

"But you don't like the vice president very much, do you, Davy?" asked Bowie, enjoying himself immensely.

"Well, the way I figure it," said Davy, "I can do more for the people gumming up the Knickerbocker works than sitting back in Tennessee railin' at 'em."

"Colonel, you're a born politician," said Houston.

"I ain't a born nothin' but a bear hunter, General. And bears is gettin' mighty scarce in my neck of the woods. Thinkin' about taking up a new sport." Crockett waited.

"What's that, Davy?" asked Bowie, knowing he set himself up.

"Well, sir," said Davy. "Y'all all know about Halley's Comet up there?" The comet had been the biggest news of the last year, besides the Moon hoax. They all nodded. "Well, way I figure it, a comet ain't nothin' but another kind of critter, scurrying around heaven, making people nervous like a panther. Well, next time one comes around, I'm gonna climb up to the top of the Alleghenies, reach up like I'm grabbing a catfish, and jerk a knot in its tail!"

They laughed. Some shook their heads.

"Way I figure it, Mr. Barnum will be glad to get one for his Congress of Oddities up there. He'd probably pay me right smart, too. Better than grubbin' stumps in west Tennessee, that's for sure."

All the guests had left except Crockett. He, Bowie, and Houston sat in overstuffed chairs, their shoes off, feet propped up on a small table.

"Damned if I ain't got the sorest bunion I've ever had," said Bowie. "Them Mexican boots are pretty, but they're tearing my feet up. Let's get us a couple good pair each before we go back, Sam."

"Might not be a bad idea," said the General. "Maybe the colonel knows where we can get some?"

"Plenty o' places, General. Memphis is about the best. Jim, you ought to try moccasins for a while."

"That's what I've been trying to tell him for six months," said Houston. "He wears 'em a week, he'll forget there's any other kind of footgear."

"Do like the General's friends, the Cherokee," said Davy. "Wear 'em all year. In the winter, just wrap some hides around them, put on some leggings. I know good men who swear by 'em."

"David," said Houston, changing the subject. "Why don't you throw this over and come on out with us? It'll be a tough fight, but it'll be worth it. You could wear all the moccasins you wanted, never have to dress up again."

"You were in politics once, General. You know how it is."

"But I saw I wasn't getting anywhere, David. Governor is about as far as I wanted to go. And it wasn't such a plum job. Texas is the place, David. There's land there that won't be touched for a hundred years, it's so big."

"Hell, I know that! You know I been supporting you all along. First thing I want when the old Knickerbocker gets elected is for us to go get Texas, bring it into the Union. But he won't do it; he ain't got the backbone. And that means y'all are gonna have a tough tussle aforehand."

"You've never been afraid of a tussle before, Crockett," said Bowie.

"Naw. And if it weren't for that damned Jackson crew, I wouldn't think a minute before joining up with you. But the Union's got a fight coming up. Nothing's gonna stop Old Hickory from naming van Buren his successor. We can't let 'em get all the power. Somebody's gotta look after your Indians, Sam."

"If we had Texas, they'd have all the land they'd *ever* need."

"If van Buren's men ever got aholt of Texas, they'd get it away from you and the Indians both, General. I ain't blind."

Houston looked at him quizzically.

"My fight's here," said Crockett. "Once I whup the Knickerbockers and the tariff people into shape, then maybe I can get around to seeing what I can do about Texas. I'd be proud to see you governor of a new state like that, General."

"If you've made up your mind, then," said Houston. "It's good to have you on our side. I know you'll do what you can for us in Congress." He added sincerely, "And if you change your mind, just saddle up and head out west and ask anybody where we are."

"Sure will, General," said Crockett, rising and putting on his boots.

"Where you going? Night's just started!" said Bowie.

"The Treasurer gets up mighty early," said Crockett. He winked at Houston. "Your general here is gonna hit some of his friends up for some of that Democrat money tomorrow."

"I'll be damned," said Bowie.

He walked Crockett to the door, his shoes still off.

"Well, you take care of yourself, Jim," said the congressman. "Get rested up real good. I had the fevers once, and they make a man so he ain't worth a suck-egg mule. And get yourself some moccasins."

"You take care, too, Davy. Maybe me and you can get together sometime and hunt those hills you like so much."

"I'd like nothing better, Jim," said Crockett. "You let me know how y'all do, will you?"

"Sure will."

Eleven months later, Jim Bowie was killed in a skirmish along the Brazos River. Davy Crockett was the Secretary of War of the United States of America.

New Year's Eve of 1838, there was a raucous party in the White House, though van Buren disapproved. Crockett knew Yankees were stuck up and didn't like people having any kind of fun. The valets had already requested him to quieten several times.

"Aw, come on, Lucius," said one of Crockett's friends to the usher. "Have a little snort."

"I better not, Mr. Parfrey. I have to attend to the other guests."

"Aw, van Buren never did like us anyway," said the friend as the valet circled through the room.

They leaned against the mantel. It still bore the scars of Jackson's inauguration ten years before, when Old Hickory's friends had thrown knives at it. For a fleeting instant, Crockett was reminded of Bowie.

"Damn, he was a fine man," said Davy.

"What?" asked Parfrey, who was having trouble standing.

"Nothing, Parfrey. I was just thinkin' that if General Houston don't hurry up and do something down there, he's gonna make a lifelong career out of tryin' to beat the Mesicans. Hell, he's been at in three years now, and ain't a whit closer than when he started."

"No damn good," said Parfrey.

"What?"

"This party's no damn good. Nothing's going on," said Parfrey.

"Well, let's liven 'er up!" said Crockett.

Parfrey gave a hog call, and they were the center of attention instantly.

"Friends!" said Crockett. "I'm gonna make good a boast I made four years ago. Follow me!"

He strode towards the door. Van Buren shook his head sadly, but followed anyway, along with the other guests.

"Lucius!" yelled Crocket. "Go to my rig and fetch me my rifle-iron!"

"Yes sir, Mr. Crockett."

The Moon shone brightly on the banks of the Potomac. There must have been two hundred people watching, talking among themselves, laughing.

Crockett, dressed in his best clothes, strode through them as if they were a thicket. He carried his rifle, powder horn, and coonskin cap.

"Gentle people of Washington," said Davy. "A time ago, I was given this here rifle, the straightest shootin' iron in the world, and I named her 'Ole Betsy.' She was given to me by the City of Philadelphia."

There were a few ragged cheers from that city's visitors.

Crockett was weaving on his feet a little bit.

"I told them people that one day I was really goin' to try 'er out. Well, I been sorta busy meantimes, and I'll do it now."

He loaded his gold inlaid rifle quickly and expertly, capped his powder horn. Then he put on his coonskin hat, gave it a little pet to straighten it.

"Don't feel right without my hat," he said.

He turned again to the assembled guests.

"Mr. President. Members of the Congress. Distinguished visitors. Yonder stands the silver Moon. It looks mighty close, but somebody was telling me it was further than ten times around the world. Well, for other rifles, that would be a mite of a reach. But not for Ole Betsy. She was forged in the city where Dr. Franklin fought with the lightning and dared the thunder. To her, that Moon ain't nothin' but a big silver dollar. And she's plugged a many of them in her time. Tonight, I'm gonna make good my boast and knock a chunk off the Moon."

He turned, strode down to the banks of the river, hefted his firearm, and pulled the trigger. A roar echoed up and down the length of the Potomac.

"Did you see me make the Man in the Moon duck?" he asked the roaring, applauding crowd. "Damn me, if this ain't a fine gun!"

Crockett tore open the dispatch which came on an April morning in 1840.

"Hot damn, Parfrey!" he yelled. "Them Mesicans has done it now! They chased General Houston all the way over into Louisiana and burned down Natchitoches and blew up our fort! It's gonna be war, Parfrey! I gotta go tell Tyler about this! Get saddled up and burn leather for Connecticut. I want Samuel Colt here by tomorrow evening. We're gonna need his guns."

Seven months later, in Coahuila, the Army of the Republic of Mexico was pulling back in a rout from breastworks around a small garrison town.

General Sam Houston, now in charge of Texican Volunteers, was urging his men on after them. Five years of frustration were behind his temper, and his horse was plunging in and out among the Texican lines. A Mexican cannonball whizzed by.

"Goddam, General, they never could shoot straight!" said a voice behind him.

Sam Houston looked around, and there was Secretary of War Crockett, dressed in buckskins, a brace of new Colt pistols in his belt, a Colt rifle across his arms, with Ole Betsy stuck in his carbine boot.

"Crockett, goddammit, what are you doing here?"

"Cain't let you have all the fun, can I, General?"

"Hell no! Where were you when I needed you?"

Crockett pointed at the line of blue-coated infantrymen chasing after the Mexican army. Artillery began to hit among the fleeing defenders.

"I figured why look for volunteers when the Union already had an Army standing around," said Crockett.

Houston laughed, and held his sides.

"Goddam, Crockett, I never thought I'd see you again."

"Save the talk for a cool spell, Sam," he said. "Right now, we got Mexicans to whup."

"Boys!" yelled Houston. "This here's Davy Crockett!"

Hats flew up the length of the line, and some of them were whipped away by snipers' bullets.

A shell exploded close by.

"Damn, boys!" said Crockett, wheeling his horse. "Let's go give 'em one for Jim Bowie!"

The men jumped and cheered and went over the abandoned breastworks.

"And one for ... for ... "

Houston whispered to him quickly.

"... for Old Deaf Smith! Travis! Fannin!"

They began running and firing, and Crockett and Houston rode to the fore. Crockett had both pistols out and was firing into the defenders who tried to make a stand at a broken wall.

The Union army was closing in to the flanks. The Texicans were yelling and screaming. Many of them had already drawn their knives fifty yards from the Mexicans.

The fire from the barricade melted, dwindled. The soldiers ran, some throwing their rifles, some trying to turn and fight.

"Hot damn!" yelled Crockett. "We got 'em goin', General. We got 'em going now."

"Let's run 'em all the way to Mexico City, boys!" yelled Houston.

And they did.

Davy Crockett had been the only member of van Buren's cabinet carried over into Harrison's cabinet. Which quickly became Tyler's cabinet on Harrison's death.

On March 20, 1845, David Crockett was sworn in as the 11th President of the United States.

He was a relatively distinguished chief executive, a little slow on foreign relations but very good on domestic issues. He had the whole Union to look after — the states, the territories of Texas and the Northern Mexicos, Indian Territory, and the Indian Sanction. He also wanted to make sure that the States bought the Russian Protections, those lands north of California all the way to the Arctic Circle. He met with the Czar's representatives in 1848, and the deed was done.

He was a good president and became an even better storyteller. He loved the Union, he watched it grow, he nurtured it as best he could, and he looked out for the little man, the homesteaders, the soldier. He caught pneumonia in the winter of 1849 and his health grew steadily worse.

"Boys," he said to the men gathered around his bedside, though most were older than he. "Remember the night I put a hole through the Moon?"

"Certainly, Mr. President," said Melville.

"Well, don't y'all forget it, you hear? This Union will run out of territory sometime, and people will want to start grabbing off more land from the Indians. Don't let 'em. Look new places. Why, hell, I figure the Moon is as good a place as any to start! When they get there, tell 'em to look for my bullet, will you, boys?"

"Sure, Mr. President," said Dan Webster. He looked at the others.

"Boys, I'm fixin' to go rassle the biggest bear I reckon anybody ever seen."

"We'll be here, Davy," said Parfrey.

"I know you will, boys. Give Pierce all the help you can, will you? He ain't a bad sort."

He died three days later, and Daniel Webster gave the eulogy. They say the stars and stripes appeared in the sky when he spoke.

The War for the Union, when it finally came, was long and bloody, and lasted nine years. It took another ten to recover. Then the nation pulled itself together, shook off its fatigue, and plunged ahead.

The Canada War lasted three years, and Queen Victoria barely kept the rest of the Empire out of it.

The Big War, the one everybody got in on, nearly sapped the strength of the generation which had grown to maturity at the turn of the century.

It was fought Rough and Tumble, No Holds Barred.

It looked like there would be a Second Big War. A bunch of young men who fooled around with rockets in an abandoned ammo depot in Berlin suddenly disappeared one day.

They soon learned to like *tacos* and *huevos rancheros.*

The Second Big War lasted nineteen days, and the earth looked a lot different when it was over. All the maps had to be changed.

The first ship touched down on the Moon on July 4, 1957.

In command were Colonel Charles Yeager and Major David Simons, both U.S.F.A.F.

White Sands Control relayed the broadcast of their landing to the whole country: the States, the Northern Mexicos, the Canadian Borders, the several Indian Nations, the Japanese Protectorate, American Germany, New Egypt, and the U.S.S.A.

And the rest of the world.

They climbed out in their spacesuits and set up the American flag, with its 111 stars and 13 stripes.

President Ira Hayes spoke his congratulations to them. He was aboard Space Station No. 2, and was anxious for their return.

After they saluted the flag, they set up a plaque in the bright lunar dust.

It said:

"Be Sure You're Right — Then Go Ahead."

Copyright information, continued from page iv:

"A Lovely Witch: A Wanderer Story" copyright © 2022 by Howard Waldrop. From *Cortana* #2 (ed. Clint Bigglestone), 1964. • "The Well of Chaos: A Wanderer Story" copyright © 2022 by Howard Waldrop. From *Cortana* #1 (ed. Clint Bigglestone), 1964. • "The Soul-Catcher" copyright © 2022 by Howard Waldrop. From the self-published chapbook *The Soul-Catcher*, The VORPAL Press, March 1966. • "Apprenticeship" copyright © 1983 by Howard Waldrop. From *Modern Stories* #1 (ed. Lewis Shiner), April 1983. • "The Adventure of the Countess's Jewels" copyright © 2022 by Howard Waldrop. From *Batwing* #1 (ed. Larry Herndon), March 1965. • "Vale Proditor!" copyright © 2022 by Howard Waldrop. From *Star-Studded Comics* #9 (ed. Larry Herndon, Howard Keltner, and Buddy Saunders), Summer 1966. • "Lunchbox" copyright © 1972 by The Condé Nast Publications, Inc. From *Analog*, May 1972. • "Onions, Charles Ives, and the Rock Novel" copyright © 1972 by New Crawdaddy Ventures. From *Crawdaddy*, 1972. • "Love Comes for the YB-49" copyright © 1972 by New Crawdaddy Ventures. From *Crawdaddy*, 1972. • "Mono No Aware" copyright © 1973 by Marvel Comics Group. From *The Haunt of Horror*, Vol. 1, No. 2, August 1973. • "Billy Big-Eyes" copyright © 1980 by Howard Waldrop. From *The Berkley Showcase Vol. 1*, edited by Victoria Schochet and John Silbersack, Berkley, April 1980. • "Unsleeping Beauty and the Beast" copyright © 1976 by Geo. W. Proctor and Steven Utley. From *Lone Star Universe*, edited by Geo. W. Proctor and Steven Utley, Heidelberg Publishers, 1976. • "My Sweet Lady Jo" copyright © 1974 by Terry Carr. From *Universe 4*, edited by Terry Carr, Random House, 1974. • "The Droog in the Green Flannel Blanket" copyright © 2022 by Howard Waldrop. From *Kosmic City Kapers* #1 (ed. Jeffrey May), 1973. • "The Great AmeriCon Novel" copyright © 2022 by Howard Waldrop. From *Kosmic City Kapers* #2 (ed. Jeffrey May), 1973. • "Cthu'lablanca and Other Lost Screenplays" copyright © 1976 by Howard Waldrop. From *MidAmeriCon Program Book*, edited by Tom Reamy, produced by Nickelodeon Graphic Arts Service, 1976. • "Chili from Yuggoth" copyright © 1983 by Howard Waldrop. From *Thrilling Monkey Tales*, Volume 1, Number 1 (ed. Bill Page), August 1983. • "The Pizza" copyright © 2023 by Howard Waldrop. This sketch, written in 1966, appears in this volume for the first time. • "Youth" copyright © 2023 by Howard Waldrop. This one-act play, written in 1966–67, appears in this volume for the first time. • "The Long Goodnight" copyright © 2023 by Howard Waldrop. This one-act play, written in 1966–67, appears in this volume for the first time. • "Davy Crockett Shoots the Moon" copyright © 2023 by Howard Waldrop. This story, written in 1972, appears in this volume for the first time.